PSYCHIC ECHOES

BOOK 2
IN THE MARY JAMESON SUPERNATURAL
THRILLER SERIES

by

J.P. ALTERS

Book cover design by: Christian Bentulan
Edited by: Zach Bohannon

ISBN: 978-1-7392374-6-2 Psychic Echoes (paperback)
ISBN: 978-1-7392374-7-9 Psychic Echoes (ebook)

www.jpaltersauthor.com

Contents

PART ONE

PROLOGUE

As the afternoon sun descends and shadows lengthen, the school building takes on an eerie quality. A hive of activity, it teams with children and their parents navigating the old-fashioned, concrete playground. It's home time, and the teachers pack up for the day, dispatching the younger children to their families with eager efficiency, their smiles weary but warm. Most of the older children leave under their own steam, and Patryk's one of them.

'See ya, Danny,' Patryk says, sharing the secret handshake they created.

'See ya tomorrow, Patryk.' Danny holds his own hand up, echoing their ritual.

Patryk heads in the opposite direction from his friend, merging into the dispersing crowd. The noise around him swells with lively chatter and end of day excitement. After checking the time on his mobile, Danny slips in his earbuds, feeling grown up. A month has passed since he's started walking to and from school alone. Soon, he'll be in secondary school, and his dad says this is 'really good practice.'

The departing sunshine still bathes his neck in warmth, but as he looks up, he notices the sky, pregnant with rain clouds. Patryk holds up one small hand, palm upwards, feeling the faintest mist of rain. He checks the time again on his phone, realising he's a couple of minutes slower than usual. With a slight jog, Patryk turns onto a tree lined residential street filled with bungalows that stand a silent witness to his hurrying. After another minute or so, he checks the time again. He can't be late getting home.

Patryk's school uniform rustles as he runs, stiff with ironing starch, and his school shoes shine in the sun as he moves. With a tut, he tries to smooth down his stubborn cowlick, annoyed as it springs back again. It makes him think of his mum's fondness for his ash-blond curls, and he rolls his eyes as he thinks about how she keeps his first baby curl in a silver tin in her wardrobe. Mum's often saying how it's sad that her baby is growing up so quickly, ten years old now. He tries to smooth down his cowlick again, growing frustrated as it sticks back up.

Lost in the classical music streaming through his earbuds, Patryk slows down, humming to himself, his rucksack slipping from his shoulder. He hoists it back up, his chest puffing out with pride. *Soon I'll be in secondary school. Got two armpit hairs now. Nearly a man.* Another glance at his phone urges him to speed up again, the classical music swirling around him spurring him on.

As Patryk continues down the street, a faint, out-of-place sound pricks his ears. He pauses, a ripple of unease coursing through him. Instinctively, he lowers the volume on his earbuds, glancing over his shoulder. The street remains as expected: quiet, lined with the bungalows of its elderly residents, devoid of other children. Seeing no-one, he shrugs, chalking it up to his imagination being triggered by the classical overtures roaring in his ears.

Resuming his walk, a sudden blur of movement catches his eye. Before he can process it, something clamps his mouth shut, stifling his startled scream. Panic surges through him, his heart pounding in his chest as he struggles against an iron grip. The once comforting music in his ears is now distant, drowned out by the pulsing sound of his own heartbeat.

The street remains silent, oblivious to the tussle that unfolds. Patryk's vision darkens, his world narrowing as the sunlit pathway transforms into the scene of his silent nightmare.

In the aftermath, the street reclaims its tranquillity. The single earbud lying forgotten in the gutter, the only testament to the boy who'd walked there just moments before.

CHAPTER 1

———

I can see that the sun has set, but think to myself how funny it is that the evening's gloom from the outside cannot encroach on our cosy flat. Our happy photographic memories brighten the cream walls. There I am in the shiny silver frame, with my fiancé, Derek, at my side. An intense barnyard owl, to my own, Jackdaw. Our youthful bodies are forever captured in different backdrops, with and without our friends. *The perfect couple. We've made many joyful moments together over the last three years.*

Glancing round the room, I stroke the velveteen lampshade of one of them, enjoying the sensation. *They make the room look so cheery, and the mirror on the wall bounces the light off it so nicely.* The mirror also reflects that same light from my shiny black hair, cut into a sleek bob, and I can see its rosy glow echoed in my cheeks.

As I stand in front of Derek, my slim hands gripping a wedding magazine, I sigh with contentment. For the last three years, Derek's been my everything. He sits, legs sprawled open as he lounges in his favourite armchair. His straight brown hair frames soulful brown eyes that stare into my grey gaze, and he grins at me. I never smiled much before I met Derek, but now, the mirror opposite me shows tiny laughter lines around my mouth. They're carefully cultivated, like my new life. I marvel at the change, gently touching the corners of my mouth. *Who would've thought this could ever happen to me, Mary Obosa Jameson?* I hold up the magazine towards Derek, showing him the photo of the two bridesmaids, dressed in pastels. 'Derek, do you want blue or pink for our bridesmaids?'

In the background, the radio plays a soft rock station. While the music's not my cup of tea, Derek likes it, so it's what we usually have on, and I can appreciate the touch of normality that's still new to me. I silently salute my spirit friend Errol, who taught me to accept this peace. Three years ago, Errol tuned his vibration to mine, becoming my friend and mentor. Gaining the psychic skills he'd taught me has been difficult and required a lot of practice, but it's been worth it.

Now, I can choose to tune out or tune in and receive non-physical spirits. Mostly, I tune out everyone except Errol. Our friendship has boundaries, but he's got an open invitation to connect with me. I still experience bouts of thankfulness for the change he's made in my quality of life. After so many years of isolation, I'm able to listen to music, read a book, or even have a non-distracted conversation. Bliss!

My fiancé, Derek, diagnosed with schizophrenia, manages his symptoms well through lifestyle changes and medication. His days of self-neglect and substance misuse are over, and he promises me he'll never wilfully stop taking his anti-psychotic medication again. Although we haven't conceived a baby yet, my life is much better than it was before, and I'm glad. We have each other and good friends. This *must* be the family I always yearned for, and now, whenever I imagine my future, a fluttery feeling fills my stomach. Life will only get sweeter, especially when we get pregnant, because that will complete our little family.

I repeat my question.

'D, you never listen to me. Do you want blue, or pink, for our bridesmaids?' I tuck a strand of my hair behind my ear, my grey gaze steady.

Derek still doesn't answer, and I follow his gaze. It's lingering on the hand I have resting on my hip. I admire my emerald engagement ring, the soft light barely revealing the faded scars on my palms.

'Your foot's tapping, Mary Jameson, but that sassy expression on your face says I might be in with a chance tonight?' Derek grins and wiggles his eyebrows, his innocent façade shattering.

I chuckle. *Actually, I was thinking how much I hate your taste in music.*

Derek stands, seeming to give my options some thought. He wears a wide grin as he folds his arms, stroking his chin.

'Oh, shut up you perv, and make a choice. Pink?' I hold up the magazine photo again. 'Or blue?'

Derek's gaze follows how mine rest a fraction longer on the little girl in blue and I know what he'll say. *He's so observant, so thoughtful.*

'Blue,' he says without hesitation.

My shoulders drop, and I pretend not to notice as he moves closer, stopping just inches away from me. We sway together to another cheesy soft rock classic. *Who wrote these lyrics?* Our eyes lock.

Warm breath fans my face as I inhale Derek's attractive, woodsy scent – a mix of pine and cedarwood. As I breathe in, he slides one of his long legs between mine. He sniffs the delicate skin at the side of my neck as he instigates dirty dancing. It tickles, and I gently push him away, staring at him. 'Why d'you always smell *so good, D*?' I ask.

'Why do you always *everything* so good, Mary?'

'Smooth talker.' I snuggle closer.

Derek raises an eyebrow. 'Early night, beautiful?'

His eyes seem bottomless, and I stare into them with a sigh. Derek has his ways, but he can be so irresistible! Kind, sweet, *and* clever, he's the perfect man to start a family with. Even after three years together, I know I'm lucky to have someone like him. It hurts that we haven't gotten pregnant yet, but I'm confident it will happen soon. Regardless of how long it takes, we already have so much more than I ever thought possible.

'Stop giving me those puppy-dog eyes, you. You know I can't say no.' I shake my head.

Derek doesn't listen, continuing to stare at me, his soon to be wife, as though I am the only girl in the world.

I let myself be drawn in by Derek's embrace, as I always do.

The magazine flutters down to the floor, forgotten as our lips meet and our clothes quickly follow them. The heat between us builds, Derek's hand running down my body, and I let out a slight moan as a loud banging on the front door startles us both.

I whip my head toward the door. 'What the hell?'

CHAPTER 2

'Who is it?' Derek calls, as he hurriedly puts on his trousers, stumbling over his feet.

'No flipping clue. It's after nine now, surely?' Frowning, I hop back into my clothes.

Derek goes to answer the door, swiping hair from his eyes. Leaning towards the sound of voices, I pick out the voice of my best friend, Marcie. At the same time, instinct makes me turn around, and I jolt reflexively. 'God, Errol. What the *hell're* you doing here? You took ten years off my life! I thought we agreed to some prior warning before you pop in?'

My spirit friend, Errol, materialises into the room with a grin, but his customary carefree expression is lacking in the carefree department. He fails to flash his gold tooth when he smiles, like he usually does. 'Hi, Mary.'

With a frown I say, 'That was a half-hearted smile, Errol, what's up?'

'Mary, I need to talk to you, tell you something.'

My head is still cocked in the direction of the hallway, and I'm finishing getting dressed, smoothing my hair down as I head towards the living room. 'What's the matter then, Errol?' I throw out over my shoulder.

Derek enters the room with Marcie trotting behind, and Errol's reply is lost. Marcie is spattering the room with her confetti-like spray of cockney patter. I can't hear what she's saying, because Errol's voice is competing with hers, but her tone sounds urgent as she talks to Derek, so I prioritise hearing what she has come to say. 'Shush, Errol,' I say. *Let me listen.*

Marcie enters the living room, her plump pink cheeks wobbling with each step, like those of a well-fed baby.

I greet Marcie, explaining the reason for my torn attention to Marcie and Derek. 'Hi, Marce. Errol's just turned up too, guys. Shush for a sec, Errol, please?' Turning away from Errol, I ignore him as he throws up his hands, instead gawping at Marcie as she strides into the room, grabbing the TV remote.

'What's happened?' I ask her.

'You ain't seen the news tonight. You've got to help.' Marcie shakes her head, switching the TV to channel three, turning up the volume.

'Me? Help with what Marcie?' I say. 'What're you talki-'

'Shh,' she says. 'You need to watch this, please, it's so terrible.' I spare Errol a quick glimpse. He's pacing around my room, but no longer trying to get my attention. Marcie then falls uncharacteristically silent. Curious, I perch on the arm of our sofa, something Derek often asks me not to do. He remains standing, and together we stare at the TV, rapt. The face of the nine o'clock news reporter fills the screen.

'A young boy, Patryk, has been reported missing in Southeast London. Patryk Challance is blonde haired, with hazel eyes, and a slight build. His parents reported him missing on Friday evening when he failed to return from school.'

My hand flies to my mouth and I hear Derek make a sympathetic noise. *How dreadful.*

A female news reporter with flame-red hair and shining green eyes is introducing the news flash. Even behind her owlish glasses, her compassion for the family is clear. I click my fingers as the face stirs a memory.

12

'I know her,' I say. '*Sarah*, something or other. She's the one who interviewed me last year, after the Rainbow Unit conspiracy broke.'

I look away from Marcie and Derek. 'Errol, stop pacing. You're distracting me.' I speak out loud, knowing I'm safe to acknowledge my non-physical friend in my present company. *After everything we went through together three years ago, Marcie and Derek know my psychic skills are the real deal.* Derek, while interested, is now unfazed by my conversations with Errol.

Marcie is always intrigued, and her eyes light up. 'Oh, Errol's here? What's he saying?'

'Hi, Errol,' Derek says.

With a quick gesture, I shush them, turning back to the TV. Errol stands still, chin down low. 'Sorry,' he mutters.

My stomach churns as I listen to the news with a heavy heart. A man enters the frame with a woman sobbing beside him. His eyes are red rimmed and swollen, and his hand-dog face appears ravaged by grief. I lean in, intent on his words.

'Patryk is a lovely, kind-hearted boy. Please bring him back to us. He's always happy to help anyone, he adores animals, and is a good boy at school. He's so very loved. Please, give him back to us. If anyone knows anything, or has seen him, I beg you...' Here, the man begins to weep, the intensity of it wracking his body. He clutches at the woman next to him.

The news reporter clears her throat and for a second, her face convulses, as though she will cry. She blinks slowly, firming her trembling lips.

'We request any member of the public who has seen Patryk, or knows anything they think pertinent to finding him, to *please*, get in touch using the number below. Call anytime. Someone will be there to answer. Help the police bring Patryk home to his family.'

Patryk's young, innocent face radiates across the television, burning the airwaves.

As we all stare at the screen, silence screams into the room. I clear my throat, dry mouthed.

Derek plucks the remote control from Marcie's nerveless hands and switches the TV off. I've been ignoring Errol til now, but now I notice again how my friend Errol seems robbed of his usual cool. His lips are moving, but there's no sound coming out. Without thinking, I grip the necklace I always wear like a talisman, asking him, 'Errol, you look distraught. What's wrong? Is Patryk in 'The Blue' already?'

'What is it?' Derek asks me, interrupting. 'What's Errol saying now?'

'I'm OK, D, it's just Errol.' I gesture at Errol, knowing although Derek and Marcie can't see him, they'll understand that I'm chatting to my spirit guide. I turn back to Errol.

Marcie's eyes light up and I know she wants to ask me questions about Errol, but I hold a hand up, asking for patience. 'You're on mute again, Errol.' My small smile evaporates. *Wait, this means that whatever Errol's trying to tell me is forbidden by the cosmos.* With a frown, I remember how my spirit friends at the Rainbow Unit were stopped by some universal power when they tried to warn me. *Errol being silenced means something big is coming, and the Universe doesn't want things changed. Shit.* I stroke the back of my neck as I study him. *This is bad. Errol's stare seems beseeching, but I don't understand why.*

Marcie can't hold her tongue anymore. 'Oh my God,' Marcie says. 'That poor kid. Those poor parents – did ya see how the Mum was just sobbing the whole way through the interview? It breaks my heart. I know we have the odd missing case on the news, but for some reason I just knew I had to show this one to you. Have you picked anything up about this case, Mary? I'm hoping you can help them?'

Can I help them? Sadly, Marcie's right. This isn't the first time I've seen a news flash concerning a missing child, but I wonder why she felt compelled to approach me regarding this one? Am I supposed to help?

Derek's gaze flies to mine. It holds the same question as Marcie's rapid-fire commentary contained. I consider Marcie's other question. *Did I 'pick up' anything...* 'Pick anything up Marcie? I'm not RadioShack.' As I think more about it, though, I realise this *is* kind of what happens. I often hear clicks before I receive visitations from non-physical entities, and it does remind me of white noise from a radio. I'm used to Errol, so now I find I barely notice the static frequency he creates in my psychic membrane when he turns up. *Maybe it's like, if you live next to a busy road, you stop hearing the traffic after a while?* 'I can't tune into every atrocity that occurs, Marcie. If I did, I'd be crazy as a box of frogs within a week.'

'Oh, Mary, I'm sorry if I came across as pushy. I just... I know you help the police with some of their unsolved cases, and I wondered if this could be one of them? Did you get any vibes or have any visions or anything?'

'No, and the police haven't called me. I work on open cases with them, but nothing with missing kids. It's terrible, though, and I hope they find him safe soon.'

Errol's resumed pacing draws my attention again and I frown at him, distracted. 'Jeez. Errol, will you stop pacing, you numpty? You'll wear out my non-physical carpet.'

Errol stops abruptly, his gaze darting around the room.

Marcie responds to my comment to Errol with surprise. 'Your friend Errol's walking up and down? Really? Do spirits do that?'

'Yes, Marce, they do. Errol, is something wrong?' I ask.

'What?' Errol says, his voice sounds strangled. Errol's eyes drop, and he lowers his head, breaking the intensity that seems to grip him. The living room light makes his afro glisten. *How does it do that?* I wonder, then shrug. *Errol's stopped trying to communicate with me, so maybe what he'd wanted to say wasn't that important after all, especially compared to the news broadcast we'd just watched.*

Derek gets up, moving towards the kitchen. 'I just hope they find that poor boy soon.'

'God. Me too. I could do with a cuppa tea if you're making one, D,' I say.

'I am,' Derek says. 'Marcie, would you like a cup of tea or coffee?'

'I'd love a tea please, Derek,' Marcie answers.

Derek nods and Marcie's dimples appear briefly before she glances back at the TV again. Her face twitches, and I can tell she's thinking about poor Patryk Challance and his family.

Eyes wide, I stare at Errol. He's wringing his hands together and rubs his arms before crossing them. His mouth opens as though speaking again, but still, no sound comes out.

With a sigh, I stare at him, but am confused when he won't meet my eye. *What's going on with him? What does he want to tell me?*

CHAPTER 3

I dash into the sunny buttercup yellow of the kitchen, sniffing appreciatively at the smell of toast. *Yum, but where the shit are my car keys?*

Derek's in there, eating breakfast and scanning his phone. He's seated at the pine table. 'You off now?' Derek glances up from his phone with a brief smile.

'I am.' I walk over to him and kiss him before grabbing a piece of his toast.

Derek grins at my theft, then a frown flickers between his eyes. 'Want to talk about yesterday? You were tossing and turning all night. You sounded really disturbed. Was it the news Marcie showed us about that little boy? It *was* heartbreaking.'

I literally haven't stopped thinking about it since I saw the news. Suddenly aware of a chill in the room, I rub my hands over the goosebumps that have risen on my arms. The action reminds me of my friend Errol last night. He'd just disappeared after Marcie'd come and shown us the news, which made me think there might be a connection between what he'd wanted to say, and the news about that poor missing boy. *Patryk, that was his name. God, his poor family. Maybe if I tried, I could do something to help? Marcie seemed to think so. Something about the idea petrifies me though... I don't want to share my worries with Derek, not after he got so unwell again last year.* With effort, I pin a smile to my face. My lips feel tight and dry. 'Devastating. I just hope they find him safe and sound soon.'

'Yeah, me too. So are you meeting the girls at Rachel's new leisure centre today?'

I nod. 'Yeah, she said we can all get a slap-up freebie lunch there after tennis too. It's nice to have loaded friends, aye?'

The kettle finishes boiling, its switch popping up. I bite into my stolen toast and grin, hoping Derek's forgotten about the lost boy, for now. 'Result! There's marmalade on this. Anyway, kettles boiled. Want me to make you a quick cup of coffee before I go?' I ask. Anticipating his answer, I pluck his 'Mr. Perfect' mug off the cup stand, pouring water into the cup and adding granules. The vague smile resting on my features flees as a thought occurs to me and I turn, asking him, 'Did you take your meds this morning, babe? The box for your anti-psych tablets wasn't on the table when I came in?'

'Of course.' Derek offers me a tight-lipped smile. '*And* I returned it to the medicine cupboard straight after.'

Knowing I've irritated him with my question, I sigh, deciding to make light of it. I swivel around to face Derek, then roll my tongue, making an 'rrr' noise.

His stiff features relax, but he's sitting up very straight in his chair.

'Oooo, D. You're so tidy. It's such a turn on.'

'Glad to hear it.' His gaze holds mine for a second, then drops back down to his phone.

'I'll be back for dinner, love,' I say.

Still focusing on his phone, Derek nods, one hand scrolling, and the other pointing to the sideboard underneath the key rack.

'Keys!' I exclaim, rolling my eyes. *What am I like? I'm always losing my keys.* 'Thanks, babe.' After grabbing my keys from the side, I move off again, wiggling my fingers and blowing Derek an air kiss. He salutes me as he watches my exit to the door. 'OK, I'll have dinner on the table for you at five. Bye, beautiful, have fun, love you.'

'Have a good day, D, love you too,' I answer, just before I slam out of the front door.

I jump into the car Derek bought me for my twenty-third birthday present. We called her 'Adrienne,' his (very similar looking) car we named 'Rocky.' Key in the ignition, I turn it over and pump the gas. As she throbs into life, I stroke the dashboard. Much like me, Adrienne is temperamental and requires special treatment before she offers her loyalty. I think I love her even more for her obstinate quirkiness. The trip doesn't take too long, but I still arrive late. As I walk towards the leisure centre that my friend Rachel owns, I spot Marcie, with our friends Sophie and her wife Rachel. Last night's news is still on my mind, and I firm my stomach muscles to help with the churning in my tummy. I wipe my sweaty palms down my leggings, then wave to them through the glass. *Can I help that little boy?*

CHAPTER 4

'**M**ary, wake up! You're dreaming!'
My breaths are coming short and fast in the tunnel, and I can barely see. I'm running down a shadowy shaft. Its walls and floor are slick with moisture, making my feet slide. There's a terrible pain in my side, a stitch maybe? and I'm panting, exhausted. I must keep going. I can't stop. In the darkness, footsteps echo as someone closes the gap between us. Whoever it is, they're coming, and coming fast. I fall over an object, sprawling onto the wet floor. My outstretched hand touches something pliable and horror dawns within me as I realise what it is. *No.*

'Mary, wake up!' Derek shouts.

My eyes open and I blink, then wipe sweat from my eyes, feeling disoriented. Is that Derek's voice in my dream, or is that him lying next to me? My gaze focuses. The room is no longer totally dark, even though it's not yet morning. His face is close to mine, and I can pick out his knotted eyebrows and pursed lips.

'You were screaming. Are you OK, beautiful? You've been screaming your head off. What the hell were you dreaming about?'

I push the hair from my face, saying, 'I dunno, but it was nasty.'

'What was it about?'

To calm down, I breathe slowly, my body quivering. *Shit, that was a bad one.* Derek strokes my cheek and I wince away. 'Something about running in a corridor? I dunno. Anyway - I'm all sweaty, babe. That can't be nice for you,' I say.

Derek snuggles closer to me, undeterred. 'Don't be silly. You know how I love it when you're all sweaty,' he says.

I strain in the gloom to see the eyebrows I guess are wiggling. My muscles relax.

'Was that it, Mary? You were running down a corridor? That doesn't sound scary. Did anything else happen?'

The churning in my stomach starts again, and I ignore it, focusing on steadying my breathing. *I mustn't worry Derek.* I swallow and clear my throat a bit before speaking again. 'Can't remember, D. I just know it scared me.' With a shrug, I change the subject, saying, 'It doesn't matter now, it's just a silly dream. Let's just get back to sleep.' *My eyelids feel heavy.*

Derek lies back down on his side and pulls me to him with care. 'Sweet dreams this time then. Love you, Mary.'

'You too, D.' I murmur as I drift back to sleep.

The morning brings the comfortable reassurance of familiarity and routine, and as we share the small bathroom, Derek's whistle makes me smile. My grey gaze meets my reflection in the mirror, and I note the positive changes in my appearance that have taken place over the last few years. *My twenty-four-year-old chest has filled out now. Thank goodness I'm not emaciated anymore.* I have an athletic build, my once hollow tummy now displaying muscle tone around the midriff. There's the pink flush of health blooming in my cheeks, and my lips seem curved into a permanent smile. My straggly, long hair is now a smart black bob that cuts along my high cheekbones like a shiny raven's wing. 'D'you have any work today?' I say the words around my toothbrush, trying not to spit out all the toothpaste I have in my mouth. While I'm brushing my teeth in front of the mirror, I admire the toned physique of my fiancé and I see he's doing the same to me. My gaze flickers down to his 'house trousers' that he refuses to call 'pyjama bottoms,' and I roll my eyes when I notice he's gripping his phone with one hand. *You and your beloved phone, D.*

'Yes, a bit. It'll only take me a few hours; I should be finished by two. Why? D'you have something in mind?' Derek answers, standing behind me brushing his teeth.

Three years ago, I would never have been so comfortable with someone this close to me. I would've needed an open door with a view to the exit. 'I was thinking a walk might be nice,' I say.

He raises an eyebrow. 'Yeah? Where should we go? The beach?'

I'm about to answer Derek when I hear my mobile ringing from the bedroom where I left it. It interrupts our happy musings and I frown. The pop song ringtone announces the identity of the caller. I assigned this contact to: 'work, work, work, work, work,' so I assume Detective Inspector Jay Santiago will be on the other end of the phone. Gargling water, I spit it out then turn to speak to Derek. 'S'OK. That's Jay. I'll call him back when I'm showered and dressed.'

'I wonder what he wants,' Derek says.

I frown, remembering the news flash about Patryk from two days ago. Since then, daily updates show that Patryk still hadn't been found. As I get undressed, I wonder what the call with the inspector, Jay, will reveal.

'Argh - Errol!' I shout as Errol appears in the doorway to the bathroom. Clasping my pyjama top, I hold it close to my chest. 'What the hell? What's happening to our boundaries, Errol?' I feel my irritation rising. Again? With my back facing Errol, I put my top back on. 'This mutha-grubba right here,' I mumble. 'I *can* revoke your open invitation, you know. We agreed, absolutely *no* bathroom visits.'

Derek's eyebrows raise. 'Has your friend dropped by unannounced again? He needs to play by the rules. He's about to get an eyeful.' Derek's tone is relaxed as, without modesty, he takes off his house trousers and steps into the shower.

Errol mouths something to me, but whatever he's saying is without sound.

My heart races. *This is the second time now. It must be like I thought on the night we learned about Patryk going missing. He's been blocked from speech by the universal powers that be, so there must be something approaching, catastrophic. Shit, what is Errol saying? This is getting jarring now.* 'What's wrong, Errol? Is it about the case? D'you want to tell me something about it?' I step closer.

Errol's eyes hold an unbearable weight and sadness. They seem to plead with me, but I'm clueless about how to help. The tortured emotion my friend is clearly enduring makes tears fill my eyes. I consider what could be wrong with him, and words that might reassure him, thinking about what he's explained to me about the Universe, and how it works. I bite my lip as I consider Errol's theory... There's a source of positivity, an invisible tapestry woven in between everyone. It holds us and the threads of our lives, with good intention acting as glue.

This positive source is everywhere in our stories, beginning, middle, and end. It is the in-between. What I call: 'The Blue.' Sometimes, inconveniently, The Blue won't permit information to be exchanged that will change the way things are fated to happen. Hence, Errol's speech being on the fritz. 'Please, Errol, I can't bear for you to be so sad and I don't know what to do. Try to let me know if I can help you in any way?' I say.

Although I aim to comfort him, he shakes his head and seems so anguished that sympathetic tears spill down my own face. His mouth opens and closes intermittently, and I can only make out the odd word. The majority of his sentences are silent, leaving me with no idea what he's saying, and what to do or say for the best.

I give Derek's silhouette a glance as his off-key singing echoes from the shower. He's oblivious to my conversation, and I stare again at Errol, desperate to say something, anything, that will ease my friend's suffering. 'I'm sorry I don't understand, Errol. I don't know what else to say. When something shit happens, sometimes it helps me to think that things'll work out for the best in the end.'

Bringing his pacing to a stop, Errol speaks, eyes wide with surprise as his voice is finally audible. 'I love you, Mary. You're all the family I have now, and all I want is to see you happy.' He glances around nervously, as if expecting someone might meet his words with disapproval.

'Thank God! I could hear you that time.' I clap my hands. 'Are you being stopped from telling me something, Errol?'

Expressions of fondness are acceptable to the Universe, it seems, but not whatever else Errol wants to tell me. He begins pacing restlessly as he speaks, eyes darting around the small room. He talks quickly, the words tumbling over each other as he rushes to get them out.

'Through our connection, I experience your love and compassion for others. The warmth of your bonds with those in your life brings me such joy and I-' Errol's speech disappears again, but his statement about bonds makes me think that his warning's not to do with Patryk after all.

'Errol? What is it for God's sake? D'you know something about what happened to Patryk, or maybe it's to do with my friends?' Along with the sudden silence, frustration fills the air. *Oh my God! Could it be about my friends?*

'Don't stress, Errol. I'll warn the gang, so they take extra care and keep a sharp eye out for any dangers. That should be ok d'you think?'

Errol rolls his eyes and kisses his teeth, making my lips curl slightly, despite my worry. 'Well, I can't think of anything else I can do, save having them all move in with me.' I lean closer to Errol, my movements fast but jerky. '*Is* there anything else I could do, Errol? *Is* it my friends' safety you're trying to warn me about?'

Errol's affection for me flows out in waves I perceive. Gold, resembling molten lava, flecked with a shell-like pink, streams from him. Love… My colour rises to meet his and unexpectedly, I beam at the feeling. 'Right, back atcha, Errol, old buddy,' I tell him.

'Less of the 'old,' please, Mary Jameson,' Errol says.

'OK. Well, I'm still not sure what else I can do, and why you even turned up like this, because the Universe or whatever won't let you tell me anything useful. Putting that aside, can you just allow a girl some privacy now, and stop jumping out at me, please? It's pissing me right off. You promised me you'd visit at decent times, at least give me a bit of warning, arse. Clear your throat or knock before showing up, like any other friend does. Sort it out.'

Just as with Marcie, my tone's never annoyed when I speak to Errol, and I reflect on how different I am from the 'me' of three years ago. *Back then, I was often angry and scared. Now, despite feeling frustration and fear at Errol's inability to pass on a coherent warning, here I am, cheering up my beloved spirit companion, telling him everything will be alright. Look at me, all 'peace, love and joy.'*

'Guru, Mary,' Errol remarks, tuning into my thought blocks.

'Stop that,' I tell him, but we both grin, worry for my friends hovering at the fringe of my outward humour like an unwanted guest at a party. *What could be coming?*

CHAPTER 5

I can tell from the ringtone it's Detective Jay Santiago phoning me again. 'Sorry I missed your call. Please leave a message. I'm busy planning my wedding, Constable Santiago.' I chuckle, breaking through the silence on the other end of the phone line.

Jay's voice sounds unamused. 'It's 'Detective Inspector,' Mary, as well you know.'

'That's Ms. Jameson to you.' I'm aware I'm winding Jay Santiago up, and a smile lurks around my face.

Jay doesn't sound amused saying, 'Tsk. Mary, stop the banter now. This is deadly serious. I need you to help me out on a case. Can you just listen without taking the piss, please?'

Jay's grief and worry reach out over the phone waves to me, dampening the joy I'm exuding. *Shit.* I purposely bar his thought blocks and self-soothe my emotions reflexively. Despite myself, my hearts sinks. I move to the bedroom for some more privacy. 'OK. What's this all about?' I ask.

'We're searching for the missing child who's plastered all over the news, but we've got no leads. I need you to meet me at the crime scene and do your thing. Find his wavelength or whatever you do. Work your magic,' Jay says.

'Like voodoo?' I quibble, but all humour has left my voice. Towards the end of his life, voodoo consumed my dad. *Not me. Now, I'm about light and love, in its purest form. I open myself up again for replenishment, aware of my constant connection to The Blue. The source of pure positive energy all beings have access to.* I close my eyes, breathing deeply and thinking about how it's where we come from and where we return to when we're released from our physical form.

The little boy, Patryk's face flashes in front of my eyes, his sweet curls laying against his blazer collar. *So young. His inconsolable parents, on my TV daily, with no new reports.* My shoulders sag. 'OK. Where is it?'

Jay gives me directions and I commit to being there in one or two hours.

'Can't you get here any sooner?' Jay asks.

'I'll leave straight away, but it depends on traffic.' I hear Jay slapping a hand over his face, revealing how stressed he is. Patryk's face flicks into my mind again, and I imagine his mum, sobbing at home. 'What's it like there, where Patryk went missing from? Are police at the area, maybe the forensic team?'

'It's cordoned off to the public, and I've posted two of my officers there. Forensics have done all they could, but they found naff all. At least we know the route Patryk took. It's a ten-minute walk, max. We've checked for CCTV in the area, had officers and police dogs walk it. We've recreated his journey, knocked on doors, etcetera. The search area is just too wide. It's a needle in a haystack situation. No evidence found on location so far. Nada.' Jay pauses, taking loud gulps and I imagine him drinking coffee from his massive mug, two handed.

Fuck-all from forensics. Poor Patryk.

'That's where you come in,' Jay says.

'You want me to walk the same route he would've taken, see if I feel anything?'

Jay sighs. 'If it's not too difficult for you.'

It will be atrocious, I'm sure. There's another long pause down the phone, and I sense it's heavy with the sadness Jay's feeling. I breathe deeply, allowing myself to connect with Jay's aura hues. Dark brown, charcoal grey, and black. I reign in my indigo and purple, and it retreats eagerly, as though wanting to avoid being tainted by Jay's colours. 'Just so you know, Jay, your aura looks like shit. Are you looking after yourself?'

'Not really.' He doesn't bother to pass off my question.

We both stay on the phone, sitting in silence, and I wipe my free hand down my trouser leg to get rid of some of the sweat. I consider the potential danger. *A missing child, likely abducted, maybe hurt, or God forbid, worse. And untrained me getting into the mix. Opening myself up to the disturbing vibrations of some sicko. Do I seriously want to get involved with this?* Patryk's young, innocent face pops into my mind's eye again, those little curls sweeping his collar. After a few moments, I nod, feeling faraway as I make up my mind. *I'll call on Errol to come with us, maybe he can help keep an eye out for me.* 'Obviously, I can't promise I'll find anything, though Jay, yeah. Is that OK?' I say.

Jay's voice is gruff, and I sense his sincerity as he tells me, 'You've helped me loads in the past with unsolved cases, Mary. I know you're the real McCoy. Don't worry, I understand your gift isn't an exact science and there're no expectations here. I'll be grateful for you just giving it a go. That's enough for me.'

After double checking the directions and noting them in my phone, I end the call and leave the bedroom to make my way to Derek – an oasis of calm, laptop set up, phone in hand. He scrutinises me as I enter the room, his eyes narrowing.

'What's the matter, Mary?' Derek asks.

I tell him about the call with Jay, explaining I need to leave for a while.

Derek sighs, running his hand through his hair. 'Animals and kids are your kryptonite, Mary. You know that, right?'

'True. I can take a lot of shit, but for God's sake, don't let me vibe on any case where the dog or the kid gets hurt. I don't think I can stand it. Perhaps I shouldn't go...' My sentence trails up at the end, and Derek doesn't miss his cue.

'I have faith in you. You're not giving yourself enough credit right now. Despite all the tragedy you've faced, you made it through. Losing your mum to cancer when you were eight, being abused by your foster parents. *Then* put back into care and being bullied at the children's home. Think of all the shit you went through in the years after. Being treated for schizophrenia and being dosed up on meds when you weren't like me or our other friends. You were actually a talented medium. *All that time*, never knowing your real self. And if you hadn't saved us all at the Rainbow Unit, we'd all be mindless zombies right now with our brains sucked out of us. We'd be doing God knows what, for the highest bidder.'

My gaze meets his, and lips curling upwards, I feel my back straighten at his encouragement.

'You're stronger than you realise, Mary, and hey, maybe this little guy's ok somewhere. Who knows?' Derek says.

'Thanks, D, you're the best. You and Jay are probably right. I just... have a bad feeling about this.' I slap a hand to my forehead. 'Oh my god, that reminds me about Errol turning up this morning. At first, because of the timing, I wondered if he was trying to warn me about something connected with this case, but then, he started talking about the bonds between friends. I think he wants to warn me about you guys keeping safe? I don't know why, but please be careful, yeah?' I retrieve my phone from my pocket and work up the message in the group text I'm in with my friends. 'I need to text Sophie, Marcie, and Rachel quickly as well, before I leave.' *Had a warning from Errol, but don't know who for. Please be careful xxx.*

Marcie works in a nursery, so she likely won't receive the message until she finishes her shift or has a break. I picture Sophie pausing her creation of whatever art creation is consuming her, removing her customary headphones, and tilting her head inquisitively as she reads the message I had sent. As soon as I text, my phone rings, displaying

Sophie's name. With a slight shake of my head, I slip the phone into my bag. *I can't answer her right now, I need to hurry up and meet Jay. Anyway, Sophie will probably call Derek for an explanation when she can't get hold of me.* Distracted as I head for the front door, I tut, doubling back to look in the living room for my keys. 'Mutha grubba,' I fumble, elbow deep in yesterday's bag.

Derek sits, scrolling on his phone, and glances at me every now and then as I call out last-minute instructions in a rush. 'Love, Sophie, Rachel, or Marcie will probably call you. It's because I've sent them a text, warning them to be careful. If you speak to them, please explain I don't know what it is they need to be careful of, but can they please just be extra alert. Errol wasn't able to spell out what the danger is.'

I find my keys in the side pocket of the bag and hold them aloft with a flourish before stopping to smile at Derek. He's not looking at me, and has his head down, scanning his phone. 'I'm going to meet Jay, now! Bye love,' I call out, moving to the door a second time.

I yank it open, then, hearing footsteps behind me, whirl around, surprised to see Derek has paused his screen time to follow me to the threshold. He wraps me in his arms and lightly kisses my unsuspecting lips. 'Bye, beautiful.'

CHAPTER 6

Traffic isn't too bad, and within the hour I spot the quiet residential street Jay had given me directions to. As I turn onto it, I speak to my companion, without taking my eyes off the road. 'Thanks for coming with me, Errol, it means a lot.'

'You can always call me if you need me, Mary. You know that,' Errol says from the passenger seat of my car.

Saying no more, I recognise Jay's car, and park just behind him. He never takes the police vehicle when we collaborate, as my involvement isn't something the Met wants advertised.

Jay's blue Skoda is nice. Average looking, clean, reliable. Like him. Errol and I walk over, and I get in beside him, giving him a smile of greeting. 'Alright, Jay?'

'Hi, Mary. You got here quickly. I hope you were driving sensibly?'

'Yes, Dad, of course I was.' I grin. A split second after my words, I freeze imperceptibly, wanting to kick myself for my poor word choice. Errol is in the back, and I know he'll have felt my mortification. It wasn't too long ago that Jay lost his son, Pepe, in a terrible drowning accident at the beach. My shoulders relax when Jay's snort of amusement comes from the driver's seat. Thank God, he hasn't seemed to have noticed what I said, and points to a large, red bricked building near the car.

I scan the building and its surrounding area. We're in a quiet, suburban neighbourhood. There's nothing around that would be likely to attract visitors. No shops or public transport nearby. No points of interest… except, the area taped off by the police, of course. I turn in my seat to look at Jay properly, sucking in a breath and pursing my lips. His eyes are rimmed with red, and there are dark pockets of skin underneath each one.

'That's his school? Patryk's?' I ask.

Jay nods.

I stare back at the school through the windscreen, defocusing my gaze while drawing in deep breaths. My eyelids flutter as I get out of the car. Already moving towards it, I hear Jay shut my door. Without checking, I know Errol will be nearby. 'Can I go to Patryk's classroom?' I ask. 'The last room he'd have been in before he finished on Friday?'

'Yeah, we should be close to it. I believe it's the one on the left-hand side.'

Closer, I'm enticed by the vivid hues that dance in front of me. I perceive the jubilance of the day, and excitement for the weekend. A smile haunts my face.

'If you must do this, at least remember what I taught you about tuning to the physical,' Errol reminds me.

I'm already so focused, that his voice doesn't make me jump. Instead, I nod, distracted.

'Are you communicating with someone? A spirit?' Jay's voice is eager. He's seen me accessing my psychic powers in the course of our other cases, but he's still not used to my habit of holding conversations out loud with invisible people.

Questions can sometimes put me off, but I nod, and hold up a hand for Jay to stop speaking. Obediently, he remains quiet as I turn to Errol, reassuring my spirit mentor that I know what to do.

I tell Errol, 'Feel the emotion I'm searching for, then it seeks the person emanating the matching signal.' Then tilt my head to one side to look at Jay, checking, 'Patryk's a cheerful boy, Jay? Happy?'

Jay's nod is slow, as though his head is as heavy as his heart when he answers, 'Yeah. Patryk's dad told me he's a well-behaved young man with special needs. Never any bother, always cheerful. Very gentle little lad, he said.' Jay's tone drops, nearly inaudible.

He's probably remembering his own son, Pepe, God rest his soul. He was only five when he drowned. My hand flutters beside my thigh, wanting to reach out to clasp Jay's hand in comfort, but I don't. *Kids and animals. I can't bear it.*

'Wrong thought-block, Mary,' Errol prompts me to refocus.

In the classroom, I shrug off the melancholy as a dog shakes off rainwater, then re-align my wavelengths. *Back to receiving that Friday feeling. The end of the week and freedom from school and weekday responsibilities.* Similar to an emotional bloodhound, I sense the trail of thoughts and follow the pathway they leave behind them. Initially, my steps seem circular, as I fixate on different thought blocks:

Fish and chips tonight.

Anime for the whole day tomorrow if I want.

Swimming, then McDonald's.

I leave the classroom, and exit the building, zig-zagging in the playground and filtering the overheard plans I pick up on, and the accompanying emotions. Absentmindedly, I turn to Jay, 'You mentioned before Patryk's on the autistic spectrum?'

'Yeah, Patryk has ASD. Aside from that, he's apparently a neat boy, polite. Oh, and he hates loud noises; they trigger him.'

Still moving, I ask, 'Trigger him how? Make him violent or upset? Did he wear noise cancelling headphones?'

Jay says, 'I don't think he's aggressive, no. His Dad said Patryk wouldn't kick off, but they would distress him. He'd clamp his hands over his ears until the sound disappeared. Patryk doesn't want to be different, so he uses earbuds. He's very proud of them, apparently.'

'Earbuds... proud...' *Got him! Patryk.* I breathe in his colours. *Bright blue. Blue for bouncing boy. Fun.* 'He's listening to classical music. He likes it.' I'm speaking aloud but am not fully aware of what I'm saying. I walk unconsciously back towards the gate, following Patryk's steps with a smile. In my mind, I hear his last thoughts.

Two armpit hairs.

Getting to be a big boy.

With a gentle twist in the air, I recreate the secret handshake Patryk and Danny share.

See ya, Danny.

See ya, Patryk.

I savour the bond between the two boys. Danny. Patryk. *The special handshake. Best friends.*

I feel the two boys split, parting ways, but their energies remain entwined. I direct my attention away from Danny and back to Patryk.

My pace is slow as I leave the school, meandering off down the street. 'He went this way,' I mumble to myself, tracking the lost boy. I smooth down Patryk's cowlick, voicing the actions I experience under my breath. 'Humming. Happy. So excited about his future. Soon be in secondary.'

Jay's voice sounds far away as he says, 'What? I didn't hear you.'

Ignoring him, I continue to trail in the psychic wake of Patryk, *Dad says it's really good practice.* Something else interferes with my vibrant pathway. I stop short, blinking in surprise at Errol, as he bars my way. I scowl at him.

'I think you should check the school building again. I don't think you've checked it properly,' Errol tells me.

'What?' I bark, worried my spirit friend will jar me out of my flow. 'Mind, Errol, you're jolting me out of Patryk's signal.'

Errol doesn't shift. Instead, he remains in my way, pointing in the opposite direction. My momentum slows, and if I'm not careful, I know I'll lose the frequency, and Patryk with it.

'What the heck, Errol? *Move*, or I'll march right through your invisible arse.'

Errol kisses his teeth but stays in my path. Then says, 'Please, Mary.' He stretches out his palm but goes on mute again.

Tutting, I still struggle to commit the ultimate rudeness and walk through my friend, so I sidestep him with no more discussion.

Instantly, I'm hit by a sledgehammer blow of raw energy. I shriek inwardly, clapping my hands over my ears and closing my eyes as I instinctively recoil against the intensity of it.

Dread flows through me as I'm inundated with a sensation of my lack of strength and powerlessness. 'No, please,' I whisper, dropping to the ground with a whump. Lost in the energy world, I don't feel the pain as my joints wallop down on hard concrete. In my peripheral vision, I spot Jay rushing over to me as Errol paces beside me like a caged tiger, mouthing words I cannot understand. Evil wraps slimy coils through my heart, its rot sending pine needles of terror throughout every region of my being. I feel it. A sick pleasure exists in the meticulous planning that went into the abduction. Even worse, there's more to come.

Daddy. Mummy.

I swallow a sob and permit myself to be helped back to my feet. Half in this reality, half in the next, I hold on to Jay's muscular arm for support. Vertigo strikes me as Patryk is propelled backwards; sight removed as they stuff him into a vehicle in one fluid motion. A human rag doll.

The sound of his cry is strange and uneven. It reminds me of when my ears need to pop when at a high elevation. My fingers move to my lobes, then I realise what's different; *Patryk has one earbud still in place. But the other?* Blinking, I stare down at the pavement. *I'm back in the room.* I clear my husky throat before speaking. 'His earbud fell out.' I rub my eyes and Jay's face becomes more focused.

His mouth is hanging open, and he remains motionless for a second, until my statement sinks in. Jay whips gloves out of his pocket before stopping down to inspect where I'm pointing. The gutter. 'Jesus Christ, Mary, you're bloody right! There *is* an earbud down here.' He returns to silence, concentrating on photographing the earbud and its position, and phones the forensic team to summon someone.

I wait for him to wrap up the conversation before I speak. 'I need to stretch my legs before we go back to the car.' Without another word, I stride off, hoping the weak sun will chase away the ice cold that now permeates my veins. I ignore the fact that my knees are knocking together as I walk and straighten my back.

CHAPTER 7

D inner was lovely, and I'm relaxed, humming as I stack the last cup in the dishwasher. But when I go to put detergent in to start the machine, I notice there aren't any tabs. 'D, did you remember to buy tea bags and dishwasher tabs yesterday?' I already know the answer. *Derek's murder for this.* Glued to his phone or laptop most of the time, he never remembers to restock the home essentials, so it usually falls to me. No answer comes from Derek in the living room. I roll my eyes. Typical, he's probably just scrolling his socials. 'Joker,' I mumble.

The supermarket in town is open until ten o'clock. I decide to do a quick trip down there to pick them up. 'Derek, have you seen my keys?' As I call out to Derek, I shut the dishwasher door with a bang, glancing around the room.

Derek appears in the kitchen doorway, anticipating my lack of car keys. He gestures to the rack I'd peered at a few seconds ago. 'You left 'em on the bathroom side yesterday,' he says. 'So, I hung them up for you.'

How come I hadn't spotted them when I looked there a minute ago? 'Oh, yeah, that's right! I was desperate for a pee when I got in.' *And I'd been even more desperate for a cry. That poor little boy, Patryk. Bless him, he'd been so innocent and terrified. In contrast, whomever had snatched him had revelled in malicious pleasure. Evil incarnate.* I swallow the lump in my throat, pinning a tight smile to my face.

Buck up, Mary Jameson. I don't want Derek to see me cry. I know he can't handle it.

Derek chuckles at my forgetfulness.

My keys jangle as I grab them, and I blow him a kiss on my way to the front door. 'What would I do without you, D?' I ask as I leave.

Derek follows me, and after I accept his gentle peck on the lips, he hands me my handbag like a prize. 'You'd spend a lot more time looking for stuff, that's for sure.' Derek closes the door behind me.

In my car, I shiver in the late evening air, jiggling my ignition key and coaxing my car, Adrienne, to start. 'Come on, bonne fille. Come on, baby, it's cold out here.'

The engine turns over with a throaty hum, as the last of the sun exchanges itself for moonlight. The night falls around me, as if it were the curtain on a stage setting.

'Success!' I twist on the hot air and click the radio to a hip hop station. Head bopping, I move off down the road, shouting along with the rap artist. My voice is loud, and I smile at the feeling of release. I don't play my music indoors because Derek says he doesn't like rap. As a night owl, I savour the freedom of being out after dark, playing my tunes. My lunch time soirees with my friends don't provide me with the same sentiment. The moon moves along the sky, perpendicular to my car. It's large and radiant, and my lips curl into a smile. With a flick, I turn the volume up, nodding my head and tapping my hand on the steering wheel all the way to the local shop. By the time I get there, my ambitious movements have warmed me up, even though my little heater only works as I arrive.

I drive up to the glass-fronted supermarket, neatly pulling into one of the diagonal parking bays outside. The other spaces are empty, and the car park is shadowy. Leaving the cheer of my car I jog to the shop, greeted by automatic doors and Motown soul music. I grin. *Nice. Let's keep this party going.* I snatch a shopping basket from the front door and enter. The glare of the florescent lights makes me squint as I enter, and I nod to the cashier.

The cashier nods back but says nothing. Instead, he continues to thumb through a comic book he has open on the counter.

Strolling around the shop, I hum along to the music being played over the speaker system. I hear the whoosh of the automatic doors and guess I'm not the only person to forget some essential items. As I continue to amble along, perusing the well-stocked shelves, I stop humming, slowing down my strolling speed as I notice the cold. With a tut to myself, I think how annoying it is that they always crank up the air conditioner in these places, regardless of the time of day, or of the temperature outside. *It's so stupid.* I rub my arms, trying to soothe away the goosebumps. A sharp stabbing pain gnaws at me, and I press my temples. *Probably dehydrated; Derek's always telling me I don't drink enough water. Tea bags. Dishwasher tabs-oooo. Biccies. I'm so easily side-tracked.* The number of products in my basket is growing, straining my arms.

I walk past different brands of rice, and remember I ran out of it a couple of days ago, when Derek wanted to make me a curry. He's been trying his hand at learning to make traditional African recipes as a gift to me, to remind me of my childhood and my mum's home cooking. A couple of months ago, I'd told him I was sad I'd forgotten the meals she used to make, and that I didn't remember any of my culture anymore to pass onto our kids, if we ever had any. Now, he searches up new recipes every month, and I end up spending loads in any food shop that boasts an international section. Although it started off as a lovely idea, a lot of the meals I haven't enjoyed, and I feel a weight of expectation from Derek that makes me feel pressured. *He likes to know I enjoy what he cooks, and I want to show appreciation; that can't be a bad thing.* I walk away from the spice shelves, determined not to put anything else in my shopping basket.

I hear a shifting in the next aisle to mine. *Someone's moving along, browsing the shelves like me. A fellow late-night shopper.* The beginnings of a migraine slice into my head again, and I stop, holding my forehead in one chilly hand.

The rustling noise indicates that the person's keeping pace with me in their aisle. I look up at the label hanging above me. *Number twenty-four.*

'Huh, that's my age,' I muse aloud, focusing on the shelves. *Breakfast bits: We need some cereal.* Rounding the corner, I'm mindful of the unseen shopper, but unexpectedly, walk straight into an empty space. I scratch my head, checking up and down the aisle. *Where did they go?*

There's a crackling in the air, similar to the atmosphere before a storm. Foreboding reaches me, and the cold in the shop makes me shiver. I glance around again, swallowing dryly, and continue to walk, slower than before. Click… click… click… the static hums in my mind like an out of tune radio station, and 'Ain't No Mountain High Enough' floods the speakers. Although I like the song, hearing it now adds to the clanging wrongness. I know what the clicking noise signifies, but I can't make anything out yet.

With a quick scan around me, my brows meet as I check for the security mirrors. They are located exactly where they're supposed to be - high on the wall in the corner of each side of the shop. Right now, there's no reflection in them, and nothing otherworldly has manifested to me either. *Maybe I'm mistaken?* My breath comes quickly, in shallow gulps, and I force myself to breathe slowly, deeply. That helps, but a gnawing sensation knots my stomach. *Something's wrong. Someone is here, I know it.* I peep behind me. *All clear.* My grip tightens on the pendant of my necklace, *my lucky charm.*

My hair sizzles, standing up on end and confusion floods me. *I've shut off my ESP, so I can't be in the receptive mode. Maybe I should put out some otherworldly feelers?* Gulping, I straighten my back and tilt my small chin up. *It's obvious I've stayed in my comfort zone for too long, I mustn't forget, I am Spartan.* I position myself to avoid the bored young man at the till, smirking. To an observer, I seem lost in thought while examining bread.

Inwardly, I open myself up to the connection with spirit, allowing my inner focus to exist without intention. Just as a cork is cast out onto the water, so I throw out my psychic net. Rusty at first, because it has been a while, it bobs along on the surface of an energy river as I wait. Something will divert its course, though it's still uncertain what. Like a wheel with no spoke, I allow my attention to stay general, its destination unspoken for.

Dread and terror rip into me out of nowhere, and an ear-splitting scream bursts into my awareness, doubling me over in shock. I jump back from the innocuous loaves of bread, crying out. In reflex, I hunch over protectively, and clap my hands over my ears, desperate to shut out the banshee noise. I search the shop for the source; no one is there. *What the hell is that?* Frantically, I keep looking around, but I can only hear the scream, and can't determine its source. A boy's shrill voice rings out and I understand it's a spirit I'm hearing, forcing its way through to me.

No! You stop it! Stop it! You're a bad person! he says.

Stop what? What's he shouting about, me? The emotion behind the demand is powerful, and filled with anger, but also contains a terrible fear. A fierce, soul wrenching agony emanates from him, assaulting my senses. It's so strong that I retch, dry heaving where I stand. I try to reject the pain and the words of the boy. *Surely, this can't be Patryk? Not with such all-encompassing rage and surging violence of emotion? It has to be someone else.* I look for the voice's owner by spinning around, but they're not visible. Hand on my tummy, I push gently, to help to steady my breathing, then focus. His fury, terror, and pain projects directly at me with a megawatt force, hitting me in a tidal wave of emotion.

Lips clamped shut, I want to scream so badly alongside the noise in my head that I have to grit my teeth together to stop myself. Inside my mouth, my fillings feel as though they're on fire, heat on heat, and vibrating. Every fibre inside me feels as on-edge as my teeth do.

The connection is closer, and although I can't see him, I feel it's a male. *Who the hell is this and what does he want?* I squint down the aisle, staring into the air. *Is it Patryk, after all?*

From a distance, he speaks. *Not Patryk.*

His words slice into the air, hanging over me like a dagger and making me jump. He's angry, vengeful, and I flinch at the unexpected statement that slashes its way into my thoughts, making me screech out loud without thinking.

Pressing my fingers to my temples, I swing around and see a male shape materialise. He's appeared at the end of the shop, behind me. At first, his features are unclear, but something about him appears 'off,' and I lean forward warily to get a better view. There seems to be something different about his face, but it's hard to tell from here…

'Jesus.' I breathe as my mind makes sense of what I'm seeing. My heart races, but I'm rooted to the spot, staring at him in horror. The blood drains from my face, leaching out into the ether and despite my fear, my heart goes out to him.

He's horribly disfigured. One side of his face is porcelain perfection, but the other side is a human patchwork of leathered, mottled pink and brown flesh. It droops down, like the liquified wax of a burned-out candle, cobbled together. My hand wavers up to my own unblemished cheek, unconsciously smoothing it. A soft breath exits my mouth, and I attempt to speak, but find that just like my friend, Errol, no sound comes out.

The boy mimics me, opening his mouth like me, and snapping his jaw shut when my mouth closes of its own volition during his grotesque parody of my horror. He grins, and smoke puffs around his face, as though he's exhaling it.

My heart continues to thud erratically against my chest as I wait on tenterhooks to see what he does next. I wipe sweaty palms on my trousers. I glance down, realising that my legs are trembling.

The boy has tufts of brown hair on a melted scalp, and although it's difficult to tell for sure at this distance, I think he has dark eyes.

There's an intense anger flowing from him, and I don't want him to come any closer. I swallow, throat dry, as he moves down the aisle towards me. The aura of menace pulsates from him in powerful vacillations, and the air surrounding me carries an electric charge that makes my hair sizzle with static, then lift.

Shuffling backward, my gaze locks onto his face. I take cautious steps, to coax the reluctant motion of my legs. *One baby step, two baby steps.* My left foot retreats first, followed by my right. Their trembling is so intense I have to use shaking hands to hoist them up for the first couple of steps. My progress is slow, and deliberate, and sweat pours in-between my shoulder blades in rivulets. The horror I'm feeling makes my perspiration seem as though it's transformed into ice water down my back, and my top clings to it.

A surge of pure hatred contorts the boy's features, twisting them into a malevolent mask.

'What did I ever do to you?' My whisper acts as a trigger, petrol on fire, and the boy's movement picks up speed. His motions are also slow and deliberate, matching mine, but where mine are wary, his are those of a predator stalking his prey.

I stop trying to disguise my retreat and blatantly walk backwards as fast as I can in a straight line. I keep my eyes glued to his actions and try to match his speed but moving away from him. The high-pitched voice of a famous Motown singer trills out of the shop's orifices.

'Come see about me-eee,' the boy demands in a sing-song voice, his brown eyes, venomous slits. His wrathful presence churns my stomach, and I heave again, this time my dinner regurgitates, burning acid up my throat. The boy hisses, and I flinch. He gathers more speed. Suddenly, he's coming straight at me from the other side of the supermarket.

'Forget this,' I shout, then pivot and run full pelt towards the guy at the till. As I sprint for freedom, action holds my panic at bay, for now at least. He's right behind me, and his anger reaches out, a fingertip away now. His emanation is stretching out to meet mine, to conquer it.

My imagination conjures up his small hands curling into vicious talons, ready to drag me back to be savaged by his nightmare face and puncture my eyes with the powerful strength that rage can give the unseen. *Or maybe he wants to take over me. Like my dad used to. No.* His presence is a hair's breadth to the back of me.

'Help! Help me!' I scream, sprinting towards the counter. As I rush towards the shop assistant, he stares at me with an almost comical expression of confusion. His head tilts as he watches me, chewing gum, and he pops a bubble, then his mouth drops open. He rises from his swivel chair slowly, letting the pages drop from his hands, then strolls around the counter, a frown still on his face. He has a walkie talkie in his hand and lifts it to his lips, speaking into it.

I hear him saying into the small black device, 'Urgent assistance needed at the counter, please.'

While he continues to talk, I let out a blood-curdling scream of release, filled with adrenaline and hysteria.

'Not Patryk' reaches out to grab me. I know he wants to smash his consciousness into mine against my will. His psychic tendrils stretch out to curve themselves into my consciousness. I get to the front of the shop, my fingertips touching the counter as though I'm a child myself, and I've reached the safety of 'home.' He fades back, like the tide leaving the shore of a beach.

Just as the shop assistant arrives at the customer's side of the counter, I fall at his feet. A wingless helicopter plummeting from the sky.

'What the hell?' he says.

I wake up, and there's a fleece folded underneath my head. Blinking, I raise a weak hand to my head to steady it. A brief scan around shows me my shopping basket has been collected from where I dropped it, and that the shop assistant has been joined by a hulking man, with features straight from the Cro-Magnon era. It's him who kneels down to me, asking in a surprisingly gentle voice, 'How do you feel, madam? Do you feel able to sit up?'

Flushing at his concern, I rise too quickly, instantly regretting it. I gulp in breaths, my gaze darting around us for the Damien child. *Get your shit together, Mary Jameson, you don't want them to call anyone. You still have a million mental health records on file. What can I say to make them chill?* 'I'm fine, so sorry. I thought I saw a rat?'

Alarm sends the gentle giant to his feet, one massive hand flying to his throat. 'A rat?' The comic reading shop assistant frowns, looking doubtful.

I nod. 'Yes, I'm deathly afraid of them, a phobia? I apologise for being a nuisance. I feel like such an idiot. Sorry.' The blood returns to my face, and I notice them glance at my pink cheeks and bashful smile.

They share a look together and the smaller guy nods. 'It's no problem, madam. Did you come in a car? Do you feel ok to drive?'

'You're so sweet. Yes I have my car just outside, but aside from feeling embarrassed, I'm absolutely fine. Thanks so much. I'll just pay for my shopping.'

The door entrance bell is set off as another customer enters the supermarket. I stand to my feet, brushing off my clothes and bum. My flush intensifies as I note the woman craning her neck in our direction. *Mind your business and just keep walking, lady.* I clear my throat, smiling politely at my two knights in shining armour. After allowing them to bag my groceries I bow out of the shop, feeling like a character from a medieval film, curtseying to nobility as I leave. Thankfully, they make no more attempts to stop me and after accepting the shock of the cold blast of outside air, I reach my car. *Who the hell was that scary-ass kid? And why was he so ferocious? Could it just be a random, pushy spirit?*

The inside of my car is bitterly cold, and my breath fogs out in front of me. I cross my fingers for good luck. They're so stiff with cold I worry the engine won't start, leaving me stranded here in the dark with only the boy with the hooked nails and melted face for company. Feeling vulnerable, my gaze flicks right and left, before I spin around to check the back seat. *All clear.* The central locking clicks as I engage it, and I cough, self-consciously.

Nibbling my lip, my shoulders twitch, shuddering. Adrienne, although temperamental, obviously feels some vehicular version of pity for me, because for once, I drive away without issue. On the drive home, I peep in the rear-view mirror of my car every few seconds. The clock tells me only forty minutes have passed since the episode at the supermarket. I glance back into the mirror at my face, grimacing. My features are tight and pasty, while my lips have taking on a bluish tinge. *Not good.* It prompts me to give myself a stern pep talk. *'Whatever happens, I can't afford to let Derek worry, his mental health can't take it. I need to sort my shit out before I get home.'* When I raise a hand to smooth my hair down, it's still shaking.

For the rest of the journey, I leave the radio off and switch the heater on full blast. It's only ten minutes or so, but it feels like the road stretches endlessly in front of me, and I glance in the rear-view mirror compulsively, checking the back seat again for an unexpected visitor. *God, it's cold in here. I just can't get warm.*

Derek's already asleep when I skitter into the bedroom, tiptoeing, so as to avoid waking him up. As I throw on my nightclothes, my gaze rakes every shadowy corner. I skip showering because I'm scared to stay in the bathroom by myself. Instead, I cut corners with my hygiene, rushing through my bedtime ministrations as quickly as I can, throwing off my clothes, then sliding next to Derek. I lift my feet away from the gap underneath the bed slats like a child, afraid a monster is lurking there in the dark. With a quick wriggle, I back up, reverse spooning Derek and squeezing myself so closely to him that a postage stamp couldn't fit in between us. I'm momentarily calmed by his strong heartbeat as I do so. He drops a kiss on my shoulder, then murmurs something unintelligible in his sleep.

My hammering heart rate slows, and his arm falls over my waist to anchor me to him.

I stroke the hair on his arm with tenderness, and lay awake for what seems like hours, biting my bottom lip with my gaze darting around mysterious shapes that shift in the room. I feel the uneasiness of my nerves, jittering out their vibration and I block them out, concentrating on the rhythm of Derek's breathing, and steadfastly shutting out the strands of fear that pour out of me like spilled vinegar, turning the air sharp with its sour tang. *Who was that angry spirit that targeted me tonight, and what did he want with me?*

CHAPTER 8

‘ H ello, beautiful,’ Derek says.
I wake up to see Derek, leaning over me with a grin and an adoring expression on his face. Sometimes, it creeps me out when he does that, but today, it feels welcome. Overnight, my equilibrium has been restored, and I give him a sleepy smile back. My voice is husky when I reply. 'Hey, handsome.'

I can hear the frown in Derek's voice. 'You were tossing and turning last night. How did you sleep?'

'Fine,' I say. *Like shit, is the actual truth.*

'Really? You've got dark circles under your eyes that say otherwise,' Derek says.

My mouth forms a circle at the cheek of him. 'Have I? What happened to calling me beautiful? I liked that more.'

Derek's chortle vibrates along the mattress, lifting my mood. 'Weather report looks good for today. Still wanna go to the beach?'

Oh, yeah! I'd forgotten he'd suggested we go on a date at the beach. I love nature. My ear-to-ear smile is authentic and all the reply he needs, but just in case he doesn't interpret my answer, I say, 'Do you need to ask?'

Derek chuckles, hugging me close, then says, 'Not really. Let's have a lazy morning, though. We didn't get to snuggle much last night because you got home late.'

Is it my guilty conscience, or does Derek's statement sound like a question? With a swallow, I say, 'Yeah, sorry about that. I told you, there was a massive queue at the petrol station.'

'Annoying, aye. Did you go to the one near the dual carriageway? People always flock to that petrol station because it's the cheapest around for miles. Honestly, what with Brexit and the effects of COVID, the cost of living has gone through the roof.'

His question is allayed, and remaining on my side, I move closer to Derek, tucking my head under his chin and curling into his lean frame. *What he doesn't know can't hurt him, as they say.* I feel my shoulders relax and press a kiss into his chest as his wiry arms encircle me more snugly.

'Do you want to invite the gang?' Derek asks.

'Nah, let's just have some *us* time. I could do with it.' *Plus, they'll ask me if I'm pregnant yet, which I am not.* Tears brim in my eyes briefly, and I swallow them down. *It'll happen.*

Derek kisses the top of my head, completely unattuned to my thoughts or mood. 'Sounds like bliss.'

As we lay there, I watch our colours merging. On a spectral level, our coupling creates a visual beauty that's breathtaking. Our colours twirl gracefully, twisting around us, similar to the ribbons of a gymnast. I sigh. *On the spectral level, we're perfect together.*

I close my eyes, not because I'm going back to sleep, but to better enjoy the iridescent lustre we generate. For a while, I inhale and exhale deeply, content, and so does Derek. Our rhythms match. *Perfectly.* We go to get ready for our day at the coast.

As we sit on the bench opposite the sea, the sand flying up around us, I look up the sky. It's a miserable grey colour that matches the tumultuous sea. *It's so cold.* My teeth are chattering, and I tug at the sleeves of my T-shirt, trying to cover my goose bumped skin. *Pointless.* 'I told you, I'm fine. I don't need your jacket.' I snap.

Derek raises his eyebrows. 'You'll freeze your little bum off. You're just being stubborn, Mary Jameson.'

I feel my eye twitch as I look at his grin and humouring tone, and my chin thrusts itself up. With effort, I press my lips together to stop my teeth from shattering by the force with which they're clicking together. 'Am not. I'm absolutely fine.' It would be too embarrassing now to admit I want to go sit in the car after I made such a big deal when he tried to help me earlier. Telling him how I don't need a man to 'save me' like some 'damsel in distress.' *Honestly, I don't know what hair had crawled up my arse and triggered me to say all that, but sometimes I wish I'd learn to shut up and back down occasionally.* I firm my lips. *Today, however, is not that day.*

'OK, that's fine, hun,' Derek says with a shrug.

We both fall quiet and the wind blasts around us, whistling loudly. Eyes narrowed against the icy blasts, I stare out at the sea. The waves are high, it's fearsome majesty triggering a feeling of loneliness that echoes in me as I watch it. Derek sits beside me wrapped up in his jacket, hunched over the phone in his hand in his usual position.

Without looking I know he's wearing the touchscreen gloves he has. *So he can still scroll.* My nostrils flare as I hunch over, shivering. A frosty gust fans my hair back, so that it flies out like the wings of a bird. Despite wrapping my arms tighter around my waist, shudders wrack my frame in response to the frigid air. The combined howling of the wind and angry sea is so loud, I don't hear Derek when he speaks again.

Flipping weather report. Useless arseholes always get it wrong. As I see his mouth moving, I realise he's talking again, and not to his phone. I turn to look at him, to help me hear.

Derek cups a hand around his mouth, enunciating, 'If your bum *does* fall off and blow away, don't worry. I'll still run down the beach to catch it, even though you're so moody today.'

'Oh, ha ha, Derek. That's *so* funny.' As I speak, I feel my cold lips curl into a sneer, and annoyance makes me grit my teeth even harder.

Our gazes meet. Derek, invulnerable to my irritation, is grinning widely, and a snort of amusement splits out of me, against my will. *I'm being an arse, but I don't really know why?* My shoulders slump as I acknowledge that's not strictly the truth because I sort of do. *I'm sour because I'm scared and feel like everything's out of my control. But that's not Derek's fault.* 'Oh, shut up, smug mug.' After a second, I sigh. 'I'm sorry, D. I dunno why I'm so moody but please, just ignore me. Let's go and grab the coat from the back seat.'

Unoffended and quick to forgive me, Derek leaps up, holding a hand down to me to pull me up. 'Don't worry about it. Why don't we dash back to the car, then eat our lunch in there so we don't get hypothermia? The view will be lovely at least,' he says.

Hand in hand, we run eagerly to Derek's car. Similar to my old jalopy, we named it 'Rocky.' It's parked away from the beach, and as we run, the movement energises me, despite the Siberian wind, pushing us along.

I turn on the radio after eating, and a soulful voice sings. I immediately switch it over, freaked out as memories of the night before at the supermarket flood back. That case has naff-all to do with me. The radio has an old-fashioned nob and even though I twiddle it, the song persists. Goosebumps reappear on my arms. Managing to change the channel, my shoulders slump with relief, but then I take in what the DJ is announcing in his smooth voice.

'Stay with us folks, 'Ain't no Mountain High Enough' is next.'

I stare at Derek, who is unaware of the sinister connotation these lyrics hold for me. He sings along with the radio, stopping as he realises I'm fiddling with the tuner. His voice is serious when he asks, 'What's the matter, Mary?'

I only shake my head, turning the station nob with more urgency. Stupid thing won't leave this channel. My head starts to pound, and I raise a shaky hand to it.

'What is it?' Derek touches my hand, gently removing it from the radio controls.

A flash flood of anger rushes through me at his action, and I wrench my hand away. Momentarily, I catch site of my reflection in the rear-view mirror, a fierce frown on my face, mouth screwed up tight. *God, I look so outraged. Derek's just being nice, he doesn't deserve this, just because I'm freaking out. It's not his fault I don't feel it's safe to share my load with him. I wish I could trust he's properly looking after himself, his mental health, and not just masking his symptoms. Like he was the last time.* I swallow, closing my eyes briefly. *This is no good. I need to find a way to squash this resentment towards him. This is what I signed up for and it is what it is. Besides, Derek is a million times nicer than I deserve. I'm really lucky to have him. I need to remember what my life was like before and be grateful.* Blowing out slowly, I clear my throat, forcing myself to speak. 'Sorry, Derek, I think I've got a headache coming.' It's only a partial lie. The music sounds shrill and threatening, causing my head to throb.

Derek clicks off the radio, first try, and the silence is a relief. Eyes round, I settle back into my seat, giving him a small smile of gratitude.

'Why didn't you just say?' he asks. 'Let's get you some painkillers, find a cosy place to eat, mooch around charity shops, and buy ourselves warmer clothes. Then we could go for a brisk walk before we leave? Blow the cobwebs away. What do you think?'

I mull this over. *That does sound tempting.* 'Sounds great. I'm up for that.'

On the drive back home much later that evening, I fall asleep, letting the waves of peace carry me away. When we arrive at the flat, I remain in a slumber, only vaguely stirring as we come to a stop. After getting out the car himself, Derek lifts me up like a baby, closing the door with his knee. Semi-conscious, I snuggle close to his chest, and he drops a kiss on the top of my head. 'Love you, Mary.'

I mumble in my sleep, and he smiles.

CHAPTER 9

————

Working from home as usual, Derek sits in his favourite work spot, at the kitchen table involved in some computer wizardry. When my mobile rings, I glance at him, motioning I will leave the room to take the call in our bedroom. I sit on our bed, filing my nails while I speak to Marcie. After the call, I stand up, about to leave the bedroom when my phone rings again. Rihanna's strident tones sing to me from the back pocket of my jeans, where I've put my phone. I look down, lifting it out slowly. With a sigh, I acknowledge my reluctance to answer its call, and sit back on my bed with a slump. 'Hi, Jay.'

My stomach lurches as I picture the spirit in the supermarket, the fury that emanated from him, and the rage twisting up the side of his face as it slid downwards. I swallow, listening intently to what Jay's saying.

'Morning, Mary. You busy?' Jay says.

The shorthand speech Jay sometimes employs used to frustrate me, but I'm no longer offended; this is just his way and I answer flippantly, 'Depends why you're asking.'

After a beat of silence, Jay says, 'Cagey. I want you to come somewhere with me, see if you can sense anything.'

I shiver, reliving the fear that had enveloped me as I sprinted down the supermarket aisle, away from the tangible rage. *The other boy… who was he, was it him?* 'Not Patryk.' *Who was he, and what did he want from me? Forget this shit. I refuse to get involved.* 'No.'

Jay's voice is louder, confused, 'No? Too busy today?'

'No… I'm not up to this, Jay. I can't do it,' I say. I'm staring upwards, half-expecting to see the boy's nightmare face glaring back at me from my ceiling. Thankfully, I don't.

There's a silence, and I know the detective is digesting my statement and coordinating his reply. I chew my lip, waiting for Jay's rebuttal.

'Why?' he asks.

'Isn't it enough for me to say no?' I snap.

'No, Mary, it's not. If I was asking you to do something for *me*, then yes, that would suffice. But a child is missing, and his life could be hanging in the balance. Think about his parents… Grieving parents.'

I pull my mobile aware from my ear and scowl at it. Jay knows I appreciate that the boy's parents aren't the only ones grieving. Jay's still reeling from the loss of his own son. My heart breaks for him. With a sigh, I return the handset back to my head, and note that my hand's shaking. *Shit.* 'Look, Jay, I can't handle it. A couple of days ago, some ghostly kid showed up and scared the shit out of me. My stomach's all kinds of twisted, and my nightmares… they're hellish. I have this nagging feeling that if I take this case, it will turn my life upside down, and I can't deal. Not now, not after everything I've been through. I've only just got my life back on track.'

With iron willpower, I resist the familiar urge to curl my fingers inwards and dig my nails into my scarred palms. *I won't let things go back to how they were. To how I was before. A prisoner to my voices, eating gone-off beans from a mouldy tin, and living in squalor. I'd rather die.* Taking a breath first, I verbalise my thoughts, telling Jay, 'I won't go back to how my life was before, Jay. I'm sorry, I just can't.' I end the call with resolve in my heavy heart, and the knot in my stomach tightens. *God, I hope Jay doesn't ask me to help again.*

Slipping the phone in the back pocket of my jeans, I wander back into the kitchen. 'Cup of tea or coffee, love?' I ask, trying to disguise a tremor with an overly chirpy tone as I return to the room.

Something in my words makes Derek shift his head aside from the laptop screen and scrutinises me for a few seconds. 'OK… what's going on?'

My face twitches, and tummy churning, I turn away so he can't see my expression. *Am I really refusing to help Jay?*

Rising, Derek hurries to my side, and face tight with worry, he says, 'Mary, what's the matter? Why're you shaking like that?'

A missing boy, he might die. A little boy. I keep thinking about what Jay said. *Oh my God, who would do that, take a little boy?* At first, my lips tremble, trying to hold their secrets in. Then, I picture the face of the boy from the supermarket, then Patryk, and his parents' heartbreak. Heat begins to rise from my core, and the quelling inside feels so great, it jars my mouth open. With eyes wide, I scrutinise Derek. *His last episode was well over a year ago now, and he's been so stable he should be able to cope with stress. Maybe it's time to trust him. He needs to hear some of what's going on.* Parting my quivering lips, I relieve myself of the entire story, telling Derek everything that's happened so far. From Errol on mute, to Jay's crime scene, to my supernatural supermarket stalker. The story falls out of me in a rush, and like a punctured balloon expelling air, I release my words until I'm spent. After I finish, I search Derek's face for a sign my recent problems are too much for him to handle, or that the stress of it all might trigger another psychotic break.

He stares back at me, his brown gaze clear and steady. There's nothing swimming in it, except concern for me. The tension inside me disperses, then suddenly, I hear a static clicking, notch by sinister notch. I force the clicking the other way, sealing my mind off. *How is this happening? The clicking signifies I am psychically open, and about to receive a visitation from the non-spiritual realm, but I'm closed to unknown visitors, so no-one should be 'knocking at my door,' so to speak.*

There's another attempt to prise open my consciousness against my will, but sweating with effort, I slam them out. I clutch at Derek as though he's my lifebuoy, keeping me afloat on a rough sea.

His hold tightens around me as he asks, 'What is it, Mary? What's going on? What's happening?'

Vertigo strikes me as my psychic membrane shifts to allow and I can't answer Derek's questions. All I can do is stare into space as I fight the forced psychic connection. *No.* I move it back, sealing it. *I'm not in the receptive mode. It can stay closed; I don't want this.* Panic stabs at me with icy claws. *Errol! Errol will help me.* I project a mental scream out to my friend. *Errol!*

Derek sees my distress and tries to ease it. 'Oh my God, what's wrong, Mary? What's going on? Stay with me, OK? Take deep breaths. Come on, Mary. You're safe, I'm right here with you.'

I shut my eyes, as though it can prevent the incoming communication. Derek's words are so close I can feel the rumble of them in my chest, but contrarily, his voice sounds far away. *I'm alone in my head and can't stop them from coming to me. No matter how much I don't want this.* I squeeze my eyes shut tighter. *Errol, come here. Help me, please.*

Errol's voice manifests beside me, 'I'm here, Mary. Are you OK? What can I do?'

My eyelids fly open, and I gasp my relief, 'Errol, thank God. Please help me, someone's forcing their way into my mind. Get it out!'

'Errol's here? Can he help with whatever this is?' Derek's head turns left and right, scanning for Errol as I beg for his help. I answer Derek quickly, then address Errol again. 'Yes, D. Errol's here. Please, Errol, help me make this creep back off, I can't take anymore.' I speak aloud to Errol, and as I do, Derek, stares at me aghast.

Errol's voice is deep, and he speaks with calm authority, 'Mary, you need to calm down! Focus on my voice Mary, tune in fully to my energy. Come to me.' Errol's gaze bores into mine as he instructs me.

With a shake of my head, I tell him, 'Yeah, but I'm losing it here, Errol. Voices pushing their way in uninvited. A spirit with a melted face stalking me in the supermarket who seems massively pissed off. You keep cutting out. My nightmares are too scary, and I can't sleep.' *And I know whoever snatched Patryk is one evil son of a bitch.*

'Mary, shhh. Concentrate on me, please. Find my signal. Follow me,' Errol says.

Releasing Derek, I place my palms against my temples. Mentally, I push against the insistent clicking in my head. *No. I'm not accepting the call. Get away from me.* With effort, I concentrate on the thread of Errol's intention. The pushing back recedes, and with effort, I gather my thoughts again, staring at the floor.

Then, I explain to Errol about the supermarket incident. As I speak, Derek studies my face. Errol clears his throat before speaking, 'Mary, do you know who this kid was, or what he wants? Any clue about who the voices are coming from?'

'No, Errol.' I shake my head violently. 'I told you, whoever this is, they just force themselves in my mind. Such rage.' My grasp tightens on my necklace, and I loosen my grip when I realise it's in danger of snapping.

Derek opens his mouth, and I know he's about to voice concern again. I stave him off with a slight shake of my head.

'But, Mary, why didn't you switch the psychic static off like I taught you?' Errol asks, scratching his head.

Eyes wide, I ask, 'Don't you think I tried that, Errol? They're still coming through, even though I shut it off. I don't understand it. I did exactly what you said and closed off my supernatural valve, so I shouldn't be in the receptive mode. But I can feel them trying to push their way through. *Click, click, click.* Forcing me open to receive them.'

57

At my words, Derek looks all around us, then pulls me close again, his hot breath on my hair.

I place my palms against his chest, bracing myself, then stepping away. 'No. Please stop, Derek, I need to concentrate on what Errol's saying.'

Errol shakes his head. 'You're wrong, *Mary*. They're not just *coming* to you. Consider everything I explained to you after the Rainbow Unit. And remember what your mum told you about frequencies? Think about your dad, before he embraced The Blue and reunited himself with it... When did he used to come to you?'

Brows crinkling, I think back before answering. 'Well... the first time was when I was in care, with abusive foster parents. My shit heel foster father paid me a visit during the night, but unlucky for him, my real dad had other ideas and was waiting for him. He took over my body to defend me. I had no memory of what went on that night, but when I came back to myself, I had bludgeoned my foster monster into a coma.' *They sent me to the children's home after that, where they all called me 'freak,' and bullied me for years.*

Derek makes soothing noises, reaching out to tuck a strand of hair behind my ear. 'Are you explaining this to Errol, babe?'

Swiping my hair back and out of Derek's tender grasp, I nod, then turn my attention back to Errol.

'Mary, do you get how the same thing's happening here?' Errol asks. 'Psychically, I mean. Think about what you're tuning into? What are your feelings when you project them?'

I peep up at Derek, concerned again about blurting out too much detail and worrying him. I've already explained, but still held some specifics back. *As troubled as I am about the impact on Derek's mental health, if I don't spell things out properly to Errol, he can't help me.* 'Well... first, something terrified me. I told you.'

'And it started when you tuned into the boy? Patryk?'

'Yeah,' I say. I picture that day again, pulling up in the car with Jay outside the school. Picking up happy weekend vibes...

but then… 'I focused on Patryk, tracking him like some kind of psychic bloodhound… then he got snatched, and I felt his t-terror and-' I falter on the last word, trailing off as I remember the jolt I'd experienced.

'What is it? What *else*, Mary?' Errol's tone holds urgency.

'When I traced Patryk, I sensed a killer. His wickedness is like a cancer; malevolent, evil. It's as though he's greedy for the suffering.' I swallow, then whisper, 'He loves it.'

Derek gathers me closer, saying, 'For God's sake, Mary, you're shaking like a leaf. What can I do?'

I shake my head, 'Nothing,' I say, turning back to Errol to ask, 'What're you thinking?'

Errol's voice is still low, helping to calm me down. 'So… have you been able to meditate with your intuition? Focus on drawing in the positive like I taught you?'

'I've been trying to, Errol, but it's not working. At the minute, it's like I'm in emotional quicksand. I'm keeping busy, hanging round with friends, with Derek. Usually, that makes me happy with no effort. Underneath it all, though, there's this constant buzz of the kidnapper's frequency, like a recurring echo in my mind. It's of that, combined with Patryk's last little scream before they snatched him. Something wants to connect with me, and they won't take no for an answer.'

Errol nods, looking solemn. 'OK. I understand, but for right now I'll help you block them like I did back in the Rainbow Unit. Then I'll see if I can find out who's doing the pushing. But in the meantime, please meditate. Elevate your frequency as much as possible. Make love, not war,' Errol quips, throwing me the peace sign and allowing me a flash of his gold tooth as he smiles.

A shadow of my usual cheeky grin crosses my face. 'I like the sound of that.'

'Alright, Mary, I'll be in touch. Can I have your permission to pop by unannounced, though?'

'Yeah, of course. Come to me whenever, I'm always open to you, Errol.'

After first touching his index finger to his forehead as a salute, Errol leaves the room, and I know he's gone, for now.

'Are we alone again now, Mary?' Derek asks.

'Yes,' I say.

Eyes wide, Derek asks, 'Does Errol know what's happening here? Or how to make it stop?'

I shake my head. 'No... but he said he'll help me block them and try to find out who *they* are–who's trying to force their way through to me against my will.'

'I may be talking out the top of my head here because I don't fully understand your psychic powers or what have you... but what if you take the case? Open yourself up to whatever it is the ghosts want to tell you? It worked out before when you did that, didn't it? At the hospital?' Derek's stiff features seem to hold an air of readiness about them, as though he's hopeful he's found the solution.

I gulp in annoyance, placing two fingers on my twitching eyelid. 'With all due respect, Derek, you're right. You *don't* understand what would be involved. It didn't all 'just work out' at the hospital. We were all nearly killed. I almost got killed. The risk I'd be taking here is massive. It would mean opening myself up to what? To whom, and what do they want from me? What if they're stronger than me, or how about they take me over and make me do things while I'm not in control, like my dad used to? What then?'

Derek steps back, palms outstretched. 'I'm sorry, OK? I was just thinking out loud and I'm sorry. You know best, but...'

I study Derek, as he shifts his weight from one foot to another. *The sound of his feet sliding against the floor is so annoying.* His sentence is left hanging, unfinished. 'But what, Derek?' I ask.

His voice is soft, but it slices through to my conscience just the same. 'Just that, as horrific as this case is, it's not like you to back down from a fight. No matter what.'

Derek's words ring inside my head, clattering around like a church bell and causing me to suck in a gigantic breath. I reel back, as though from a blow. Then, jaw clenched, I straighten, staring at him. 'I can't believe you just said that to me. What the hell do you know about what it's like for me?' *God, can he be any more insensitive? What the hell does he know about it, anyway? What does Derek really know about me, what it's like to be me?*

Derek, seeing the grim set of my face, hastens to pacify me, adding, 'Although I totally get everything you've said, of course.'

I continue to glare at him, experiencing such rage I struggle to catch my breath. I put one hand up, palm towards his face to silence him. 'I can't even speak to you right now.' *You arse.* Without another word, I turn on my heel, marching towards our bedroom. I flop onto my bed, staring at the ceiling. The act reminds me of my loneliness at The Rainbow Unit. When there was only me left. With a sigh, I do what Errol had directed me to do. *Focus on the good things.* With great effort, I concentrate on pulling forward in my memory the picnics, walks in the woods, days at the beach, and cuddles that Derek and I have shared over the last three years.

Then, Derek's actual words reverberate in my mind, hanging in front of my eyes like pictures on a screen. The truth of what he's saying strikes me. *Derek's right. This isn't like me. It is really scary, but why am I reacting so differently to this situation?*

'Kids and animals…' I sigh. *I can't stand anything bad to happen to them.*

I haul a deep breath in. *Shit. Who am I and what happened to me that cut off my balls?*

CHAPTER 10

S itting up straight on Marcie's sofa, I stare from the DVD cases to my friend's face, and back again. It's our regular, bestie's movie night. Marcie's getting the popcorn, and synchronised, we both curl up on the sofa putting our feet up in a side 'V' shape.

As the movie gets darker and more depressing, I keep glancing at Marcie, confused. *She said it was a love story.* Noticing my stare, she smiles at me, her dimple peeping in her cheek, angelically. Frowning, I watch the screen again. *What the hell is this bag of misery?* 'When is this shit gonna get funny, Marce?' I ask.

'Won't be too much longer, I reckon. Keep watching,' Marcie says.

Two and a half hours later, as the credits roll up, I stare wordlessly at Marcie. My lips are stuck to my dry mouth, and I swallow.

Marcie's eyes sparkle.

Mine squint, then widen, my lips forming a perfect 'O.' All at once, I comprehend what's happened. 'Oh, *you little* cow-bag,' I say.

Marcie grins, confirming she duped me.

'I can't believe I trusted you, you con merchant. You knew exactly what that film was that whole time didn't you?' The question is rhetorical; Marcie's mirthful expression says it all.

She doesn't deny my accusation and instead throws her head back and starts laughing. Her giggles peal out into the deathly silent living room.

I lob the scatter cushions at her one by one. 'You rotten cow, that was *so* out of order. That's the last time I trust you, Miss Marcie! You wait and see.'

Marcie's unrepentant. 'Sorry, I couldn't resist. I thought you'd twig on before the end of the film. You should've seen your face. You kept looking at me, all confused. I nearly peed myself laughing, I swear.'

'Is that why you went to the toilet so many times? I thought you were upset! You little crook.' I pick up a cushion from her floor to wallop her with it again. It doesn't stop her from letting out a huge belly laugh, triggering my hilarity button at the same time. Together, we hoot and cackle.

My mobile rings, and the ringtone tells me it's Jay. Instantly, my amusement dries up, and I wipe suddenly clammy hands down my thighs. Marcie's giggling peter's out, the smile dropping from her face. 'Are you gonna take it Mare?'

I shake my head, telling her, 'No. I can't.'

'But, Mare, what about-' Marcie's question cuts off, but I know what she wants to say. *What about Patryk.* My shoulders sag.

'Can I take it in your bedroom, please?' I say.

Quelled by the heavy tone in my voice, and lack of expression in my face, Marcie nods, not speaking. I take my mobile to Marcie's bedroom, sitting on her bed and staring at it as though it were a venomous snake about to strike. Standing up, I make the call. As soon as Jay answers, I begin pacing up and down.

True to form, Jay does not waste any time on small talk coming straight to the point.

After a brief, 'It's Jay here, is that you, Mary?' he moves straight into, 'We still haven't found anything about Patryk's disappearance. I have to give another press release and I've got nothing to tell them. I need your help with this, Mary, desperately.' His voice is hoarse, a result of his all-night drinking coffee and smoking cigarettes while he looked into case leads. Probably that was part of the reason his wife Fiona left him. But only part.

'Jay, I told you. I can't do it.'

'What? Because Casper visited you and gave you a bit of a scare? Come on, Mary, belt up for God's sake. Because of that, you're going to leave a little boy God knows where, with who knows what's happening to him? Leave his parents in pain forever, seeing him round every corner? Waiting for him to come home?'

I push my hair back off my face with a shaking hand, and, closing my eyes, hope in vain to shut out his words as they attack my conscience. 'Look, Jay, you're the police, not me. It's not my responsibility?' I hear my tone lifting at the end of my sentence, as though I'm asking him a question.

Jay curses under his breath. 'Not your responsibility? You're a human being, aren't you? And I believed a decent one at that. In fact, I would've bet my last pound that despite all your wise cracks and your potty mouth, you wouldn't have been able to turn your back on someone who needed you. Especially not a young child. Consider his mum. Think about what this is doing to her. Think how it would have affected yours.'

Jay's words cause me to suck in a sharp breath through my teeth. 'Fuck off, Jay.'

'Alright, that was a low blow, but I'm not apologising for it. You know what's at stake, Mary, and I'll do anything, say anything, to get you on board. I need you to unearth something. You're the only one who can help me drum up clues with this. We've got sweet nothing at every avenue of our investigation.'

'And whose fault is that?' My voice raises in frustration. 'Mine?'

'No... no, you're not to blame. But if you can help, why wouldn't you? I'm not ok with all that hippy, tree hugging bull crap about letting people choose. If you possess the ability to do something good, you should do it. Because it's the right thing to do.'

I shut my eyes, wishing I could blot out the image of Jay flashing into my mind's eye. Jay wearily sweeping a hand across his face. He twists his wedding ring with the thumb of the same hand. Although I know he and Fiona have been apart since Pepe's funeral, he still hasn't taken it off. Her absence has left him free to become consumed by his job, staying up working most nights. I visualise him working, eating readymade dinners in front of the television whilst poring over photos of crime scenes, looking for any clue he's missed. Going over notes, statements of relatives, neighbours, friends, teachers, relentlessly.

That 'think about the mum' comment bugs me. *That was well out of order, and Jay knows it.*

My own mum's solemn features float into my memory, and I sigh deeply, not wanting to think about another mum suffering. I purposely relax my shoulders. 'Bastard.' My tone is gruff, affectionate. 'OK, I'll do it.' *Even though I know I'll regret this.*

Jay's tone is jubilant as he answers me, 'Yes! Thank you. You won't regret this, Mary, I swear. This case has a lot of media eyes on it, so I need to be stringent about keeping your involvement quiet. We'll fly you under the radar like we have before.'

'Whatever, Jay. Don't sugar-coat it. I'm not stupid. I know this is going to be shit.'

I'm not joking. A feeling of dark, impending doom settles upon me as soon as I agree to work on the case with Jay. I sigh. 'So, when and where are we meeting then?' I ask.

'We're going to Patryk's family home. Tomorrow at ten; I'll text you the address.'

My heart thuds, and I ignore the churning of my stomach. *I'm doing the right thing, but this feels so wrong and I don't know why.*

PART TWO

CHAPTER ONE

A middle-aged blonde answers the door of her house, and I immediately recognise Patryk's mother from the news. While she's appeared in subsequent television reports about her missing son, it's the first one I watched that sticks in my mind. So stricken with grief, she could hardly stand. All angles and legs, Patryk's mum's face is drawn and taut. Yet the swirls of grey and pink in her aura hint at a softness and vulnerability underneath her steely exterior. She's on the brink.

'What do you want?' she snaps, her sapphire blue gaze darting from me to Jay, a clear warning to leave.

'Hello, ma'am,' Jay begins. 'I'm Detective Inspector Jay Santiago. We've spoken before. This is my associate, Mary Jameson. May we come in please, Mrs. Challance?' Jay displays his police ID through the porch window. Patryk's mum's eyes round, and her face pales, but she gestures us inside, hand trembling. My heart breaks for her. I can see that our presence has triggered her distress. She fears the reason we've come, and I hasten to reassure her.

'We're not here with any new updates, Mrs. Challance. We just have a few more questions, I'm afraid.'

'Of course. Anything you need, Detective. Please come through.'

We follow her, and I notice the way her A-line skirt swings loosely as she walks. On screen, she seemed taller, more imposing. But in person, she looks shorter, as though the weight of her grief has been grinding her down, compressing her. But I know I'm being fanciful.

The sitting room is plush, spotless—a stark contrast to the places I'm used to. Suppressing instincts to check exits and potential weapons, I offer Mrs. Challance a polite, rehearsed smile. The gravity of the situation hits me hard. *Her ten-year-old son is missing.* I swallow, squaring my shoulders and lifting my chin. *This is going to be difficult.* As I gather my thoughts, she breaks the silence, addressing Jay. Twisting her wedding ring, Mrs. Challance says, 'What else do you need from us?'

Avoiding a direct answer for now, Jay answers her. 'We truly appreciate all you've shared with us so far, Mrs. Challance.'

'Please, call me Iryna. Can I get you something to eat or drink?'

Jay shakes his head with a smile. 'Thank you, Iryna. We just have some questions, and if possible, may we look around, specifically in your son's room?'

A frowning silence meets Jay's words, a hint of confusion and reluctance clear. Sensing her hesitation, I interject, 'It'll help us build a clearer profile of Patryk. By understanding his home environment, we can better predict his reactions in different situations.'

Her discomfort eases slightly, and she nods, her gaze drifting as though looking for something to ground her. Recognising her need for distraction, I decide it's best to let her focus on something, allowing us to proceed with our tasks.

'Actually, Iryna, could I trouble you for a cup of tea, after all?' I use my most polite voice. *My mum would be proud.*

Our hostess quickly stands, her hands absently smoothing down her skirt.

'Of course! I'm sorry I seem to have forgotten your names… but, anyway, I'll bring you biscuits… and cake. I have so much cake; Patryk adores it. David tells me not to keep making it but…' Iryna's chin wobbles as she wrestles with her emotions.

'You want to have some here in case he comes home?' I suggest softly.

The depth of her grief nearly overwhelms me, making me blink back tears. Wordlessly, I reach out to touch her hand. When I connect with spirits, our souls merge, and I absorb their memories and feelings, but with Iryna, a living person, the experience is different. As she squeezes my hand, I'm reminded of my mother's hardworking hands, and can make a fair guess about what's on Iryna's mind.

She nods, a determined glint in her eye.

'I'll get the tea. Please, feel free to explore. Do whatever you need; I just want my son back.'

After she leaves, Jay and I exchange a glance. He points upstairs, and I nod. Let's get this show on the road.

I breathe in and out deeply, feeling my way up each step as I go.

'As a reminder, Mary, Patryk was last seen leaving school at three thirty-five PM. His school is a ten-minute walk from here and his parents expected him home by three forty-five. They contacted the authorities just after four PM.'

Jay's voice fades as I approach Patryk's room.

As I do, I notice a hint of blue energy seeping out from beneath a door.

'Why touch the door like that, Mary? With the back of your hand?'

I explain, 'I'm testing the energy before I go in. It's safe.'

Jay slips on some gloves while he searches the drawers. I stand in the room's centre, noting the white and red decor. Red and white. Favourite football team. I turn slowly in a circle as I tune into his vibration. If I close my eyes, I can see better. My eyelids drift down, and immediately, I feel a zing of electricity through my body that makes my fillings feel sensitive. Then I hear the clicks.

'*You need to help him,*' a voice says.

With a sudden jolt, my eyes snap open to meet the watery blue gaze of the speaker. In front of me stands a woman, her broad face, withered as an old oak, is framed by a headscarf, and she's wearing a long, flowing skirt teamed with a high collared blouse, covered by an apron. Her accent mirrors Iryna's, but her English is less polished. She speaks again. '*Help my Patryk. He has much pain. He is good boy.*'

A frown creases my face and I ask her, 'Are you related to Patryk?'

'*I am his grandmother, Monika.*'

I nod. 'I'm trying to help find him, Monika. Do you have anything you can tell me that might help?' *If you even can - stupid cosmic law making everything more difficult.*

Patryk's grandmother remains silent for some time, head cocked to one side before replying. 'He is always good boy. He has the autism. Some people know this and-'

I frown as the clanging shut of a wardrobe door intrudes on our conversation. 'The kidnapper targeted him because of his autism?'

Patryk's grandmother becomes blurry, and although I observe her lips moving, her voice is silent. *OK. This seems like a simple case of stupid cosmic law at work. As happened with Errol when he tried to tell me something, the Universe must be shutting Monika up. So, I'll take her mute response as a 'yes.'*

I can see Monika attempting to answer for a while before she gives up. '*Please. You have to help him.*'

I nod. 'I'll try my best.' I allow myself to refocus on my physical companion, Jay.

'Who was that, were you talking to a ghost?' Jay has paused his search and is looking at me with a hopeful expression.

Nodding, I tell him, 'Yeah, Patryk's grandmother.'

Jay's eyes widen with hope. 'Shit, what did she say? Anything I can use?'

I shake my head. 'Sorry, don't think so. Her name is Monika, and she said that Patryk is in pain, that he's autistic, and is a good boy. She just wanted to ask me to help him, really.' My shoulders slump. *Kids and animals... I can't stand when bad things happen to kids or animals.* I nibble my bottom lip as I think. *Was there anything useful she told me?* My eyes widen hopefully, and I ask Jay, 'Could there be a link between the kidnapping and autism?'

My friend's mouth is downturned. 'I don't know, Mary. Could be? I'll search again, see if I can turn anything up. You probably don't know this, but a lot of autistic children go missing every year. They either do a runner, or they just... go missing.'

I scowl at Jay's words. 'What? Do you mean this happens even more to kids who have autism, than those who don't have autism?'

Jay's slow nod and sad features are answer enough.

'A load more?' I ask.

'A shit load more,' he says.

Taken aback, I stare at him, aghast, 'How come?' I ask.

Jay shrugs. 'Well, each case is unique. But I connected with a lady from a safeguarding hub a few years back. She said kids with autism can struggle with recognising danger, and often wander off to play in risky places.'

'What kind of risky places, Jay?'

'Er... rivers, ponds, construction sites, traffic.'

I close my eyes, placing a hand against my stomach. 'Oh my God.'

'And then there are the sickos...' he says.

I shake my head slightly, gritting my teeth. I don't think I can bear to hear any more about it right now.

'Would you like another tea?' Iryna calls up from the bottom of the stairs, cutting our grim conversation short.

'We'd love one, thank you,' Jay calls, then asks me, 'Want to take a break?'

I nod, swallowing the dryness in my throat and move towards the door. Jay follows behind me as we go downstairs to join our hostess.

Photos of Patryk on the wall punctuate the staircase at varying stages of his school journey. I guess they're in chronological order, because the first one looks like a nursery picture.

We sit back down in the sparkling living room, and the silence is suddenly painful.

I clear my throat, then scan the room, avoiding Iryna's red-rimmed eyes. 'You have a lovely home.' I smile and touch my mouth as though squeezing my lips shut. *I just saw your mum upstairs, Iryna. She wants me to help Patryk, but I don't think I can.* I purse my lips. I can't say those words.

Iryna is concentrating on the safe delivery of the ornate silver tray she carries to us. She's ladened it with a pot of tea, milk in a jug, and some cakes on delicate doilies. It all looks very appetising. Iryna's wish to make us comfortable sweeps out to me tentatively and I smile, sinking further into my chair, whilst absorbing what impressions I can glean from the environment. 'Is that Patryk with you, when he was a baby?'

Iryna nods, looking at the large photo on the mantlepiece. Walking over to the picture, she picks it up. 'He was such a beautiful baby. Everyone thought he was a girl.' Iryna gives a choked laugh, then rests a hand on her stomach briefly. I feel the weight of her yearning stretch out towards me and shuffle my bottom back in my seat.

'Is Patryk your only child?' Jay asks.

Iryna doesn't seem offended by his question, and shakes her head, mouth downturned. 'Yes, Sadly. I would've loved a big family, but I have a condition which meant I couldn't. The doctors told me I couldn't have children. Then along came Patryk. He's my gift from God.'

I shift in my seat again, restless. Something about what she said was bugging me, but I don't know what. I can see her love for her son shining out from her and radiating within her. It's pure and uncorrupted.

Jay clears his throat, then asks, 'Please, Iryna, if you wouldn't mind, can you tell us again what happened on the day Patryk went missing?' he continues. 'Was there anything unusual about that day you can think of?'

Iryna sighs, sitting back down heavily. She gestures to the tea and cakes and when she answers Jay, her voice is dry and slower than before, as if she's exhausted. 'Please, Detective, drink your tea before it gets cold. No, nothing out of the ordinary happened during the day, that we know of. Patryk went to school on time like a good boy. I went to work. His father went to work. We all left on time.'

Jay says, 'And can I ask, where were you and your husband at the time Patryk went missing? Was there anything different about Patryk's behaviour that morning?'

'No. I came home from work and waited for Patryk, as always. But… he never came. He's such a good little boy, and he's always so good with being on time.' Iryna's voice cracks on the last sentence, and Jay waits a few minutes before his next question.

'And I understand he's autistic?'

At Jay's question, Iryna frowns, and her chin tilts up. 'Yes, that's right. Patryk's our gift from God.' She repeats her comment from earlier, but this time, her tone is firm.

Jay nods. 'I'm sure he is, ma'am. Please understand, I mean nothing offensive by asking you these questions, but I must ask them.'

'You've asked them already when we spoke on the phone the first time. We're not stupid, we've told you everything we know already.' Iryna's expression is stiff, and she crosses her arms tightly, back straight.

Jay shakes his head and sets his face in neutral, non-threatening. 'I know, and I'm very sorry. It's nothing against you and your husband. I'm just making sure there's nothing I missed.' Jay's voice is like warm treacle and seems to melt something in Iryna.

Her shoulders relax, and she allows him a tiny smile. She loosens her arms and unlocks her gaze to include me again. 'I get it, Detective.' Iryna sighs again. 'The paediatrician diagnosed Patryk with autistic spectrum disorder. I don't know about that, but what I do know is he's a good boy and has always been quiet and well behaved. As a baby, he never cried, just wanted to be close. He's neat with his toys and obedient at school.'

Jay smiles, nodding, then asks, 'Does he do any extra-curricular activities?'

'Tons, Patryk loves his football. We take him swimming every Wednesday, he's a real water baby.' Iryna smiles as though holding a memory of her son splashing away. 'Patryk also went to a social group every Friday. It's for other children who sometimes... struggle.'

Iryna looks defensive, and Jay frowns, confused, but I guess what Iryna wants to say, and ask her. 'The other children are also diagnosed with ASD?'

Patryk's mum turns to me, nodding. She seems relieved as I frame the words. *Maybe just like there's sometimes a reluctance to talk about a diagnosis of a mental health condition, there's a similar stigma attached to neurological disorders?*

'Yes. And other conditions. ADHD,' Iryna says.

'Does Patryk like going there?' Jay asks, changing the subject briefly.

Iryna smiles, more naturally this time. 'Yes, he loves it. It's a peaceful place, and he always comes home happy, with a ton of drawings he'd done. His good friend Danny also goes to group. They're very close.'

'Danny–that's Patryk's *best* friend, isn't he?' I cut in.

'Yes, he's also a wonderful boy, but very different to Patryk. Talks all the time.' Iryna laughs, but with fondness, not unkindly.

Jay smiles briefly, asking, 'Did Patryk ever say anything about anyone troubling him at school? Outside of school?'

Iryna shivers. 'No. Not at all. Everyone who knows Patryk adores him. He's such a lovely boy.' Iryna's bottom lip quivers, as Jay and I look at each other, and I see Jay's eyebrows raise in query.

I shake my head imperceptibly. *There's nothing more I need to see or feel here.* We give our thanks to Iryna for her time and Jay gives her a business card. 'In case you think of anything you think might be important, or if you have questions for me,' he tells her as we leave.

Feeling disheartened, I say, 'I'm sorry, Jay. I wasn't much help in there.' My shoulders are slumped as we walk back to the car, then simultaneously slide into our seats.

'Don't be silly. You came, and you tried. That's the main thing. Even though I don't suspect them of any wrongdoing, the parents are being investigated at the moment,' Jay shares. He was right not to tell me before we went in there because I am horrified and stare at him aghast.

'Don't look at me like that. It's standard procedure. No stone unturned and all that.'

I continue to gawp at Jay, a picture of Iryna in my mind, touching the photo of her son. So full of love. 'But Iryna's a lovely mum.'

Jay rolls his eyes. 'If you only knew how many times *it actually is the parents.*' He sighs. 'Anyway, I'll look again at the possibility of an autism link. Thanks for that.'

'But I haven't done anything.' *I feel like a fraud.*

Jay shrugs, then starts up the car and revs it. 'I told you. It's not about that. It's enough that you're trying. That's all we can do. Appreciate it. Cheers.'

I nod. *Why hadn't I sensed something more?*

'We'll find something; we have to catch a break soon,' Jay says without taking his gaze from the road.

CHAPTER TWO

'Jesus Christ, Mary! Wake up! Mary, please, wake up! Wake up, Mary!'

My blood-curdling scream stalls in my throat and I come to, awakening to a massive disturbance that shakes the bed, and Derek's panicky demands.

'The little boy was there with someone. It was so horrible. He frightened me so much, Derek.' I stifle a sob, knowing this will push Derek over the edge with worry.

He strokes my forehead and doesn't mention that it's damp with sweat. Again.

'In the house. With the soup. But he'd already done things. Terrible things. And she's so horrible. Did she know? I'm not sure, I couldn't see. It was so tense, so awful, God.'

'Baby, what're you saying? I can't understand you. You're not making much sense.'

I catch myself on a sob again. *Derek doesn't need to deal with my shit. I mustn't lean on him, no matter what. He can't take it.*

'It's ok, love. I know it was just a silly nightmare.' I try to make my tone sincere and believable. 'No big deal.'

I can make out Derek's frown, even in this darkness. 'Mary, you know you can always talk to me, right?'

'Uh-huh, of course.' *Or not.* 'Let's just have spoons and go back to sleep now, babe.' I settle the conversation.

'Mary, you keep having these dreams. It's obviously connected to this case, don't you think?'

Derek's arm is at my waist, securing me to him and I relax slightly, telling him, 'Sort of, but it's probably just my mind sorting out information I'm learning.'

'Mary, you're waking up screaming. That's not right.'

'Derek, it's fine. They're just bad dreams. A boy's gone missing. You know I love kids. Of course, I'm going to have nightmares. Please, let's not go on about my dream. I'm trying to put it out of my mind for now. It'll make them worse. Please D, let's just try to go back to sleep.'

Derek is silent, but I feel his uneasiness, and hope he's not worrying too much about me. With everything going on, the last thing I need to do is push Derek into having an episode by pouring all this emotional strain on him.

Still too scared to close my eyes, I stare at the wall, suspiciously peering into the dark. *What's that stretching out towards me across the ceiling? A hand?* I squint to make the shape out, but don't raise my head off the bed to check. *No. It's only the shadow of something innocent.* My aura leaks out, grey and faint crimson. *There was red in the dream… No!* I shut the thought out.

A sharp creak outside the door makes me hold my breath and, heart pounding, I push even closer to Derek. His solid warmth soothes me. *When am I going to stop jumping at shadows?* It's just air in the pipes, that's all. My hands slide up to cup my ears, and I concentrate on tuning into the feel of Derek's love for me, drawing satisfaction from the iridescence that dances all around us. My shallow panting gradually becomes deeper and slower, but I still don't close my eyes again for a long, long time.

The next morning, I'm pulling on my other sandal when my phone sings out with a familiar ringtone. It's Jay. I walk, wriggling my foot into the shoe, trying to unfold the back of it as I step. 'Hi, Jay, I'm just on my way out to meet Eileen. What's up?'

It was through the psychiatric nurse, Eileen Macintosh, that Jay had first become acquainted with my psychic abilities. He'd been at the station on the night I'd called on Eileen to save me at The Rainbow Unit. She'd come to my rescue, and with her, brought uniformed police and one police officer without uniform: Jay.

'Hi, Mary. I have to go to the hospital this morning, but can you come down to the station again this afternoon? We've had some new developments, and I'd like to go through some leads with you.'

I stop hopping into my footwear and stop moving, shocked by Jay's words. Derek materialises in the doorway. He's raising a brow in askance at my still posture. I raise a palm in his direction, holding him off with a smile.

'Hospital, why? Are you ok, what's the matter?' I ask Jay.

'Oh, I'm fine. The hospital's not for me. A friend on the force had a nasty accident and I need to visit him.'

He didn't say 'want.' He said 'need.' Duty. That is pure Jay. But he's also about kindness.

I release the breath I am holding, and my shoulders relax. 'Oh, OK. Sorry about your friend, Jay, but I'm glad you're alright though. So, what did you want me to do when I come then?'

'Well, it's like I said, I'd like to share some information with you, maybe talk about clues and evidence I have, theories I have about the case. Then you tell me what kind of vibes you get?'

I glance at Derek, who's blatantly listening to my side of the conversation. He has his head cocked, rapt.

'What am I, a psychic detective now? Why don't you just ask your police colleagues to go through that stuff with you?' Sandals both on properly now, I pace up and down the small hallway of the flat. I know my tone is sullen, but I don't change it.

Jay is silent for a while, and guilt gnaws at me. I drag in a deep sigh. 'Sorry for snapping, Jay. I didn't get much sleep again last night.'

As usual, Jay's quick to catch on, asking, 'Did you have another one of your nightmares, Mary?'

Yes, Jay, it was a nightmare of epic proportions. I glance at Derek, remembering he's still here, listening. 'You could say that, Jay.'

Jay's speech picks up speed, and his question's breathless with sudden enthusiasm, 'Did you get anything come through I can use?'

'Wow, Jay, thanks for the concern. I'm fine, really.'

Jay sounds contrite as he apologises, 'Sorry, Mary. I meant, are you OK?'

Knowing how much Jay must be restraining himself from his usual rapid-fire questions, my shoulders relax, and I sigh, relenting. 'It's OK, Jay, we can talk about it.'

'Great. So, what happened then, Mary?'

With another quick glance at Derek, I move into the bedroom for some privacy while I speak to Jay. Then, I think back to last night trying to remember details. It's difficult, because I have been purposely pushing those details to the back of my mind since waking. *Damn! Should've written it all down.* 'It's all a bit cloudy now to be honest, but I think I was in a kitchen, and someone was cooking and talking to me. They were asking me something, but I wasn't *me*. I was a little boy.'

Jay's question is immediate, 'The same boy who scared you at the supermarket?'

'Not sure. Maybe I was him or maybe some boy about the same age.' There's a hesitancy in my words.

'Anyway, then what?' Jay asks.

I try to explain, my words hesitant. 'There were questions being asked, and I was getting angry. Really full of rage, and I felt hatred. I simmered with it.'

'Yeah?' Jay asks.

I cast my mind back, frowning with effort. 'I was doing a drawing as well.'

In full inspector mode, Jay says, 'Can you tell me what you, this little boy, looked like? Or the person who was in the kitchen with you?'

I rub my forehead. 'I didn't see me really from the outside.'

Continuing his line of questioning, Jay asks me, 'Were there any reflective surfaces in the room with you that you might have glanced at? A window maybe? Any shiny objects that you saw - cups, saucepans, spoons?'

I shake my head again and smooth my bob back behind my ear. 'No, sorry Jay. I was sitting down at a table. It had a gingham tablecloth if that helps. Sorry. I know it sounds lame.'

Jay doesn't respond to my apology, instead asking me, 'What was the room like? It was a kitchen you said… was it big or small? What could you see around you?'

I think for a few seconds, rubbing the back of my neck while I answer. 'It was a large kitchen. There were old-fashioned cupboards around me, quaker style.'

'You said you were drawing. What was the paper and pen like? Any initials or unusual characteristics about them? What hand were you holding the pen with?'

I picture sitting back at the table. 'It was a high table. The paper is thick, and off white. It was quality paper. It would be expensive to buy. The pencil I was using is the same. It felt lightweight in my hand, and the colour on the paper it left was deep and vivid. Not like the light colour I remember coming out of the cheap colouring pencils I used as a child.'

'What was the colour of the drawing?'

I swallow. 'Red… Lots and lots of red.' I put my fingertips to my eye to stem the twitching.

'Of course it was,' Jay says with a sigh. 'OK, Mary… so can you come down later then?'

I look at my watch and think yearningly of my brunch with my friend Eileen. Time with Eileen always helps. She's kind, calm, and collected. Perfect, as she's a community psychiatric nurse, as well as my dear friend and idol. 'Yeah, OK. I'll see you about two.' I hear the reluctance in my tone.

'Why not any earlier?' Jay asks.

'Because I'm meeting Eileen for our monthly brunch today, that's why.'

There's a loud silence.

'Oh… and er… how's Eileen? Is she… Did she say anything?'

I hold the phone away from my ear, looking at it with a frown on my face. 'Huh? Say anything about what?'

'Nothing, me. No, nothing. Just… nothing.' Jay's sigh is as loud as his silence was. 'Give her my regards.'

My lip curls up. *Huh?* 'Why don't you give her your own regards? I thought you two were friends.'

I strain to hear what Jay mumbles, then I blink as he says in an uncharacteristically loud voice, 'Come after the brunch. Bye.'

CHAPTER THREE

S tanding inside the hotel lobby where I'm meeting Eileen, I lift my gaze to scan around me. The large stained-glass windows bathe the interior with a gorgeous orange and turquoise glow. The floor is old-fashioned, parquet, and my heeled sandals make a satisfying sound as I walk. Out of deference to the occasion, I have forgone my usual casual attire, and put on a long, pretty sundress with the sandals. Although the foyer is empty, when I follow the directions to the hotel restaurant, I round the corner into a hub of civilised activity. Well-dressed diners fill every table, and their animated conversations create a hum that fills the large space. I lock out my psychic senses. *The last thing I want to experience right now is overload.*

Scanning the room quickly, I see my friend's arrived early and I wave gaily. I know Eileen's wanted us to try this restaurant for a couple of months, so I *could* attribute her earliness to an eagerness to test the food out. However, Eileen usually arrives at our meet ups before me. She spots me and stands up, a huge smile on her face, waving her enthusiasm. Three years ago, after years of suffering and self-neglect, the truth had finally set me free. Eileen was there to help me pick up the pieces, leading the way to wellness. It was her I had based my current persona on.

A proud Scot, Eileen, is a no-nonsense, attractive professional in her late forties, and is everything I aspire to be. She tucks her bobbed hair behind her ear, and I mirror the wide smile that's plastered on her face. We greet each other with a fierce hug, and she puts me at arm's width away from her so she can admire me better.

'Mmm, Eileen, you always smell so lovely. Like the most gorgeous apples ever,' I say, savouring the clean, appealing scent Eileen always releases.

'And you look even more beautiful every time I see you, Mary Jameson.'

I blush, staring at the floor. 'Get away, no I don't.'

Eileen doesn't argue with me. Instead, I hear the scrape of a chair leg as she pulls it out. I look up and see her gesturing for me to take a seat.

'C'mon, let's sit down and order. I can't wait to eat; I've been wanting to get us reservations here for ages. Plus, I'm starving.' Eileen says.

We grin at each other and sit down.

'Jay sends his regards,' I say.

Eileen nods, but she drops her gaze from mine for a second. 'How's he doing?'

'What's with you two? Have you fallen out or something?'

Eileen remains quiet, but shakes her head. I shrug, then answer her question.

'How's Jay doing? Well, not great, actually, Eileen. We're working on another case together.'

Eileen smiles. 'Another serious robbery or burglary they want you to find clues for?'

This time, I don't smile back. Instead, I shake my head.

'Nah. It's a missing child.'

Eileen gasps. 'Not that poor boy that's been all over the telly?'

I lean forward, then glance around quickly before speaking. Even with this amount of background noise, you never know who's nearby, watching or listening to your conversation. Eileen also leans forward, ready to listen.

85

'Yes,' I whisper.

'Jesus Christ, Mary.'

'I know. It's so sad.'

'Have you found anything yet? Has Jay's team got anything?' Eileen asks.

A waiter arrives at the table with a carafe of water on a tray. We fall silent as he turns over our glasses and pours us a glass each. 'Can I offer you ladies anything to drink?' He has a clipped London accent.

'I'll have a jasmine tea, please,' I ask.

Eileen smiles at him. 'I'll have a breakfast tea,' she says.

The tablecloth is heavy linen, and I smooth over it with my fingertips, matching Eileen's polite smile as we watch the waiter. He removes the wine menu with an air of disappointment. Neither of us are day drinkers. He puts the food menus in front of us, then steps away from the table with a snap in his step, and Eileen and I both lean forward, jumping back into our conversation. Eileen sometimes works with the police and with Jay, so I'm confident I can trust her, although I must still be careful about how much I reveal to my friend as she's not working on this case. 'So, I can't share much with you, but I'm trying to help. Jay has asked me to go there later today to look at some clues.'

'This could be a very troubling case for you. I know you've helped Jay out before, using your gift, but this isn't what you're used to.' Her voice is low and serious, and I match it.

'I hear what you're saying. I know.' *Animals and kids.* 'In fact, I didn't want to get into this case, but I sort of didn't have a choice. I had a forced spiritual visitation, also... I've been having terrible nightmares.'

My friend's brow wrinkles. 'A forced visitation? What nightmares? What happens in them?' she asks me.

The waiter reappears, offering a polite cough. After taking a brief look at the menus, we order.

Eileen returns to our conversation. 'Look you. My Jo thought of you as the daughter we never got to have, and over the last couple of years, I've come to feel the same. You know I worry about you.'

She sighs and with a smile, I rest my hand over hers, saying, 'Please don't worry, Eileen. I'll be OK, honestly; I can take it.'

'Can I help? Is there anything I could do to help the investigation? Or to help you while the investigation is going on?'

'Thanks for the offer, Eileen. I might have the odd question for you, like usual. If that's OK.'

Eileen nods, and she says, 'Of course. I'll be here for you whenever you need me.' Her brow furrows, then she says, 'How're things with you and Derek now? Is he still making you find all the ingredients for your traditional meals?'

My smile is tight as I take a moment to sip from my water glass. I nod, feeling defensive. 'It's very sweet of him.'

Eileen picks up her own water glass, but says nothing for a while, then, 'You both moved in together very quickly, lass.'

I blow outwards, guessing what my friend's about to say, 'Eileen, please don't start with that again.'

'Start what? It's the truth, Mary. You don't act like your real self around him. You can't listen to the music you like, you don't eat what you want, you don't even swear anymore!'

'Chicken chasseur?' We both look at the waiter as he interrupts us to present our food with a flourish.

There's an awkward silence for a few seconds, then Eileen exclaims, 'Well, this looks nice.'

With a smile, I thank the waiter, admiring my grilled chicken and quinoa salad, then I address Eileen's comments. 'You're wrong. I *can* do all of those things if I want to, Eileen. Derek isn't controlling, he's very sweet, perfect, and I love him. We love each other.'

'I'm not saying that Derek isn't a sweet young man, I believe he is. What worries me is that you're so caught up in the idea of having this 'perfect' life, and with the idea that the real you isn't good enough for him. My concern is, if you're not giving Derek the opportunity to know you, *properly*, and if you aren't being your wonderful, authentic 'you,' then Mary darling, how can he truly love you? How can you have a real, honest relationship with each other?'

The ring of truth in Eileen's question hits me in the gut, but saying nothing, I chew my quinoa salad even though it tastes like sawdust. I wash it down with water, wishing I'd ordered wine.

Eileen sighs, saying, 'I'm only saying this out of love for you, Mary. I want you to be happy. If that's with your Derek, well then, I'm happy for you, but trust me, you need to let him get to know the real Mary Obosa Jameson. Or your marriage will be built on smoke and mirrors.'

Bitter tears fill my eyes and I blink them away. Nostrils flaring, my head jerks angrily up at Eileen, but a wave of love comes at me, like a force field. Immediately, my anger's neutralised by the strength and purity of her affection for me. *Everything she's said is truth, and I know it's said in love.* It's my turn to drop my gaze to the tablecloth.

We settle back into eating our lunch, and for a short time, except for noises of appreciation, our table is quiet again. After a while, we both lean back in our seats, satisfied.

'Now then, Mary. Tell me about this 'forced visitation.' What did you mean by that?'

Nothing gets past Eileen. 'The first time was at the supermarket. It was late, and I'd just pop in there for a couple of bits. Then, I thought I heard a noise. But maybe I only *thought* I did. This boy manifested. He appeared without me calling him, or opening myself, and then he screamed and ran at me. Full pelt.'

Eileen's appalled, '*What*? Oh my God, Mary! Did he say anything? What did you do?'

'What do you think I did? I shit myself and ran like hell.'

Eileen whistled under her breath. 'Don't blame you. What did he scream at you, Mary?'

'I dunno.' I shrug, looking off into the distance and trying to remember, then shake my head. 'Nah. It's no good, I can't remember it all now, Eileen. I've done too good a job at erasing it from my memory.'

'Can I offer you both any desserts? Or drinks?' the waiter asks.

Eileen and I visibly jump in our seats, then Eileen lets out an embarrassed giggle, then says, 'I think we can find some space for that, don't you, Mary?'

I smile, nodding my agreement.

Several minutes pass as we admire the selection of tempting desserts until the waiter leaves. Eileen leans forward, asking me, 'So does this scary boy want to hurt you? Who is he?'

'I can't tell if he wants to hurt me, just that he projects so much rage and hatred, it's terrifying. I'm not sure who he is, but he's not Patryk.'

Eileen holds my gaze across the table and all the noise from the other diners disappears.

'Mary, this boy going missing is a terrible tragedy, but please, don't destroy yourself working to find him. If you need to, it's ok to say it's too much. Remember that you're important too.'

She suddenly gawps over my shoulder, clapping her hands and I see the waiter approaching in my peripheral vision. 'Now, that's a dessert!' she says, adding conspiratorially, 'Pavlova looks good too.'

'Yeah, it does.' A sudden frown creases my brow as I realise I've dominated our conversation with my worries and news. *What's been happening in Eileen's life?* I smile, leaning towards my friend. 'Anyway, that's enough of my whinging. What's happening with you at the minute, Eileen? How's work?'

Eileen's green eyes shimmer intensely, and she draws closer.

'Why don't we *not* talk shop. I refuse to think about what's lacking in my life. How's the pavlova?'

My mouth is full, and I nod, covering my mouth and saying, 'It's as good as it looks.'

We both smile, but neither one of us acknowledge that the table is jigging because of my foot tapping restlessly underneath it.

CHAPTER FOUR

A fter purchasing a car park ticket, I head into the police station to see Jay. He's told me that I'm expected, and he's been very particular about how many officers he's given my name to. A stocky, bald constable is manning the police station counter behind the Perspex glass I'm waiting in front of. 'Look, it's Enola Holmes,' he says with a smirk.

Hilarious. It seems Jay wasn't particular enough when he was handing out my details if this idiot's in the know. He stares at me with a blank expression on his face and raised eyebrows. Recognising his unfriendliness, I give him a tight-lipped smile.

'Yes?' he barks, staring me in the eyes unblinkingly.

'As I said, my name's Mary Jameson. I'm here to see Detective Inspector Santiago.'

'And you think he'll be expecting *you*?'

'Hopefully, but I suggest you contact him and find out.' I smile sweetly. *Nob jockey.* I watch him speak into the receiver, and whatever Jay says to him prompts his bloodshot gaze flying to mine. He pushes a buzzer, and a door opens, allowing me access to the police station.

'Thanks,' I mumble.

Standing with a hand cupped to an oversize ear he asks, 'What's that?'

Cor, what is his problem? Nostrils flaring, I withhold the urge to flip him the middle finger. *Nope, stand down Mary... I will not revert.*

I am reformed. Derek has reformed me. I won't punch this bozo in the throat as soon as he opens the door. It would totally piss Jay off if I did that. Or maybe not? This guy seems a right arsehole. Eileen has told me many times that people can only upset me if I give them permission to. So, I don't consent.

When the officer opens the door, I'm smiling politely. Disappointment floats out of his aura, and he frowns his suspicion at me. *Knew it! He wants me to be upset. Well, thanks, cock knocker; now I know exactly how to handle you. I'll kill him with kindness.* My smile widens, and I assume my professional persona again. 'Thanks so much.'

His smirk vanishes, and he grunts an acknowledgment of my greeting. 'Just come through.' His instruction is terse and thrown out over his shoulder.

I follow his rigid back, and only my iron will prevent me from sticking my middle finger up behind him. That, and the fact they operate CCTV cameras in the station. 'I'm afraid I didn't catch your name officer. *My* name's Mary.' I say.

'Paul,' comes the sullen response. *Wow, so gracious Paul.*

'Paul, great. Thanks for showing me to Detective Inspector Santiago.'

We enter a large room that contains Jay and other officers, all typing into keyboards and staring into monitors at their desks.

Paul stands still, awaiting another instruction.

Jay looks up briefly, saying, 'Cheers, Paul. Thanks for showing Mary in.'

'Boss.' The constable walks out and I frown at his back, swallowing my dislike for him.

As I start to sit down in an empty chair, Jay says, 'Don't bother getting comfortable, Mary. I want to show you some stuff on our system, so I need to find us an interview room with a computer. I want to show you a few things on our system.'

'Alright,' I tell Jay, straightening up again and watching while he tidies his desk before stepping round it to join me. He gestures to the door. 'Let's go, Mary.'

My mouth hangs slightly open as I gawp at the open office that we move through. As we walk, I see several glass offices that ring around the rows of desks, but they all look occupied with people in meetings. After we weave through the lined-up tables and officers, we come to an odd bridge that leads us into an old, brick-walled building with narrow corridors and parquet flooring.

'We'll try through here, Mary.' Jay says.

'This place is a maze, and it looks so different to the other part,' I comment, mouth still gaping as I look around me.

Jay nods. 'Yeah. They attached a new building onto the old station. This part's around two hundred years old.'

Still following Jay's back, I tap him on his shoulder. 'That's why the hallways are so skinny?'

'Yeah. It's a bit claustrophobic, aye?' Jay says.

Just a tad. 'Yeah,' I say, then, 'Is there a ladies' toilet, please, Jay? I need to spend a penny.'

Jay takes me to a vestibule, pointing a short way down the corridor.

'Over there,' he says. 'The loos are down there.'

'Cheers.' I spare him a last glance, as he leans against the wall just outside the ladies facilities.

When inside, I check the toilets for cleanliness before choosing one. The cast iron fittings and peeling paint on the walls inform me I'm in the older part of the building.

'No expense spared,' I murmur, heading into a cubicle and clanging the door shut. The door has a small, ancient looking lock that I slide into the barrel to engage. It's stiff, taking effort because of the rust. Perhaps it's because I am centring my energies on this task that I don't notice the temperature dropping. As I crouch, hovering over the toilet seat, I exhale. Frowning, I realise that my

93

breath's visible. 'Shit, it's cold in here, boy,' I mumble. *Government cutbacks. They really could not spring for heating in here to normalise the temperature. Tight arses. It must be nigh on sub-zero in here, the cheapskates.*

As I'm finishing up, I pause, cocking my head to one side. *Is that someone whistling outside?*

I hold my breath. Straining my ears, knickers still bunched in my hands. *It's nothing.*

'Old building.' I shrug, reaching out to flush the toilet. It's a metal chain flush that dangles down beside the black cistern. 'Jesus. It's like, from the nineteen eighties or something.'

The door rattles in its frame, and I frown clearing my throat. 'Someone's in here. There's a reason the door's locked, mate.' I smooth down my summer dress, then rub the goosebumps that have risen on my ice-cold arms. 'Brr.'

The door shudders violently in its frame again, testing my patience. 'Oi! Hello? Piss off and find another bog, yeah?' I reach out to unlock the door, but my hand stops before it settles on the lock. *It's quivering as though it has a mind of its own.*

'Hello?' I call, staring in front of me. My exhalations hang like a cloud in the quiet space, and I wait to see if anything occurs. The door shakes again with force after a second of quiet. *I closed off my abilities at the hotel so I could enjoy my meal. What will I see if I open up my psychic senses again? Who will be there?*

My hand trembles as I rest the back of it against the door and close my eyes, shivering. It's so cold. Chewing on my lip, I mull over my choices with lightning speed, weighing up both sides. *To remain closed off to the spirit world makes me vulnerable to surprise, but if I open myself up psychically, God knows what waits there for me. But at least I'd know what I'm dealing with.*

Squaring my shoulders, my chest swells high with the next inhalation I take. *OK. Get a grip, Mary Jameson. I am not a woose. I know deep down there's nothing to fear. It's all just a matter of frequencies, like radio stations. Some radio stations play nothing except drum and bass, and I like it. Some stations are all cheesy pop music, and I dislike that, most of the time. It's all just a matter of choice. I only have to tune into the station I want to connect with, and that's it.* Feeling tranquil now, my attention drifts and I cast it about aimlessly. *The vibration I draw will match my neutrality and pull my focus in. I am in the receptive mode, and I will allow.* Click... Click… Click.

There's a disturbance in the air surrounding me. It tells me I'm not alone. *Someone's in the small cubicle with me, but I can't see them yet.* There's anger and rage in the energy coming through. I suck in a breath. *It's that boy from the supermarket again, pushing his way through to me. The one who wants to smash and destroy whatever gets in his pathway. Or whomever. He's dangerous.*

'Stop it now!' he booms.

His shout in my ear is powerful, ruffling my hair. Despite the metal and iron surroundings, his voice does not carry or echo. It's both loud and intimate at the same time.

'Argh.' I jump, while reflexively clapping my hands over my ears.

Turning towards the source of the voice, my gaze picks up the increase of charged particles in front of me. It's almost like a haze of dust at first, then more and more of the speckles appear, coagulating into the form of a boy. He begins to manifest directly in front of me. His body's twisted, and hangs mid-air, a foot from the floor, his mangled face level with mine.

I remove shaking hands from my ears, placing them over my mouth. *Dear God, no.* This boy is the melted horror story of a twisted imagination. As he coalesces, he moves closer and closer, and I push back against the cold metal door. My eyes roll back in my head, as breath thready, I fight against losing consciousness. My hands are sweaty, as I grip my pendant necklace like a talisman, praying for him to go away.

The boy's odour is foul and fills the space we share. The smell of stagnant water and malodorous wounds rushes into all six of my senses, and I release my pendant so I can cover my mouth, retching as it hits my stomach. Pus drips from a threatening face and he comes closer, hemming me in. His mouth, shapeless and yawning on one side, opens impossibly wide. He's about to devour me like a snake engorges itself with a mouse.

'Bollocks to this,' I say.

My arm stretches behind me, and trembling, I feel around for the door lock. My dithering hands are so sweaty my fingertips are slick, but I locate and decipher the mechanism, sliding the bolt open. It's stiff, resisting my efforts, but after a couple of seconds, my desperation for freedom wins out and it moves across. Without hesitation, I yank at the handle, banging it against my head in my eagerness to escape this living nightmare.

As I escape, the boy lets out a chilling scream that pierces the air, but I waste no time looking back. Sprinting towards the hallway door, I notice the mirrors above each sink pulsate, bulging one by one. I instinctively cover my head, bracing for the expected shattering being brought on by the vibration and strength of his cry. It doesn't come. Reaching the door, I slam it shut behind me, leaning against the wall, taking shuddering breaths.

I wipe the sweat and tears from my eyes with the back of my hand. The corridor is empty except for Jay, and I make my way towards him. My legs feel weak and are trembling under my summer dress.

He glances up from his phone then double takes, staring at me with his mouth open. Deep gratitude to see him swells inside me and my bottom lip wobbles.

'Mary,' Jay says. 'What the hell happened to you?'

'That little shit scared the snot out of me again,' I mumble as I reach him, then collapse in front of his surprised face.

CHAPTER FIVE

'So, then what?' Jay says, watching me as though I'm a butterfly pinned to a display board. I release my pendant so I can press my hands to my fiery face. My bashful gaze scans the small interview room, escaping Jay's scrutiny. It's empty of any distinguishing characteristics, containing only a table with a computer and phone on it, and a chair on either side of the table. There aren't any windows for me to stare out of, so I'm forced to look back at Jay. 'Thanks for carrying me to this room. I feel like such a dick. How embarrassing.'

Jay scoots his chair closer. 'I didn't manage on my own; a PCSO helped me. And don't be silly, you've got nothing to be embarrassed about. Sounds like you've gone through a terrifying experience.'

'Clearly, yeah.' I look around again briefly with a strained smile on my face for Jay.

He leans forward, resting his warm hand over mine. 'Seriously. Now, carry on with the rest of the story, please.'

Jay's back to business, and I stare upwards, gripping my pendant again, as I search my memory. With a shaky breath, I recount the incident in the ladies' toilets for the benefit of my detective friend.

'Was it definitely the same boy you saw at the supermarket?' Jay asks.

My head feels weak as I nod. 'Absolutely.'

'What did he say?'

With a frown, I consider, saying, 'Something like… 'No, stop it,' or, 'Don't do that,' I think?'

'Well, which one was it? Cast your mind back… take your time, Mary. This is important.'

I cast a furtive glance at the door, imagining I see small glowing particles gathering. Blinking, I force myself to draw in deep breaths and close my eyes. *Jay's here with me, and I'm safe.*

'It was, 'Stop it now.' That's what he said.'

'OK, that's great. Now, you said he appeared to you. What did he look like? Can you describe him to me?'

My stomach quivers in revolt and we're interrupted by a knock on the door. Jay grimaces. 'What is it?' he snaps.

An unblemished face peeks in. 'Sorry, Detective Inspector. I brought the lady a glass of water.'

'Thanks, just leave it there,' Jay instructs him, returning his attention to me without giving the young lad another glance before he leaves.

As soon as it's offered to me, I grab the water, gulping it down as though I've been wandering in the desert for forty nights.

'You OK?' Jay asks.

I nod and blow outwards with such force that my lips vibrate. 'Yeah.'

'So, d'you think this is the kid you dreamt of? The one who was sitting at the kitchen table with the drawings or whatnot?'

I shrug. 'I dunno… maybe?'

Jay frowns and my nostrils flare. 'Look, I said I don't know, alright, Jay? If you prefer, I can sit here, agree with you, and bullshit you all day long?'

He puts his hands up, palms outward. 'My bad, Mary. I'm just wondering aloud, I suppose.'

'Yeah, well, you're winding me up. I *think* it was the kid from the supermarket, but don't *know* if that's the kitchen kid.'

It's Jay's turn to snort at the phrase, "The kitchen kid?' Is that what we're calling him now?'

'Yeah. The kitchen kid.' I give a small smile, feeling the grip of fear lesson as Jay rolls his eyes.

'Well, that's agreed then. How do we find out more about this 'kitchen kid?' You're the psychic.'

My smile disappears and I stare off into the distance. 'I am, yeah… leave it with me, I'll sort something out, Jay.' *I can see if I could tune Patryk's grandma again, or I could ask Errol to help. Where's he been lately? It's been ages since I've heard from him, and he was supposed to be looking into things for me.*

'How about I make you a cuppa, then we can go back into the main office together and grab a table? There might be one free now. I still have something important to tell you, and we need to go through some clues I've got. See if you get any vibes off them.'

I nod my head and stand. 'Alright, yeah. I'll have three sugars in mine, please…'

Jay's eyebrows shoot up, then back down again. 'That to help with the shock?'

I nod. 'Yes, I hear it's good for that.'

He holds the door open for me, and we both step over the threshold, walking down the hall into the main office. The hum of conversation is immediate, and I'm surprised because I remember how quiet I'd considered the shared room to be when I first arrived. God, that seemed like a million years ago now. When was that? I lift my arm to glance at my watch. An hour ago.

We go to the compact kitchen, and I watch Jay take out what we need while the kettle boils. He scratches the back of his neck, then kneads at his neck-shoulder muscles.

'What is it you have to tell me, Jay?' I ask.

He doesn't turn around, but I notice his back and shoulders stiffen at my question. After a moment, Jay makes a slight rumbling noise in his throat, before explaining in a quiet voice, 'The body of a young boy was found, washed up in a canal. It's not Patryk, but I think it might be the body of another missing boy we had a while back. A little boy called John Barrington-Miller.'

'Oh my God, that's terrible!' With a frown, I ask, 'But why do you think his death might be connected with Patryk?'

'Because of what you said, Mary. That there might be a connection with autism. John was also autistic, and it's a bit of a coincidence we've found him now.'

I gasp, one hand flying to my throat. 'This is heartbreaking. So there's a link, do you think?'

Jay nods. 'It's a possibility, and if their disappearances are connected, then there's even more chance that Patryk's life is in danger.'

Silence falls on us like a blanket, smothering us both with its heavy weight of sorrow. *Oh my God.* After taking a moment to absorb that a boy is dead, I murmur, head shaking left to right. 'Oh my God, Jay, it's just so terrible. What happened to him?' *That poor boy, his family must be devastated.*

A woman pops her head into the room, takes in Jay and me, then leaves.

'I'll talk to you more about it when we're back in the office,' Jay says turning to face me, two steaming mugs in hand. Jay passes me my tea, then gestures for me to leave the room in front of him, saying, 'After you then, Mary. Let's go see what we can see.'

I wait at the doorway for Jay to take the lead because I don't know the way, and shake my head in answer to his question. 'So are we getting any hunches about Patryk's parents? Either of them, or both?'

Following him into the main office, I answer, 'Er, no. We are not receiving any hunches.' I chew my lip. *That's not strictly true, is it, Mary?* I question myself. We reach a desk in the main office, and both sit down facing each other.

'What is it?' Jay asks, clearly noticing my troubled expression.

I sigh. 'Well, there is something. A feeling I'm getting… about the mum.'

Jay's eyebrows fly up, and he inhales rapidly as though he's about to extol a long hypothesis about Iryna's involvement with her son's disappearance.

I shake my head. 'No, Jay, it's not in the way you think. I can't put my finger on it, but I know there's a link between Patryk going missing and his mum. I just don't know what the link is, sorry.' My gaze drops to my sandals, and I'm momentarily surprised to see them shod in open toe heels. *Oh, yeah, that's right. This morning started out much differently.* I look at my watch. *It'd been nice to see Eileen, but lunch with her seems like it happened a million years ago now.*

Jay reaches out and pats me on the shoulder, then cradles his large mug. I notice it says: 'What is meant to be will always find a way.' The quote causes me to break into a wry smile. *Little does he know, right?*

'Don't be sorry, Mary. I told you before; it's enough that you're trying, believe me. Let's put a pin in your feeling for now. We'll explore it later. So, I've looked at the possibility of a connection between the two boys. John went missing several months ago, which is why I didn't automatically connect them. Both boys *are* on the autistic spectrum, but the first boy, John, was more affected with his communication than the other. He was also a frequent wanderer and often escaped from the family home despite their precautions and supervision. He even went missing from school once. When our investigation found no evidence of foul play or abduction, everyone assumed he'd wandered off again, and would be discovered at some point. All of which was tragic, but understandable. Sadly, now we've found his body and examined it, we've been able to *correctly* connect the dots and realise the truth.'

After clearing my throat, I reach out for the cup on the desk in front of me. 'How did they know for definite, anyway? That there was foul play involved, I mean,' I ask.

Jay gazes away, looking out into the main office. Following his lead and gazing at his colleagues, I become aware again of the chatter that surrounds us. I swing back to stare at him. 'What?' It's my turn to ask.

Jay's face is solemn as he answers, 'Because there were signs of torture on the body.'

My face twitches as a snapshot of the melting candle wax features, dripping globules of skin, flashes before my eyes. I shiver, and say, 'This boy, John, he was burnt, wasn't he? The boy they found…the murderer burnt his face and body before he killed him then dumped him in the water.' My voice is melancholy because I'm not asking Jay if this is the case. I'm thinking out loud. As I refocus on Jay's face, I watch his mouth make an 'O' of surprise and his attention snaps back to me.

'My God, Mary, how did you….' Jay breaks off what he's saying as I give him a knowing stare. 'Wait- do you think this is the kid that's been stalking you?'

'One hundred percent. He said he was 'not Patryk…' so I guess we've finally ID'd my spirit stalker. What I don't know is why he's so angry with me, or what he wants me to do. Errol was supposed to be looking into that, but he's gone AWOL.' *So weird, Errol has been with me these last three years, and my intuition lets me know the deep connection that we share between us is real and powerful. What's stopping him from being at my side right now, when I need him?* I shrug. 'Well, I suppose we don't really need Errol right now, anyway. What d'you want me to do?'

Jay takes a gulp of his own beverage before plonking it down. He removes a folder out of the locked filing cabinet beside him. 'I know it's a massive ask, but I'd like you to visit the canal where John was found, then go with me to visit his parents. First though, I thought you could look at some photos of both boys.'

Jeez, this is so messed up. I'm going to the scene where the body of a child was found then going to see his grieving parents. Despite my stomach churning painfully at the thought, after a brief hesitation I nod, shifting my chair closer to the table and leaning my head round to see the computer model.

Jay shakes his head, giving me a small smile, and says, 'We do keep all our files on the computer, but I thought it'd be better for you to view the physical photos.'

'Yeah, it might be helpful. I can get like a resonance sometimes, even with my senses locked down a bit. Did the families give you these pictures, or are they reprints?'

'Judging by the newness of the photographs, they're copies, reprints they gave. Why? Does it matter?' Jay says.

After I think about it, I tell him, 'It seems like it might, yeah. Objects a person has touched give me a stronger vibe. It's like peering into a mirror that's steamed up after a shower, compared to looking in one that's clear.'

'Can't be helped,' Jay murmurs with a shrug, then reaches back into the folder, retrieving more pictures of John and Patryk, both in different locations. He passes them to me with care.

'Cheers.' My heart races and my nostrils flare. I focus on breathing slowly and regaining a calm momentum. I handle the photos with slow precision, and Jay remains silent, not mentioning the slight tremor in my hands as I hold them. Closing my eyes, I drift, verbalising what I see, 'He was in a deserted work yard. A construction site maybe? He's fascinated by the cables. They're massive and brightly coloured. The crates are yellow - he likes yellow, it draws his attention. I hear him humming, then talking to himself... saying the names of songs out loud, the words of songs, but he's not singing. He's reciting the lyrics, but the tune all sounds the same. Monosyllabic tone.'

'Huh?' Jay says.

My eyelids open, and I stare at Jay. 'His tone, it was monosyllabic. Oh, never mind, it doesn't matter...'

103

'What else are you getting?' Jay asks as he reaches for a folder, then puts a pile of photos between us.

Closing my eyes again, I grope along the table for the next one. 'John's eating an ice cream. His parents were there, and they were happy that day. They were standing by the water slide, and they all got soaked. Ice creams, too.' A brief smile flits across my face, but then I frown. 'John gets angry easily, frustrated, but that day he's happy.'

This ordeal isn't over yet, so I put out my hand for a few more snaps that I see of John in the pile and scrutinise them. All the pictures capture idyllic moments. John on holiday eating a giant ice cream. A happy theme park outing. John on the garden swing with his mum and the frame of the setting sun behind him. John and his mum playing with an ambitious giant puzzle. His first day at school, clothes immaculate, and John wearing a proud expression on his face. I pick up the second pile of pictures, and Patryk's face fills my vision. Without realising it, I stop all conscious thought and rush towards an altered state. My eyelids flutter like a clockwork doll as my eyes roll back in my head. The love of his mother encircles John; it's strong and pure. I catch the scent left by the bond of the rich and unwavering love between them. John is beloved by his parents, and in particular, his mum. Patryk and his mum have a relationship that mirrors John's with his mother. I focus again on Jay's face and for a second my mouth remains slack, then I click my fingers.

'Their love is the key that links them,' I say.

Jay leans back in his chair, rocking it back on two legs. 'Very cryptic.'

'Alright, sarcey,' As I try to consolidate my thoughts, my fingers lightly twist my pendant back and forth. 'I meant I don't think autism *is* the link between the boys, actually. I think that love is.'

'Enlighten me,' Jay says.

'Both these boys have really loving mums. Nurturing and protective. I feel their bonds. I'm getting pictures of afternoons splashing in puddles, encouraging the boys with their homework and remaining patient, but most of all I can feel how strong the mother-son bond is. Both mums are incredibly loving.'

'Go on.' Jay sounds tense.

I scoot forward in my chair, catching my tongue between my teeth as I consider how to explain my intuitions to a layman. 'OK, so John has these perfect parents, and so did Patryk. They weren't the phoney type of 'social media perfect' either. These mums and dads didn't just switch their attention off when no one was looking. They were the 'still really nice when the kid wakes them up at three a.m.,' kind of parents. With both boys... the dad's lovely, but the mum is super nice.'

A frown creases Jay's face. 'So what? How does that help us find the killer?'

I search my friend's eyes before I answer. 'Because the killer also knew that.'

'How?' Jay demands.

Scratching my head, I lower my gaze to drop to the photographs once more and my shoulders slump, deflated. 'I dunno.'

'Yet,' Jay says, steel in his voice. 'We don't know *yet*, but we will. Mary, I'm sorry to drag you into all this, but I need your help. I know it will be difficult, but we should go now to where we found John's body.'

The horror of Jay's words causes me to flinch, and I close my eyes for a moment, calming my breathing. *What kind of hellish visions are likely to fill my mind when I open my psychic eye where the body of a young boy was dumped? Then, as a thought occurs to me, I feel disgusted with myself for my selfishness. How tough must this be for Jay, after little Pepe's death.*

CHAPTER SIX

H aving taken separate cars, I park up on the gravelly road, and set off to catch up to Jay's strides. As our footsteps synch up, they echo dully against the concrete of the canal bridge we're walking along. I navigate the path carefully.

We come to a halt, slowing as we approach a yellow taped section of the bridge. Jay is standing still at the edge of the bridge, pointing over the rails into the water. He says, 'John's body was discovered around here, in this canal. Someone doing routine checks spotted his body, and it was recovered. So far, forensics have found no DNA or evidence of any kind on the lad, and they're not too hopeful. Probably because of the location he was found.'

'What do you mean? Why would the location make a difference, Jay?'

At my question, Jay turns around to face me, explaining, 'This particular canal is a hydropower canal. The power of the moving water is harnessed and used to generate electricity. The killer probably dropped John in a river somewhere, realising it was a feeder to a hydropower canal. They must've been clever, realising the consistent flow of water would wash away any evidence. Not only that, but there's the mechanical objects, gates, turbines that would've caused further damage.'

My eyes mist over. 'That poor boy,' I say, feeling choked. If it was John who was breaking through my psychic membrane, I could certainly understand his rage, although not why it's being directed at me. 'So what can I do, Jay?'

'Well, we can't safely get down there, so we're a bit limited with what we're able to do here. But I thought we'd stand over the area, see if you sense anything.'

With a shrug, I nod. 'That's fine, Jay. I'll try.'

'That's all any of us can do, Mary. I'll go and speak to the officers over there, give you some space to concentrate.' Jay moves over to a man in uniform and quickly appears lost in conversation.

Taking my attention from Jay, I stare over the bridge. I press my slick fingertips to my temples and take in a deep breath as I try to find my equilibrium. My stomach churns and I wrap my arms around my midriff for a few seconds. It feels like I have swallowed a bag full of electric eels. My senses reel themselves out, but they're snagged by nothing. Except...

My eyes fly open. 'Errol! What the hell're you doing here?' I say.

'I thought I'd check in with you, Mary,' Errol says.

He snags my attention, and a frown passes over my face like a cloud over the sun. 'Thanks, but Errol, I need to focus here. Can we catch up later, please?' I ask.

'Sure, Mary, no problem. I won't say anything, I'll just be around if you need me.'

I nod absentmindedly. 'Cool.' My focus comes back quicker this time, as I open myself to the receptive mode. *Nothing.* My throat feels constricted, and I wipe beads of sweat from my upper lip. *Shit. There must be something. Come on.* After what seems like hours of trying, I allow my eyelids to unfurl, gazing sadly at Jay as he approaches me.

He looks at my slumped shoulders and rests one warm hand on my shoulder. 'It's ok, Mary, you tried,' Jay says.

'Sorry, Jay. I just don't know what's happening lately. I'm all out of whack.' *Am I doing something wrong here? Why didn't this work?*

CHAPTER SEVEN

The sprawling, detached houses indicate the area where John's family home is located is an affluent one. Despite this, as I pull up behind Jay, a dark shadow seems to hang over me, reaching out like a gnarled hand. A chill of unease creeps up my spine as I stare up at the windows that line the street. *Is that someone looking out?* I shake my head, hoping to make my feeling of foreboding disappear like the glitter in a snow globe. 'Get a grip, Mary Jameson. Just get in there,' I command myself. Getting out of my car, I march up to Jay's Skoda, smiling at Jay as he leans over to open the door for me from the inside.

'You made good time, Mary,' he says.

Without speaking, I take a seat next to Jay, waiting for him to explain.

'John's parents, Izzy and Michael Barrington-Miller, were notified yesterday when his body was found and identified from his dental records. They're expecting us today, but I've not given them any other information about why we're here.'

'And why are we here, Jay?' I ask, sighing deeply. *I'm not even sure if I can help anymore.*

He stares ahead, answering me with a dull voice, 'So you can try to sense something that might help the investigation, Mary. I have to try *everything* at our disposal.'

As we roll forward, I stare ahead of me, brows rising in surprise. There's a barrier resembling a toll tunnel placed just before the turnoff to the Barrington-Miller's house.

Jay stops at the small hut placed next to the barrier, lowering his window, and I look in askance at the guard.

A woman dressed in a worn T-shirt sits on a chair scrolling on her raised mobile phone. She pauses her scrolling and stares at us with a questioning expression on her face.

Jay leans forward to give our names, and the names of the people we're visiting.

Placing her mobile down on her lap with a sigh, the guard speaks into a walkie-talkie. She's been told to expect us, and after a few seconds of mumbling, our visit's confirmed. The woman pushes a button under her counter, raising the barrier, and gives us a lazy wave as she grants us access. We drive slowly through the exclusive roads, both looking left and right.

'Wow… they live in a gated community, Jay? I didn't even know these were a thing here in the UK?'

Jay's lips twist. 'Yeah, it's not just the Americans. How the hell did John escape so many times when there's someone guarding the gate then?'

I shrug as we continue to cruise along, obeying the ten mph speed limit signs. 'That barrier woman doesn't seem particularly into her job. Maybe she was playing with her phone like that when John went missing. Or maybe little John was good at going unnoticed.' My mouth droops. *Sadly, he wasn't undetectable enough; someone noticed him.* I snatch a glance in the rear-view mirror, half expecting John to be sitting there, his horrifically maimed face leering at me. Instead, I rear back in my seat when I catch sight of Errol, sitting in the back.

'Hi, Mary,' Errol says.

'Jesus Christ, Errol! Don't scare me like that. Shit.' At my shout, Jay swerves the car slightly, surprised. I press a hand to my chest, feeling its rapid palpitations in response to my friend's sudden appearance.

'Mary, Jeez, that was dangerous. You made me jump,' Jay says.

'Sorry, Jay, Errol made *me* jump as well.' I turn to the back seat again, addressing Errol. 'Errol, don't be an idiot next time. Wear a bell or something.'

'Sorry, Mary,' Errol says. His chin's lowered so I can't see the expression on his face, and I frown.

We come to a halt and Jay turns off the engine then removes his seat belt. Before opening the door, he glances at me askance as I remain unmoving.

Nibbling at my lower lip, I make a decision, saying, 'Can you give me and Errol a couple of minutes please, Jay?'

At my request, Jay pauses, hand on the door lever. He throws a look over his shoulder at the seat behind me. My lips twitch. *He's looking in the wrong direction for my spirit guide, although to be fair, he had a fifty-fifty chance of getting it right.*

'Where did you go after we spoke at the canal, Errol?' I ask.

Errol shrugs. 'Oh, you know, around.'

Swivelling in my chair, I squint at my friend. 'Around?' *What's going on here?* 'Did you find out anything? About who's trying to push their way through to me?'

Errol looks away, then back again. 'No, I'm sorry. Look, Mary, why don't we leave here and go back to yours for a powwow?'

Jay's head is moving back and forth between the two of us. It distracts me from Errol. It's as though Jay's watching a tennis match.

'Leave? What the bloody hell're you talking about, Errol?' I ask. 'You think I should leave without speaking with John's parents?' Suspicion is clear in my tone as I study Errol, eyebrows knotted. *What's he playing at?* 'Why would you suggest that?' I ask, frowning.

Errol's gaze drops from mine, and for a second, I imagine he flickers.

With a tut, I reach for my handle and Jay and I both get out of the car. Standing on the pavement now, I turn, addressing Errol, and my voice abrupt, I say, 'Don't be a mug, Errol, why would I do that? C'mon, Jay, let's go.'

'Mary.' Errol's voice is raspy as he calls my name, and my body tenses at the urgency in his voice and I whip round, leaning forward to study him. He sounds serious, but I can hear Jay's foot tapping on the floor. *'What is it, Errol, we've got to go?'*

Errol's pained face is still and silent, remaining congruent with his aura. It drifts out to me in grey and tattered gold ribbons. *He loves me, and he's agonising about something.* Jay is getting impatient, but Errol still holds my attention, and my concern.

'Hurry up, Mary, they're waiting for us,' Jay says.

'You're surrounded by love, Mary, please always remember that,' Errol says.

'Yeah, thanks for that, Errol. That old chestnut,' I mumble, then tsk underneath my breath as I catch up to Jay, arriving outside John's family home. While we were in transit, Jay had phoned Izzy Barrington-Miller, so I know she's definitely expecting us. Seeing a woman poised at the doorstep, I note the tight, but polite smile, drawn face and hands twisting in front of her and guess she's Izzy Miller.

A quick check over my shoulder tells me Errol's vanished.

'Errol's gone,' I hiss, updating my friend out of the corner of my mouth.

Jay glances back at the car, even though he wouldn't be able to see anything anyway. As we approach the house, Jay and I greet the diminutive lady framed by the door, introducing ourselves.

'Detective… Ms Jameson… I'm Izzy Barrington-Miller. Please come in. Michael's working from home today, and I'm afraid he's in the middle of an online meeting. Luckily though, he expects to be free in about forty-five minutes. He'll join us then.'

Izzy speaks in a slow, cultured tone, and her manner is welcoming but her eyes are wide, and her expression seems blank. Up close, I see her eyes are red rimmed and swollen. My heart squeezes as I guess it's from crying. *Izzy looks like she's in shock, or not fully present.*

As we did at the Challance's house, we follow John's mother, Izzy into the lounge. She offers us seats, a slight tremor in the hand she gestures with. The room's large and impressive in a completely different way to Patryk's home. The Barrington-Millers own a spacious house in a highly selective area. Although it's not a mansion, they're clearly affluent.

'Can I offer you tea or coffee?' Izzy asks.

'No thanks,' I answer with a smile to soften my refusal.

'Oh, please, Mrs. Barrington-Miller, don't go to any trouble,' Jay chimes in. His suave response makes my polite, no frills 'no thanks' seem abrupt.

My eyebrows raise and I check it's him who just spoke. *Wow… Jay really has his professional game on.*

'Please, call me Izzy. It's no trouble. There's a tray ready. Somewhere. I can get it.'

'OK, then thank you, Mrs. Barrington-Miller,' Jay says. 'Tea for both of us would be great.'

Izzy smiles at Jay's reply, then realises we're both still standing and gestures again to the sofa. 'Take a seat do, I shan't be long.' Izzy exits the room with an aimless gait, as though she's not really sure why or where she's going.

We both watch her leave, then glance at the two-seater sofa and the three-seater sofa, simultaneously choosing the three-seater. Jay moves closer to me so we can speak without being overheard. In a low voice, he asks me, 'Did Errol say anything helpful?'

'No, I don't think he knows anything, and he was being weird,' I whisper.

'Well, when you see him again, ask him some more questions, Mary,' Jay rasps, quietly.

112

A massive sigh racks my body, as I agree, and our conversation's put on pause by the rattle of a tea tray.

'Here we are,' Izzy announces as she returns.

I notice that although her tone's breezy, her smile is strained as she leans over the refreshments and her hands shake. *Ah, she looks so brittle, like spun sugar, as if you reached out to touch her she might snap.*

'Sorry it took me so long, I couldn't find the Madeira?' Izzy's voice quivers on the last word.

'Thank you, Izzy,' Jay says. 'It's very kind of you.'

'You're welcome, Detective.' Izzy offers me a cup and saucer, which rattle in her hand as she passes them to me. I accept with thanks.

Jay's sharp eyes flick to my flared nostrils, and I know he'll also have clocked the tremor in my own hands when I accepted my drink. The recently strange behaviour of my spirit guide is having an effect on me. Little Mary's beloved face zings into my mind's eye, and I shy away from the feeling of déjà vu. Errol's out of character flakiness is reminding me of how my spirit friends seemed to have abandoned me at the Rainbow Unit. When really, they were helping me, but weren't able to tell me how or what they were doing. *What the hell's happening, Errol? What exactly are you keeping secret from me?*

It's difficult to impart my desire to get out of here and go to John's room whilst being discreet, so I stare at Jay until I catch his eye, then jerk my head toward upstairs. *I need to connect with anyone from the spirit world who can help me find out what happened to those boys.* Jay shakes his head and mouths, 'Too soon,' then, he stands, touching Izzy lightly on the arm as he addresses her, 'We appreciate you giving us your time today, Izzy, thank you.'

Izzy stops arranging slices of cake on the tray to look at us absently. 'It's for John. It's something we can do for John.' Her face crumples just as she slumps down into the two-seater sofa opposite us, and a sharp spear of her pain pierces my heart. *No, Mary, don't follow her emotional trail, it's unbearable.* I close my eyes momentarily, then swallow and clear my throat.

Izzy hunches over in her seat, covering her face with her hands. She stays quiet, and I blink away tears of compassion.

'So, we've already spoken, and you're aware of the recent, tragic discovery of John's body,' Jay says. 'Words don't seem enough, but we are so, so, sorry for your loss. We... I want you to know we're still working to find out what happened to your John. I won't stop until we do, I promise.'

Back straight, Izzy removes her hands from her face, and nods at the start of Jay's statement, but at the mention of her son's name, her chin wobbles, and the composed construct of her face collapses. I see her raw grief and despair; it's palpable.

A man with his tie slung over his shoulder interrupts our sad trilogy, striding into the room. He joins Izzy on the sofa, putting his arm round her, and clasping her to him as he turns his face to us.

'Michael.' Izzy sighs his name like a prayer whispered into the wind.

Michael unwraps one arm from his wife, and she moves closer to him. I can scarcely bear to look at her face; she looks dazed.

'Have you had any updates concerning what happened to our son?' Although clipped, Michael's tone is not unfriendly, but he'd obviously overheard what Jay had said to his wife.

I allow my gaze to fall to the floor. Michael emanates a deep sadness that drags my heart down even further.

'No,' Jay says. 'But as I was just telling Izzy, we're still looking, and we intend to leave no avenue unexplored.'

'Huh... no stone unturned, that kind of thing, aye?'

Jay nods, answering, 'Exactly.'

'Well, we've already told the police everything we know, so I can't think what you could possibly want with us today?' Michael had been working in another part of the house, but judging by the tired eyes matching his wife's, and the nervous twitch on one side of his face, Michael's also suffering.

'Well, we wondered if we could have another look in John's bedroom,' Jay says.

Michael furrows his brow. 'But what's the point of that? It's been months since he first went missing. Didn't you chaps have forensics in there already?'

'Yes, we did, but sometimes we like to revisit all the information we gathered, just in case there's anything we missed the first time.'

'You mean because you all thought he'd just run away again, you hadn't bothered looking into what actually happened to our son. Until it was too late?'

Jay's head goes back as though he has taken a punch to the jaw. 'No, Mr. Barrington-Miller, that's *not* what I meant. I'm sure a very thorough job was done. It's partly because we may have been searching for clues, based on the information we had then… and looking through a different lens.'

'So, you're saying you didn't think my son had just run off and had a terrible accident, then leave it at that?'

'That was one possibility we considered; I agree. But please let me reassure you, it wasn't the only line of enquiry we followed.'

A measured silence settles in the room while the two men stare at each other.

Michael nods, clearing his throat, and he and Izzy touch hands briefly. 'Understood. So, how can we help?'

'Well, if we could look in John's room, that would be very helpful. If you could collect some photos of his favourite places, or things to do, that would be useful too.'

'We can do that for you, Officer,' Michael says.

Izzy interrupts, her tone curious, 'What for? We've already given you photos, haven't we?'

'You have, and that was extremely kind of you. It's just so we can see if there's any place or link we previously missed. That's all, Izzy.'

Jay smiles as he says this, and Izzy nods with alacrity, reminding me of a baby bird, catching sight of its mother.

'Oh.' Izzy smooths back her hair absentmindedly before she addresses us. It's faintly tussled from where she's leant against her husband's shoulder. 'Then, of course, Detective, that's fine.'

Her husband drops a kiss on the top of her head, then interjects. 'Izzy, would you like me to show the officers upstairs?'

'Ah, I'm not an officer,' I say.

The couple stands, and Izzy looks surprised, asking, 'You're not? Then why are you here?'

'Ms. Jameson is a specialist consultant that works with the force when needed,' Jay answers her question, his voice strong and confident.

'I see,' Izzy says listlessly, staying where she is.

Michael makes no comment, but moves upstairs, taking us to John's bedroom. When we arrive outside the second door along the hall, he clears his throat, 'Izzy slept in here when John first went missing. I couldn't get her out of the room for the first few months. Now, we find it's best if she doesn't go in here anymore.'

I get a clear sense of the powerful anguish that holds him in its grip. I wish I could soothe him, but I know this pain is too raw, his grief too deep. If I did offer sympathy, it was most likely he'd react with anger, telling me to get the hell out of his house. *The best thing I can do is find out what happened to their son, and who did it.* 'Is this John's room?' I ask.

Michael flinches slightly at the sound of his son's name, but that's the only sign he gives of his suffering.

'Yes, it is. Is there anything you'd like, or can I leave you two to get on?' Michael barks out the question. I don't take offence.

'There's nothing else we need, Michael,' Jay says. 'I'm not certain how long this will take but please, don't mind us.'

'We'll let you know as soon as we finish,' I add.

'Sure, no problem. Take as much time as you want,' Michael tells us, then quickly descends the stairs, leaving me and Jay to enter.

Jay stands in front of me, and I'm silently grateful for his positioning. After the fright fest month I'm experiencing, Jay can take some of the grey hairs.

I peer around his shoulder into the room, involuntarily giving a silent whistle. It's spacious, resembling two double rooms merged. A lit display cabinet holds construction themed toys, and someone has made the bed with linen from a well-known steam engine character. The entire place is co-ordinated with matching accessories. As I glance at the small toys, lovingly displayed, my heart strings pang and tears prickle my eyes, threatening to drop.

'The Barrington-Millers aren't short of a bob or two, are they?' Jay says, breaking into my sadness.

I narrow my swimming eyes, asking, 'What's a bob?' I ignore how constricted my voice sounds.

'Are you kidding, Mary?' Jay asks, frowning.

'No. What is it?' I shrug, 'I genuinely don't know.'

'It was an old English currency,' Jay says.

With another shrug, I sniff, blinking back tears, then, after clearing my throat, I step closer to a chest of drawers, opening it to peer inside. 'I've never heard of it. Is it like euros?' I glance up as I ask Jay my question. His conversation's helping to divert me from crying, and I engage with it gratefully.

Jay sighs, slapping his palm on his forehead, then down over his face. 'No. It's a slang term for a shilling. Haven't you heard of shillings, Mary?' The kindness in his eyes confirms that he saw I was close to tears and is making small talk to try to lighten the atmosphere.

'Oh, yeah, I know what they are. You mean like 'shillings, pounds and pence' or something?'

My companion gives a derisive sound. 'Yeah... how old am I again?'

A tiny smile curls my lips. 'Not sure, but do you still ride to work on a penny farthing bike?'

'Wind-up merchant,' Jay says, then nods. 'OK. Come on, Mary, let's focus now.'

With a nod, I push the drawer in, walking around the room as I attempt to push myself into a receptive flow state. I twist my engagement ring as I think what's best to do. *Maybe I'll pick up something if I keep touching John's belongings?*

'Have you found anything yet?' Errol's appearance startles me.

'Jesus, Errol! What the hell?' *I hope Izzy and Michael didn't hear me shout out.*

'Ow, Mary!' Jay squeals. 'That was my foot!'

I stare down realising I trod on Jay's foot when I stumbled in shock. Jay hunkers down slightly as he bends to rub it. 'Oh, sorry, Jay. Errol scared the shit out of me again.'

'Does he have information about the case?' Jay asks me.

I glance at Errol, who stands watching us both. '*Do* you have any info, Errol?' I ask him.

Errol shakes his head. 'There's nothing I can tell you, Mary.'

'Then what are you doing here?' I realise my tone sounds short, but I don't care. I need to concentrate on this.

Errol holds his hands up. 'I just wanted to touch base with you, check on your progress, and give you an update. See if I can help?'

I shrug. 'Only with what I asked you to look into. Did you ever find out who it is that's trying to hotwire my brain?'

'Nope.' Errol shakes his head, looking around, and I screw my face up.

'Well, I think it's probable that John is the boy who chased me down in the supermarket that night. He might be the same one I dreamed of, the scary one who was at the kitchen table, thinking bad things,' I tell Errol.

Errol tugs at his earlobe, then wipes his ghostly hands down his faded jeans. I frown, confused. 'What's up, E? You seem troubled? Have you remembered something?'

'Is your friend able to tell us anything?' Jay interrupts us, his tone lifting up at the end, with hope.

'Nada,' Errol says, and like an interpreter, I shake my head, demonstrating Errol's negative response for Jay's sake. My gaze slips away from Errol, following Jay's departing back as he strides off to busy himself with detective work.

'OK, fair enough,' I say to Errol, 'Then d'ya mind if I get on with what we're doing here then, please? There's a lot to get on with by the looks of all these shelves.'

'You're not kidding, Mary. This is a walk-in wardrobe,' Jay comments from the other side of the room, where he's searching the wardrobe.

Giving up my attempts to centre myself, I open the nearest chest of drawers and start doing the same. I have to trust I'll have an intuition about important clues, even if I'm not *fully* open to my mediumship.

Errol stands in front of the construction toys, arms crossed as he admires the tiny figures and miniature vehicles and equipment. Someone raps on the door.

'Izzy would like to know if either of you would like another drink?' Michael asks.

We've only just had one, but then again, maybe it's good for Izzy to be distracted with a task while we're up here. 'Could I just have some warm water, please?' I ask.

Micheal looks over at Jay. 'Of course, Inspector Santiago?'

Jay pauses his search. 'I'll have coffee please, Michael.'

'No problem. Back in a tic,' Michael says.

I sit cross-legged on the thick shag pile carpet, and Jay crouches beside me, his knees cracking as he lowers himself.

'Got anything?'

Jay shakes his head. 'Nope. Not a thing I wasn't aware of already. I really hoped that you'd sense some information.'

My heart sinks, and shoulders slumping I answer Jay, 'No such luck yet. I'm sorry, Jay. I don't understand it; I would've thought John would be more likely to make himself visible to me here, at his home?' I wrap my arms around my waist. 'That poor kid.' *I feel sick, I can't believe we haven't found anything at all, and no sign of John. In his own home? What am I doing wrong?*

Jay is lost in thought, staring at his knees, when Michael's knock interrupts our heavy silence. Errol remains with us, but the sorrow edged into his usually smooth face reveals his shared sense of our pain and disappointment.

Jay sighs, then reaches over to tap my arm, 'Thanks for trying, Mary. I know this must've taken some guts for you.'

The tumult in my stomach increases and with effort, I swallow the lump that's lodged in my throat. Tears blur my eyes as I mumble, 'Cheers for saying that, Jay. I'm gutted it didn't work.' *Why didn't John appear to us here? Is it my fault? Did my fear of him block him?*

Unaware of our despondency, Michael serves us refreshments in the doorway, before retreating downstairs, and Jay frowns, his contemplation of our host's swift retreat.

Guessing what he's thinking, I shake my head. 'No, he's not acting suspiciously, Jay. It's because his grief is too deep. He literally can't bear to be in here.' *If anyone can understand, I know it's Jay.*

CHAPTER EIGHT

I n the dark of my bedroom, I hear Derek quietly addressing me, and stop my restless shifting in our bed.

'What is it, beautiful? You haven't stopped tossing and turning all night.'

I struggle to speak over the loud beating of my heart. 'My head's pounding, and I'm freezing cold.'

'Want me to get you a drink and some tablets?' Derek sounds half-drunk with tiredness, his words slurring. More awake now and feeling guilty for disturbing him, I sit up, smoothing the hair out of my eyes, nibbling my bottom lip. 'I'm sorry I woke you up, love. I'll go get a drink and some pain killers myself. You just go back to sleep.'

'You sure?' Derek asks, but he sounds like he's already halfway back to sleep.

'Yes, of course, don't worry. It'd be good for me to get up and walk around,' I whisper, and after dropping a gentle kiss on his forehead, I get off the bed, taking my dressing gown from the back of the door, and shuffling into my fluffy slippers on the way out. *My flipping head. Maybe it's dehydration?*

The fridge door illuminates the room as I remove the apple juice, swigging the rest of it straight from the carton. From the corner of my eye, I glimpse a figure standing in the dark. The carton drops out of my hands, and I open my mouth to scream, but no sound comes out. I realise it's Errol, frozen to the spot, staring at me. Heart in my mouth, I husk out, 'What the actual hell, Errol?'

'I'm sorry,' he says.

'Sorry doesn't give me back the ten years you just took off my life with that scary arse shit. *Jesus*,' I hiss. 'Look at the state of the floor now.' I grab the kitchen roll and disinfectant spray from the side, muttering under my breath. While I crouch down to clean up the spilled juice, Errol holds his hands out, pacifying me. I ask, 'What are you doing here, anyway, Errol?'

'What do you mean?' he asks.

'I mean, what the hell are you doing here in the middle of the night, Errol?'

'I just wanted to check on you, Mary, that's all.'

Pausing the cleaning of the floor I squint at him, my face sour with disbelief. 'Check on me? At midnight? Are you having a spirit embolism or something? What the hell is wrong with you?' I shove my hair back out of my eyes and get back to cleaning up the mess. Anger lends me more energy, so I finish within minutes. When it's all done, I straighten again, throwing the rubbish in the bin. I bypass Errol, who's staring at his hands in silence, and head to the medicine box we keep in one of the kitchen drawers.

'My head's killing me.' After swallowing two pain relieving tablets, I turn back to my friend, frowning. Suspicion stabs me, and I stomp up close to Errol, peering into his face. He's avoiding my gaze. My eyes widen as my suspicion solidifies into a coherent idea. *Mutha grubba.* 'You were blocking John today, weren't you?' I hiss the question at Errol.

Errol's eyes shoot back to mine, and the horror on his face confirms my hypothesis.

'Oh my God, Errol. *Why* would you block him? Is it because he's dangerous or something? What in the *hell* is going on?'

'I'm sorry, Mary. I can't explain,' he says, staring at the ground.

'You *bastard*. You can't explain? What about at the canal - did you block John then too? Have you been steering me in the wrong direction this entire time?'

Not looking up from the floor, Errol puts some space in between us, and I guess his answer.

'Oh, you are *totally* out of order. Didn't you used a be a science teacher or something? And didn't you take a Hippocratic oath?'

This prompts Errol to look up from the floor, and he says, 'I was a quantum physics lecturer, one of the most respected in my field until I got unwell. Anyway, it's *doctors* who take the Hippocratic oath, not teachers.'

'Whatever, Errol, no one gives a shit; the point is, I thought I could trust you. You totally screwed me over, Errol. How could you do that to me?' My voice breaks, and Errol rushes back over to comfort me. He doesn't touch me, but I feel his love, mixed with a deep sadness, swirling out towards me. Rejecting it with a shake of my head, I step back, clenching and unclenching my fists as I study him. 'No. I can't believe you snaked me out, Errol. After everything we've been through. *You of all people.*'

'I wish I could explain, Mary, but I can't. All I can say is that I love you, and rightly or wrongly, everything I have done – or not done – is because of that love.'

Ignoring the pounding in my ears, I grit my teeth, then an idea occurs to me, and I focus on Errol. 'Prove it,' I demand.

'How?' he asks.

'Merge with me,' I demand, holding my palm upwards to face him. It's been a while since we merged. Back when Errol was helping me to learn some techniques, I'd found it easier to absorb information that way.

This time, however, Errol steps back in a rush, as though avoiding a hot poker.

'Oh, you lying git! If you weren't already dead, I'd kill you.' I walk slowly closer to him, trying to close the gap between us, and he backs off further. 'What the hell're you up to, Errol?'

'I'm sorry, Mary. I can't explain, but I'm trying to help.'

'You're *sorry*, Errol? Well, I'm *sorry* that I can't trust you. I feel like I don't even know you anymore.'

The agonised look in Errol's eyes strikes a twinge of guilt into me. *Why would Errol block information that could help John, Patryk? Since when has Errol worked against me?* I scrutinise his features, remaining silent and looking into his crestfallen expression, his words churning over in my mind. My heart keeps coming back to the fact that I know my friend genuinely loves me. He said that everything he's been doing is out of love for me.

My gaze flies back to his concerned one as mind racing, I put two and two together. 'You've been trying to save me from something bad that you think will happen, haven't you?'

Errol covers his mouth, stepping away from me again.

'That's why you keep flickering and going on mute. You want to warn me properly about it, only the Universe won't allow you to tell me anything momentously life changing. It would upset the balance too much. That's it, isn't it, Errol?'

Errol rasps out, 'Mary, don't. I love you very much. You're like a little sister to me.'

'What, annoying and bratty?' Even though I'm still angry, I can't stop my quick retort.

Unexpectedly, Errol grins and his gold tooth pops into view for the first time in weeks. He moves closer to me again. 'Many a true word there, Mary.'

'That's why you can't merge with me, isn't it? Because the Universe wouldn't allow it? Tell me, Errol. Just yes or no.'

'Mary… please. You know I can't say anything, and you're breaking my heart.' Errol snatches looks from left to right, as though scared the Universe is going to hear him and come running in to bitch-slap him.

'Well, I want you to stop all this nonsense. If the Universe wants whatever this event is to happen, we both know fate will make it take place, no matter what you do. All you're doing by getting in my way is pissing me off in the meantime.'

'Mary, no… you don't understand.'

'Understand what?' I ask, hands on hips.

Errol shakes his head, and his lips tightly purse like a small boy, determined to keep a secret he's desperate to tell.

'It won't work anyway, Errol, no matter what you hope, and these are *kids* we're talking about. You know how I feel about kids and animals. I can't bear bad things to happen to them.'

'I'm sorry, Mary. Really I am. Is that everything now? Do you forgive me?' Errol scrubs a hand down over his face, then looks at me, his mouth downturned. He seems defeated.

'No, that's not all. I also want you to realise you've messed up big time, because now I don't trust you. You'd better stop blocking whoever is trying to get through to me, because you're only making things harder and if I can't piece this together, it leaves me *and those kids* vulnerable to a killer.' I tell him.

Errol looks sickened by the thought, and his horror brings another line of argument in my head. It pops up like the switch on a toaster-*ping!*

Chin tilted upwards, I demand, 'Anyway, how do you know what you're doing isn't the cause of whatever you're trying to avoid?'

'No… no way, it can't be. Please don't even suggest that, Mary.'

'Well, I *will* suggest it, Errol. Stop getting in the way and just help me find this kid. You might see some possibilities, but neither one of us really knows what we're dealing with here, or what action sets which future into motion.'

My words cause Errol to bury his face in his hands. *He seems overcome with emotion. Urgh. I can't bear to see it.* Making a face,

I relent, moving closer to my friend, unable to see him suffering so much. 'Well, alright, let's just draw a line under it now E. I don't want you to have a meltdown about it. Just butt out from now on, OK? Remember what you've taught me; we're not *the Universe,* but we're all *part of* the Universe, and what we do affects everyone and everything.' My back's straight, and I stare at my friend, then glance at the clock on the wall. I only have a few hours now before Derek gets up for the day. 'Alright, now I really need to go get this psychic show on the road. Will you check in with me more regularly, please? In case any spirits come and kick my arse?'

'OK, sure,' Errol says.

'Don't interfere this time though, OK?' I warn him with narrowed eyes. Errol nods, briefly closes his eyes, then offers me a tentative smile. He hasn't agreed. I rub my forehead, resting my index and middle finger at my temples. *This frigging headache, why won't it go?*

CHAPTER NINE

'D, I forgot to mention, I messaged Sophie and Marcie earlier. I've decided I need some time off the case, you know, get out the house for a bit this evening.' *I feel selfish, but I know if I don't take my mind off poor John, and finding Patryk even for a little while, I'll lose it.*

'Good idea, Mary. You know I was just planning on staying in to watch the rugby tonight myself. What're you ladies going to do, and when're you leaving?' Derek takes the heaviest bag of food shopping from me as we walk from the car to the house.

Rooting through my handbag, I find the key and open the door, telling Derek, 'Marcie suggested the cinema. No-one's sure what we wanna watch, but the showing times are all at four, so I'm swinging by to pick up Marcie, then we'll meet Sophie and Rachel there. If we get there just before, we can decide and queue up.'

'Sounds like a plan, but you don't have too long, so you'd better shake a leg. I'll put the shopping away while you get ready.'

After thanking Derek, I head upstairs to freshen up, humming under my breath as I go. *Some girlie time will be just the thing to relax me.*

An hour later I'm standing in the queue with my friends, Marcie, Rachel, and Sophie, chatting about which film we want to watch.

'Rach, why're you wearing the face mask? We don't have to wear them anymore,' I ask Rachel.

'Yeah, it just looks weird now,' Sophie tells her, Rachel.

Hands on hips, Rachel turns to address us, mask in place. She repositions the elastic around her ears. 'COVID still exists, and I won't take risks.'

Sophie rolls her eyes, smirking. 'Well, I'm not wearing one and we're married, so I could get it and pass it to you. Plus, you don't wear them when we play tennis.'

'That's different. I make sure there aren't many others playing when we're there. Also, it's a massive area. They cram the cinema with lots of people in proximity. And everyone probably sits there with their mouths open. Just don't worry about what I'm doing, anyway. What film are we thinking now?'

We all check the board and discuss our choices again. Rachel isn't happy.

'But I don't like action movies,' she says, chin up.

Sophie touches her arm, appealing to her, 'But, Rach, it's this, or the period drama.'

'Well, I pick the period drama then,' Rachel states, unmoved.

We all stare at Rachel, emanating various sounds of disgust.

'Come on, Rach, we all have to take turns to choose the films, you know that,' I say, trying to be the voice of reason.

Rachel, purses her lips, but her chin isn't tilted so high now as she says, 'Hmm.'

'You picked the last one we saw together, Rach,' Sophie says, then reminds her wife, 'Remember, we're here to cheer up Mary.'

My friends all shift their gazes to me, and I look down, picking at my top self-consciously. 'Er, d'ya mind? I'm not an exhibition at the zoo.'

'Sorry, Mare.' Rachel says, gaze dropping.

Sophie turns her attention back to Rachel, silently staring at her. Rachel throws her hands up.

'Yeah, alright, I'm sorry everyone. Just ignore me. I was being high maintenance. God knows it doesn't really matter what we watch, anyway. We usually just whisper to each other, then Marcie talks over the film, anyway.'

'Hey!' Marcie says.

'Just kidding, Marcie. Let's get these tickets. My treat for being such an arse.'

We all exchange smiles, expressing gratitude towards Rachel for her generosity. Then, we advance in the ticket queue, walk up to the self-serve machine, and purchase our tickets. We go in. Our local cinema is big and plush, and it looks like the film has already started by the time we get there. Using our phones to navigate the many stairs in the dark, moving along the row with sheepish apologies all round.

'Mis-timed that, didn't we?' I mumble as we slide into our seats.

Once seated, we get comfy, settling in to watch the screen, but it's not long before the fidgeting starts.

'Can I have some of your popcorn, Soph?' Marcie whispers.

'If you swap me for some of your fizzy sweets,' Sophie answers in a hushed tone.

I grin. *I was right. This banter with my friends is exactly what I need. The only person missing is Eileen.* I yawn, covering my hand with my mouth.

'You tired, Mary?' Even in the dark, Rachel's observant.

Yes, I've been having nightmares that're so bad I wake up screaming, and I can't remember properly what they're about. No. I'll keep my mouth shut, I don't want to worry my friends unnecessarily. Instead, I say in a sotto voice, 'Sitting in the dark makes me feel sleepy.'

'Shhh,' the woman in front of me says, looking over her shoulder.

I grit my teeth. *What a misog.*

The movie soon grips us all in its suspense, and at first, I don't notice any difference in my environment. A feeling, almost like forgetting something, occurs to me at first, and I peer into the surrounding dark. I look to my left, where the only vacant seat remains. *Nothing there, only the darkness.*

Despite eating popcorn and trying to immerse myself in the movie, a strange feeling distracts me, and I look to my left again. Goosebumps cover my arms as I turn to stare at the space beside me.

Marcie, seeing my silhouette move, leans over asking, 'What's the matter?'

'Nothing,' I lie. *Something.*

The woman in front makes another shushing noise, and as the screen lights up, I see her putting her finger to her lips like old-fashioned librarians used to do.

Ignoring the creeping sense of panic rising inside me, I face the front again, acting like I'm still watching the film. But I can't pay attention and my gaze darts all around me.

'Brr, it's freezing in here,' Marcie says.

Rachel's silhouette moves closer to Marcie as she whispers to her, 'It's the air con. Why don't you put your hoodie on, Marce? It's in the bag. Pass me mine out of there as well, please, Sophie.'

'Will you all be quiet? I *will* call the attendant,' the annoyed woman says.

My nostrils flare briefly, but I shake my head, clearing my thoughts. *I have other fish to fry at the moment.* I can hear the clicking, and I know what it means. Ignoring the woman, Marcie and Rachel put their hoodies on, and we all fall silent again.

A feeling that a presence arrives forces me to stare into the gloom. *Something's watching me, and it's malevolent.* Fear paralyses me, and I can't bring myself to turn away or break its focus. Head pounding, I press my hand to my temple, but it does nothing to stem the pain. The clicking noise reverberates in my mind like the hands of a grandfather clock. *It might be the spirit of John Barrington-Miller. The little boy. Maybe. It might be better to face whoever it is? Like Derek said ages ago, things got better at the Rainbow Unit when I opened myself to the non-physical. If I can just get hold of this terror racing through me, I might be able to do that.* Taking deep breaths, I close my eyes and, when I feel I have some measure of control again, I slowly turn my head to the left, then yelp.

John has manifested, and he's waiting for me, in the dark. He blasts me with such unbridled rage and pain, that I reel back in my seat at the sheer primitive strength of it. Shaking, I let out a bloodcurdling scream. As I clamber up in my chair, desperate to get away from John's uncontrollable fury, I careen into Marcie's side. All my composure's vanished.

'Mary, what is it?' Marcie tries to put an arm around me, but as my fear takes hold of me, it's like she's grabbing hold of a bar of soap.

I register shocked murmurs from the people around me in the audience, hearing exclamations of, 'What the hell?' 'What's going on?' and 'Who's that?'

'Mary! For God's sake, what's wrong?' Sophie's questioning rings out over the commotion.

'Mary, what is it?' 'Mary!' I don't know who says what, but hear Marcie and Rachel both call out to me. I can't respond.

'Right, that's *it!*' the woman in front says as she stands up, storming out of the screening room.

'OhmyGodohmyGod,' I continue to sob, lost in my psychic horror. Other movie-goers shout out, some concerned, some annoyed, and a few people bawl out, mirroring my wailing. Marcie and I bang heads as I scrabble to get to safety, crying out all the while as I move closer to her. John looms nearer, his melted face howling, small hands reaching out like claws as though he's going to tear off my features. Not understanding what's happening to me, Marcie wraps me in her arms, trying to calm me down and I struggle to get out of her clasp like a wild animal who's been restrained. As quickly as it started, the air of menace disappears, and John's nightmarish visage vanishes from view. My racing heart still hammers in my chest, but my breathing, quick and laboured, starts to calm down almost as soon as I look around and see John's gone.

The lights come on in the theatre, and the annoyed woman returns with an attendant in tow, demanding our immediate ejection from the cinema. However, it seems the attendant's priority is my well-being, and he enquires if I need anything, asking what happened. I lower my head, humiliated. *How embarrassing, get me the hell out of here.*

Leaving the cinema, I shield my eyes from the bright daytime and take a few seconds to adjust to the rush hour noise, then I apologise. 'Guys, I'm so sorry I ruined it for you. How mortifying.'

'Don't be stupid, Mary, in my eyes you saved me from an absolutely dire film. But what on earth happened in there?' Rachel enquires.

As I try to avoid colliding with another pedestrian walking on the pavement, I realise Marcie has me in a deadlock hold and isn't letting go. She's held onto me since the cinema, and although I feel like a big baby, it's helping my heart rate to come down from the clouds. Head hanging sheepishly down, I try to explain what happened as my friends crowd me, all worried, clambering to find out.

'So, it's all related to this case? But why didn't you tell us about it?' Marcie asks.

'I'm sure it's all connected to the case. I've been keeping it schtum because I didn't want to break confidentiality.' *Plus I don't like anyone knowing when I'm out of my depth and petrified of the spirit of a small boy.* I flinch away from the cutting edge of vinegar in my thoughts, justifying my fear with the memory of the level of rage John seems to have towards me.

'Then why don't you open yourself up to the spirit world with us there too? If you do it when we're all together, you've not broken any confidences, plus, we won't let anything bad get you.'

Marcie's suggestion has me gawping at her, mouth open. The idea is novel to me; *I hadn't thought of that before.*

'Mary, don't be scared. We'll protect you.' Marcie's voice is earnest, bringing a swell of tears. *I may not deserve you in my life, Marcie, but I'm so grateful we're friends.*

'Yeah, Mary, Marcie's got this,' Sophie says, mouth turning up as she hugs Marcie.

'God save us all,' Rachel chimes in, crossing herself with a grin.

Although we all know that Marcie would put herself in traffic for any one of us, the idea of our sweet Marcie becoming anyone's protector is so ridiculous we all giggle at the notion, Marcie included.

'Let's go to mine and Rachel's,' Sophie says. 'While we're all there, you can call out into the spirit world and see who answers.'

'When, now?' I ask, ignoring the crack in my voice.

'Yeah, now, Mary. What're you waiting for?' Marcie's voice brooks no argument.

My eyes meet hers, and she gives my shivering arm a squeeze. *Get a grip, Mary Obosa Jameson. Get your shit together.*

CHAPTER TEN

Rachel clicks the remote control, and the electronic gates at the entrance of their driveway open. I'd picked up Marcie and taken her to the cinema, so the two of us are in my car, Adrienne. We'd followed Sophie and Rachel home. As we bump along their winding driveway, Marcie and I both admire their sleek executive car as we trail behind them.

'How the other half live, aye Marcie?'

'I know, right, Mary? That Audi is proper nice. Look at this massive house? And can you imagine having a driveway this long?'

'Yeah, this place is gorgeous,' I agree.

We both smile, pleased for our friends. *If anyone should enjoy the finer things in life, it should be them. They both work so hard and have been through so much.* Although I'm feeling calmer than when I was in the cinema, I keep checking the rear-view mirror in case John's reflection's waiting there for me.

Coming to a stop outside the house, I click the ignition off and get out of the car to join our hostesses. After crunching our way along the gravelled drive, Marcie and I make admiring noises, cooing about their impressive home.

'Wow ladies, this is stunning. Soph, when did you put this water feature in? It's gorgeous,' I say.

Sophie gazes at her wife, asking her, 'It was a couple of weeks ago, wasn't it, Rachel?'

'Didn't we tell you about it?' Rachel frowns, scratching her head as she checks with us.

Marcie and I look at each other, and both shake our heads.

'Don't think so,' Marcie says.

I shrug. 'You might've done, and I forgot. There's been a lot going on lately.'

'Looks like there has been, yeah,' Sophie says, looking into my eyes. My gaze drops from hers, and I scuff my feet along the gravel like a child who's in trouble. I don't need to read Sophie's aura to guess what she's thinking. I can see it in her face. I should've told them what's been happening. *But I've been too scared to share it because that would've made the dangers even more real.*

'Anyway. Let's get inside, it's turning nippy out now,' Rachel suggests, typing a keycode into the door.

As we follow our friends into their house, I gaze all around me, admiring the décor. Marcie walks beside me, surveying our plush surroundings, her mouth a perfect circle.

'It's been a while since we've been round, hasn't it guys?' Marcie comments to our hosts. Rachel nods, then walks down the hallway, calling, 'We can go in here.'

We all follow Rachel into the room, and she connects her phone to the house's Bluetooth, making music swell out. I glance at Sophie. Rachel's put one of Sophie's favourite blues albums on, and the mellow sounds float out into the living room.

'I'll be back in a sec. Make yourselves comfortable,' Rachel says, before walking into an adjoining room.

After a few minutes, we're greeted by a clanging noise. The kitchen adjoins the room we've entered, and Rachel strides out of it. When she returns, she's holding two large candles, a lighter, a felt-tip pen, and a large, flat, cardboard lid, ripped from an empty pizza box.

Marcie beams, taking in the box, and asks Rachel, 'You want to order pizza?'

'Nope. I thought we could use all this stuff to have a séance. Then, Mary can open herself up to the spirits and we can be there to protect her,' she replies, tone serious as she transfers her gaze to me.

My right eye twitches, and automatically, my fingers stray up to still the motion as I address Rachel. 'I don't think that's a good idea, Rach. Just because I'm a medium doesn't mean I automatically know how to hold a séance. It might not work, you know.'

'So? Who said you need to know about it? I'm sure we can figure it out together. Anyway, you have a gift, Mary, so we'll have better odds with reaching someone on the other side, and if it doesn't work, it doesn't work.'

'Er… yes, Rach. But who knows *who* we might reach?' Sophie's words trigger a nervous titter from Marcie, and an impatient head toss from her wife, who turns to answer her.

'Oh, come on, ladies, let's just try this, shall we? From what Mary says, she's not getting any joy from the other methods she's tried,' Rachel says.

My foot taps on the marble effect floor, and I twist my lips while I consider Rachel's suggestion. *A séance. Well, it might be alright if they're with me, and if Errol isn't here blocking me, then maybe I can find something out.* 'So, you're saying you think I need to switch it up?' I check, holding Rachel's direct gaze.

'Well, what did I once hear somewhere… that the definition of madness is doing the same thing again and again and expecting a different result?' Rachel replies.

The saying strikes a chord in me, and I nod at her, making my decision. 'Alright, Rach. To help those kids, I'll try anything. But… how do we start? Any ideas anyone?'

'Maybe we should make a circle?' Marcie suggests.

We all agree with Marcie's suggestion, and Rachel busies herself, appropriating cushions from the sofa and arranging them on the floor. It's not comfortable, but better than if they had sat on the shiny modern flooring.

'Right, now I think we should set up the stuff, like in the movies,' Marcie says.

Rachel crosses her arms. 'Good idea, Marcie, then Mary can do her stuff and get some answers while we're here to protect her.'

My brows raise and I feel my back straighten at the brusqueness of her tone, but then I relax again. *Rachel is used to giving orders, and she can sound abrupt, but she's got a heart of gold and will fiercely protect those she cares about. To the death.* Obviously thinking along the same lines, Sophie gazes at Rachel with a tender smile gracing her lips. Rachel's face softens as she glances back at her, and I sigh. *I miss Derek. OK, enough. Get a grip, Mary Jameson, stay on task.*

'Ok… well, Marcie is our resident film guru here,' Rachel says. 'So, Marcie, what do they usually say in seances or whatever in the movies?'

Marcie leans forward, grinning devilishly, saying, 'Is anybody there?'

A ripple of nervous giggling moves through our circle, then Marcie sits up straight, ready to direct us.

'Well… first, if we're going to ask questions, we can use that cardboard to make a ouija board. We need to write the alphabet and other stuff on it, oh, and get something to use a pointer for the letters.'

'Great, that's what I was thinking, but I forgot about a pointer. Will a glass do?' Rachel asks.

'Perfect.' Marcie answers, in a business-like tone, reminiscent of Rachel herself.

Within a few seconds, Rachel gets up and is back with a glass in hand.

Marcie scribbles yes and no, the alphabet, boy and girl, and then writes numbers one to ten on the lid of the box.

As we watch her form the last digit, Rachel interrupts her concentration. 'OK, what's next?'

'Well, next they usually make a circle and get some candles going. Then, they say a protective prayer,' Marcie answers.

'How do they say it?' Sophie enquires, leaning towards Marcie.

'Yeah – and what do they pray for?' I ask, trying to remember scenes from films.

We're interrupted by miaowing and rustling sounds from a cat in the kitchen and turn toward the noise.

'That's just Tibbles,' Rachel says, turning to Sophie. 'Did you feed him when we came in, Sophie?'

Sophie shakes her head. 'Nah, I just came in and sat straight down in here with these two.'

'Alright, hang on.' Rachel gets up from where we're sitting, moving lithely into the kitchen. The slam of cupboard doors punctuate the silence while we wait.

'Remember, never break the circle!' Marcie calls out with drama in her voice, making us chuckle.

Rachel returns to her original place on the floor, holding Marcie and Sophie's hands with loose fingers.

'Wait, Rachel, first we need to light the candles and say the prayer,' Marcie says.

'Can I have that one that smells like the ocean over here? I love that one. What d'you think we should we say then, Marce?' I ask her again as she hadn't answered me the first time I asked.

'Don't worry about what to say, Mare, I've seen loads of horror films. I'll just make something up, then you can all copy me.' Marcie hands me a candle, saying, 'Here, Mary, take this one, just don't put it too near our circle.'

I nod with appreciation at Marcie's take charge attitude. *I don't think I've ever seen her this confident; it's nice to see. Maybe she should take it up as a hobby.* A shiver runs through me as I think about this some more. *Like my dad did? My dad. When he was alive, he'd turned to voodoo and the occult after losing his mediumship skills. I wonder... Had he done seances and used a ouija board, too? Is it even safe for someone like me to do this?* Squaring my shoulders, I tilt my chin up.

My friends are here with me, and I'm confident they'll help where they can. 'OK, Marcie, let's give it a whirl,' I say, chin up.

'Yes, you lead us, Marce,' Sophie says, in a quiet voice.

Marcie clears her throat, her features set and composed. I resist the urge to release her clammy hand and wipe my own down the leg of my jeans.

'We're here today with good intentions,' Marcie says. 'We ask for loving guidance, and for protection of the beloved departed.' She looks around the circle at us. 'Repeat it, ladies.'

'We come with good intentions, and we ask for protection from the beloved departed,' we say in unison.

Marcie continues. 'We have someone here who's gifted. Her name is Mary, and she can speak with you, the beloved departed. Mary would like to ask you some questions. Do you agree?'

'Uh-oh, look at the candle,' Sophie says.

'Oh my God,' Rachel gasps.

I simply breathe in, transfixed as I stare at the candle.

The flame nearest to me increases, flickering towards Marcie.

'We'll let go of hands now to touch the glass pointer. If you can, please make the candle flicker to show you understand?' Marcie's voice sounds relaxed, as though she's having a casual chat with someone she's met down at the pub.

'And agree... I think the spirits have to agree,' I add.

'Sorry, that's right, Mary. Spirits, please make the candle flicker, to show you understand, and you agree to us communicating with you in that way,' Marcie amends her previous statement as a response to my request, then we all stare at the flame with bated breath.

It flickers noticeably and as one we transfer our touch from each other to the glass, touching it with our fingertips.

'Mary will now open herself to speak with you,' Marcie says. 'And we would like to use the board for our specific questions.'

As the fear suddenly grips me, I become aware of a strange urge to burst into laughter, and a smile twitches on my face. My tiny crack of a grin grows, but Marcie's voice stems my hysteria before it takes hold, sluicing me like a bucketful of ice water.

'Stop smiling, Mary. Think about those kids.' Marcie sounds cutting, and unlike her usual chirpy tone.

'Alright, Marce, it's just nerves.' *God, Marcie, have a heart. I wasn't really finding this funny. Not really, it's just the way my terror is expressing itself. And I am terrified.* I can admit that now. Mouth now straight, I clear my throat, then take a deep breath. *Marcie's right, I need to put aside my fear and focus on those boys.* After casting about for neutrality, I feel more centred. *There... This is the right frequency zone now; I can feel it.*

'Someone's trying to reach me,' I say. 'I think it's a boy. Please tell us, is that correct?' My question sounds loud and theatrical in the silent room.

The glass jerks and we all cry out, removing our hands without thinking.

We put them back after a few seconds, touching the object tentatively, as though it's an un-defused bomb. There's a charge in the air, and I shiver, immediately feeling the hairs on my arms rise. An icy finger runs down my back and I push back my shoulders, forcing myself to remain still.

The glass slides along the cardboard, and eyes now wide open, we all stare down at it. All four of us gasp.

'It's gone to yes!' Marcie says. 'It *is* a boy, and what's it spelling now? It's moving again.' She adds.

'Shush, Marcie, I'm trying to read what it's spelling out,' Rachel orders, eyes wide.

The candles flicker, and I lean forward, closer to the homemade ouija board, so I can track the glass's movement. We all say the letters aloud.

'I-A-M-J-O-H-N-G-E-T-H-Y-M-O-R-I-W-I-L-C-U-M.'

'I am Johnget?' Marcie says. 'What does that mean? What's a 'Johnget' when it's at home?'

I shake my head. 'No, Marcie, I think it's 'I am John…' the little boy whose house Jay, and I went to visit.'

The glass jerks to 'yes' without a question being asked. Somehow, I knew John would come here.

'What does 'Thymore Wilcum' mean, Marcie?' Rachel asks. 'Is that the killer's name, do you think? Can John say what happened to him?'

'OK, Rach, hang on. John, can you tell us… was it a man who took you?' Marcie asks for clarification from the spirit connecting with us.

The glass moves to 'yes' immediately, then 'no' and I frown in confusion. Then I ask, 'Do you know who took you, John?'

The glass moves to 'no' and my shoulders slump.

'That would've been far too easy,' Rachel says.

'Shush, Rach, you might put him off,' Sophie says.

Rachel turns her gaze to the floor, 'You're right. Sorry,' she mumbles.

Ignoring the distraction of conversation, I focus on breathwork as Errol had taught me, inhaling and exhaling joy and love, and settling my mind and emotions as I do so. 'Can you show me anything about the place they took you to, John?' I ask.

A deep silence engulfs our circle, and my heartbeat quickens. My eyes have been mostly closed while I focus, but now I open them. Love surrounds me, shimmering in the air like golden strands of candy floss being spun. My friends fear for me, but their support offers me the strongest and most intricately woven protection possible. John is filled with rage, confusion, and pain. He wants revenge, but I know he can't take it out on me, not while my friends safeguard me with their presence. With a deep breath, I tell him, 'OK, John… show me.'

Something shifts, and I experience a sudden drop, my stomach lurching. Red dots drift in front of my eyes and waves of dizziness assail me. Someone muffles my mouth by taping it shut, and although I open my eyes, I see nothing. Something's over my head, tied tightly around my neck. The motion sickness I'm suffering from tells me I'm travelling in a vehicle. My body slides back, banging against something hard, and I cry out through dry lips. We're going up hills - big ones. *Mummy… where's my mummy?* Bile rises behind the tape, keeping my mouth closed. *No, please, I want my mummy and daddy.*

The memory stops with an abruptness of a light switching on in the dark. The next thing I'm aware of is a searing pain on my cheeks. I want to scratch my face off to stop the pain, anything, please. *Why are they doing this?* My skin sizzles like when Mummy cooks in the frying pan on a Saturday morning. *But it's my face!*

He's making me scream. I hear laughter at my agony, and then it ebbs, and I fly, still full of rage. Hate and anger. Denial of The Blue. A light… *Mary is her name. She will help me; I will make her!*

'Mary, Jesus Christ, stop!' I hear Rachel shouting, and I feel her slap me round the face. All at once, I become aware of Marcie and Sophie's screams, which, together with Rachel's slap, snap me out of my connection with John.

My trembling hand holds my injured cheek, and Marcie wipes away the tears that soak my face, and I touch them myself, feeling like I'm sleepwalking.

'I'm sorry, Mary, we couldn't get you out of it, and I didn't know what else to do,' Rachel said, giving me a brief hug.

'In the movies, they usually just roll their eyes a bit, but you went full 'exorcist' on us. You were screaming the place down like you were being murdered. The candle flame went about two metres in the air, the glass was spinning, it was so scary. Rachel said we needed to wake you up no matter what, and that's when the living room windows blew in,' Marcie tells me, dragging in a huge breath afterwards.

'Yeah, and they're reinforced, so you owe us a bomb.' Marcie's update and Sophie's dry comment afterwards, send my gaze darting to the windows. The debris that greets my eyes makes my mouth fall open in shock.

'Oh my God, you guys, I'm so sorry,' I say. *What've I done?*

Noisy sobs burst out of me with a suddenness that makes my friends veer back, gawping at me, their own mouths open. Then, as one, they move in close, to support me, and I catch my breath again, steadying myself. 'He took that little boy,' I say. 'Somewhere far away. He burnt John's face, just for kicks. That sicko was enjoying it. He was laughing at his agony. John's right: I need to help him. I have to catch this bastard, no matter what.' Then, I collapse against Marcie, sobbing again at the memory of it. The arms of Rachel and Sophie also encircle us, and I catch sight of golden threads solidifying in the psychic field around us all.

'What about me? You don't speak about my Patryk yet.' There'd been no clicking sound to announce her, but Patryk's grandmother Monika now stands beside John. She's staring at us with a pragmatic expression on her face.

'Crying does not help. Call the policeman and tell about John. Find my grandson,' Monika instructs me, her face stern.

How the hell're all these spirits hacking into my psychic system?

CHAPTER ELEVEN

J ay answers his phone after a couple of rings, and as usual, wastes no time with greetings. 'Mary. What's wrong - has something happened?' he asks.

Marcie's hand tightens on my free one as I speak into my phone, 'I held a séance tonight, and I think I might have some details to tell you about Patryk's disappearance. I'm staying here with the girls for a bit and it's late now, but I'd like to get together tomorrow to talk about it, please?'

'You did what? A séance? What details did you find out? Can't we just talk about it now?' Jay asks.

Psychic replays of tonight's visions assault me again, and fear and hopelessness well up inside me, making my head spin. My legs tremble, and as I sway, I let go of Marcie's hand to steady myself against the wall.

After some deep breaths, I manage to answer Jay. In a voice flat and quiet, I say, 'I'm sorry, Jay, but I really can't, my head's scrambled. Just let me get my shit together, then we can speak properly tomorrow. Please?' *Much as I want to help, I don't think I'd be making much sense right now.*

Jay's silent for a couple of seconds, then says gruffly, 'Alright. If you can't manage it, you can't. Tomorrow though, Mary, first thing, yes?'

I catch Rachel and Sophie exchanging eye contact, and Sophie steps closer to me, mouthing, 'Are you ok?'

After a brief nod to Sophie and a tight smile for Rachel and Marcie, I focus again on the conversation. Whatever's in my facial expression seems to relieve the pinched set of Rachel's face. Sophie blows a breath out, then walks past me, switching the lights on.

Rachel strides out of the room, then returns after a couple of minutes, bringing us all a cup of tea from a tray. The hand I extend to take my mug shakes so much that I give up, gesturing for Rachel to place it on the nearby table for me. Although I see her sharp eyes narrow, she puts it on the table without comment. Sophie's settled on a chair now and says, 'The carpenter's on her way now. She said she'd be here within the hour.'

'She?' Rachel asks. 'Who'd you get? What happened to Rob? I like him.'

'I like him, too, but he was busy, so he gave me Sky's number,' Sophie answers.

Marcie hasn't stopped staring into my face, with an intensity that makes me awkwardly shift my feet. Sophie and Rachel finish their exchange, then all three of my friends stare at me wordlessly, making me uncomfortable.

I consider Jay's question again, answering, 'Yes, Jay, I'll see you tomorrow, early.'

'Shall I come to you?' he asks.

Nibbling at my lower lip, I turn my back to them, walking a short distance away on still wobbly legs. I remain in the same room.

'Yes, that's fine, Jay. Come to my place.' My voice is still sore from screaming and I pick up the hot tea to soothe it, sipping. Unexpectedly, it's sweet and my eyebrows fly up. *Hmm, I like it.*

'Brilliant, Mary!' Jay's tone is enthusiastic.

'Thanks, Jay. Oh, yeah, tomorrow I'm meant to be seeing Eileen again. I'd like to talk about this case with her, see if she has any ideas, if that's alright. Maybe she can come round when you do, all three of us together, just like old times?' I hear the wistful note in my voice, and I'm surprised. It reminds me of a child asking an adult for a really big present.

The line's silent and unconsciously, my sixth sense unravels itself, creeping down to Jay. *He's feeling awkward, holding himself back. There's a strong emotion Jay feels about Eileen. He likes her. A lot.* I reel my awareness back, reminding myself it's wrong to spy on my friends. I've promised I'd never invade their thoughts or feelings without their permission. Once you start down that road of corruption, I imagine you can't stop, kind of like those scabs on my hands I used to pick away at, then wish I hadn't.

'Ask Eileen if she's ok with me tagging along first please. If she's OK with it, that'll be great.' Jay's tone is unusually gruff.

'Alright, will do,' I reassure him.

'Oh, and Mary? What you've done tonight is amazing. I know your visions are genuine, so I'm really hopeful this will lead to something. Thank you,' Jay says, then ends the call, and I turn back to my friends. They're all silent, concentrating on my conversation with the detective.

'What did your detective friend say?' Rachel questions me, wariness in her tone. I don't need to be psychic to tell that she's worried for me.

I shrug. 'He said we can talk about it all tomorrow. He's coming to mine with Eileen.' I notice all three of my friends faces relax when I mention Eileen will be present. We all like and trust her.

'Maybe we could do this séance thing again another time? It really helped me to have you guys surrounding me tonight, thank you.' My voice falters, then breaks off. It's strained from screaming and crying.

Marcie flies to me, ringlets bouncing as she hauls me to her, filled with fierce emotion on my behalf. 'We'll always be here when you need us, Mare. That was so scary, I nearly peed my pants. If I were you, I wouldn't ever want to contact ghosts again. God, it was petrifying, especially when you started screaming and we couldn't stop you. I was so close to freaking out. It was *proper scary.'*

I nod, white faced. *Yep, it was. Proper scary.*

CHAPTER TWELVE

The beeping of my morning alarm feels painful, and I wake up feeling as though I'd only slept for a moment before it'd gone off.

I shut one eye as I squint at the time on my phone. 'Shit, it's just after six. That's too early,' I mumble. Then, confused, I reach over to my beside table, to switch off the siren. *What's happening? It's not working.* With a huff, I push myself up in the bed, ignoring Derek's grumbling.

'Do Jay and Eileen have to come round today, Mary?'

As the noise from my phone stops I breathe a sigh of relief, admitting to myself I'm still exhausted from the séance last night. Part of me wishes I hadn't agreed to meet with Jay and Eileen today, but this has to be done. Rubbing the sleep from my eyes, I wriggle into a more upright position, staring at my phone as though it's a poisonous snake. The ringtone registers belatedly and I understand. *It wasn't my alarm. That was Jay calling.*

Derek's protests are almost absorbed into the background as he complains, 'You were out til late yesterday. Can't you take a break?' His voice is soft, but it grates on me, even as sweat breaks out on my brow.

Why is Jay calling me this early? I turn to Derek, answering him abruptly, 'You know what's at stake, D. We're making headway. We have to keep going while we still have a chance to save Patryk.'

Every minute counts. I wince as I catch sight of Monika's morose face, staring at me from the corner of my bedroom. She came back with me from the séance and now just appears at will. *What's she doing here still?* I flick a glance at Derek. *It won't be helpful to tell him I'm being haunted by the ghost of Patryk's grandmother. I mean, what's he supposed to do with that kind of information? Nah, best if I say nothing.* 'Anyway, Jay just rang me, so I'd better phone him back,' I tell Derek. Without acknowledging Monika, and avoiding Derek's gobsmacked expression, I get up, heading for the bathroom grimacing. *Monika makes me feel so bad, I wish she'd go away.* Guilt prickles me for my selfish thought and ashamed, my gaze drops to my feet as I walk. *Until I've done everything I can to find Patryk and get him home to his parents, I don't have the right to stay in bed and enjoy lie-ins anyway.*

After I use the toilet and wash my hands, I ring Jay. Jay answers my call on the first ring, barking out my name tersely, his voice sounding loud in my ear. Wasting no time in getting to the point, Jay says, 'Mary, glad you called back. Listen, I want to hear about what happened at the séance, but before we catch up, I need to tell you something. An eye witness just phoned in a sighting of Patryk. I'll check it out this afternoon and I want you to come with me when I do.'

Shocked, I gasp out loud my mouth falling open, and exclaim, 'Oh my God, Jay. Does it seem like a legit witness? What did they say?'

'It's promising. The person claimed to've seen Patryk near the entrance of a building, accompanied by a tall person. They didn't say much about who was with Patryk, but they did give information about details on Patryk's uniform that wasn't released to the general public. Can you believe it? I need to investigate. Will you go with me?' Jay asks.

My heart hammers so fiercely I'm suddenly scared it might break its way through my ribcage. *Could today be the day we find Patryk?* Dry mouthed, I nod in reply, then as I stare into my own eyes in the mirror opposite, I realise Jay can't see me. My voice is squeaky as I vocalise my answer, 'Yeah, sure. Where to?' I ask.

'Do you know the old Forbes Arms pub, near Woolwich ferry?'

'Yeah, I think I know where the ferry is, Jay. Is the Forbes pub the old rusty building to the right of the ferry that's a canary yellow colour?' I wave a hand over the steamed-up mirror. Initially I'd intended to run the shower until the water was warm, but now the condensation has filled the entire bathroom. Leaning to the right of me, I click the extractor fan on to reduce the steam and clear the air. I leave the shower on though, as I don't want Derek to hear my conversation.

Jay speaks into my ear again, 'That's right, Mary, that's the one. Now can you tell me what happened last night please?'

The weight of his question presses down on me, slumping my shoulders. 'Well, it's definitely John, and we need to get the sicko responsible for his death. He's a sadistic psycho of the first degree.'

'Poor kid. We'll catch this monster,' Jay assures me, resolve unwavering, 'did John reveal anything that might help our investigation? What else did he say?'

A turbulent breath escapes me, my nostrils flaring as I press a trembling hand against my forehead, bracing myself to recall the horror again. I recount the chilling details to Jay: John's abduction, having his head covered and being unable to see, the disorienting journey in a spacious vehicle, his battle with nausea and finally, the unimaginable torture by fire that John endured.

Jay, ever the meticulous detective, interjects occasionally to confirm details or seek clarification. 'Wait, so John felt sick? Was this before he was taken, or did it develop during the journey?' 'How long did this ordeal last?' 'Do you recall a continuous movement, or was there a period of stillness, perhaps when you were aware of the sound of an engine idling?'

A sudden flash of memory illuminates another piece of the puzzle, and I wrinkle my nose as I remember something else. 'There

150

was another message he gave via the ouija board. He said 'gethymore wilcum.' We couldn't figure out what it meant, maybe 'get Thymore Wilcum?' I don't know if that name means anything to you? Is it something you could investigate?'

After a moment's reflection, Jay says, 'I'll look into it now. And thank you, Mary. You've given me lots of leads to explore before we meet up later. Would half one work for you?'

'That's fine Jay, yeah,' I tell him.

'Great, and Mary, I really appreciate your help.'

I shake my head to clear it, then gratefully realise Monika has disappeared. 'Laters, Jay.' I say. Feeling nauseous I step into the shower, turning it to the cooler setting. The blood pounds in my ears as I wash, and I put one hand to the wall to steady myself. *Derek's not going to like this, but I have to go.* A tentative smile of wonder curves my lips. *There's a chance we could find Patryk.*

Sometime later, having spent most of the morning reassuring Derek with regards to my safety and mollifying him with a promise to be home in time for dinner, I get in my car. The cold makes me shiver as I hunker over the steering wheel. A quick search on maps provides the optimal route to get to the Forbes pub, and after I've programmed my phone map to direct me, I cover my eyes with icy hands, rubbing them together and blowing on them while I wait for the windscreen to de-mist. After sending a text to Jay to let him know I'm on my way, I fasten my seat belt and when it's safe, pull away from the curb. *Here we go.*

As I spot Jay's familiar car, a feeling of safety settles the knots of anxiety that have been building in waves since I received his call. He's parked in the car park in front of the desolate building, and our two vehicles are the only ones there. It doesn't take me long to pull up and jump into Jay's unlocked car and slide into the seat beside him. My 'Hey, Jay,' is breathless, belying the nerves I'm assailed with.

Jay's face is solemn, and his greeting is as serious as the heavy atmosphere in his car, 'Morning, Mary.' He turns to study me saying, 'Thanks again for meeting me today, and for the details you passed to me regarding the séance. I found out some information that's really promising. You're a star for doing all this, you know that?'

Heat floods to my cheeks and I know that colour is staining my face in the daylight. I shrug off Jay's thanks. 'Whatever. So what did you find out? What're we doing?' I ask.

'I plan to talk to you about what I found out after we've been inside here. For now, let's concentrate on this.' Jay looks at me for askance, and when I shrug, he continues, 'I've accessed the floor plans, and taken a look around the area. Because of the massive fences and barbed wire at the top, there's no access to anywhere except the front entrance to this pub. So we'll get inside, scout around, and it'd be good if you check for any psychic clues about the place. Once we've done that, we can give Eileen a ring. Then, I'll update you both. It's been busy today.'

'Hopefully there's some good news?' I say, inwardly praying.

It's Jay's turn to shrug, and he says, 'We've turned up some promising leads. We'll talk as soon as we've checked round here.' Jay sighs, gazing out the window at our surroundings, 'The eyewitness account might turn out to be false. The person didn't give their name, or agree to give any personal details when they called it in.'

'Did they say why?' My trembling lip feels tender as I nibble it, so I press them together instead.

Jay rubs his face, and even though he's seated, I see there's a weary slant to his shoulders, as though they can't bear any more weight. He says, 'They said they have a past they don't want looked into.'

In the small confines of the car, our eyes meet. We both know how suspect that statement sounds.

I say, 'On the way here I was thinking, how come they're only just phoning the police now? Patryk's little face has been plastered everywhere over the last couple of weeks.'

As though he's expecting this question, Jay answers immediately, 'The officer who took the call asked the same thing. The witness told them they thought nothing much about seeing the two of them here until they found out about Patryk's disappearance when they returned from an overseas trip.'

'Hmmm,' I say, mulling the statement over in my mind. *Seems a bit dodgy.*

'I know. It sounds fishy, but this caller knew Patryk's school blazer had a particular emblem on it, and we didn't release that information to the public. We kept some details back, so we'd be able to tell the more promising reports from the false ones. Sadly, we get a ton of those.'

I follow Jay as he exits the car. Arriving outside the pub, we both stand still, staring up at the desolate yellow eyesore. The property stands alone, two storeys, isolated in the street, all the other buildings having been demolished years ago. Ivy snakes up the crumbling walls, stretching up like sinister brown talons attached to its sides. The paint is old and weary, the once sunny colour now corrupted, patchy and flaked. As we look up at the darkened windows, I notice some of them are broken, the shattered glass staring back at us like open, mawing mouths with jagged teeth. The birdsong I could still hear when we were in the car park, is silent now we're at the building, and the unnatural quiet adds to the trepidation growing inside me. *This is a horrible area.* Using my thumb, I twist my engagement ring round and round, then wipe my sweaty palms down my jean legs. Part of me doesn't want to think of a little boy in a place like this, but the rest of me still prays we find Patryk here today.

Jay blows outwards, and I comment, 'Well, this is a real palace, aye?'

'Hmm,' he says, lifting the crowbar he brought with him from the car.

'After you,' I tell him, gesturing for him to go in front of me.

A wry smile graces his serious features, bringing an answering grin to my face. When he moves, I walk beside him and we stand at the door, Jay slotting the crowbar into place in the corner of the old-fashioned door.

With a frown I ask him, 'Won't you get into trouble for that? Don't you need to get permission or something?'

'Nope. I'm going in there to save a life. Hopefully, anyway. If an officer enters with an intention to save a life or prevent injury to someone, or to prevent damage to the property we don't need a court order,' he says.

Shuffling from one foot to another as Jay readies himself to prise the creaky old-fashioned door open, I snort at the last sentence, saying, 'Bit late for the damage part, judging by the state of the outside.'

As we speak, the door swings open, without the encouragement Jay had been about to offer with his crowbar.

'Huh, it was open already,' I say, and we both peer inside.

The interior of the premises defies the light, clinging to the darkness and shadows instead. Sharing an uneasy glance with Jay, he enters first, then I cautiously step over the threshold, my gaze darting left and right as we go.

The first thing I notice is the smell. Despite the unlocked door, there's a strong scent, the musty odour of a property that's been closed off and locked up for a long time. It hits me squarely as we move further into the first room. In response, my stomach curdles at the offensive scent, and I rest a hand over my nostrils and mouth. 'It stinks in here!' I say.

'Hmm,' Jay's voice is muffled by the hand I guess is covering his mouth and nose, as mine is. Jay's other hand reaches out to my arm, and he says, 'Wait here a minute, Mary, we need to get used to the darkness.'

That is literally the last thing I want to do. My body quivers in protest as we stand still while we become acclimated to the gloom. Rigidly alert, I listen out for danger, my head cocked. As if on cue, I hear a creak on the tall stairs that face us, and as one, Jay and I head towards the sound.

In order to be fully present and focus in the moment, I shut myself off to the receptive mode, instead, concentrating on the shadows that dance and beckon in the corners of the room. *It's just because we're moving, that's all.* Still, now my eyes have accustomed to the lack of light, I can make out Jay's head jerking in the same directions as mine do. Stealthily, we tip-toe to the stairs, painstakingly creeping up them one foot at a time. The staircase is tall, to accommodate the high-ceilinged spaces.

Ominous creaks sound from the different rooms, and I swivel to face the noises, but see nothing out of place. *Now isn't the time to unlock my psychic tuning fork and make myself vulnerable, but I'll need to soon.* We move deeper along the upstairs hallway, with Jay systematically opening doors to the empty, disused bedrooms and checking for any sign of Patryk or foul play. He asks me, 'Once we've checked through and made sure it's safe you can do your thing. OK, Mary?'

I give Jay a quick nod but don't speak.

The smashed glass in the windows and on the floor seem to emphasise the emptiness of the void we've entered, and Jay whispers to me, his hushed voice echoing in the barren hallway we're hovering in, cobwebs wafting in the chill breeze that's coming from the windows.

'I don't think we're going to find anything visually, Mary. There's only one more roo-' Jay's sentence is cut off as I squeak enthusiastically.

'Jay, look!' Without thinking I run into the room I'd cast my gaze over as Jay had spoken. *A blazer!*

'Hang on, Mary,' Jay says, but it's too late, I'm already sprinting to the blazer I catch sight of. The piece of clothing lays on a chair near the window and I grab it. Disappointed, I stare down at the black cardigan in my hand until a loud, cracking noise jolts my gaze up – *Is that thunder?* Then quickly back down again as my feet suddenly freefall, my body height drops, and all at once, I realise what's happening.

'Mary!' Jay shouts, and I scream.

The floorboards immediately in front of the chair are broken, and I'm plummeting through, about to drop an entire floor.

Instinctually, my arms fly up like a child demanding to be picked up, and I grip onto the hand Jay clamps onto my wrist. White lipped, I claw at his arm, desperate for purchase as my legs flail, suspended in between floors. 'Jay, help,' I pant, fear striking me and making my palms slick.

Leaning over, knees bent, Jay uses both hands to haul me up and grim faced, I wrap my arms tightly around his neck, shuddering with an overhang of terror.

'Are you hurt anywhere, Mary? Did you hurt yourself?' he asks, concerned.

Unable to speak at first, I allow myself to be supported by Jay back over to the doorway, shaking my head as I compose myself. 'No, I just nearly shit myself that's all,' I say.

Jay's reply is a relieved snort, and we walk downstairs. He pulls up an old, cobwebbed bar stool for each of us and we both sit in contemplative silence. After a while I murmur, 'It wasn't even a blazer when I picked it up. It was a bloody cardigan.'

My companion's eyebrows raise, and a tiny smile haunts his face. 'That was rotten luck, Mary,' he says. 'Are you sure you weren't injured at all?'

'I'm fine, Jay, not a scratch. Just got the wind knocked out of me,' I tell him, voice confident. Inwardly, I'm quailing. It occurs to me the hole in the floor may have been deliberately set up. *Am I just being suspicious?*

Jay obviously considers the same question, saying, 'I'll ask forensics to come and check over for any recent evidence, in case that was deliberately staged. You never know. We did receive a call tipping us off.'

Yes, you never know. 'I'll see if I can sense anything here, Jay.'

'Great,' he says.

My lacklustre shuffling around the pub feels anticlimactic, and after a frustrating twenty minutes of trying to get into the right frequency, I feel a gentle tap on my shoulders.

'Give it up, Mary. You tried, but you look done in. There's obviously nothing here you can feel out. Let's get back to the car and call Eileen with that update,' Jay says.

CHAPTER THIRTEEN

O nce we're settled back in the car, Jay reaches into the bag
he retrieved from the boot, extracting a large envelope.
Then, he gets out his mobile phone and, holding it up slightly, video
calls Eileen. Her clear, crisp greeting mirrors her green gaze, and
although my heart's still racing from what happened at the pub, I
smile, relaxing against my seat. Jay wastes no time in filling in Eileen
about the outcome to our investigation of the old pub. Then he
moves on, all business. 'Anyway, Eileen, thanks for taking the time
to speak with us, I'm grateful to you two. Hopefully, I won't keep you
too long today,' he says, continuing, 'Just to give you both an update,
after I spoke with you, Mary, I started working on narrowing down
suspects. After a bit of work, we've now whittled it down to five likely
suspects to check from that area,' Jay tells us.

'What? That's amazing, Jay. How'd you do that?' I ask, frowning
my puzzlement.

'We used John's last known whereabouts as a starting location,
and you told us we were looking for large vehicles. We traced the
possible routes from where John was last seen travelling. Then we
checked CCTV footage for large vehicles out of that area around the
time he went missing. We have three that went towards Holloway
Road and onto the A four one four two, two that went to Romford,
then were last seen on CCTV footage taking the M eleven slip road

toward Cambridge. All the rest stayed local in or around London, so we don't need to worry about them.'

With a frown, I puzzle over Jay's statement. He sounds very definite. 'Why don't we have to worry about the London vans?'

Eileen asks, 'Ah - because I gave John's parents a call and asked them about the travel sickness timings. His mum said John would get sick after about two hours of being in a vehicle.'

Gobsmacked, I stare at Eileen saying, 'Did you, Eileen? God, you're amazing. What did they say? Didn't they think it was an odd question, by the way?' I ask her. *How did she even know how to phrase that? It was so gutsy of her.* My eye twitches at the idea of calling grieving parents to enquire about the time it took for their dead son's travel sickness to kick in, but I know Eileen would've known just what to say.

As I raise my fingers to still the motion of my twitching eyelid, Jay comments, 'Probably, but you know Eileen, she can charm the birds from the trees.'

My brow strays upwards and I nod in agreement, my gaze straying back to Jay. *Eileen is charming, yes, but I had no clue Jay noticed these kinds of things.*

'Anyway, lass, after Izzy told me that information, Jay was able to pinpoint a radius,' Eileen tells me, not commenting on Jay's compliment.

Jay clears his throat, explaining, 'So we were able to use two hours as a minimum window of time driven, which would likely take us outside of London. There are also speed limits that helped to work things out. Plus, Mary, you described being driven. You *didn't* say you were stuck in traffic, or stationary, so they must've been moving. Hence, we don't need to look at any vehicles that remained in London.'

'That makes sense,' I say, eyes wide.

'I pinpointed locations that are outside of a two-hour drive radius from John's last seen location. Then I got that search to intersect with our search conducted for large vehicles. From the areas we focused on, during the two hours after John went missing, there were a few vans and large cars recorded as moving. I've narrowed down the results to five vehicles –or rather, to five suspects.'

My heartbeat picks up pace, and my mouth seems suddenly dry. I run my hand over my hair to smooth it down, pushing it behind my ear.

'That's great news, Jay. Any suspects for me to put my feelers out for?' I ask, squinting from the sunshine that has started to penetrate the cars windscreen.

'Yes.' Jay picks up the envelope he'd placed on his lap a short while ago, opening it, taking out a handful of photographs. After holding it up to his phone to show to Eileen, Jay presents one to me. Glancing again at Eileen he says, 'I thought we could all look at these five people. Mary, I'll give you basic information about them, without saying whom I suspect and why. I think it's best if I don't pass on bias to you. If you get a sense about someone, we'll focus on that individual, then I'll see if we can find a link between them and the victims.'

'I think that's smart,' Eileen says from Jay's phone. 'Mary would be less likely to give skewed results that way.'

'Cool with me,' I say, closing my eyes and taking a brief moment to bask in the sun that's now warming the windscreen and filtering onto my face. With a nod, I open my eyes again, gazing at Jay and straightening in my seat. 'OK, let's get down to business then, aye?'

Jay nods, then taps on the photo he gave me. 'Right. So first we have Simon Redford. He's a twenty-one-year-old law student from Cambridge. He drives a VW van.' Jay hands me another picture and I present it briefly to the phone and Eileen before looking myself. Jay continues, 'Then there's Phil Moyce. He's fifty-two and a farmer from Taunton. He drives a Land Rover.'

I study the two men closely, examining their features while Jay gets another picture ready to offer me, flicking it in front of Eileen for a few seconds before offering it to me. 'Next we've got Jason Deres, he's a twenty-eight-year-old plumber from Exeter who drives a Ford, and then we have David James, a taxi driver from Plymouth. He drives a Mercedes-Benz.' Jay places his mobile phone into the dashboard holder, then clicks his knuckles.

'And the fifth?' Eileen asks from her new vantage point as I stare at Jay, my hand extended for another photo.

After flashing it at Eileen, he passes it to me, and I look down at the image. Jay says, 'Lastly, there's Joan Sante from Minehead. She has a mobile snack van, which she was driving on that day.'

'Let's have a look then,' I say.

Eileen and Jay stare at me while I organise the pictures, shuffling them in my hands. I take time studying the face in the photograph on top. 'Simon Redford is a twenty-one-year-old student? He looks way older,' I muse.

'He's studying law, and he's from an old money family,' Jay says.

'Didn't we think the killer might be well-off?' Eileen asks.

'Yes, we did,' I answer Eileen slowly, because it feels as though I'm already far away mentally. Without another word, I tune them both out, casting my mind adrift. Emotions neutral, I focus on Simon's face, as though it's burned into my retina.

Simon's pink, floppy jowls and beady eyes stare back at me from behind my eyelids. Formal attire on a sunny day. *He looks like he'd be a barrel of laughs at a party. Not.* 'It's not him. I don't think so, anyway,' I say.

'Percent, if you had to give one?' Jay asks.

'Seventy percent sure, thirty percent not?' I say.

Satisfied with my answer, Jay passes me another envelope, not giving me time to read whatever's written in the file. 'Next one.'

'Who's this?' Eileen enquires, leaning forward on camera.

'Jason Deres, the plumber from Exeter,' Jay says.

161

With one hand gripping the photo, I lean in close to it, concentrating on Jason's chiselled features and piercing blue eyes for a while before speaking.

'He looks like he should be on the cover of one of those romance novels,' I say, surprised, showing his image to Eileen again. She murmurs agreement, and Jay sighs. 'Mary, please focus on the task.'

'It's not him, and I'm ninety percent sure before you ask,' I tell Jay, anticipating his question.

Head down, I examine the next photo in the pile. It's the female and Jay identifies her.

'Joan Sante, thirty-three,' he says.

'The mobile food lady?' I ask.

'The snacks van, yes. She lives in Minehead,' Jay confirms.

The photograph captures Joan's ruffled hair and uncomplicated grin. I stare at a woman in her thirties with a careless, cheerful demeanour. *It'd be hard to find someone who looks less like a killer.* I shake my head. 'Definitely not.' With a sigh, I shuffle to the next photo, scrutinising the man in the picture.

'David James, forty-one-year-old taxi driver from Plymouth. What do you think, Mary?' Jay asks.

With a shake of my head, I answer, 'He looks proper smug, but I'm not getting any killer vibes from him so far.'

The sound of traffic interrupts my concentration and I swivel round to glance at the road. *Traffic's building up now, it must be getting later.* I stare back down at the photo again, examining the forty-one-year-old in the photo once more. My stomach gives me no odd sensation. *It isn't him. He's OK looking - not a total Jason, but also not a complete Simon, either.* David's short, but well kept, clearly not a stranger to exercise. He's propped against his Mercedes-Benz van, wearing well-fitting jeans, a tight T-shirt, and a smirk. I flash the picture at Eileen, suspended in the phone frame, so she can also have a look.

'Hmph. He does look pleased with himself, doesn't he?' Eileen says. 'Is he well off? How much is that van worth? It looks expensive.'

Jay answers Eileen's question, scratching his head, 'For that year, you'd be looking at around thirty to forty thousand.'

My whistle sounds loud in the car's acoustics, and I wince, realising I have the beginnings of another headache. *Flipping headaches.* The bright sun of earlier is starting to fade, much like me. *Time's getting on.* I glance at my watch.

'I need to keep an eye on the time. I promised Derek I'd be back home for dinner.' Even though food's the last thing on my mind right now, gratitude swells inside me because I have someone of my own in my life who cares enough about me to worry.

'We only have one more left,' Jay says. 'The fifty-two-year-old farmer from Taunton. Phil Moyce.'

There's a tugging sensation in my stomach as soon as I receive the photo in my hand. Silently, I examine Phil Moyce. A feeling of electric shocks tickles the fingers that hold his likeness increasing my scrutiny.

He has the ruddy complexion of someone who spends most of his time out in the elements, which I'd expect of a farmer. In the picture, he's walking across his yard. Nondescript face and clothes, there's nothing in there that should make me suspicious. However, the pulling sensation in my tummy says otherwise. 'There's something off about this one, and not just the fact that his eyes look like piss holes in the snow.'

Jay's face screws up, looking pained. 'Mary, please,' he says.

I shrug. 'Sorry, Jay, it's my bitch Tourette's. Can't help myself.'

Jay's drained sigh makes me feel some remorse at taxing him when I know he's busy, but Eileen's snort of amusement brings an answering grin to my pale face.

'Stop encouraging her, Eileen,' Jay says. 'She's bad enough as it is.' He turns his attention back to me. 'So, Mary, d'you think Phil might be our guy?'

'Maybe. I'm getting a feeling he's a wrong'un somehow. That's all I can say about it at the minute, but now I have a face and a name in mind. I could always do another séance and see what I come up with? I just need to hope the Universe doesn't gag the spirits.'

Jay scrunches his face. 'Huh?'

With a glance at the car ceiling, I contemplate how to explain 'cosmic law' to my friend, who is a concrete thinking police officer. *Well, he is clever, and has called me in to work with him, so that proves he's not that concrete in his thinking after all.*

I turn to him explaining, 'See, sometimes the non-physical are so connected with us physical beings and our happiness they want to help us. They might be tempted to advise us, so it avoids certain traumatic events from happening, and that could make a massive difference to destiny.'

Jay's lips curl down either side. 'Like… they might want to give you the winning lottery numbers?'

'Yeah, I wish. More like they might *want* to warn you not to get on a train they know will derail and paralyse you for life.'

Eileen throws in, 'So, what's the Universe's problem with that? We'd avoid the big sad in life; that'd be a good thing, right?'

'Wrong. What if you're a medical student, and you were supposed to become paralysed because it inspired you to find a cure for paralysis? Or because you inspired someone else to do that. Or because in the future you go to physio sessions where you met the love of your life, and *your progeny* change the world.'

'Well, that's miserable. You're saying there's a plan for everything and there's an ultimate power that controls fate?' As I watch, Jay's features all tighten, and his mouth firms into a thin line.

My nod confirms Jay's interpretation, and too late, I realise my words have incensed him, and I instantly know why. Eileen meets my eyes, and mine fill with tears. *His son. Without meaning to, I've just said to Jay that the Universe could have allowed his death to be stopped. But didn't. That's so fucked up and unfair, it should never have happened.*

My eyes close on the pain clear in my friend's face, and when I open them again, I can see that Eileen has her hand resting on her heart. Jay and Eileen gaze into each other's eyes via the video link, in a way that makes me suspect they're silently communicating. As I watch, Jay's loud breathing quietens again, and his shoulders slump, releasing his pent-up anger.

'OK… enough about the Universe. Back to the case,' he says, breaking eye contact with Eileen. 'I think we should take a look at these suspects in a slightly different way. Mary, would you take these photos and do another séance? Can I come this time too though?'

My mouth drops open. 'You want to come to my next séance?'

He glances at Eileen before he answers. 'Maybe we should both go Eileen, and your other friends too, Mary, of course.'

Now we're getting somewhere. I might also call on Errol, see if he can help. He seems to be back onside again. 'Sounds like a good idea, Jay, I'll let you know what time when I get home. I check my watch again. 'Shit, it's getting late, I really need to get back. Will you let me know the outcome here though, Jay? I mean, if forensics turn anything up from this place?'

Jay nods and checks his own watch. 'Of course, and I should probably get off too, ladies. I appreciate all your help today, Mary. You've been great. Thanks to you, too, Leenie.'

'Don't mention it Jay,' I tell him.

Eileen chimes in, 'No problem, Jay, anytime,' then, 'Bye, lass. Don't mind me, but you look a bit pale, Mary. You make sure you look after yourself and rest up when you get in.'

'I'm fine, Eileen, don't worry. I'll let you both know about the séance. Will you both let me know if you uncover anything?' I ask, hand on the door-opening lever.

As I return to my own car, my back straightens and I frown, swivelling slowly in Jay's direction. '*Leenie?*' As I drive home, I think about Jay's nickname for Eileen, and the two of them making eye contact. The way they didn't see each other for a while, then were all teenage uncertainty about their reception. Jay's been single for over a year now, and Eileen's a widow, having lost my beloved spiritual uncle, Jo, years ago. I remain silent while I drive, a replay of verbal and non-verbal clues flitting through my mind. For a second, my open-mouth gawks back at me in my rear-view mirror, then a slow smile spreads over my face as a lightbulb goes off in my head.

Adrienne seems to purr knowingly, in agreement with my realisation.

'Hold the phone - they have a 'thing'!'

PART THREE

CHAPTER ONE

Back at home, Derek hovers, face tight as I take off my jacket. His lips are pressed shut, and as I glance at him quickly, I get the inkling that he's desperate to ask me what happened. After I've put my shoes and jacket in the cupboard I turn around to give Derek a hug, asking him, 'How was your day, D?'

Derek frowns down at me. 'Never mind my day. How are you, Mary, and how did it go today?' I wince as his arms tighten around my waist and he continues, 'Did you find anything out? Are you alright?'

With a sigh I accept Derek's questioning as I snuggle my face into his chest, absorbing his attractive woodsy scent as I reflect on what happened. 'It went well, actually. We made a lot of headway.'

I tip my chin up to smile at Derek, feeling suddenly good about that. We *had* made some progress on the case today, and I think we'd all been pleased with the amount of leads that Jay could now follow up on. Something draws my attention to look over Derek's shoulder and my eyes widen as I realise my dearly departed friend has arrived. *How long has Errol been standing there?* 'Errol! Where the hell've you been?'

Errol's perfectly spherical afro glints under the lighting, and a smile spans his even features.

I'm not smiling though, and step away from Derek to move closer to Errol.

'Errol's here?' Derek asks.

Jaw clenched, I nod confirmation to Derek, then demand, 'Seriously, Errol, where the shit *have* you been? It's been *ages*.'

'I'm sorry, Mary, I know the last time we met there was a bit of bad blood between us, and I know I messed up. It's nothing like that this time. I've been away trying to help.'

Derek moves to my side, staring in the vicinity I'm directing my voice to. He touches my arm to get my attention back, then asks, 'Is it cool with you if I go online while you have your catch up with the invisible man here?'

Absentmindedly I answer Derek, 'Yeah, of course, whatever, Derek,' then turn to Errol. 'We'll talk in the bedroom,' I say. Errol's face is a picture of offence and I guess it's because of Derek's tongue in cheek reference to him as 'the invisible man.' With a grin, I move off, gesturing for Errol to follow me.

As he follows, Errol mumbles under his breath, and as we enter the bedroom, I put a hand over my mouth to hide my smile as I hear him kiss his teeth. I sit on my bed, looking up at him.

'I take it back,' Errol says. 'Maybe Derek's not so cool after all. 'Invisible man,' cheek.'

'Whatever. Just go on and spill whatever it is the Universe will allow you to say, my friend.'

'Well, I'm obviously limited to what I can tell you, but I've been tackling it as best I can from this side,' Errol says.

I tilt my head as I regard Errol. 'Really? Is that even possible? How does it work?'

'I use you as the link. It's like how I taught you to focus your attention. Except, once I've stabilised my emotions and I'm on that frequency, the intention I send out is a vision of you. By holding onto this vision of you in my thoughts and keeping a positive emotional frequency, individuals who're in harmony with me will be drawn to me. Then we can form a connection.'

Mouth dropping open I consider Errol's claims, hit by the idea that there's so much about the world that I don't yet know, 'Wow, that's so mind blowing. So, who'd ya get?' I bounce slightly on the bed, making me feel like an enthusiastic child, and Errol sighs, his warm, golden reels of love floating out to me.

'I'll try to say, but just understand, I probably won't be able to tell you, you know, because the Universe will likely silence me.'

The hope inside my chest deflates as Errol silently mouths the name of whoever he is trying to mention. His pixelated face makes it impossible for me to lip read. *Whatever, universe.*

With a shrug I say, 'Well, that blows, but it's okay. It's not like I need to know all the details for things to fall into place. It'll work out alright in the end, anyway. Won't it Errol?'

He's silent for several moments, so I prompt him, 'Errol?'

'Er… yes, eventually. But Mary, the Universe sees the overall picture. It may not turn out how we expect or want it to immediately. For some of us, things unfold in this lifetime, or maybe in the next, and there's always a thread connecting everything.'

Feeling comforted by Errol's words, I lay on my bed, on my tummy, swinging my feet up and down. My hand props up my chin as I consider my friend, pondering his last statement. 'D'ya mean like that old film?' I ask. '*The Butterfly Effect?*'

Errol gives me an eye roll, and protests, '*Old* film? What the hell, if that's old, I must be ancient! But no, not really. I'm talking about *coherence* and *superposition*. Have you heard of those terms?'

'Nope,' I say.

With a smile on his face, Errol steeples his hands together in thought. 'Well, the quantum world supposes everything's made of particles, and these particles have wave functions.'

'Like sound waves?' I ask. *Even I've heard of those.*

'Sort of. There are different quantum effects, like kinds of interaction or interference, and these effects need the waves to be coherent with each other, to be co-ordinated.'

My head hurts, and I scratch my scalp. *He's losing me.*

'Superposition is when a particle is in two or more states at the same time,' he says.

'Errol, my friend, you're going way over my head. Do I need to know the ins and outs of a cat's arsehole? Or can we bottom line this shit?'

'Mary, you're such a charmer. OK, basically, it's what I said the first time. Everything is connected.'

CHAPTER TWO

After propping up the phone on the sideboard so I can see properly during our video call, it's almost like my friend Sophie is in the room with me.

'Hi, Soph, it's been a minute - how's things? Did you get the windows sorted OK? I'm so sorry about what happened. I feel terrible.'

Sophie's lips curl into a smile and she shakes her head gently. 'Don't worry about that, babe. Rach had that all sorted the next day. Our insurance covered it.'

'Well, I do feel terrible about it. If your insurance goes up because of it or anything, just let me know and I'll pay the difference. I'm so sorry.' I bite my lip, imagining the price of repair.

'Shut up, will you, Mary? We both told you not to worry about it, and we meant it, honestly. It wasn't your fault anyway. How're things with you and Derek?' Sophie casually waves my offer away.

As if hearing his name called, Derek pops his head round the corner of the kitchen door, whistling. He stops when he sees I'm on a video call and puts a hand to his mouth. 'Sorry.'

'Relax, handsome, it's just your bestie - see?' I tilt the phone towards Derek so he can see Sophie and they wave to each other, swapping greetings. He leans closer to the screen to talk to his friend.

'Hi, Sophie, how're you doing over there at the mansion?' Derek asks.

Sophie grins. 'We're doing fine, thanks. Are we going to have our usual get together soon?'

Derek nods, smiling. 'That'll be nice, I'll text you and we can talk dates. Say hi to Rach for me.'

Sophie nods, and waves as Derek leaves, then alone again, Sophie and I share a grin. *A man of few words on the phone is my Derek.*

'So, were you just calling for a catch-up? What's happening with that poor missing boy - any news?' Sophie asks.

'My detective friend Jay's been able to gather a few clues from our séance that he can follow up on. That's why I'm ringing really. I need to set up another séance with the ouija board as soon as possible. Would you and Rachel be up to doing one again?'

Within the frame of the phone, I watch as Sophie's pretty face goes slack for a moment. For a second or so, she doesn't speak. I feel a thin bead of sweat appear above my upper lip and swipe it away. *Oh my God, I might have to do it without them. It might just be me and Jay doing this. And what if Eileen doesn't want to be part of it either? Jay's my friend, but Eileen, Sophie, Rachel, and Marcie are my family. Bonds forged by trauma hit different.*

Sophie frowns, and her next words bring a lump to my throat. 'Of course, we're up to it, Mary. Us three will always have your back. You know that, right?'

The knot in my stomach releases. *Thank God.* I nibble my bottom lip to stop it wobbling, as gratitude swells inside me. 'Thanks, Soph, it means a lot.'

'Listen, we're here for you. Whenever you need us, whatever you need. Anyway, it was kind of exciting. It's definitely different from our usual night out, aye?'

'Slightly, yeah.' I clear my throat and say, 'I'll text Marcie, and this time, Eileen and Jay want to be a part of it as well.'

'Jay wants to hear it from the horse's mouth, aye?' Sophie guesses, brows raised.

'Yeah, something like that. If he comes with me, he can ask the questions he wants and get the answers straight away. Cut out the middleman.' I clap my hand over my mouth. 'Oh my God, but what about your windows? You've only just got them fixed.'

Sophie hesitates before answering. 'I told you to stop worrying about the stupid windows. We don't care. However, maybe for safety's sake, this time, we can do it in the den, out the back of the house. It's comfy, and it just has the one small window, so it won't cost tons to replace if it gets blown out.'

Biting my bottom lip, I check again, 'Soph, are you sure?'

'Mary, of course. Anyway, Rachel would never forgive me if I turned you down when you need us. Also, she's realised she loves a séance.'

As relieved as I am that my friends will all be by my side, my palms are slick with sweat as I reposition my slipping phone on the side. *I can't believe I'm going to do this again. How have I changed my future by agreeing to this?*

'Okay, if we say tomorrow at seven, is that alright, Soph? I'll call Jay, Eileen, and Marcie to let them know,' I ask, cementing the arrangements.

'That'll be great, no worries, Mary. I'll tell Rach so we can get prepared.'

A smile of affection flits across my face. 'Please thank her for me. You're both amazing to do this.' I swallow the lump in my throat. *God, I love you guys.*

'No problem, Mary, see ya.'

'Laters,' I tell her, shutting off the call.

CHAPTER THREE

A fter opening her front door, Rachel glides quickly ahead of me, Marcie, Derek, Jay, and Eileen. She leads us to the back room where Sophie sits, waiting. The room's large and stylish, and the walls are decorated in white. Diametrically opposed to each other are large white sofas and two cerise armchairs that add a splash of colour to the space. A shiny white cabinet lies off to the right, and there are speakers in the ceiling. Reggae music plays softly from them, and I recognise the songs are by one of my favourite groups.

'Sheesh, this is some 'den,' Sophie,' I say, impressed.

'Yeah, and oh my God, you got that cool sofa and armchair set we saw the other month,' Marcie says. 'It looks so nice in here. Proper plush - is it comfy? I bet it's comfy.'

'Try it and see for yourself,' Sophie offers Marcie with a smile. Used to Marcie's gregariousness, the rest of us take a seat and Rachel opens the lid of a double piano stool, pulling out an aged wooden box.

Jay, always curious, leans forward to better study the box, asking, 'What's that?'

With a gasp, Marcie interrupts, asking, 'Is that a *real* ouija board?' At Rachel's nod of confirmation, Marcie continues, 'It looks so old... how old is it, Rachel? I bet it's got a really amazing history; did you ask them about it when you bought it?'

'It was six pound fifty from a local charity shop, so not that impressive, Marcie,' Rachel answers with a brief smile.

Although Marcie's interested in the wooden box, she's also still extolling the benefits of the sofa, so only half listening to Rachel's reply.

Sophie shrugs, then says, 'Have a proper look at it if you like, guys. Rach, where'd you put the drinks or whatever?'

Rachel points to the white unit. 'I put some canned drinks and crisps in there. Everyone, please just help yourself whenever you want. Because of what happened last time, I thought it safer not to have hot drinks or glasses out.'

We all nod. *Good thinking.*

Jay shifts so he faces me and automatically, I tense. Eileen moves closer to me, patting my hand. She gives it a light squeeze before letting it go, then says, 'So, how do we kick things off?'

An awkward atmosphere sets in as we look at each other, thinking back on the last time we did this.

'Marcie, you're the horror film buff, and you came through last time. Why don't you start the proceedings tonight. How do we start this again?' I ask my friend.

Derek rests his hand on the tense muscles of my leg, and the warmth and weight of it feels reassuring.

Marcie doesn't hesitate, 'Well, in the movies, they always say a ouija board shouldn't be kept in the house. They reckon it can become a portal that attracts demons, or evil spirits who're trapped and want to scare the living.'

My throat's dry and I swallow, thinking about the drinks in the cabinet. *Well, there shouldn't be any problem then; we're only using it to contact a murdered little boy who's filled with rage and is stalking me. Also, this shit is definitely being kept inside the house.*

I wipe sweaty palms down my thighs surreptitiously, then put a hand to my neck to fondle the necklace my mum gave me.

177

Derek puts his arm around me, sensing my unease, then turns slightly to Marcie. 'Ready, Marcie?'

'OK, everyone, here goes. We ask that our angel guardians watch over us. We come here today with good intentions, and we ask for the protection of our ancestors, and for the protection and help of our spirit guardians or angel guardians. Amen.'

In unison, we mumble, 'Amen.'

A familiar voice comes from the side of me, '*What're you doing, Mary?*'

I feel myself flinch, and open my eyes, tracking the source. 'Errol! What're you doing here?' One of my eyes peeps open, as I whisper to my friend. I open both eyes, searching for him. Moving round so he's standing opposite me, Errol raises his eyebrows and glances around the room in his relaxed fashion. '*I asked first.*'

'Is your spirit guide Errol here, Mary?' Marcie asks. 'Can I talk to him - will he hear me?'

'Yeah, Marcie, he's here, you can ask him what you like,' I say, watching Marcie's earnest expression as she pushes a handful of ringlets back off her cheek.

'Errol, we're trying to find the little boy who appeared to Mary before. Can you see him?' Marcie asks.

Errol's wry gaze holds mine. '*I take it Marcie doesn't know about the Universe shutting me up?*' he says.

There's no time to explain all of that crap. 'No, Marcie, Errol can't see him. Hold up for a bit, guys, sorry. I need to chat with him.' I don't wait for a response, and from my seat, I begin a conversation with Errol. Everyone here's used to my conversations with the other side. After how Errol was messing me up before, I'm still suspicious of his motives for joining tonight.

'What're you doing here, Errol?' I ask.

'It's your fault for projecting so loudly, Mary. I heard your call and followed your thought blocks here. After what happened last time, I just wanted to make sure you're safe, and that no other spirit-being jumps in, or worse, takes you over uninvited.'

'Ah, that's so sweet, Errol. OK, you can stay, but don't *fudge* this up for us, OK?'

Errol nods once. 'I promise,' he says.

'Thank you.' I turn my attention back to my friends who watch raptly. 'Errol's just here to keep an eye out for us. Let's get back to it, guys.'

Marcie clears her throat, and I do the same, heart pounding. I peep over at Errol, standing in the corner with a watchful expression. His presence makes me feel better, and I shut my eyes again with more confidence.

Derek's shoulders are touching mine to one side, and Marcie's on the other. I can feel Eileen, Rachel, and Sophie's intentions towards me, zigzagging like lines of electricity in my direction. It creates a cradle of safety and well-being that increases my feeling of security. *My friends are the best.*

In my mind, I call him. 'John. John Barrington-Miller, can you come to us? We want to help you, John.' Now, Jay and I are pretty certain about the identity of our séance informant, and I'd shared this with my friends earlier, however, I still jump as Marcie, in tune with my silent intentions, says out loud, 'John Barrington-Miller. We want to help you find peace, John. Can you hear us?'

The pointer jerks underneath my fingers, and we gasp collectively. It moves to '*YES*.' After a quick glance around, I don't see John but realise Errol's moved and is now standing to attention just behind me. *He reminds me of a Busby guard outside the Queen's palace. Well, actually it's the King's palace now, as Her Royal Highness has crossed over, bless her.*

'John, is that you again?' Marcie whispers.

The pointer moves quickly to '*YES*' and I catch my breath, glancing around the board. I can't see any signs of an apparition and lean forward to address the ouija. 'John, we want to find out who hurt you. Did you see who did this to you?' My head moves sharply to follow the pointer.

'*NO*'

'Mary, I think you're asking the wrong questions. Can I try?' Jay is on the edge of his seat and speaks in a voice that's hushed and urgent.

I nod, answering, 'Of course, Jay. John, this is Jay. He's a policeman, and he wants to help. He is going to ask you some questions now.'

Collectively, we gasp as the planchette moves slowly this time. It goes to: '*YES*'.

A sharp pain rickets its way into my temple. Click, click, click. The static comes and my headache clears like the sun bursting out over a rain cloud. *John? Not only him. I can't see John, but I know there's a feminine energy that's with him this time. He's not alone.*

Jay continues with his line of questioning, 'Did you see the make or colour of the car that took you, John?'

'*B-L-A-K*'

'Black? It was a black car?'

'*YES*'

Eileen gasps and I remember that the suspects cars were all black. My attention is briefly snagged as I register Rachel's awed 'Oh my God,' but then I turn my focus back on the board, and the answers to Jay's questions.

Jay speaks again, his voice quiet, calm, 'John, do you know what make?'

'*NO*'

Derek's hand closes on mine as my shoulders slump, and my disappointed gaze meets Marcie's.

Eileen breaks the despondent silence saying, 'Knowing the make of the car might be something an adult would've made note of. A small boy could've noticed a smaller thing in the environment. Some minor detail that was close to him that drew his attention.'

Jay nods, straight away asking, 'Were there any landmarks you saw nearby or on the way to where they took you, John? Anything we can look for to identify the killer?'

'YES'

'F-L-O-U-R-S'

Rachel spells out the letters as they circle the board and repeats them aloud. 'I think John's spelling is off. But remember his age…I bet he means he saw flowers. Ask him if that's correct, Jay.'

'John, is that right? Did you see flowers?' I ask.

'YES'

Staring at Sophie, my gaze drops to the sketch pad that's Sophie's constant companion and I catch my bottom lip between my teeth as an idea occurs to me. *OK, now here's something I can work with, but it's probably gonna suck for me.* I lick my dry lips before voicing my suggestion. They're sticking to my teeth.

'What about if Sophie lends me her pad, and I try to channel John to do some automatic writing?' I ask. 'That way, I can receive a picture of the flowers he saw, and maybe we can tie them to a particular location.'

'No way, Mary. Absolutely not,' Derek bursts out. Gazing at him, I take in his rigid posture and clenched jaw. I stroke the back of his hand lightly, saying, 'It'll be fine, Derek. Please don't worry.'

Derek shuts his eyes, and I can see a vein throbbing at his temple.

'D'you think you could even do that, lassie?' Eileen asks.

With a shrug, I answer Eileen, 'I think so. I've never actually tried it before, but I can't see why not. Sophie, can I borrow your pad and pen for a bit, please?'

'For God's sake Mary, think about it first. This sounds dangerous,' Derek says.

Sophie hands over the requested items slowly, glancing at Derek as she does so, and her hesitancy triggers a nervousness inside me. Nibbling my lip, I smooth my hair behind my ears, then take a deep breath in.

'Let's do this,' I say.

Eileen's clear green gaze holds mine, intense as she sits forward saying, 'Mary, I agree with your Derek. I don't think this is a good idea. If this is John, God alone knows what he's been through, and what experiences you'll open yourself up to.'

My jaw clenches so tightly I can feel the strain all the way up to my ears, but I shake my head. 'I know you're worried about me, Eileen, but my mind's set. I think this will help.'

I can feel Derek's stiff form pressing uncomfortably close into my side, and I turn to look at him again with what I hope is a reassuring smile. 'It'll be ok, D. You'll see.' *Maybe. Hopefully.*

Derek holds my hand with an almost painful pressure, but he doesn't protest again.

'Mary, this sounds well dodgy. Are you sure?' Marcie asks, her blue eyes like saucers.

I shrug again, telling her, 'It's not that different to what I did before really - I'll just be holding a sketch pad this time, no biggie.'

Eileen's frown tells me she's still not happy about my plan, and her words confirm it. 'If you *have* to open yourself up to John, I suggest you only allow a vision of these flowers to be transmitted to you. If you can, allow nothing else. You only need one thing at a time, or it may overload you. We can't tell about the magnitude of the emotions attached to this, and the effect it'll have on you psychologically, OK?'

'OK, mother hen, I hear you,' I say, trying to be casual. I swipe surreptitiously at the beads of sweat that have started to gather on my forehead.

Jay leans forward across the table, enthusiastically exclaiming, 'This is unbelievable, Mary. What a cracking idea! Now, maybe once you've got a picture of the flowers, ask John if he can show you the killer.'

I realise that Errol's still here, and he's pacing around the room. As he notices my attention on him, he cautions me, '*No. Remember what Eileen just said, Mary. Just the flowers.*'

God, now Errol's chiming in as well. I throw him the peace sign. I'll be keeping it tight, I don't want to let in any more than I have to. Who knows what else is out there that I could tune in to?

The tense atmosphere in the room defuses, and Marcie wipes her hands down her corduroy pinafore dress before asking, 'Can I get another drink please, Rachel?'

With a sweeping gesture Rachel says, 'Of course, Marcie. Please guys, everyone just help yourselves to whatever you like before we start this.'

After a few minutes of bustle and normality, I feel as though I've got my shit together again. I put myself into a relaxed state and am enjoying the love swirls my friends and I are creating. Its beautiful tapestry is mesmerising, adding to my Zen-like calm.

Taking the drink Derek's holding out to me, I gulp it, savouring the fresh taste, then smile crookedly into the sudden silence that has fallen on the room like an anvil.

'Lighten up, guys. Let's just get on with it,' I tell them, deciding it's now or never. 'John, if you can hear me, I want you to show me the flowers, please. I'm opening myself up to you now, but only to see the flowers, John. I'm open to that.' As I call to John, it builds up a resonance inside me that increases in vibration like ripples in a pond. *John. Flowers. What did the flowers look like?* I don't speak the words out loud again because that will distract my emotional frequency. Plus, there's no need.

Flowers flit one by one in and out of my mind, in front of my eyes, then moving to the right, out of view. The pad and pen are in my lap, and I'm loosely holding them.

Suddenly, John's thoughts grip me like a vice, and I hunch over the pad, fingers clenched on the pen so tightly that they turn white.

A single flower floods my consciousness. Its round, pretty petals filling my mind and moving my hand to recreate its likeness. No sound or thought disturbs me. *One flower. One flower. One flower. One flower.*

'Mary,' Derek says. 'Baby, that's enough. It's done now; you can stop.'

Jay's voice registers, but it sounds further away than Derek's, 'John. *That's enough.* You ease off her now, boy, or we can't help you. Let Mary go.'

The pointer moves along the board with a sharp scraping noise.

'*GOODBYE*' it spells.

My fingers release, and I slump over the pad like a wet dishrag, vaguely aware that my friends have all jumped up from their seats and are crowding around me.

'OhmyGod, Mary, are you alright?' Marcie crushes me in a hug.

'I'm fine, but loosen up a bit so I can breathe please, Marce?' My mouth is dry, and I feel a bit woozy for a few moments, so I flap my hands weakly near my face.

Eileen, recognising the gesture, instructs everyone to give me space, and Rachel jumps up to get me a drink, which I accept thankfully.

'That was amazing,' Eileen says looking at Jay. 'Do you think you'll be able to triangulate the flowers like this that grow in the areas the suspects live in?'

Jay nods. 'That's what I'm hoping.' He looks over at me as I gulp my drink. Derek and Marcie are fanning me, and Sophie and Eileen are quietly studying the pictures that now occupy the pad. 'Thanks for doing this, Mary. I know it can't have been easy, but this is pure gold.'

'We *can* save Patryk. Can't we, Jay?' I ask. To my own ears, my voice sounds small and childlike. *The pain I felt from poor John lingers inside me like a psychic hangover. It's almost unbearable to think about it. I need to hear Jay say this.*

Jay nods, his face solemn. 'We *will* save Patryk.'

Even in my exhausted state, I can hear the note of doubt in Jay's voice, even though he'd said what he knew I needed to hear. *Please, God, please. Let us find Patryk in time.*

CHAPTER FOUR

'How come you let me sleep so long?' I pout as I pad into the kitchen to switch on the kettle. Derek's hunched over his mobile phone and is scrolling avidly. As I enter, he looks up from the small black screen, eyeing up my T-shirt and knickers with an appreciative smile. He answers me, 'You must've needed it, Mary. You've been burning the candle at both ends lately.'

The word 'candle' reminds me of the séance, and a shiver runs through me, leaving its cold residue in the pit of my stomach. Without acknowledging that Derek's correct, I walk past the morose faces of Monika and poor John to switch the kettle on. They've both been with me, haunting me since the séance, so I'm no longer shocked to see them. *How had I ever been scared of little John? He actually just breaks my heart now.*

'So, I can juggle my appointments round so we can do something today, Mary? I think you could do with some time away from this case. Don't you?' Derek says.

Drawing in a deep breath, I remain silent, one hand raking through my hair. I'm saved from answering by the ring tone that's now so expected I almost imagine I hear it. Derek points to my phone on the table and my lips curl up at the corners as I give him a thumbs up in thanks. *So, that's where I left it!*

After answering the call, Jay's voice sounds in my ear, 'Mary, if I email you a link today, do you know how to take a video conference call? I want to set up a quick one with you, me, and Eileen.'

'Jay, I live with a computer expert. Yes. I can click on a link. What time do you want to meet online?' I say, voice dry. A brief memory flickers behind my eyes of me working through Derek's step-by-step instructions to start a computer. *How things change.*

'I'll send the link now, but will you be able to join the meeting in an hour?' Jay asks.

With a nod into the mouthpiece, I answer, 'Yeah. No worries. See you then.'

Derek's stare is intense, his deep brown eyes burning into my grey ones like hot coal. After a stretched moment of silence, he concentrates on his phone, repositioning it in his hand again and resuming his clicking and scrolling.

With deft movements around the kitchen I make myself a quick breakfast, then leave to get ready for the day. Monika and John trail silently behind me, a grim reminder of my responsibilities.

When my tablet's set up in my bedroom, I click on the link Jay sent, waiting for the meeting to launch. While I wait, I get the photographs of the five suspects out of my handbag and look at them. Eileen's greeting jolts my attention back to the screen, her warmth making my heart swell. Jay's gruff, 'Mary,' makes me smile. 'Hey, guys,' I tell them.

Wasting no time, Jay explains he's been working all night on the existing and new leads and wants to update us both. After a moment to digest the information, we start to discuss what he's learned. Eileen explains that she's got the details from Jay and accessed the National Health Service records. 'As a CPN I have access to the NHS database. I thought I'd look up the suspects and see if there's any interesting physical or mental health records held on there.'

I nod, waiting for her or Jay to expand on their findings.

'So out of the five, two of the suspects have a forensic history,' Eileen says.

'Don't tell me; Simon Redford and Joan Sante,' Jay guesses.

Eileen shakes her head, saying, 'Close, Jay, but no cigar. Joan Sante, yes. But also, Jason Deres.'

I frown, scratching my now recovered head. 'Wasn't Joan that nice one with the snacks wagon? You're saying *she's* got a forensic history, really? What'd she do?'

Jay nods, confirming, 'She committed arson.'

Eileen breaks in, adding context, 'Joan was apparently a bit of a hellion when she was younger and visited a hostel for young people. One night, when she was under the influence, she set light to her bedroom. Luckily, she didn't hurt anyone, and she never had to serve any time. For a few years, she was under a community order, with a requirement for substance misuse treatment. Joan seems to've straightened out nicely. Has a husband and two kids of her own. There's been nothing recorded about her since to suggest otherwise. As far as health systems show anyway – do you have anything, Jay?'

Jay shakes his head, saying, 'No, nothing.' He's holding photos of the suspects, and picks up Joan's picture, studying her again while stroking his chin.

I ask Jay, 'How'd you guess Joan was one of the two? And also, why'd you think the other one was Simon?'

The video link shows Jay, snug in his favourite armchair, leaning back, smug. 'That's easy. It's always the ones you least suspect. In this little suspect party, that would be Joan and Simon. They seem the most innocent.'

'Well, that's sad.' I sniff.

'Yes, but it's still true,' Jay comments.

Stroking my earlobe, I ask, 'So how about Jason then? What's his history?'

I notice Jay's gaze drops, and watch as he takes a deep breath in. 'Breaking and entering, then abducting his ex-girlfriend and holding her hostage for seven hours.'

'What?' Shocked, my eyes turn big as saucers as I stare at the cocky, good-looking plumber in the photo I'm holding. I look at Eileen, saying, 'No way! And what, he's just walking free out here? Just… working in other people's homes, all… free and stuff? That can't be right, can it?' I aim my last question at Jay.

He smashes his lips together, sucking in another deep breath, then says, 'Well, it's what happened. The guy committed the offence within the context of his mental health,' Jay says, and Eileen breaks in to explain.

'The courts were lenient because Jason never *physically* harmed his ex. He was treated, and when he got better, he was a free man. Obviously, *MAPPA* monitored him for some time, but… Jason served his time in a medium secure psychiatric unit and has officially recovered.'

I realise as a community psychiatric nurse Eileen is used to hearing stories like this. *Still, what Jason did sounds like something out of a horror film to me.* I shiver, saying, 'God, that's scary. I hope the ex is OK; how horrific for her. What's 'MAPPA' mean Jay?'

'Oh, it stands for *Multi Agency Public Protection Arrangements,*' *Jay explains.* 'They monitor offenders who have had convictions for violent or sexual crimes. They're supposed to assess and manage risk while monitoring the individual.'

Jay frowns, asking Eileen, 'How often were they seeing him?'

Gaze sliding upwards, Eileen considers his question, before answering. 'Once or twice a year. They had him down as level one. Low-medium risk.'

Jay taps the photograph that's in his hand, then holds it up so I can see the image he's looking at. He asks me, 'Do you get anything from Jason?'

189

'Well, I felt something uncomfortable, but definitely not a serial killer frequency. I think he must be clean now, although now that I know his background, I get the creeps. Aside from all that, I'm getting no otherworldly alarms going off. It makes you wonder just who's sitting next to you on the bus and stuff, though, doesn't it?' I say.

'I never get the bus,' Jay says. The device he's using for the video link is set some way away so I can see as he shuffles the pictures on the table in front of him. Jason's image lies on top of the pile. 'OK, so picking up from there, Jason's kept himself clean since the crime I just told you about. He works as a self-employed plumber and owns his own vehicle. He doesn't have a significant other, but his social media shows him as a bit of a 'jack the lad type.' There're lots of pictures of him, posing with pretty women in bars. Also, his Ford minivan is black.'

'That's too easy,' I say quickly.

'Yeah, I have to agree with the lassie. It seems too clear cut, it's never gonna be him.' At Eileen's words, Jay's mouth droops down at the sides, and he throws Jason's picture back down onto the table. 'Well, I know what we said before, but sometimes it *is* the obvious ones, so I think we shouldn't rule him out. Anyway, Joan doesn't have so much as a parking ticket, and her mobile snack truck is actually more of a charcoal, not pure black. We'll keep Jason first on our radar.'

My heart rate picks up as I feel the momentum start to build. I answer Jay, 'Yeah, for sure. What about the rest? What did you find out?'

Shuffling to the end of his chair, he explains, 'Well, on top of what we already know, Simon is a law student at a prestigious university. He's from old money, but his branch of the family has run through most of their legacy. He keeps his nose clean. Had a couple of girlfriends in the past, and there's no record of any criminal or deviant behaviour.'

One glance at the weak-chinned, narrow-shouldered tie wearer tells me everything I need to know. *That toff is not our child abductor, that's for sure.* I cross my legs on my bed, Buddha style, growing nearer to the diminishing bundle of information. 'Who's next?' I ask.

Jay holds up another photo. Although he left the originals with me and printed copies, he shows the picture to the camera for Eileen's benefit because she doesn't have a copy. 'Next, we have David James, from Plymouth. He's got one ex-wife and two kids that don't live with him. He has a clean driver's license, no prior or current offences.'

Eileen asks Jay, 'Ah, OK, and isn't he the mini-cab driver or something?'

The photograph contains a smirking David, propped against his luxury people carrier.

'Still think David looks like a right smug git,' I say with a sniff of disdain. 'Honestly, where did you get these photos from again?' I enquire.

'Social media is the easiest source, you know how people love to put a million photos up on their accounts,' Jay says. 'We also have access to central database identification, and anything that's public record.'

'Clever thinking,' Eileen says, and I see Jay's cheeks warm.

Jay says gruffly, 'Thanks, Eileen.'

Eileen's offhand compliment seems to have derailed Jay's train of thought for a second or two and I take the opportunity to reflect on their relationship. Jay's nice, and he's been suffering a long time. First, from losing his little boy, and then from the loss of his wife, Fiona. Eileen's a legend. If anyone deserves some happiness, it's him and my dearest Eileen.

'That only leaves Phil Moyce,' Jay says. 'He's the fifty-two-year-old farmer from Taunton. He has two divorces in his past, but no kids. Phil doesn't have social media, and there are no convictions or anything else noteworthy in his past.'

Eileen leans closer to her screen, decreeing, 'Hmm. If my dear old granny were to look at him, she'd say his eyes were too close together and he's not to be trusted.'

'Well, with all due respect to your dear old granny, Eileen, we're going to need a bit more evidence to go on than that.' Jay looks at me. 'Mary, you got anything else for me to explore?'

Even as I stretch my hand out to the photo on my lap, palm flat, I feel the vibration it emanates. My ears hurt, and my fillings ring out in painful sympathy, converging with the frequency. Clapping one hand over my ear, I eyeball the picture of Phil Moyce. Eileen and Jay glance at each other, then stare back at me. 'There's something *off* about him, we'll have to pin him to the top of our suspect list,' I say, as my stomach rolls, making me feel nauseous.

'*And* he drives a black Land Rover. OK, great, now we're getting somewhere.' Jay wipes a hand over his mouth, firing questions at me in quick succession. 'Can you give me something more, Mary? Can you see him and any of the victims? Does he take them to his home? He lives on a farm and it's in quite a remote location, so he has the perfect place to hole up with his victims after he abducts them.'

Eileen intercedes firmly, holding a palm up to the camera, 'Whoa, Jay, will ya slow down for a sec?' Eileen says, voice calm. 'All Mary said was that she feels uneasy about him; that could mean a million different things. Let's give Mary space to do her thing, give her time to feel her way for a bit.'

Jay nods, and after a few seconds, the crease of his frown unfurls leaving his forehead as smooth as butter. *Damn, she's good.* I nibble at my lip as I admire Eileen. *She has such presence.* I notice Eileen's accent seems to get more pronounced when she gets upset. *Other than Eileen becoming more Scottish, I'd never know she's emotional about anything. Nothing seems to faze her. She always knows just what to say.* I bring the photo closer to my face, ignoring the increase in vibration the act brings.

A tight silence is broken when Jay says, 'You're right, Eileen.' telling me, 'Mary, please take your time and study all the photos. Eileen and I will be online here, ready to note down any info that occurs to you whenever you're ready.'

I nod, then after a while I say, 'This guy is the only chap that makes me feel physically sick, and when I look at his picture, all I see are flowers. Not the same flower I saw during the séance, but that doesn't mean much.'

'Not mean much? How d'you mean, Mary?' Eileen asks.

I look upwards as I unpack my thoughts. 'What if the flowers weren't literal flowers? I'm new to all this séance business, so I don't know how I'm supposed to take the information I receive. What if the flower I saw is *John's idea* of what the flower looked like? Our memories play tricks on us, don't they? So, what if John's remembering it differently than how it actually was? Or, maybe what John showed me was an interpretation of his memory, and the flowers symbolise the killer is a farmer? Or something like that.' I put my finger on the picture of the suspect as I consider. 'Nah, I definitely think this guy, Phil, is well dodgy. My stomach turns over every time I look at him. It's gotta be him.'

The noise of Jay slapping his thigh makes me jump, and I see him smile for a brief second, before muttering with a scowl, 'That's great, but now, how do I get him?'

My brows fly upwards at his mumbled question. 'Do I look like a police officer? That's your department, mate. Can't you go in there to get evidence, or do a stakeout, then grab him or something?'

Jay says, 'It doesn't work like that, Mary. We'd need probable cause to justify any surveillance, and to enter his property we'd need a search warrant granted by the courts. We have the CCTV footage placing his vehicle at the time and place of the likely scene of the abduction, but I think we need more.'

After a moment, I have a thought. 'So this might be a stupid idea, but what if we have our own unofficial mini stakeout first?

Kind of like a preliminary surveillance, to get some clue about his habits and stuff?'

Jay rubs his chin. 'That might work. Of course, we can't be seen, but I could at least say I had probable cause to check in with him. And while we did that, if we saw something that made us suspicious, then it might be enough.'

'But are you sure that would be legal, Jay? Eileen asks. 'Isn't it against Human Rights? The right to private and family life, or something?'

Jay frowns at Eileen and his mouth turns down again, like a pantomime artist. 'Who cares about the killers' rights? Weren't those kids entitled to the right to live?'

Quick as a flash, Eileen fires back, 'But you don't even know this guy *is* the killer yet.'

Jay shakes his head, 'Mary said-'

'All Mary said was Phil Moyce gives her a bad feeling. There're a million reasons that could be, without one of them being he's a serial killer. You should know that, Jay.'

At Eileen's words, a deep silence fills the room and I swallow, staring down at my fingernails. I feel like a child caught up in the middle of their parents' argument. I consider Eileen's statement. What she said is true. I do*n't know* Phil is who we're looking for. 'Eileen's right,' I say. 'Phil *is* making me feel like shit, and none of the other suspects are giving me that same vibe, but I'm not certain he's the killer. All I can tell you is that I feel a sense he's doing dreadful things, things that make his vibrations feel… wrong.'

Eileen puts her hands up to the camera. 'Just to be clear to you both, I'm not saying it *isn't* Phil Moyce. I just want us to acknowledge that we all feel personal about this case, and we need to go about this professionally. We have to be clever about this. If we don't, we could risk having inadmissible evidence in court, or end up being prosecuted ourselves. Couldn't we, Jay?'

'You know the answer to those questions already.' Jay closes his eyes briefly with a deep sigh, then opens them again. 'As usual, you're right. Yes, and then the killer could get off. But give me some credit, will you Eileen? I've been doing this job for how many years now? I think I know something about how to poke around without ruffling feathers.'

Eileen's taut features soften, and I notice their heads tilt the same way, mirroring each other's body language. My head swings from one to the other during their interaction, but I make no comment. *Ah, they're so cute.*

'So, without a court order I have enough justification with the CCTV footage to introduce myself, and to ask a question or two,' Jay says. 'I'll need to do that for all the suspects anyway, but we can prioritise Phil. We'll watch him for a little while beforehand, nothing official. I'm hoping Mary will get more of a feel for him when we're there in person.'

As Jay lays out his plan, Eileen nods, they're both still focused on the case and finding Patryk, but underneath that I'm aware of the smoky tendrils of red that stretch out, twirling between them. *Passion.*

'So, what's Taunton like?' I ask. 'And when are we going there?'

CHAPTER FIVE

A s we walk along the pathway in the local park, I stretch out a hand to touch the leaves, taking joy from the sound of the rustling trees, sighing on the gentle breeze. Derek clicks his fingers, obviously remembering something. 'Oh yes,' He says, 'I saw a *really* nice property online yesterday. It's in Hampshire, and not too far out from London. Just what we're looking for.'

'Really? Is it a two-bed, or a three-bed house? How close is it to the sea?'

'It's a three-bed house, semi-detached, and a short walk to the beach, it said.'

I clap my hands and turn to Derek with a grin. 'Send it to me and I'll have a look. Is it near a park as well? I've always loved a park.'

'Not me.'

'D, what? You don't love the park? But we come here so often… you've never said?' I stop for a second, so I can look at Derek properly and he shrugs, unconcerned.

He drops a light kiss on the top of my head, then says, 'It's not a big deal. It isn't like I hate the park. I just don't love it, or being out in nature, like you do. I'm more of a stay inside my house tech geek. Besides, it doesn't matter where I am, as long as I'm with you.' He takes my hand again and we resume our stroll.

Derek's statement has put a massive lump in my throat, and I don't speak for a while, instead, listening to the pretty birdsong trilling out around us.

A sudden wind teases at my clothes, and I realise the fragility of them. I grip Derek closer, clutching at the waist of his hoodie, to siphon his warmth.

He rubs my arms, but it doesn't ease the goosebumps down. 'Cold?' He asks.

'Yeah. Suddenly, it's really chilly.'

'Let's get moving again. We'll soon warm up.' He suggests.

Striding briskly along now, I slip one of my icy hands into Derek's pocket for heat. The chirping of a nearby bird captures my attention and I exclaim, pointing at where it sits in a tree, 'Ah, look at that, it's a robin redbreast, D. They're so cute. Did you know some people think robins carry the souls of loved ones?'

'No, I've never heard that. That's just weird. Aren't they a bit too tiny for that?'

I roll my eyes. 'Idiot. The soul doesn't have concrete substance like that, smart arse. It's not big or small, it's like air. Air is everywhere, but is it big or small?'

Derek scratches his head. 'I don't know. I've never thought about it, to be honest. But… do they?'

I frown, confused, 'Do they what?' I ask.

'Do they carry the souls of loved one's coming to visit?' Derek asks.

The robin and I make eye contact as we draw closer. Instead of walking past, I slow my steps, peering at it. My breathing slows, and my eyelids droop. *Something's on the tip of my tongue, but I don't know what.*

'Mary?' Derek prompts me.

My eyelids flutter open, focusing on him and his question, 'Huh? Maybe? Sometimes… sometimes I think they do.' Tears brim up, and I dash them away, confused. With a shrug, I slide my hand into Derek's again. *Maybe I'm just tired or something?*

'So, finish telling me about your plans to go to Taunton,' Derek says.

'We're doing our own mini stakeout, then we'll question the suspect, just like in the movies! Hopefully not like one where the sassy female lead gets slaughtered by the serial killer.'

'Please don't joke, Mary.' Derek's tone is serious, and as I recognise the worry in it, guilt prickles me. 'Sorry love. Poor joke. We'll be fine. It'll be just like we're spies or something.'

He runs his spare hand through his hair, then asks, 'Spies? Why?'

I make a conscious effort to keep my tone light, not wanting to add to Derek's worry, 'Well, because we'll go to see the suspect, and watch him in his house before we speak to him.'

Derek's frown is unimpressed with my attempts to ease his concerns and his tone doesn't match mine. 'Why're you surveilling him in person? Do you have legal permission for that? Can't you just do it remotely?'

'Well, from what Jay said, I think he's being careful not to break any laws. We both will be. Wait, you can do that-surveil people remotely?'

'Someone like me could.' Derek grins. 'Without being caught, too. I'm not too sure Jay could, though.'

A quick flash of Jay, using his phone's messaging system with deliberate intention comes into my mind and I nod, snorting. 'You're not wrong. He knows how to use his system, but he only knows the basics. More than me, but definitely less than you. *Everyone* knows less than you.'

'Sweet talker. So, I know you can't do it yet, but when you get the legal OK for surveillance, tell Jay I'm happy to give advice if needed. Although I'm sure the police team has everything they need.'

With a sigh I adjust my pace to Derek's, allowing for his longer strides by picking up my tempo and trotting along, 'You're so cool,' I say.

Derek's profile smirks as he agrees with me, 'Yes, I am.'

'We can ring Jay up and tell him the good news when we get home. We'll be the ultimate crime fighting duo; Mary and D in the house. Taking names and kicking arse, PI besties forever.'

'Besties with benefits.' As Derek wiggles his eyebrows with a grin, we chuckle, hustling down the path home that suddenly seems darker.

'What're you like, D?' I smile, shaking my head ruefully at his one-track mind, wishing I could shake away the sense of foreboding that shadows me persistently.

CHAPTER SIX

J ay and I are silent as we trudge up the long, steep road surrounded by endless green fields, and I mumble under my breath, 'Why's everywhere up a fucking hill here in Devon? How's this even possible? It's like we're stuck in that eighties film. You know the one where the guy walks down the stairs and he's going up the staircase, then he goes down'em and move up'em. Where even are we now, are we close to Phil Moyce's farm?'

Jay shakes his head. 'D'you mean Legend?' Jay answers, then consults the map app on his phone. 'Our location is just North-East of the Devon border and yes, we're nearly there now.'

'What does that mean?' I huff and puff as we keep marching, murmuring to myself, 'I'll have calves like a rugby player by the time we're done.'

'I doubt that, Mary. I told you our location because Devon's hilly.'

'Devon's hilly. Fucking Taunton's not too flat either is it, Jay?' Coming to a stop at the top of the hill, I hunch over, pinching the stitch in my side with one palm. When the pain eases, I use the same hand to put my weight on Jay's shoulder while I catch my breath. *How is Jay coping with this trek so much better than me? I thought I was fairly fit.*

With a deep sigh, Jay says, 'You know, Mary... you swear too much.'

My middle finger raises slowly, out of frame at first, as I do not look at it. It lifts, as though independent of me, but then Jay catches sight of it with his peripheral vision. He laughs out loud.

'You're hell, I swear. What would Eileen say if she were here?'

'She'd say, 'You tell him, wee lassie.''

'But, why would she say it with a French accent? I'm confused.'

For a second, I frown, the joke going over my head, like the clouds passing over the moon. Then, as I realise Jay is teasing me, I give a shout out of laughter. 'Shut up, Jay! My Scottish accent is mint.'

'Yeah, right. Anyway, let's get back to it now. Look over there at those houses. They're people's farms, with their land ringing them. See that massive one on the left there? That's Phil Moyce's farm. Shall we go down there, say hello?'

As the birds chirp, I look around and check out the farmland. A few pretty farmhouses, and Phil's is all the way to the right. It's the largest, ringed by what looks like a spacious driveway and yard, in the centre of fields.

'Sure, let's see what we can see.'

'That's the stuff, Mary. Come on.'

We head towards the farm, the silence between us comforting. Once we near the boundaries of Phil's property, I grit my teeth. As we reach the edge of the fields, I shut my eyes. I can feel them rolling backwards in my head as I try to breathe myself open to Phil's aura. I turn to Jay.

'We're not close enough yet. I don't sense anything.'

'We'll head in closer,' Jay reassures me. 'Let's do a recce around the perimeter first. The grass here is pretty tall. Once we've finished our walk, we can knock and introduce ourselves. If we pose a few questions out in the open, you'll have the chance to do your stuff.'

'What's a recce?' I ask, frowning. 'Sounds like some kind of dance.'

Jay smiles. 'Sorry, sometimes I forget you're new to all this. It's short for reconnaissance. It's the term we all use when we're scoping out an area. You know, you're quite a good detective. Ever think about being on the force?'

'No thanks, Jay. Remember, I don't play well with others. Plus, we both know how I feel about being told what to do.'

'Well, think about it. If you ever change your mind, let me know and I'll pull some strings.'

With brows raised and a close-lipped smile pinned to my face, I reach out to pat Jay on the back. 'Yeah, cheers for that. I appreciate it. I'm good though.'

Jay's snort of laughter stops any awkwardness that might have fallen over me, and I grin in response. *Thanks, but no thanks.*

'Whatever, ingrate. C'mon, Mary, let's get going again, shall we?'

'Yeah, let's go, Joe.' Saying the name 'Joe' caused an unexpected sliver of loss to jolt through my heart. It's been three years, but I still miss my non-physical family. Jo, a kind man with a fatherly air, had been a proud Ghanian, and a doctor. He'd also been Eileen's husband when he was alive, so my connection to him remained. Sometimes, though, I longed for him to be beside me. All of us together, like it used to be, but happy. Him, Little Mary, Lou, and Dolores. My dearly departed family. But they'd all moved on. They went home to experience further joy, being reabsorbed into The Blue. I swipe my damp eyes with the cuff of my fleece.

Without missing a beat, Jay asks, 'What's up?'

'Huh? Nothing?'

Jay doesn't let it go, scrutinising me with quiet professionalism. 'Then why did you just wipe your eyes? Were you crying Mary?'

Jeez. Does nothing get past you, Jay? 'No, I wasn't, Jay. I just got something in my eye, alright? I'm fine, let's go.'

'OK, let me know if anything's up though, yes?'

'I will. Now please shut up about it and let me concentrate.' I glimpse something out of the corner of my eye. 'Hang on, what's that over there? Is it moving?'

We both stop, standing still in the field, and I breathe in the smell of fresh air and the sounds of nature all around us. Momentarily, I'm transported back to that first time I stepped out into the garden, back at The Rainbow Unit. Before all the misery and terror.

'We're still a few minutes' walk from the farms building itself,' Jay says.

I notice a moving black dot in the distance and point it out to Jay. 'Look. There. What *is* that?'

'Get behind me, Mary. Right now.'

Eyes squinting, I cock my head as I peer out to where Jay's staring. 'Why?' I ask, 'What do you think it is? I can't tell from here, but it does look like it's coming closer.'

When he realises I haven't changed position, Jay moves in front of me. He casts around the long grass, straightening with a sturdy-looking stick in his hand. My brows lift.

I screw my face up, confused as I ask him, 'What're you gonna do with that?'

'Look down there again, Mary. Do you see what it is now?'

We both redirect our attention to the black dot, this time tracking the direction of Jay's arm, not mine.

My mouth drops open, and I mutter, 'That is one big mama jamma of a dog, Jay.'

A stocky Rottweiler plods towards us through the grass, and I shift my feet.

Interpreting my instinctive reaction, Jay says, 'Don't run, Mary. That'd be the worst thing you could do.'

Brows lifted I say, 'You sure about that?'

'Yes. Trust me. Stay still and do *not* make eye contact with it.' Jay's voice is low and gritty as he answers belying his apprehension.

I don't blame him, it's taking an iron willpower not to respond to the air of menace our steadily approaching visitor exudes. I desperately want to sprint away. I hiss out the corner of my mouth, 'What about shitting my pants, Jay? Can I do that?'

'Shh.'

The dog is here, and instinctively, I admire its coat and form. It's a beautiful specimen, the powerful muscles defined as it stands, examining us both with a confident reserve. My nerves jangle as I sense it is deciding. Hmmm… shall I tear the nice man and woman limb from limb, or *not?* Rooted to the spot, both Jay and I hold our breath, waiting to see what the dog will decide. It looks back at the farm, then at me, and its lip curls up for an instant. *Shit.* I rock up onto the balls of my feet, ready to run for my life.

Out of nowhere a familiar voice says, 'Here, boy. Come see me. Come to Errol, that's it. *There's* a good boy.'

The dog's ears twitch, then he switches his focus to where Errol stands a few feet to the left of me. My ghostly friend is capturing the attention of the canine guard effortlessly. Errol's voice is upbeat and full of his trademark laconic warmth. The dog, suddenly playful, bounds over to him, tongue lolling out the side of his mouth. Within seconds, he is wagging his tail and dropping to expose his belly for a spectral tummy rub.

Jay's mouth drops open, and I realise he has no clue that Errol's here and is helping to neutralise the dog. Not wanting to disturb the bonding session that's occurring and perhaps upset our canine visitor, I whisper to Jay, 'It's ok. Errol's here, the dog loves him.'

Jay and I regard each other, eyebrows high on our foreheads, then stare at the dog.

Switching my gaze back to Errol and his hound-dog friend, I grin, taking in the situation's surrealness. Even though he knows Errol's materialised, to Jay, it must look like the huge and previously petrifying dog is playing with thin air, having just averted his energies to nothing on a whim. As it occurs to me that those energies might change back on a different whim a shiver runs down my sweaty spine, and Errol beckons to me, 'Come over here Mary, let me introduce you to my friend. He's a really lovely boy underneath, and he's got a really mean daddy. Don't you, boy?'

'Errol's telling me to go over and say hello,' I tell Jay, then I move towards Errol, and realise Jay's hand grips me.

'Mary, don't,' he says through clenched teeth. Sweat beads out from his hairline, dripping down his face.

'Chill out, Jay, it's fine. My friend Errol is here. He says I should go over there.'

Jay and I make eye contact, and I can see the tension in his body and features. I imagine he's torn between the reality he sees and what I'm telling him is occurring. 'Are you sure, Mary? Really?' he says.

'Yeah, really, so let go of my arm, uncle weirdo. *I'll* tell *you* when it's safe to move.'

A wry expression appears on Jay's face, then his shoulders relax as he nods. He releases his fingers, letting go of me. *He trusts what I'm telling him.*

With a bended knee and a slow hand outstretched for sniffing, I allow Errol to introduce me to our new friend. Jay's shoulders have relaxed somewhat now, and he's just observing me with an alert, watchful air. Warmth spreads through me as I open myself to the frequencies immediately surrounding us. Feeling the dog's surprised joy touches me and prompts me to overcome the last of my fears and scratch his belly. He rolls around in ecstasy immediately, making me laugh out loud. 'That's it, doggo. You're a good boy, aren't you? Sweet boy. D'you know his name, Errol?'

'No, but I can sense he's not loved by his owners. Not mistreated physically, but not loved. Luckily, like most animals, he's hypersensitive to us, departed, and responds well to us. Good thing, aye, Mary?'

My hearts throbs for the dog, and feeling simpatico for him, I stroke his velvety ears. *Sounds exactly like my childhood. Lonely. Well, my childhood after the age of eight when I lost my lovely mum, anyway.* 'I'm going to call you Toto. Shall we go down with Toto, Errol? Or will that get him punished, do you think?'

'What's happening, Mary? Is the dog safe now?' Jay asks.

205

'Is it safe for Jay to move now?' I check with Errol.

He answers, his voice easy. 'Yes, tell Jay to come over here and make friends. We won't go together though. His owner's obviously making a statement with one of these types of dogs roaming around his land. With that in mind, I think Toto's owner would punish him for not ripping you both to pieces. I'll go back with him first, then you and Jay can make your way there afterwards. When you get to the farm, I'll call him and divert his attention elsewhere again, so he doesn't greet you and get beaten.'

'Oh my God, beaten? What a monster.' Outrage swells in my chest on behalf of Toto. Errol encourages him to go home, and he seems to understand that we're sending him on his way. He's hesitant, making eye contact with me and whining slightly. His reluctance to leave us fills my eyes with tears and makes my bottom lip tremble slightly. Despite this, Toto goes with Errol.

As we walk closer to the farm, I spot a group of wire fenced large cages with dirt runs inside and realise it must be a set of outdoor kennels at the corner of the farm. My stomach churns Toto probably lives there. *He isn't even living inside the house, for God's sake. Disgusting*. We walk nearer, scoping it out as we go.

'There are lots of cars on site,' Jay says.

I nod, and keeping my voice low, say, 'Yeah, I thought that as well. What do you think it means?'

Jay also keeps his voice quiet, 'Don't know. I mean, often criminals have lots of people, customers, groupies, and security types hanging around. The profile for a serial killer is different; they're typically loners. It's not usual for them to hang around in packs.'

I scan my surroundings as we walk, thinking how weird it is I can revert to my old, *hyper-vigilant Mary* persona so readily. Scanning for threats, noting entrances and exits, identifying any objects I could use as a weapon if I need to. My right hand moves to twirl my engagement ring, then I put a hand to my neck, touching the necklace my mum gave me. I take a deep breath. Sensing... There's a sourness here. It's rotten. 'There's a lot of corruption here. A kind of lingering sourness surrounds the main building. We need to be very careful,' I tell Jay. My stomach churns and my eyelids flutter. My peripheral vision registers a smaller building. A shed. I stop walking, holding out my arm to stop Jay from moving past me.

Turning sharply at my gesture, he says, 'What is it, Mary? Can you feel or see something else?'

I point to the shed that stands to the front, right of us, telling Jay, 'Let's go have a look in there, Jay. It's… wrong.'

'OK, but let's go slowly Mary. We've already met one pedigree friend. Who knows how many more there might be onsite?'

After a nod of agreement, I rub my temples. My head feels like it's stuffed with cotton wool again, with sharp slicing pains striking at me. I still scan the yard as we move towards the dark entrance of the large shed. It looks old and disused, but I know it's not. There are random sentences from people in the shed drifting out to us as we stand just outside the door. Jay and I lock eyes as we listen, alarmed by what we're hearing.

'If we hurry and mix this shit up quicker, maybe Phil will let us have a couple of pills thrown in for free.'

'No fucking chance, mate.' My head turns left, following the voice of the other speaker, 'Phil cuts it up with dog de-wormer to make it stretch a bit more, he's not just gonna lob some over to you for nothing. You know what he's like.'

Another man muses, 'It still makes good Molly anyway, so who gives a shit?' Then, with a seamlessness that surprises me, my mind switches into receptive mode, colliding with this man's thought blocks. He thinks, 'Maybe if I take a bit more of this, I won't mind so much what they do to me on camera tonight? *Maybe*….'

A pressure shifts, clearing my muggy head as I understand the snatches of conversation I'm bumping into psychically, mixed with what the men and women in the shed are saying out loud. At once, it all clicks into place, horrifying me.

Jay, although he wasn't privy to the depravity hinted at in the last speaker's thoughts and feelings of repulsion and shame, he's heard enough to know that we're in a bad situation. He leans towards me hissing urgently, 'Mary, we're in a really bad spot here. I'm sorry. I should've dug a bit deeper before bringing you out here. By the sounds of it, Phil's a drug dealer and judging by the looks of it, quite a prosperous one. We're on a drug farm.'

Agreeing with a nod, I swallow, saying, 'I know. But that's not all, Jay.' Casting a glance at Jay, I explain what the thoughts of the last man have shown me, saying, 'Phil Moyce isn't a serial killer, Jay. You're right, he's a drug dealer. A ruthless one at that. He also runs some girls and an amateur film producer. He's a vile piece of humanity. He uses the drugs to trap people, then either blackmails or exploits them when they're hooked.'

Quick on the uptake, Jay nods upwards discreetly. 'There's CCTV. Up high, near the spotlights on the roof. Phil will know soon that we're here. If he doesn't know already. People like him don't play around with nosy trespassers. Anyone who sticks their noses into places like this usually just vanishes.'

A picture of a freshly dug dirt grave out in the woods flashes into my mind, and I know it's what Jay's scared of. A very real possibility. Feeling my heart race, I wipe damp palms down my thighs. 'Shit. Do we have time to run?'

We look at each other as Jay answers, 'No. Phil will definitely have security, and he's gonna be pissed and wondering who we are.'

Jay turns sideways slightly, allowing himself a view behind us.

'What can we do? I still think we should run now. I'm pretty sure he's not the one who took Patryk.'

Jay shakes his head, replying, 'No, definitely don't run. The door to the main house behind you just opened. We probably have a couple of minutes at most before we have some very hostile company. I need to send an SOS text to a friend for some off-the-books back up in case they try to disappear us. *Now.*' With a steady hand, Jay sends his message out to the ether, and I curse the psychic awareness that tells me we're both praying Phil Moyce does not employ expensive signal jamming equipment. *Shit.*

The sound of aggressive shouting accompanied by many feet, swiftly running behind us, causes us to pivot round sharply. From the house, there are a group of men, squat and powerful looking, with several growling rottweiler dogs in tow. As they come closer, teeth bared, I notice Toto's not with the pack, and that the men's faces are peppered with broken noses and scars. Amongst them, Phil's ruddy cheeks and rough-hewn face are recognisable from the photos we've both seen. Feeling suffocated by the air of menace they exude, I jam trembling lips shut and suck oxygen in and out through flared nostrils. Phil and his group bristle round us, cutting off any means of escape. *Please God, let Jay have gotten his text out to someone before these gangsters got here.* The low, guttural growls of the dogs at the heels of the humans with them, prompts beads of sweat on my upper lip.

Amidst the warning snarls of the canine security guards, Phil shouts at us, 'Who the fuck're you, and what do you think you're doing on my land?'

Seeming undaunted, Jay calls out, 'Mr. Moyce, we're hoping you can help us. I'm a police officer,' pulling out his identification as his men encircle us.

Shit, we're surrounded, what're we gonna do? Knees shaking and heart racing, I correct my stance so my head is lowered, and my arms can block a blow if it comes. Fists clenched by my sides, I say nothing, and try to block out the collective air of menace as I study Phil's face from underneath my lashes. The photograph had showed an outdoorsy looking man with nondescript features. It had not depicted him accurately. Phil looks as though he were carved out of a slab of granite. Above his broken nose his blue eyes glare at Jay and me with a calculating gaze that reminds me of a raptor. It makes my skin crawl and my eye twitch.

Despite my fearful thoughts my chin rises, and my nostrils continue to flare as I pick up the threat Phil presents. This guy expels a grimy trail of aura slime that triggers bile that burns its way up my throat. After overhearing the thoughts and memories of the guys in the shed, I know that if we don't leave here quickly, depraved and vicious ideas are going to start occurring to Phil. And I also know from those thought blocks, that once an idea occurs to Phil, he sees it through. Automatically, I shift my feet, moving backwards, away from his filth. *It's intolerable.*

Phil's voice sounds as dead as the look in his eyes, and he says with nonchalance, 'Police? Great, but I didn't see you flash a warrant with that ID, bud. So I'll ask you one more time. What *the fuck* are you doing on my land?' The blandness of Phil's tone somehow makes it even more intimidating, and although he addresses Jay, Phil stares into my face, and the lascivious glint in them brings a sour taste to the back of my mouth. Uncaring, Phil's gaze sweeps my chest with a slow insolence, before dropping it to my crotch, and back up to my face again.

What a sicko. A dull flush of rage colours my cheeks, pushing back the panic that's starting to rise inside me. Phil is dirty, dangerous, and my instinct is warning me to get away from him. Fast. My hand lifts to my eye to slow the twitch plaguing me. All at once, I feel another presence, and glance surreptitiously to register a familiar face. Relief fills me, and I blow out a sigh of pent-up anxiety and tension. *Errol's here.*

'This guy is one disgusting dirt bag, isn't he, Mary?' Errol says. 'I've just had to make Toto stay in his kennel. I think he wants to protect us. He's really soppy.'

It's taken me a long time to be able to do it, but I'm thankful I'm able to avoid responding to my spirit friend. I know my face doesn't respond to any spiritual chatter and shows no sign of any internal conversation. Phil and Jay will be unaware of Errol's presence, as long as I don't speak out loud to him. Hope blooms in my heart, like the flowers we're here in search of.

'No warrant, Mr. Moyce,' Jay responds respectfully. 'We haven't come to search your property, sir. We're in the area, asking you and your neighbours a few questions about a child kidnapping. You may have witnessed something helpful without realising it. Do you have time to assist us, please?'

Phil's bald head lolls back, and I see his eyes flicker to me before returning to Jay. I swallow dryly, pushing out the pictures that I have inadvertently tuned in to. *He wants to do bad things to me. Terrible things.* My hand goes first to the necklace, and then to twist my engagement ring. *Dirty bastard.*

'Easy, Mary.' Errol stills me, sensing my rising ire as quickly as my pulse rate increases. My chest struggles to contain the pounding of my heart and, stepping back further, I relax back out of this dirtbag's frequency. The conflicting emotions inside me are making this damned eye twitch go ballistic.

Phil raises his eyebrows. 'A kid got taken? Nothin' to do with me. I don't know nothin' about that.'

Replying as though Phil's asked for more information, Jay says, 'Well, if I can just give you a few details about the crime. A young child was abducted from South London and we're following up some information that brought us to this area,' Jay says.

Not acknowledging Jay's statement, Phil stares at him straight faced with shoulders squared. 'What - to my farm?'

The air thrums with menace, and the feeling of danger increases, catching fire like a match striking dry tinder. My fists clench at my sides, and I rock lightly on the balls of my feet, ready to sprint away.

Phil steps forward, chin jutting upwards, but Jay maintains some distance between them by moving backwards with fluidity. Speaking in a composed tone, Jay tells Phil, 'Please, Mr. Moyce, allow me to apologise for intruding and reassure you again that we're here visiting everyone in this area.'

'Yeah? So what were you doing down this end then, sneaking around my shed? Why not just knock on the front door?' Phil is loud and belligerent, and the gravel we're standing on crunches as his goons shuffle closer en masse. The dogs' growls start to include the odd snap into the air, as the pitch of Phil's ire cranks up a notch. Both men and dogs remind me of a pack of hyenas, just waiting for the chance to pick at the remains of a carcass.

Unexpectedly, Jay releases a small chuckle. Jaw dropped, my head swerves in his direction and I blink at my companion. His laugh sounds genuine and sheepish. In a voice that sounds steady, but somewhat embarrassed, Jay says, 'That's purely to do with my stupidity, I'm afraid. We're from London you see, so we're used to little flats and small buildings. I don't think I've ever actually been on a huge farm like this before. In my naivety I thought that building was the main one until my colleague pointed out the main house.'

Eyes rounded by surprise, I watch as Jay's gaze meets Phils, lifting his palms up and shrugging. Somehow he manages to convey a sincerity that almost makes me believe him myself, even though I know the truth.

The blow-up I'm dreading doesn't come, as Jay's explanation miraculously soothes away Phil's well-developed sense of threat with his well-oiled professionalism. My mouth rounds in awe as I witness Jay's self-deprecating language and a calm tone of voice to control the situation.

Phil's shoulders relax and his frown melts away. He rolls his eyes, and a smirk appears on his face. 'Down,' he orders the dogs.

He's swallowed it! What kind of mind-trick is this? I see Errol's lips twitch. *God damn it, Errol, what've I told you about tuning into my thought blocks?* Out the corner of my eye I catch Errol's head dipping, and I know he's grinning.

CHAPTER SEVEN

J ay, quick to press the advantage of Phil's less threatening body language, says, 'So would you mind if we ask you some questions then, Mr. Moyce?'

'Told you. Haven't seen nothing,' Phil answers, and his brooding air intensifies.

Eyes narrowing, I take another step back, trying not to make my apprehension obvious. I've been around enough wolves in the past to respond with instinctual wariness and I know that fear draws people like Phil like blood on water. On red alert for trouble, I run through a mental checklist for danger, scanning the area covertly as I do so. *Maybe find a stick to ward off the dogs. Don't get within Phil's arm's reach. Be prepared to fight or run. See what I can use around me for defence. My engagement ring is precious, so I don't want to damage it by hitting anyone. I think I have a pen in my pocket. A quick jab to the eye or to his ear if I get cornered would do the trick, give me the chance to get away.* As I give my pocket a gentle tap, the slight action draws Phil's attention to me again, his gaze zooming in on me. I feel a small growl of response deep in my throat. *Back off, you perve.*

'Can I show you a photo first please, sir, of the little boy?' Jay asks. 'You may have seen him without realising, and it might jog your memory. My colleague, Mary, has the picture.' He turns to me. 'Do you mind showing Mr. Moyce the photo?'

Actually, Jay, I do mind. I'd forgotten this was the plan, and now I don't want to get within five feet of this man, let alone pass him a picture. Phil's aural signature makes me want to puke my guts up. But this was the plan. I recognise that although remaining distant from Phil keeps me safer, we've come all the way here so I can get within touching distance of Phil Moyce. So then I can get a sense of him and what's in his mind, and check if he's the one that took Patryk. *Only I don't really want to see what he's about, and I already know why.* Tight lipped, I force my feet to move nearer to Phil, they shift with slow obedience. At the same time, I reach into my bag and find the picture of Patryk. As I get closer, the taint of corruption oozes from him, and it takes me massive effort to override my reluctance for this man to touch even a photograph of Patryk. Phil's arrogant smirk makes me want to smack him in his face, but I swallow my urge to resort to violence when feeling threatened.

Phil shakes his head without taking a serious look at the photo. 'Nope, never seen him.' He says.

You're not even facing the picture you cock knocker. Wipe that shit-eating grin off your face and look, arsehole.

'Er… can you take another look please, sir?' Jay asks. 'Maybe if my colleague explains when and where this young man was last seen, it might help to refresh Mr. Moyce's' memory.'

Phil's jaw drops at the audacity of Jay, and after a second's frozen silence, Phil smirks and gives a nod for the benefit of his entourage. 'Go ahead, babes.'

The over-friendly endearment makes my stomach roll and swallowing a dry heave, I say, 'Of course,' keeping my tone bland. My mind's filled with the thoughts of others. *The longer we stay here, the more likely we won't be allowed to leave.* Forcing my heartbeat to slow down, I begin, explaining when and where Patryk was last seen, ending with another description of him in the photograph I'm showing him as I speak. 'Patryk's ten years old and was dressed in his school uniform when he disappeared. You can see what he looks like in the picture. It's a really good likeness we've been told. Please could you take another look, Mr. Moyce?' Feeling my way into the receptive mode, it's a conscious effort for my eyes to remain open as I speak, but I manage somehow. After centring myself, I cast my awareness outside of myself deliberately, seeking information. *We need to know this, it's why we've come all this way.* Phil's psychic presence feels like I'm wading through treacle with weighted boots or sifting through a sewer on my hands and knees. It's both painstaking and disgusting. As I keep my focus on his colours, his thought blocks assail me. Unsurprised, I note they're filled with violence, depravity, and greed. I see Phil's pride and satisfaction in his steadily building criminal empire. There are names of drugs, names of contacts, networks… it all crowds into my mind and I push past them, until pictures of plant leaves snag my attention. Then I know for sure he is *not* the one we're searching for. These are different plants, and definitely not the flower John scored into my mind during the séance. These relate to Phil's production of narcotics.

My heart sinks. For Patryk. For John. *Phil's dirty, a real nasty piece of work. But he's not an abductor or murderer of small children. So we're back to square one.* I give a slight shake of my head, and although it is tiny, without checking, I know Jay will've caught the gesture and will correctly interpret it. *Phil Moyce is not the one we're looking for. He didn't take Patryk. I know it.* A car trundles up in the distance, and we all turn to see who the new arrival is.

'Who the fuck's that?' Phil says angrily, not mincing his words as a vehicle pulls up in the yard. Phil's men encircle him at once, puffed up and raring. As the car door opens, Phil and his companions all reach behind their backs and with a gasp of dismay, I guess they're retrieving weapons. Snaps and snarls resume and the hench dogs stand to attention, ready to attack.

Jay's voice is honey once more, quickly telling them, 'Apologies again, Mr. Moyce. That's my colleague come to give us a lift. I should've said. We had to abandon our vehicle a little way away. We got a flat. Turns out our car wasn't used to the countryside either.'

His statement does nothing to disperse the tension. Backs rigid, Phil and his men remain stiff, hands behind their backs. They don't reply, busy tracking the movement of the car and its driver in silence. As we all watch, an attractive man in his fifties gets out of the vehicle. He approaches us with an upright march that makes the gravel snap and crunch as he walks towards us. There is no doubting he's a man of uniform, even if he's not wearing it right now.

Saying nothing, Phil's eyes squint and his jaw juts out again. His eyes darken, the iris filling his eyes. I'm reminded of a shark.

The newcomer calls out jovially as he walks towards us, 'Hi, Detective, I got your message about your flat tyre. I came to give you a lift. Sorry. Don't have much time as the team are waiting on me. Is this a good time?'

Jay nods, turning to Phil. 'Certainly is. Mr. Moyce, this is Mr. Clive Saxon, the best Inspector in England. Inspector, this is Mr. Moyce. We'll be able to get out of your hair now.'

Cool as a cucumber, Clive Saxon stops in front of Phil, a confident air about him as replies to Jay's introduction. 'Cheque's in the post. Good to meet you, Mr. Moyce. OK to go now then, Detective, yes? Busy schedule today.'

'You want to leave?' Phil asks Jay. His question is quiet, but the ripples of it cast waves of ominous dread out to his uninvited guests.

Jay had anticipated this as soon as he'd known about the drug production. However, he maintains an air of casualness, an easy smile on his face. After a second of silence, Jay says, 'Yes, we'll be going now, Mr Moyce, but I'll leave you my card. Please do contact me if you remember anything. Thanks for your time.' Without waiting, Jay places one hand between my shoulder blades, gently propelling me towards Clive's car. He follows, leaving Clive to bring up the rear.

Before I go, I see Phil's piggy eyes slide to the large work shed. Sending out an echo wave of psychic enquiry, I'm comforted to know that he's weighing up his options. If Clive wasn't here, he'd have much better odds of 'disappearing' us, his unwanted guests, but with another visitor here from the long arm of the law, Phil's chances of that were considerably less. Without argument, he smiles and nods goodbye. Despite his outward civility, Phil doesn't extend his hand, and none of us offer him ours. Adding my goodbye to Jay and Clive's, we beat a hasty retreat to the unmarked car. *Fuck you very much, Mr. Moyce, and goodnight.*

With a shaking hand, I wipe beads of sweat from my upper lip and forehead. *Phew, that was close.*

As soon as we get into Clive's car, Jay says, 'Mary, this is Clive. Clive, this is Mary.' After this brief introduction, we fall silent for the few minutes it takes to get from Clive's car to ours. As we pull away from the drug-farm, I ask the two men, 'How did you know what to say? About the flat tyre?'

Clive says, 'Our established cover-story.'

I gaze at Jay, inquisitive and he explains, 'Clive and I have a pre-arranged excuse ready for if we send out the SOS text with a location. He knows to say the reason for collecting us, and I know to say it before he was within ear-reach. It helps people to swallow the lie if we both mention it separately.'

Impressed, I nod, then fall silent, observing Clive. He drives confidently, continuously scanning the patchwork green of the fields as they recede in his mirror. We pull up to where we parked just a short while earlier, springing from the confines of the vehicle and standing in the large, open car park.

Gazing at me Clive asks Jay, 'So, this is the young lady you mentioned?'

'Yes. This is Mary,' Jay says.

I'm so grateful for Clive's intervention, I'm willing to forgive the fact he's asking Jay who I am, instead of just asking me directly and give Clive a wide smile of relief.

Clive holds out his hand to me. 'Pleasure,' he says, as I grasp his hand.

The firmness of Clive's handshake doesn't surprise me, but I am jolted by the strong connection to Clive that leaps through me like lightning in a plasma globe. Flinching, I withdraw from Clive's greeting, and as I reel backwards I pinch my nostrils to relieve them of the acrid burning I can smell. Stumbling on coltish legs, I manage to prop myself against the car, panting in shock. *What the hell?*

'What's the matter, Mary?' Jay asks, wearing a puzzled frown.

Clive looks confused, asking me, 'Are you OK?'

Ignoring their concern, I stare down at my feet. Feeling the ground shift beneath them I inhale deeply, pushing the strange kaleidoscope of images out of my mind. *What's wrong with me? Who did I see? Were they Clive's family or something? Maybe his kids when they were little, or his grandbabies? Why am I so drawn to them?* Shutting my eyes I concentrate on breathing slowly and deeply. *Calm. Down. It doesn't matter who I saw. This has just been a freaky day, and disappointing, too. My mediumship skills are probably just blown out, or on the fritz.* With determination, I close myself down mentally. *I am not in the receptive mode.* Then, when I'm gathered again, I raise my eyes to meet Clive's and Jay's curious stares.

'Yeah,' I say. 'All OK.'

'Great,' Jay says. 'We'll get back to the flat I rented for me and Mary, but first Mary, want to fill me in on our prime suspect, why he's *not* the one?'

I *knew* Jay had caught my head shake, indicating Phil wasn't the one we were looking for. I waste no time explaining, 'I saw in a vision that Phil Moyce is an up-and-coming dealer, a pimp, and a small-time porn director, but he never touches kids. That's about the only thing he has going for him. His stepdad had an eye for his younger sister, so that's where he draws his line.'

As Jay and I exchange information, Clive gawps at us. 'Astounding,' he says. 'Mind telling me how you know this information, young lady?'

I shrug, then glance at Jay, hoping he'll expand. He doesn't disappoint.

'Long story, old friend,' Jay says, answering for me. 'Want to follow us back to the flat? We can explain everything there.'

'Absolutely. This is unbelievable. Lead the way and I'll follow you in my vehicle. Haven't got long though. Can't stay. I'll come back for the explanation but have a meeting at fourteen hundred hours.'

'We'll make it a quick debrief then,' Jay says.

After we shut the car doors, and drive away, we head for the flat. A snatched check of the wing mirror reassures me that Jay's friend is following behind us. Closing my eyes I lean back against the cushioned head rest. I savour the secure feeling that seeing Clive trailing us gives me. *Strange.*

We come to a stop outside our rented accommodation and before I manage to open the door, Clive's there holding it open for me. Head sweeping left to right, it takes me a few moments to realise he's surveying the lonely area for any potential threats. You can take the man out of the force, but you can't take the force out of the man. The two of them exchange pleasantries as we walk up to the accommodation and I unashamedly ear wig on their conversation.

'That was a risky visit then, no?' Clive asks Jay.

'Yep, it was a risk. Thanks, Clive. For having my back. Especially as it was in an unofficial capacity. Means a lot.'

Clive smiles tightly, giving Jay a brief nod. 'Think nothing of it. Owe you one anyway. More than one, actually.'

Jay nods, and I notice he and Clive make eye contact. 'Let's get inside,' Jay says.

Whilst we walk to the flat, I study our cavalry in more detail. Tall and slim, Clive Saxon looks around the same age as Jay, late forties, or early fifties. Still attractive, with close cut Sandy blonde hair and blue eyes, he reminds me of Clint Eastwood, and has an air of vitality and strength that many men his junior lack.

The small flat is unassuming, but clean, and we've only booked it for one night's stay. Once in, the two men make their version of chit chat.

After visiting the toilet, I put the kettle on. 'I'm parched,' I say. 'Anyone want a tea?' Clive and Jay both accept with alacrity, and as the kettle boils I sit at the small table listening as they catch up with each other.

'How's Adam doing?' Jay asks Clive. 'Sorry I haven't been to see him this week. I've had a lot going on.'

'My boy's impatient to get back to work. Getting there though. In physio now. Doing well.'

Jay smiles, pleased. 'Yeah? That's great news. His legs were still in casts when I visited two weeks ago.'

'Hmph. Yes. Leaps and bounds,' Clive says, respect evident in his voice.

Jay claps Clive on the back in a gentle fashion. 'He's like his old man: one tough cookie.'

'Adam's your son?' I ask, interrupting.

Pride glints in Clive's eyes, and he nods.

CHAPTER EIGHT

W hile I make the tea, Jay moves from polite catch up to explaining about my mediumship gifts to his friend.

Clive stares at me intermittently throughout Jay's monologue and says, 'Amazing. Evidenced?'

Although I only met Clive a few hours ago, I don't take offence to his question.

Jay nods with slow confidence, 'We've worked on several cold cases together over the last three years. When the clues run cold, I call Mary. She never fails. Aside from that, the night we met, Mary proved herself.'

'How?' Clive asks, stroking his chin as he divides his attention between the two of us.

'Mary told us personal details about a colleague who was in the room,' Jay says. 'Out the blue, Mary spoke about memories she'd been told by my colleague's dead husband. Said he'd told her.'

Clive's brows raise. 'And you trust your colleague's judgment?'

'One hundred percent.'

'Hmmm, I can understand that,' Clive says. 'Eileen *has* got her head screwed on.'

My gaze flies to Jay's face in time to see him blink, taken aback. 'Still the best detective in England, I see, Clive. Yes it was Eileen,' he says.

Clive gives Jay a silent salute. 'So, what now?'

'Now, Mary and I scrutinise the other suspects.'

As I put fresh mugs of tea down in front of the two men I interrupt, aghast, 'But what about Phil Moyce? We can't allow him to just go on, doing terrible things, surely?'

Clive smiles briefly. 'I shouldn't worry about that. I'm sure he's already on the radar of other agencies. If he's not, he soon will be, I'll make sure of that.' He shoots a look at his watch.

My shoulders relax, and I breathe a sigh of relief. 'Really?'

Clive breaks into another quick smile. 'Really. Phil's activities will not go unnoticed.' Clive glances at his watch again, then gulps down the rest of his drink. 'Right, you two. Thanks for the tea. Must go. Mary, nice to meet you.'

'Nice to meet you, too, Clive, and thanks for coming to our rescue,' I say. *It'd been touch and go if we were going to get to leave for a moment.*

Clive is motionless for a second, and his gaze glints. I bite my lip, guessing he's noted that I wave at him instead of holding out my hand for a parting handshake. He doesn't comment on this though, instead, turning to Jay, palm outstretched in anticipation. Jay bids him goodbye.

'Bye, Clive, and again… thanks a million. As soon as we stumbled on that shed and understood what was going on at that farm, I knew we could have trouble getting out of there. Moyce was very suspicious of us at first and it could've gone very wrong. You saved our bacon.'

'Tosh. Anytime. Sorry. Right you two. Really must dash. Can't be late I'm afraid.'

With a smile, Jay says, 'It's been a pleasure, Clive. Let's have a proper catch up though, and soon. Maybe next time I visit your Adam, you could come along too?'

Clive nods. 'Sounds like a plan. Cheerio, Jay, Mary.'

As we wave off Clive at the front door, my bottom lip trembles slightly and I touch it, frowning. *What is this wobbly feeling about?*

Maybe I'm hormonal. Even though I've already taken a pregnancy test this month, maybe I should do another one? Hope sparks inside me, and a smile lingers, turning up the corners of my mouth. *I've got a handful of pregnancy test kits indoors; I can check again as soon as I get back.*

Jay's car pulls up next to where I parked mine, and suddenly weary, I'm glad he declined my offer to take turns driving. After wiping a palm over my face, I ask Jay, 'So, what's the plan for the rest of the week? Which suspects are we checking out next?'

'Let's get the least suspicious ones out of the way first, shall we?'

With a shrug I ask, 'You mean you want to go see the nice lady fire bug and the toff first? Fine. When d'ya want to go?' Although my shoulders slump with tiredness, as I stare at the entrance to mine and Derek's flat, I feel my enthusiasm reignite. *Maybe this time's different. Have we made a baby finally?*

'Yes, we'll see Joan and Simon both tomorrow, one after the other. If we go at the crack of dawn, we should be able to fit them in on the same day. It's down the M Five, about a four or five-hour drive.'

Five hours! 'Lovely.' I push my hair out of my eyes with a tut. It grows so quickly. 'OK, whatever. Let's just get this done, aye? Want to meet at mine at about six again?'

'Sounds good. You'd better go, I can see you're exhausted - you look done in. I'll check if any new reports have come in from the station and go over the case files again tonight. And thanks again for everything today, Mary.'

The sun set a long time ago, and I'm straining to see in the gloom of the car. Even so, Jay so recognises something in my face that makes him smile. 'You go on and get in to Derek now, Mary. Get some rest, and thank you for coming. You did great. I'll see you bright and early out here, first thing.'

'No worries, Jay. Night.' I skip out of the car, rejuvenated at the possibility of experiencing a positive pregnancy test. As I dig in my bag for my door key, my concentration makes me unaware of my surroundings. Which is why I jump so violently when Errol speaks from behind me.

'Mary. I'm here for you.'

'*Jesus Christ,* Errol, what the actual shit?' I say, rounding on him, my cheeks flushed with fury. *Is Errol trying to give me a heart attack or something?*

Derek must have heard my key in the door, because he opens it to give me a soft kiss on my lips in greeting. 'Er... Hi, beautiful, I take it you're *not* talking to *me?*'

After we pull apart, my nostrils tingle. *Hmm. Something yummy's cooking.* A spicy scent wafts out to greet me, and I grin as I take in the apron Derek's wearing, tied round his waist. In the hallway, I slip my shoes off, exchanging them for my slippers.

'Sorry D, I was talking to Errol, the jump-scare master from the other side. I'm going to have a shower quickly. Is that glorious smell coming from the kitchen our dinner?'

'It most definitely is.' Derek hugs me close again, and with my eyes shut, I breathe in his woodsy, masculine scent. It's distinguishable to me, even with the smell of dinner flooding the flat. 'Tonight, we have Amiwo, with chicken, and fried onion and tomatoes. I hope you like it.'

Another meal I vaguely remember from my childhood. *That is so sweet.* With a shake of my head, I wrap my arms around his waist, staring into his large, soulful eyes. 'You're the absolute Carlsberg of fiancés, I swear. Thank you, Derek.'

'It's my pleasure. Now, if madame will excuse me, I must check on tonight's meal. And do say hello to your spirit friend from me, won't you?' Derek offers the air beside me a quick salute, making both Errol and I grin.

As I move towards my bedroom, Errol says, 'I do like Derek. He's pretty cool.'

With a nod I agree, 'Yeah, Derek's the boomshackalak. Now what the hell are you jumping out on me again for? You nearly made me shit myself for real that time.'

'Sorry, don't mind me, Mary, I thought I heard you call me that's all. Sorry.'

My bedroom door's open and I enter, picking up my fluffy bathrobe from the back of the door. I give Errol the side eye as I walk past him, shutting the bathroom door in his face. Grabbing two pregnancy tests from their home in the bathroom cabinet, I force myself to take calming breaths. Five minutes later, I'm disguising my heartbroken sobs with the noise of the shower.

I take so long Derek calls out to check on me. Only when I'm certain the water has taken away the red puffiness from my eyes, and that the knot in my throat has relaxed, I turn off the shower. When I step out over the bath and dry off, Errol's waiting. Concern for my well-being must have overridden his bathroom space etiquette. As I put my dressing gown on, I study him with a tut. He is standing near the sink, head down, staring at the bathmat on the floor. His distress rolls out towards me as I pick up the negative tests and wrap them in toilet roll, before binning them.

My sigh is heavy as I tell him, 'It's OK, friend, don't suffer so much on my behalf. Maybe next month. It will happen, Errol, no biggie.'

Without raising his head, Errol answers me, his voice sounding like he harbours a throat filled with straw. 'That's true, Mary. It *will* happen one day, you'll see.'

As he speaks I'm brushing my hair, and I lift my chin and push my shoulders back, practicing a wry smile in front of the mirror. *I need to get my game face on, I refuse to burden Derek with my sadness.* All at once, Errol's statement sinks in, making me my breath catch and my gaze flies to his in the mirror. *The Universe is allowing me some hope, it seems. It did not shut Errol up.* My chest swells with joy. *It will happen. I knew it.* 'In that case, put a smile on your face then, Errol, it looks like a slapped arse. I'm about to have my dinner. You'll put me off eating with that sour puss staring at me.'

Errol rolls his eyes, giving me a quick salute as he disappears from the room. 'Have a nice evening, Mary, and give my regards to Derek.'

Errol's words have given me the gift of renewed hope. Feeling a weight's been lifted from my shoulders, I head out to join my fiancé, saying, 'That's much better, I needed that shower. So mon Chéri, what exactly is 'Amiwo' again? It sounds familiar, but I can't properly remember.'

My question prompts Derek to puff out his chest, and looking pleased with himself he says, 'You'll see. Come and sit down at the table. I'll serve dinner up, and you can tell me all about what's been happening in the last couple of days.'

My lips twist and I wrinkle my nose. *Derek's not gonna like it when I explain I need to be away again for another day or so.*

CHAPTER NINE

J ay and I have been inside this car for nearly five hours now. Visiting Joan Sante's house gave us a brief reprieve, but now we're back in Jay's car. My nose curls as I smell the stale sandwiches and cheese-and-onion crisps we ate earlier.

Jay shrugs. 'So, you got nothing from Joan, aye?'

'Well, I wouldn't say *nothing*… she has her secrets,' I tell him.

'She does? Like what?' Jay's excited all at once, and I watch as his eyes flick from my face to the road.

'Watch the road, for God's sake. Nothing exciting, just regular relationship stuff, feelings about her marriage and stuff.' *Joan had been thinking of leaving her husband, but she is worried it will mess up her kids. The cheery-looking snacks-wagon seller is having an affair with someone, and the two of them are in love. Memories of her own messed-up childhood plague her. Joan is petrified of causing any trauma to her children.* I'm not telling Jay any of that. I can feel it's not important to the case, and that she has no connection with Patryk, or with the harm of any child. The malevolence I'd sensed when I tracked Patryk near his school had nothing to do with the kind-hearted Joan. 'It definitely isn't her,' I say, feeling relieved as I say it. I liked Joan. She was respectful to us when we came to see her, and although she wasn't being honest in her relationship, she's torn and filled with guilt. Joan is suffering because she wants to do the right thing for everyone. *Poor cow.*

'Oh,' Jay says, sighing.

'Well, don't sound so disappointed. That should please you. With her *and* Phil Moyce out of the innings. It narrows down the suspect list considerably.'

Jay removes one hand from the wheel, scratches his ear, tugging at the lobe while he ponders my question. 'I suppose. It's just I know it can't be Simon, so that leaves the plumber and the taxi driver. We can go there tomorrow or the next day. Depends how knackered we are after the visit to Simon.'

'OK, off to Cambridge we go then. But can you try to open this window first, please? It stinks in this car, and this button's jammed.'

Jay presses his control panel, and the window swishes down with immediate obedience. Without a word, he grins, indicating to pull out onto the road.

Typical. I grin too with a shrug. 'So, remind me about who we're going to see next please, Jay. Simon someone? All I remember was that I thought he looked stuck-up from his photo, but I don't know why I thought that.'

'Probably because of that weak chin he's got in the pictures. It has, 'upper-class inbreeding' written all over it. Shouldn't stereotype though, I suppose. Simon Redford is a twenty-one-year-old law student, currently in his third year at Oxford. No known issues, criminal background, no driving violations. According to Eileen there's no forensic history either. He seems clean as a whistle.'

'Cool. And it's about a five-hour drive again, isn't it?'

'Yep.' Jay picks up speed, entering the motorway and focusing on safely joining the traffic flow.

After a brief rummage in my bag, I check out the time on my mobile, telling Jay, 'I'm gonna give Derek a call, then I might have a couple of hours shut-eye. Let me know if you change your mind and want me to take a spot at the wheel, OK?'

'Will do, Mary. Say hi to Derek from me.'

'Yeah, OK.' Absentminded, I click my phone open and scroll to contacts. *How do I not know anyone's number off by heart; disgraceful.*

CHAPTER TEN

W e hurry along the park's concrete pathway, heads down from the rain. The park's beautiful, but it's a lonely place, the rainy weather ensuring that our meeting with Simon is solitary. Luckily, I put my long, waterproof coat on, and when we come to the first bench along the path, I sit down on it. Even through my wet weather clothing, the cold transfers itself to me. Jay, in his padded jacket, doesn't sit down, hovering in front of me. He's tilting his chin down, keeping most of the rain out of his eyes.

My frown clears as I realise why he's standing up, and after a quick dig around in my handbag, I pass him a carrier bag.

Jay raises his brow. 'What's that for?'

'Sit on that,' I smirk. *So childish, Mary, but I couldn't resist the pun.*

With an eye roll, Jay accepts the bag I shove at him, and after putting it underneath his derriere, he sits down. He holds his palm out into the rain. 'I think it's stopping, anyway. I'm starving; don't suppose you have a three-course meal in there, or an umbrella, do you?'

'Sadly, no. My surname's *Jameson,* not *Poppins*. Why did Simon pick here, d'you think?'

'Probably didn't want to be seen fraternising with the likes of us, I expect.' Jay shrugs, unconcerned.

With a grin I say, 'Yeah, no-one likes the '*po-po,*' do they?'

Jay gives a shout of laughter, but a scowl accompanies it. "Po-po,' how d'you come up with those words?' He shakes his head, like a parent rebuking their child for mischief, when they really want to laugh.

'American television shows. When I've got the time, I love 'em. Don't you?' My phone rings. 'Oh shit, let me get that.'

'You can call them back. Here comes our Master Redford now.' Jay nods towards the portly man in a snug suit and raincoat, hurrying along the pathway towards us. We're the only people on the path, so even though he's far enough away to be out of ear shot, our view of his approach is unobstructed.

Even still, I'm careful to whisper as I say to Jay, 'What's he wearing a shirt and tie for anyway? It makes him look like a stuffed sausage. Is he coming straight from work or something?'

'No, I think he always dresses like that. It's what he's wearing in all the photos I got.'

'Hmm.' *Sad-arse, though I don't know why I'm bothered. Who cares what this guy wears?*

'Mary, shh.'

After a few minutes of watching his scurrying progress, Simon Redford reaches us, and Jay stands up to greet him, so I do the same. I don't extend my hand as Jay does; I'll save the contact for later.

'Mr. Redford, pleased to meet you,' Jay says as the man accepts his handshake. 'Thank you so much for agreeing to join us today. We'll try not to take up much of your time.'

Simon's soft face, buck teeth and receding chin do little for him, and the way he narrows his already small eyes puts me in mind of Phil Moyce's piggy ones. Except his attitude isn't lascivious - it's arrogant. From underneath his floppy dark hair, his gaze jerks from Jay to me.

'Who's *she*?' Simon says.

The question obviously relates to me, but Simon directs it to Jay, as though I'm not important enough to answer. *Feisty little shit.* Back straight, I bite my lip and draw in a calming breath.

'Well, hello, Mr. Redford, it's nice to meet you. My name is Mary Jameson, and I'm a colleague of Detective Inspector Santiago's.'

Simon demands, 'What kind of colleague? Which department are you in?'

What's wrong with this guy? I give Jay the side-eye, willing him to intervene, so I can avoid a misstep. *Oh, yes, Master Redford is one stuck-up, entitled prick. That's for sure. Obviously thinks he's some kind of posh Billy Big-Balls, with the right to push us women around.* I wonder if my deep breathing is audible to Jay, and guess it probably is because he intercepts the question.

'Ms. Jameson is just here to take some notes, Mr. Redford. I'm guessing you're concerned about confidentiality? I can assure you, Ms. Jameson has signed a waiver. There's nothing *else* you're concerned about, is there, Mr. Redford?' I observe as Jay subtly changes his posture, altering his demeanour to become more commanding in his presence. Jay's scrutinising our guest and his stare, previously affable and relaxed, now drills into Simon's, demonstrating his authority.

Different from when he was addressing me, Simon's feet shuffle as he shifts his weight from left to right. He looks intimidated, scared. *Ah, I see. So, he's a bully and a coward.*

'So, would you like to speak here, or go somewhere more comfortable? The police station, maybe?' Jay asks Simon.

'My apologies, Officer. I meant nothing by my question, I assure you. Here will be fine, Detective.'

Jay nods. 'Great. I can see you're wearing a raincoat, so please take a seat beside my colleague whilst she takes notes.'

The way Jay regained control of the conversation gives me a warm feeling of satisfaction and makes me duck my head and hide my smile as I sit back down. As soon as I seat myself I grimace. *Shitty bench is numbing my bum cheeks.* Jay remains standing, but I catch his quick side glance warning me to readjust my expression, and I lean down, taking out a writing pad and a pen. It's stopped raining now, so I unzip my damp coat, and lay the pad on my dry lap. The act helps me to smooth out all traces of smugness from my expression. Out of the blue, I wish Eileen was here also, so our little trio could be complete. She would have shared a moment with me, despite Jay's stern gaze.

'Mary, would you mind showing Mr Redford here the photographs please?'

'Of course, Detective,' I say obediently. My bag is considerably less full than usual, as I cleared it out last night. As a result, it only takes a second or two before I pass Simon the pictures. I watch him stare at the photos, shaking his head then laying them on his lap, uninterested. I'm sucked into a kaleidoscope of images that comes in and out of focus.

Simon, young, looking up at the ceiling of his ramshackle mansion. I hear the ping-ponging noise of water dripping into the saucepans on the floor as they collect rainfall from the holey roof. Simon, a bit more mature, gazing at his affluent relatives elegant three-storey house with envy. Also, hero-worship. Simon's letter of acceptance to a prestigious university, the fees and accommodation costs weighing on him like gravity. Bills pushing him down with worry. How will he afford it? How will he afford it… and then… Release! It's not him, he's not the killer, but…

Simon draws back, startled as my gaze gleams bright grey, and I realise I'm staring him directly in the eyes, without speaking. He stammers, faltering with whatever he's saying about the photo to Jay, until I cloak my burning gaze with my eyelashes. I return my attention to the writing pad I'm using as a prop. Only I haven't just used the pad as a prop. I'm amazed when I notice I've written on it.

His car.

Inadvertently, I see my examination of Simon's watery features is unnerving him again. I know his car is important, but I don't understand how. It may not be my place, but I feel I have to say something, 'Does anyone else have access to your car?' I ask. 'Or have you ever reported it as stolen, perhaps?'

Simon's mouth opens wide, and he leans back, staring at me. 'How the hell did you know that?'

Jay's head whips down to look at me, and without losing a second, he crouches down in front of the bench Simon and I are sitting on, taking up the mantle of my line of questioning. 'We're asking the questions, thank you, Mr. Redford. Now, if you wouldn't mind, please, will you answer my colleague? Has your car ever been stolen, or have you ever lent it to anyone?'

Simon's soft chin wobbles as he swallows, and he pushes a swathe of floppy hair back from his sweaty face. 'Well, yes, I have, but I don't see how that's any of your business.'

Jay raises his brow. 'Oh, really? So, to recap, we explained to you about your car being seen in the vicinity of a serious crime, at the same time and date of said crime. However, you're saying you can't see we might have a probable cause to question you about the whereabouts of your car. *Or* to ask who has access to it? Is that what you're saying, Mr. Redford?' Jay doesn't give Simon a chance to answer, continuing to say, 'Now, concerning *your* whereabouts. Can you remember what you were doing on that day, at around that time, Mr. Redford?' Jay leans in closer to Simon, creating an atmosphere of intimacy and intimidation.

Simon's eyes flit between my face and Jay's while his pasty complexion turns a blotchy salmon pink. I ensure my facial expression matches Jay's stalwart one, and that I'm giving nothing away.

A tap-tap-tapping sound draws my attention, and I glance down to see Simon's hard-soled shoes knocking against the concrete path. It reminds me of the noise the water made in my vision, as it dripped from the ceiling of his family home. I glance at his bouncing leg and see his shaky hand move to his knee to still the jiggling. *My, my, he is nervous.*

A brief silence rests between us all, and the singing of the birds serves as a cheery background for our frozen tableau. We wait for

Simon to elaborate, faces closed and tongues silent as Jay and I stare at him. He pushes his hair back again, then clears his throat.

'I only lent it to my cousin. I let him borrow it sometimes when he needs to run down to London. You're not seriously suggesting that *Ollie* would do anything criminal, are you? He's one of the *Redford-Bowles*, for God's sake.'

'How often does your cousin borrow your car, Mr. Redford? And do you recall the dates that you lent the car to him, and the purpose he gave for needing it?'

'But... he's Oliver *Redford-Bowles*!' Simon erupts, standing up with his fists clenched by his side. As he shoots to his feet, the photos he'd left carelessly on his lap flutter to the bench and

Jay also gets to his feet. My eyebrows entrench themselves somewhere near my hairline, and on the floor, my foot twitches. With a heroic strength, I force back the childish urge to kick this pretentious idiot in the shins. 'Oliver *Redford-Bowles*...' *No-one cares, you stuck-up idiot.*

Jay sighs. 'Apologies, Mr. Redford, but that name means nothing to me, unfortunately. Do I take it from your repetition of the name the family is renowned?'

Simon's chin wobbles in outrage, reminding me of a Thanksgiving turkey. 'Urgh. *Of course,* they're renowned. They have generation upon generation of financial wizardry in their lineage, and Ollie is no different. He's often featured in magazines because of his exemplar investments.'

'He's good with money, then? Wealthy?' Jay's question earns a look of pitying disgust from Simon, his eyes heavy with derision as he clearly feels a renewed arrogance.

'Yes. I should say he is *'good with money.'* He's an extremely affluent investment banker, legendary in his circles, in fact.' Simon smirks at Jay, making my nostrils flare and my hackles rise. *Alright arse, it was just a question.*

235

Jay smiles, asking in a mild voice, 'So, er… if your cousin is so well off then, Simon, why do you suppose he needs to borrow *your* car? Why doesn't he have one of his own?'

'He does have one!'

Jay smiles. '*Really*? But then why would he choose to use yours?'

My lips purse and I see Jay's eyebrows have risen to match the position of mine. Simon blusters, his Adam's apple wobbling, and his eyes casting about. A quick glance down shows me that Simon's foot's tapping on the spot. *Oh-ho, mister smug… gotcha.*

'He… I don't know! Maybe it's not convenient? He might do it as a favour to help me out?'

'A favour to help you? What kind of favour?' Jay draws nearer to Simon's, who drops his gaze.

'He pays me,' Simon whispers.

Jay asks, 'For your car? How much?'

'Two thousand.'

My jaw falls open, and my intake of breath garners the attention of both men as I can't help but interrupt, 'Two thousand pounds? Every time he uses your car? And you say your cousin's good with money?'

'He knows I struggle. My family is somewhat less… affluent than Ollie's branch, and I think he knows and wants to help me.'

Jay nods, saying, 'You '*think*' he knows that? Or do you *actually* know that?'

The law student remains silent, crossing his arms.

'Can you give us your cousin's address please, Mr. Redford?' Jay says, every inch the police official.

Simon draws himself upright, and I see the buttons on his shirt strain as his chest puffs out. Voice cold, he says, 'This is *not* what I agreed to discuss today with you. I'm afraid I'm not prepared to answer any more of your questions without proper legal representation present. Now, if you'll excuse me, I have work to do.'

You mean a cousin to warn, or an essay to write?

Jay stands, as do I. When Jay extends his hand Simon doesn't take it, leaving it hanging in the rain. Jay says cordially, 'Thank you for your time today, Mr. Redford. We appreciate your help with this matter. We may be in touch again.'

Without another word, Simon scurries back along the way he came. He's hunched forward again, and the tails of his raincoat flap in the breeze as he races along. Simon reminds me of a fly caught in a spider web that is being retracted.

'Well, he was a dick,' I say.

Jay's snort agrees with me. 'How do you feel about going back home for today, while I get official permission to approach this rich cousin of Simon's? If he's as loaded as our Master Redford suggested, there's bound to be some push-back. He won't want us poking around. Then, in a day or so, we find this Oliver character. Ask him a couple of questions?'

'You mean 'Oliver *Redford-Bowles,* for God's sake!"

Jay chuckles, as do I, until the first big fat glob of rain plops down onto my head.

CHAPTER ELEVEN

D erek's wiry arms encircle me, and the mattress creaks as I snuggle into his side. His breath is warm on the back of my neck and despite the topic of our conversation, it tickles me, making me smile. 'So, Jay's having the police look into this other guy-the cousin?' he asks.

I nod. 'Yeah. It should take a day or so. Plus, Jay got permission for Eileen to help a bit as well, so that's good. We should have a bit of time together before I have to leave.'

'Well, I've been thinking about that Mary. Remember when I offered to help with surveillance advice before? Could I help out now? With this new suspect?'

My heartbeat picks up its pace suddenly, with no provocation. *It's funny how it does that sometimes, for no reason.* I clamp my arms around Derek's, gluing myself to him in our cosy bed. 'Well, he has a team for that, but thanks, love. I'm not sure if he'd get official permission. But if he could, you'd be willing to do that?'

'Of course! I'm not blowing my trumpet, but I doubt there's anyone better at it than I am on Jay's team.'

I put my fingers up, making a steeple and mime playing a trumpet. 'Do-do-de-do,' I say.

'Alright, it was blowing my own trumpet. But also...'

Waiting for Derek to finish his sentence, I frown into the dark silence of the room, relaxing my eyes as I see the familiar swirling colours that we make together. 'Also what?' I ask.

'If it means I get to be with you more, then I'll happily volunteer. You've been so busy lately we haven't been spending much time together.'

'Ah, D. You're so romantic.'

We both chuckle, and I close my eyes as Derek smooths my hair away from my nape and presses a kiss into the crease it was shielding.

'So,' he says. 'About that baby making.'

My smile lights up the darkness, and I turn to face my fiancé. 'Thought you'd never ask,' I say, and we become lost in one another.

'Jesus Christ, Mary. *Mary, stop!*' Derek shouts the words, suddenly waking me.

We're both sitting upright on our bed. I open my eyes to realise he's scooped me into his arms, and is rocking me backwards and forwards, his voice fierce and uncharacteristically loud. The motion reminds me of being at the psychiatric hospital and experiencing acute distress. Uncomfortable that I'm worrying Derek, I hasten to reassure him. *I mustn't burden or worry him; I don't want him to become unwell again. I need him.* His heartbeat races against my own.

'It's OK, Derek. It was just a stupid dream. I'm awake now. I'm really sorry.'

'A dream? Sounded like you were having another humdinger of a nightmare. This is getting ridiculous. What was it about? Can you remember?'

'There was a giant, reddish moon hanging in the sky. I heard my voice saying, 'The blood-red moon,' over and over. I don't know why that was so scary, but apparently, it was. Stupid. I'm sorry I woke you up, love.' The moon in my dream was a full one, cloaked in a beautiful mist of reddish gold. My voice has a robotic quality I can hear myself as I speak. It reminds me of the recordings you hear

239

on an auto responder for companies. It sounds emotionless, and its emptiness chills me, making me shiver. Immediately, Derek wraps the surrounding covers around me, rubbing my forearms like a parent warms a small child.

Derek asks, 'Do you fancy a hot chocolate or something? Help us get back to sleep?'

'That sounds lovely. I'll make it though, as an apology for waking you up. Do you want one?'

'No apology needed, beautiful, ever. We can make the hot chocolate together, c'mon.'

Derek guides me up from the bed and gets up. With a foot, he slides my slippers closer to the bed, and passes me my dressing gown. He shuffles into his own slippers, then stretches out a hand to me, pulling me up.

'We can talk to Jay about me unofficially joining the case early tomorrow morning, and maybe you can also talk to your friend Errol about these dreams.'

Good idea, although he probably won't be able to tell me anything if my nightmare was important. I sigh. Sometimes, I wonder if there is any point in my 'gift.' Maybe they should have called me Cassandra.

The next morning we stand in Jay's basic home office, amidst the hard copy case files that he has lain out over his desk. We can't see anything because they all have numbered folders, and I have to force my attention away from them. I can feel my eyelids close as random words spring into my mind. *No.* I clench my small hands into fists. *Not now. I will not 'allow.'*

Jay, unaware of my inner turmoil, is shaking a handful of peanuts in his own fist, throwing them in his mouth with an unerring accuracy. He squints at me, then at Derek. 'So, Mary mentioned you're willing to come on board with the cyber stuff, Derek. Help the case along.'

'If you think I could be of some use.'

'You'd definitely be of some use; we'd be glad to have you behind the wings. I'm already well aware of your professional reputation. Top in your field, Derek. There'd be some bureaucracy to go through first, of course. It's not the same situation as our Mary, because we have to be more discreet with her suggestions. But we *can* take and investigate any concerns she reports. We have our own specialist police team for surveillance you see, but I'd still be grateful for your advice on how to proceed, in addition. Obviously, you need to sign a confidentiality contract, and a disclaimer as well, of course.'

My chest puffs out with pride on Derek's behalf. 'Top in his field.' *My fiancé.* I smile at him, still the cat who got the cream, and he gives my hand a loving squeeze.

'We have to be very careful, legally, with this man,' Jay says. 'A quick internet search explained why our Master Redford was name-dropping his cousin's name so heavily. This Oliver chap is wealthy, and renowned in financial circles. We need to get proper evidence if we're going to pursue this officially. It has to be watertight in court. That includes the justification for any investigation I carry out, and the application of it. We need to be smart here.'

'That's exactly what I've been telling you all along. I'm glad to see some of it has sunk in, after all,' Eileen says as she enters Jay's office breezily.

'Eileen!' I gasp, swinging around to hug my friend. 'What're you doing here?' I ask. A quick look at the clock tells me it's just before 9 a.m., and as Jay hadn't gone to let Eileen in, she must've been already here when we'd arrived. *At 8.30.*

Eileen's sea-green gaze glimmers, then drops, and she gives a delicate cough.

After a second of confusion, my eyes widen, and a quick glance at Derek's knowing grin tells me he has also caught on. *Eileen must've stayed the night at Jay's.* I beam at my two dear friends, chuckling at the opposite reactions to my gasp of understanding. Eileen's lips twitch, and I watch as a flush travels upwards from Jay's neck, all the way up to his mortified face.

Eileen shrugs, saying, 'I sort of… stayed over.'

'Uh-*huh*. You guys had a *sleepover*, aye?' Derek lifts his eyebrows.

'Shut up, Derek.' Jay's swift comment has the rest of us laughing out loud, and as his face floods an even darker crimson, sympathy twitches inside me. *Jay's usually so chill.* Then I consider Jay's personality and realise why this conversation's probably difficult for him. *The hard copy files, the respectful manner. The wedding ring he still wears.* The thought sobers me, making the smile leave my face. *Jay's old school. He likes these things to be private. I'd better shut Derek up and help him out.* I give Derek a quick elbow to the ribs, making his chuckles come to an abrupt end, then I change the subject, 'So, it's settled then, Jay? Can we both be involved in the case? Officially?' I ask.

Jay looks at me with such gratitude my heart melts. I resist the urge to pat him, knowing that a few years ago, if someone had aimed such a gesture at me, I probably would have punched them.

Eileen, astute as ever, goes along with the abrupt shift in direction, acknowledging the alteration with nothing more than a brief brow raise. 'Derek, you're helping out with the computer stuff, I take it?' she asks.

'That's the plan, yes, Eileen. I just need to get the official go ahead from the powers that be and have the right bureaucratic boxes ticked, but as Derek's such a respected professional in his field, I doubt there'll be any problems. Well, we'll work our way around any advice you give, Derek. I'm sure it'll be agreed. Has Mary told you this guy's in Hampshire?'

'No, she didn't mention that. Are you thinking of going there, scoping him out?'

Jay nods, saying, 'Yes, definitely, but I'd like to go there for a few days this time. Intuition tells me that I really need to take my time with this suspect. Also, he's loaded so we need to be extra careful.'

All business, Derek grants Jay a nod of accord. 'OK, let us know when you'd like to go and Mary and me can organise a place to stay. Do you have any other info about this chap, Jay?'

Jay shakes his head. 'Not much. Adopted at aged nine by a rich family. Soon after the adoption took place, his adoptive father died in a car accident, leaving the adoptive mother to raise Redford-Bowles alone. Initial reports show him as a troublesome child. Went to boarding school where he towed the line and excelled. Highly intelligent and works as an investment banker.'

Eileen frowns, asking, 'What happened to his adopted mum?'

Jay shrugs. 'She's dead. Died when Oliver was fourteen.'

'And his biological mum?' I ask.

Jay answers, 'There's little on record about her. Sadly all pre-adoption paperwork seems to have vanished. All that's known is that by the time he was adopted she was deceased.'

A shiver runs through me, and Derek slips his hand into mine, knowing I'm empathising with the loss of a mum. I'd been eight, and it had taken me many years to come to terms with the grief, although I still miss her. Something niggles at me. 'How did she die, his adoptive mum?' I ask.

'Heart attack, why?' Jay, as usual, is quick off the mark, answering straight away.

'Not sure. It might be nothing, but it felt like I got some resonance there. Do you have a photo of Oliver, then?'

'Well, sort of, but sadly, there are no personal ones. Only the ones we found in a couple of those money magazines. The guy's a recluse. No social media accounts for me to trawl through, no paparazzi pictures of him, holidaying with some floozie.'

Eileen snorts at Jay's out-of-date phrase, making his face heat again. His awkwardness is so sharp that although I'm not actively reading him, it swims out to meet me, the embarrassment tainting the air and my eyes squint in reaction. I shut it out. *Thou shalt not read thy friends.* 'Can I look?' I ask.

'Sure. I have them here, ready for you.' Jay moves a folder out of the way, and the pictures are lying under them.

Oliver Redford-Bowles cuts a dashing figure on the page. Fitted, expensive suits. Possessing good-looking, chiselled features along with sandy coloured hair and almond-shaped brown eyes. There's no resemblance to his cousin Simon, with his floppy hair, poorly fitting suits, and overbite. But then, there wouldn't have been, what with him being adopted.

'Hmm… he's quite distinguished looking, isn't he?' Eileen says in a neutral tone of voice. Closer to us now, she leans in to see, and I notice Jay holding his breath as her bob swings forward, brushing his forehead.

I put my head down to hide my knowing smile, and Derek and I share an undercover look. Focusing once more on the two magazine articles Jay passed to me, I silently agree with Eileen's judgement. *Oliver Redford-Bowles is a striking-looking guy, and I have a feeling there must be a ton going on underneath that smooth exterior.* I place my hand over the likeness, closing my eyes to help my concentration. *Drifting…* I pick up coins, changing hands. It's raining. Then a thought block, 'Work is shit, can't wait 'til the weekend.' Likely belonging to the people who've just touched the magazine as it moved from person to person. With a sigh I say, 'I'm not getting anything helpful, Jay. I think the image is too far removed from the actual person. It holds no vibration from touch, and there's no memory of the photo linked to it, either. There's nothing for me to hold on to psychically, if you like.'

Jay says, 'That's disappointing, but I'm sure you'll get something when you get closer to him, in person. When would you two be ready to head down to Hampshire? Would you like the force to organise your accommodation?'

Without thinking I answer Jay, 'No, it's fine, Jay. If you let me have Oliver's home address, I'll find somewhere close-ish and book it up for us.'

Derek holds my hand saying, 'We can go tomorrow.' Derek turns to Jay asking, 'Will that allow you enough time to get the warrant sorted for us to look into this Oliver guy, along with your team, of course?'

Jay screws up his face, shrugging. 'Hopefully. Can't say for sure.' As he speaks, Jay flicks through the pages of a writing pad. Then he writes something down on a page, tears it out and hands it to me. 'That's the address we have for Oliver,' he says.

As I take the piece of paper from Jay, my stomach turns over feeling as though it's housing an eel in there. Anxious thoughts scrabble around my mind like a hamster in a cage. *It's just nerves; I can block them out.*

CHAPTER TWELVE

'This isn't the way to the flat I rented, Derek?' I stare out of the window as Hampshire's picturesque fields, houses, and village squares flash past our car window. It's only taken us two hours to drive to Hampshire, and we'd nearly reached the rented accommodation that I'd booked us so we could help out with investigating Oliver Redford-Bowles. Unfortunately, Derek had ignored my instruction to get off the M3 and had stayed on for the next junction. Now, we're driving along an unknown A-road in the wrong area. 'You'll have to find somewhere to turn round, Derek,' I tell him.

Derek smiles and nods, but when the road widens sufficiently, doesn't take the opportunity to turn around.

'D, where are you going? You could've turned there,' I say, confused.

Derek keeps his eyes on the road, but slows his speed, pulling into a residential turning that leads to a close. A ring of tidy-looking houses sit amongst tastefully cultivated lawns. 'So, I have a surprise for you, Mary.'

Puzzled, I scratch my head, staring out the window. *It's lovely here but why's he stopped?* 'Why've you stopped here, Derek? I can't see any coffee shops or anything?' I crane my neck around, scanning the cul-de-sac. The close we arrive at is quiet, and the leaves of the tall birch trees that surround the houses seem to twinkle in the breeze. They make a soft, rustling noise that sounds to me like gentle applause. I draw in a deep breath. *Hmm. This is really nice. Peace. Tranquillity. We drove past a park at the corner, maybe we could go for a quick walk there. Hang on!* I double take at Derek, and he grins, knowing straight away that I've realised where we are.

'You've brought me to see the house I liked! Oh my God, Derek, I love it!'

'Yeah, this is the one. I thought seeing as we're not starting things with Jay til tomorrow, we could squeeze a viewing in today. I called the estate agent, who called the owner, and here we are.'

Gratitude swells in my heart til it threatens to burst from my chest. In the confines of the car I throw my arms round Derek's neck, kissing him reverently. 'You're amazing. Thank you. This is the nicest surprise I've ever had. It's so beautiful here, the area. It seems peaceful in this close, and all the houses are so pretty – don't you think?'

'Yeah, I do. Plus it's also near the sea and the New Forest like you like, Mary.'

A memory of Derek telling me he didn't really care about being near the park pops into my head, triggering a sick feeling of guilt. *Will he resent me for dragging him away from city life?* Aghast, I stare at Derek, catching my bottom lip with my teeth. 'But what about you, D? What about what you like? You need to be happy, too. What do you ideally want? There must be something.'

'I told you before, I honestly don't care, Mary. Whatever you fancy, I'm on board.'

'There's got to be something you want in our future home. You can't give me all the choice with this decision.'

With a smile, Derek shakes his head, shrugging his shoulders in an easy motion. 'Just you. Literally, I couldn't care a fig about the house. As long as there're good travel links nearby, we can get a good internet service, and you're in the house with me, then I'll be happy.

'You're the best,' I say, my eyes brimming with tears.

'Yes, I am. Now let's get in there and see what this house is like on the inside, shall we?'

After standing on tiptoes to kiss Derek, I link arms with him, and we stroll towards the house in the centre of the close. It has a small driveway out front, with hanging baskets and flowerpots outside, overspilling with abundance.

An elderly lady opens the door with a smile of welcome on her face. She holds out her hand, and automatically, I take it. Homely contentment pulses out to me, making me smile as the lady stares into my grey eyes. 'Hello, dears, you must be Mary and Derek? I'm Vivian, the current owner. I understand you've come from London. What a long journey! Would you like to use the loo, or can I offer you a drink?'

We decline Vivian's kind offers, and a song swells into my heart as soon as we step into the hallway. I can feel the embrace of the house, accepting us. My gaze meets Derek's. *This is the one.*

'I've had a lot of good times here, with my husband Gerald - God rest his soul, and with my daughter, Charlotte. She and her husband moved a couple of years ago to live in Spain. Lotty had a baby boy last year, and I want to be with them. Do you have children?'

'Not yet, no. But soon, hopefully,' I say, feeling her yearning as she mentions her daughter.

'Ah, it will happen, I'm sure. Everything comes when it's meant to. Would you like to have a wander around by yourself? I'm happy for you to go in every room.' At my eager nod, Vivian smiles, her faded blue eyes twinkling with life. 'If you like it, there's no buying chain either, dears. I could be ready to sell and move out next week if you wanted.'

After we tour the house we see ourselves out, and I find myself dragging my feet, forcing myself to walk away from the house. As we get back inside the car, I shift in my seat, staring at Derek. 'I loved it, so much, D. What did you think? Did you love it as well?' I ask.

'It was nice, yes. The home has a pleasant feeling about it, and Vivian said there's no chain. Want me to put an offer in with the estate agent?'

'Oh, my God! Really? Do you mean it? Can we?' I hold my breath for Derek's answer. I've never been aware of wanting something so badly before and part of me is waiting for my balloon of hope to be popped.

At Derek's easy nod, I fling my arms around his neck, showering him with kisses. 'Thank you, thank you. I love that house so much! Are you sure though, D? Can we really afford it -and are you sure you like it?'

Because of previous trauma we experienced at the hands of a medical professional, both Derek and I had received a large financial settlement. Besides this, Derek earns a very good wage, and insists I don't have to work at all. However, I insist on continuing with my 'consultancy' role with the police as it makes me feel like I'm helping people, plus, it earns me a reasonable amount, albeit sporadically. Despite this, solo, my lump sum and modest earnings are not mortgage worthy. Derek will also have to agree to a mortgage for us to be able to buy this house.

He strokes my face, staring into my eyes with intensity. 'Happy wife, happy life.'

We both grin, and I set upon Derek again, kissing his face as many times as I can, in as many different places as possible. 'You're the best fiancé ever!' I tell him.

'Well, that settles it. I'll give the estate agents a ring with an offer right now.'

'You're amazing,' I repeat. 'While you're doing that, I'll re-enter that bed-and-breakfast address for tonight in my phone maps.'

Derek leans over to the back seat, grabbing his mobile from the jacket that's lying behind us. A few minutes of conversation with the estate agent confirms there is no chain, and that everything should be straightforward. Vivian obviously liked us as much as we liked her and the house. She'd called her agent as soon as we'd left, to instruct them to accept an offer from us if it was at the asking price. I swallow a huge lump in my throat as the realisation hits me. *This is going to be our home. We're going to be a proper family.*

Joy is threatening to burst out of me, and I hug myself as Derek finishes the call. *We've just been in our family home.*

Later that night, as we sit in the room we'd rented, in front of the gas fire, my legs comfortably hanging over Derek's, I say, 'It's a funny coincidence the guy we're going to check out lives in Hampshire, too, isn't it?'

'Well, yes, although he lives in a completely different part of Hampshire. His place is right in the New Forest. Shall we drive up to his area early tomorrow to have a look? Scope him out on the quiet, before Jay and Eileen get down?'

I nod. 'Yes, that's not a bad idea, Derek. I might find it easier to receive if there are fewer people around me interfering with the signal.'

'OK, and maybe we can stop for a meal on the way back. I'm sure there are loads of nice places along the way,' Derek says.

I twist my engagement ring between my thumb and ring finger, then warm my hands by the fire for a few minutes. 'I haven't seen Errol for a while again. I can't help but feel he's up to something.'

Derek frowns. 'Something bad or good? I thought he was your friend?'

'He is my friend; I know that for sure. But he's been suspiciously absent for ages again. He usually checks in now and then if I don't call on him.'

Derek stands up, pulling me with him as he goes. I click the fire off reluctantly and follow Derek towards the bathroom.

'Let's get ready for bed,' Derek says. 'Maybe you should give old Errol a spectral shout-out? I'm sure it's nothing. Maybe he's got himself a ghostie girlfriend, and he's busy getting it on in the other life.'

'What's with all the alliteration?' I ask with a smile.

'Hey, smart Alec, what's with all the big words?' Derek says.

I snort, then pause in the middle of grabbing my toothbrush. With one hand over my mouth, I turn to Derek. 'Derek, did you take your meds this morning? I can't remember.'

'Yes. I've told you before, Mary, you don't need to keep worrying. I'm fine.'

'I'm sorry, Derek, I know you're good at remembering. It's just because I know how important it is, I worry. And I don't understand why you won't just have the depot injection like Marcie, Sophie, and Rachel every month?'

Derek shrugs, and his mouth turns down at the corners. 'I know the depot's a good idea for loads of people, but I just don't like to hand over control so completely. You might think the other reason I don't want the depot is silly, but… when I take my medication in tablet form, it makes it feel more like an everyday thing to do that everyone does. You know, like… I'm just taking vitamin supplements in the morning with my breakfast, or something. All good folks. Nothing strange here.'

My eyes squint as I listen between the lines of Dereks words. Emotion wells up inside me, and still gripping my toothbrush, I address his reflection in the mirror saying, 'D. taking your medication *is* a normal thing to do. You're absolutely perfect, just the way you are.'

Derek clears his throat and drops a kiss on my head. 'Isn't that line from a famous romantic film?'

The unexpected comment clears the intensity of the moment and makes me laugh out loud. 'Flipping Marcie. She's screwed up my mind with all that shit she keeps making me watch.'

'How *is* Marcie? We haven't heard from her in a while.'

We pull apart, and Derek passes me the toothpaste. We're in front of the mirror, stacked behind each other in the tiny bathroom. I speak around a mouth full of foam. 'Marcie's good, I think. She dropped me a text yesterday on her way round Rachel and Sophie's. She said all's good in the hood.'

Derek nods. 'Great. Let's have an early night then,' he says.

CHAPTER THIRTEEN

D erek's car, Rocky, zooms along the country lanes framing the lush waves of green fields on each side. Occasional sprinklings of wildflowers decorate the landscape, their pretty colours dancing in the light summer breeze.

Despite the weight of the case we're here to help with, I can feel that being surrounded by nature is having a rejuvenating effect on my outlook. 'Look, Derek, the flowers all look like they're waving at us as we drive by,' I say, smiling.

Derek chuckles. 'The scenery's beautiful in Hampshire, isn't it, Mary?'

'It certainly is,' I agree, then I point out the window. 'Look D, sheep!'

Derek grins at my enthusiasm, and I fall quiet again before pushing the button to open my window. In the car's silence, it makes a satisfying *voooooom* sound. Feeling centred, I lean out of the window, inhaling the fresh air with a goofy smile on my face.

'You love it here, don't you, Mary?'

'Yes, I've been looking at the local neighbourhood social media group. They're offering to volunteer on there, swapping information about services, and talking about wild swimming. I want to do that, too. We'll be near lots of clean rivers when we move down here.' *It'll be perfect for raising our kids.*

'That sounds nice, beautiful. Whatever you want. So, what did Jay say this morning when you rang him?'

I depress the button again and my window zips up. With a sigh, I turn the radio on, putting a classical station on and keeping it low. *Maintain my chill mood. It will help with whatever's to come.* 'He said he's looked into Oliver and can't find anything on him. Apparently, the guy looks clean, a pillar of the community. Ultra-respectable.'

'Hmm. They're the worst ones sometimes. Remember the good doctor, Adelia Sinclair? Anyway, we'll have to think of an excuse to get you close to him.'

'Jay said Oliver plays Bowles for a private club once a week. He should be there.'

I screw my face up, worrying about the effects of others on my psychic energy. *What if there are too many people there, and I can't distinguish this Oliver guy's aura?* As I think the question, I realise how pessimistic I'm being. *After all, I don't actually know it'll be him we're looking for. We still have two other suspects to look into. Who knows, we might get there, and Oliver Redford-Bowles' turns out to be a genuine diamond of a man. Nice, kind, noble. Yeah, right, because rich people are always like that.* My lips twitch.

'What's funny?' Derek asks.

'How can you tell I'm thinking about something funny?' I say. 'Watch the road, buster.'

'I'm always watching you, Mary, remember that.'

'Mmm, how creepy,' I say, then place my hand upon his as it rests on the steering wheel, savouring the connection buzzing between us. When we touch, I absorb the pleasure that grows in concentric circles of positive feeling. With a content sigh, I turn back to admiring the scenery.

'So pretty here. I feel so blessed,' I say, as our navigation system announces we have reached our destination.

'You find grandson. Find Patryk.' Monika's monosyllabic voice says from the back seat. A quick glance tells me she's sitting in the back and John's still with her. *Oh for crying out loud! Can't they leave me alone for a while? I told them I'm looking. What more do they want?*

'It's tiny, isn't it? I'll look for somewhere unobtrusive to park.'

'Yes, lovely. Really picturesque. What about over there? That looks like a car park, near the enormous field with the horses over there?' I point, quickly stretching out my arm to the left.

Derek pulls into the open parking, and we step out of the car onto the gravel. We both stretch out, arms up, stiff after the journey, and I yawn.

'Tired, baby? Will you be OK to do this? I bet it takes a lot out of you.'

'Yeah, I'll be fine. I'm not planning on hugging up to the man. I'll just get in his vicinity. Close enough to see if anything drifts out to me or not. I dunno, it's not a science, but I think I'll know what I'm looking for when I see it. Or him.'

'OK, let's go for a wander around the village, find this Bowles place, see what we can see.'

'See what we can see,' I repeat. The phrase reminds me of Jay. Then Eileen's attractive face flashes into my mind, and the shadow of a smile passes over my face.

The village is small and quaint, with cottages dotted along. There are a few streets leading off the main road, which have private property signs up.

'Hmmm... exclusive,' I remark.

'Any idea whereabouts the club is?' Derek asks.

'Turn right.' As my phone speaks, I hold it up to Derek's face, waggling it. 'I'm on it already. I got Jay to text me the address when we were on our way here.'

Derek gives an impressed nod of his head, and we follow the instructions until we arrive at an immaculately cut hedge. Simultaneously, we look at each other with raised brows. 'Remind you of anywhere?' he says.

255

'Yeah...' I nod. 'The Rainbow Unit's grounds all over again. Freaky. Maybe all rich people have similar tastes in landscaping, aye?'

'Well, maybe, but thinking about it, maybe not all. Rachel and Sophie are loaded, and they have a cool, artsy back garden with funky art in it and stuff. No symmetrical hedges or colour-coded flower borders there.'

With a nod, I agree with Derek, slipping my hand into his. It's eerily reminiscent of the perfection that was the grounds at *The Rainbow Unit*. I shake my head, clearing my dark memories like glitter in a snow globe. Then I search for the entrance, craning my neck as I glance round.

'Let's pretend we're looking at properties nearby, and want to scope out different locations,' Derek says. 'We'll give them the names Jay told us to use for the flat: Teresa and Henry.'

'Good idea.' With a squeeze of his arm, I walk towards the entrance, and he moves with me like the trail from a boat.

There's a young woman in a small reception kiosk and I step up to her saying, 'Hi, we're Teresa and Henry James. We're hoping to move to this area soon, so we thought we'd take a look at what's available socially.' I smile widely, holding her gaze for a few seconds, before lowering it. When I do, I notice she's wearing a name badge that says *Daisy*.

'How lovely! Here at the Bowles Club we welcome prospective members. I'd be happy to offer you a day here free of charge, complete with a complementary lunch for you both?'

'Oh my goodness that's so generous - we'd love that, Daisy, thank you so much,' I exclaim. Then I lean forward, conspiratorially, 'I don't suppose we'd be able to have a look round at all would we? The grounds looked so beautiful - didn't they, Henry?' I say, warming to my 'country club persona.' My lips twitch when I see Derek stare at me blankly. *He's forgotten who Henry is.*

'I'd be happy to give you a tour, Mr. and Mrs. James.' With a smile, Daisy offers us a guided tour of the premises. She chats casually as we go from one high-ceilinged room to another, smiling greetings to members as we walk around, confident the club will impress. *I don't blame her. This shit looks super nice. Open fire, Chesterfields in a common room, antique leather-bound books on the shelves. Bowles club. Old money, baby. Old school.* Behind Daisy, I stop mid-step, clutching at my stomach as it suddenly lurches violently. Panicked, my gaze flies to Derek's, and I grip his forearm with desperation.

'What?' he hisses.

I feel the blood draining from my face like the water from a bath, and my attention follows suit, swirling, swirling, down and down. Until it connects. My eyelids lower, feeling heavy. Almost too burdensome for me to open, as though they're anchored down with matching lead weights. *Shit.* Nausea rises and I heave, retching weakly and shivering in disgust.

Slight as the noise is, it causes the young girl showing us around to turn to me enquiringly, brows raised and a polite smile on her face. The cheerful expression disappears, and she looks aghast, her gaze moving from my tight face with its ice-white complexion, to my tense grip on Derek's arm. 'What's wrong, Mrs. James? You've gone white as a sheet! Is anything the matter?' the guide asks.

Er... I'm going to say yes, sweet cheeks. With a Herculean effort I give Daisy a slight nod and wave her concern away, making a fanning gesture as though I'm just hot. At the same time, I instinctively scan for the source of my dis-ease. A lighthouse beacon scanning the horizon for interlopers. Out of nowhere a psychic gut-punch doubles me over, and my knees tremble, threatening to buckle completely.

Daisy gasps, and I hear her worriedly call my name, but it sounds far away, as though my ears are stuffed with cotton wool. I drag in deep breaths of oxygen, trying to stop myself from losing consciousness.

Across the gentleman's room, Oliver Bowles-Redford's brown eyes glimmer across the space that thankfully separates us. As our gazes meet, my fingertips dig even deeper into Derek's arm, and he places a protective hand around the back of my shoulders, drawing me closer to him. 'What's the matter, baby?' he whispers.

'Here,' I hiss.

Our gazes meet, locking, and I know Derek understands what ails me. *The killer is here, and it's the man we came here to check out.* 'Daisy, I think my wife could do with a spot of fresh air. Is there somewhere quiet outside we could go?' Derek says.

'Of course, I'm so sorry, Mrs. James. Please come with me, and I'll escort you out to the veranda. Can I get you a glass of water, madam? Or would either of you like a cup of tea or coffee?'

Visceral images slice into my mind's eye, and I choke out a plea, wanting nothing but to escape from them. What the hell has this psycho been doing? The flower that John shows me pours into me, filling the space behind my eyes with its innocuous Hawaiian vibe. My breaths pant out raggedly, as I'd imagine they would for a woman in labour. *Chance would be a fine thing.*

Whilst making soothing platitudes, and murmurs of concern, Daisy takes us to comfortable seating on a veranda framed with a wooden balustrade, and a view of an impossibly perfect lawn.

The short distance this puts between me and Oliver helps me to establish my equilibrium again and I straighten up, blowing out in relief. 'Bowling green?' I ask.

'Yes, that's our bowling green. People come from miles around to use it. Please take a seat. I won't be long.' Daisy's solicitude is authentic, and she hurries away, checking back over her shoulder as she goes.

'It's him, then? Oliver what's his face is the killer?' Derek asks in a low voice as soon as Daisy leaves us.

'A hundred percent. God, it was clear as day. The space is so dark surrounding him. His deeds, his... soul, maybe? They're intertwined, and so corrupt and murky. And that flower was there, too, but I don't know why. The one that John showed me.'

Derek leans forward, whispering, 'The one you saw at the séance?'

I nod, confirming. I'm not surprised Derek has remembered which flower I'm talking about. He has a mind like a steel trap and remembers everything. As I consider the flower, and the flitting images I saw when my mind connected with Oliver's, my fingers move to twist my engagement ring, then my necklace. I try to explain my visions to Derek.

'What do you think it means?' Derek asks.

Thinking about Derek's question, I touch my forehead, unconsciously trying to smooth my furrowed brow. 'I'm not sure, but I think it's important. I don't understand why, but I just know it is. The flower definitely fits somewhere in the puzzle and it's a gigantic piece.'

'Did you see anything else? Or get any strange feelings about it?'

The hand at my forehead starts to shake, making me feel like a Victorian lady of the house going into a swoon. 'It's difficult to make sense of what I experience, D, but the flower came first, and it kept floating back throughout our psychic link… there's something to do with a mother, maybe his? I'm not sure. Disappointment and worry… him feeling overwhelmingly smug and arrogant. Then screaming… and so *much* pain.' As I speak, my stomach lurches again.

Phone already in his hand, Derek assumes a take charge attitude. 'Right, I think we should call Jay right now and see if he can do anything with any of that information. Maybe he should feed your drawing of that flower into some AI software or something? See if it gets any hits. If you're OK now, Mary, I think we should leave now. Unless you want to go back to see if you get anything else from Oliver?'

'You're kidding, right? I've had all I can take for now, thanks. After experiencing that, I pray we don't need to see him ever again. Fingers crossed, Jay can dig us something up on him, without us having to get involved with surveillance or whatever. I don't think I could stomach it.'

Derek and I return to our feet, and I steady myself on the wooden rail, feeling its smooth solidity underneath my hands. Using my abdomen to force myself to take deep, slow breaths, I concentrate on pushing air in and out. Once I'm feeling more centred, I give Derek a nod and we leave.

As we move back through the gentleman's room, I scour our surroundings for Oliver. Thankfully, I can't see Oliver, but my lips curl up as I spot Daisy. She's carrying a glass of water with ice and sliced lemon floating in it. 'Sorry I took so long. Here's your water, Mrs. James. Are you sure I couldn't get either of you a cup of tea or coffee?'

'Oh, thank you, Daisy, but no,' Derek says. 'We've decided to head off now. I think Teresa here will feel better if we get some food inside her.'

Daisy's frown clears, and she smiles. 'Oh, but we have a chef onsite who creates a fantastic selection of meals. You're welcome to dine here.'

Derek smiles. 'That's very kind of you, but no thank you, Daisy. Another time we'd be glad to accept your invitation.'

As she sees us to the exit, Daisy's smile, which had been flickering throughout our polite refusal, blinks back onto full wattage. 'I understand, I always want to get home when I'm feeling poorly too. Thank you for coming to see us. I hope you feel better soon, Mrs. James, and if you do, we'd be happy to see you again in the future if you decide to visit us again.'

As we walk away, my phone vibrates in my bag, and rings out a familiar tune. It's Jay. Still a bit unsteady, I rummage around for it as Derek rolls his eyes at my usual inability to find my property. Without a word, he takes my bag from me, plucks my mobile out and passes it to me.

I answer it. 'Hi, Jay. Guess what? I've got some news for you that I think you're going to like.'

PART FOUR

CHAPTER ONE

D erek and I stroll around our future home, holding hands. My mouth is open, and my grey eyes are round with wonder as we move from room to room. 'I can't believe it,' I say, 'It's like a dream. Vivian seems as happy as we are to push this exchange through quickly. Did they really say we could complete the sale as early as next month?'

'They did, yes, and it is lovely. Although, the whole house could do with a lick of paint, the garden's completely overgrown and the bathroom needs updating.' Derek says.

I roll my eyes at his pragmatism. 'That's OK, we can just take our time. We'll have all the time in the world to get it sorted once it's ours.'

Our conversation's cut short by Rihanna's singing trills from my handbag. I'd left it hanging on the hallway coat hook, so I rush to go and take the call. 'It's Jay,' I say, hurrying for the phone. It was only yesterday since we last spoke. Surely, he hasn't found out anything yet, it's been too soon. When I answer the call, Jay's voice sounds full of urgency.

'Hello, Mary? Thanks to you and Derek, we've had a massive breakthrough,' he says.

'What? Why - what happened?'

'It was the flower. You know, the one you said was really important. Derek suggested that we feed the picture you drew into

AI software and see what it came up with. I can't believe we hadn't thought of that before! Guess where we found it?'

I scratch my head, tugging at my earlobe as I consider. 'I dunno, where?'

'On the tabletop of a VW camper van! Its design fits the picture of what John showed you perfectly. We had enough with the CCTV footage we had to search the van, and when we got forensics in there, we found strands of hair in it. Turned out, they matched John's hair and the hair of one other. Oliver and Simon both voluntarily submitted to strand DNA tests. That proved their hair was also in the van. Big surprise, aye? Simon stated it was obvious he and his cousin would have hair strands in the van, because they both use it. He said anyone could've transferred John's hair strands to the van, from any place.'

With a shiver, I think about how Oliver will now be on red alert. I ask Jay, nibbling my lip, 'Will this put Patryk in even more danger?' I say. *Oh my God, will he kill him now, hide the evidence?*

'I don't think so,' Jay says. 'Oliver can't be certain of what we know. For all he knows we're suspecting Simon as the kidnapper. After all, that's obviously why he's been using his cousin's car instead of his own. What he doesn't know is that we have you, and we *know* it's him. Plus, he has no clue that what with the fact Patryk's missing, together with my suspicion that Oliver may have him somewhere, was enough for me to get a special warrant to surveil him. You and lover-boy still up to help?'

As though she hears me call her grandson's name, Monika appears, alongside John. They're both mute, but Monika's dour visage and the pained misery in John's face make me shiver. As I picture Oliver's glimmering eyes, hiding the corruption in his simmering soul, fear grips me again. To be near that evil man. 'Oh my God.' My whisper sounds like a scream in the silent hallway. *Nope. No way.* I don't want to put myself anywhere *near* that sicko Oliver.

I flinch as I feel a hand in my hair, and whipping around, I breathe a sigh of relief to see it's Derek. His slim fingers smooth the hair from my face and tuck it behind my ear. 'What's the matter, beautiful?' he whispers, dropping a kiss on the back of my neck.

Monika and John watch on, silently. My hand covering the phone, I mouth an aside to him, not wanting Vivian to hear any of our discussion. 'The police've got some evidence on Oliver, and Jay's asking if we can help.'

'I'm in if you are,' Derek says.

I think for a moment before uncovering the phone again. 'Derek said he'll help, and I'm...' *What exactly am I? Scared shitless? Like I have a really bad feeling about all this? If I spoke to Eileen, she'd say to hell with the case, just tell Jay to piss off, and go with my gut instinct. But then I'd have to live with that. And with Monika and John appearing whenever they feel like it, young John with his mangled rage and tortured face, and Monika, with her sour face like a bulldog chewing a wasp.* My sigh is so deep, it seems to come from the soles of my feet.

Impatient, Jay asks, 'What is it, Mary? Are you alright to pitch in?'

'Yeah. I'll help too,' I say. *Why does it feel like I just put the final nail in my own coffin?*

'Great news - brilliant! Thank you both so much. Listen, I'll brief you both again in a couple of hours. Things're moving fast here.' Jay's voice is hopeful and imparts his joy at the developments. He sounds so elated that it *nearly* balances the melancholy that Errol's silent form holds, as he materialises in the doorway next to Monika and John, watching us.

Nearly. I swallow, throat suddenly dry.

Errol's figure blinks, once... twice... three times, and then he is gone. *Vanished, like a cosmic hiccup.* A second later, Monika and John evaporate too. My eye twitches and my hand drifts up to stem the movement. *This is so messed up.*

265

The drive to visit Jay and his small team doesn't take long. An entire house was booked in order to preserve the security and confidentiality of the investigation, and the whole police team are residing here. After several minutes of discussion, they all look impressed by Derek's professional air. My fiancé, usually soft and reserved, has assumed a take-charge manner, confident in his abilities.

'OK, so we're posing as a couple who're staying in a rented place Mary found us. As per your request, Jay, we're using aliases, Teresa and Henry James, and pretending to everyone that we're looking for a property in this village,' Derek says. 'Can I ask what kind of surveillance you're instigating? Do you have a surveillance van, or will you plant a device on his property? You could also just surveil remotely?'

I slip my hand into Derek's, staring up and blinking as I recognise the arsehole police officer, Paul. *Why's he even here? He's just a nasty, annoying, prick – he might even put me off what I need to do.* While the police tech guy communicates with Derek in what seems like another language, I suck in a deep breath. 'We can conduct interception of communication equipment interference.' Derek and the other man, Ethan, bandy around what I guess are industry terms, while I gawp in awe.

Voice confident, Derek says, 'Thanks, Ethan, for filling me in. I have a bit more of an idea about what's being done now. Jay, would you mind letting me know what's happening with the rest of the plan?'

'So, the rest of the team I'm keeping quite small, but we'll conduct direct surveillance. You know, tailing the suspect, taking photographs, video for evidence. Watching who Oliver interacts with and where they go. I understand you'll be hacking into all of his internet interactions for us, but I'd also like something planted inside the house. Then I can listen in. We've borrowed a device that uses radio waves to pinpoint bodies through walls. It doesn't provide an image, but it can show movement, so if there's anyone breathing inside his house, we'll know about it. Hopefully, the device we put in there will give us more to go on.'

Derek nods, then with a smile says, 'By the way, if you wanted me to help, I wouldn't actually need a surveillance van. I've got my own equipment.'

Jay smiles, nodding. 'Oh, I don't doubt that, Derek. Not to worry, though, we'll be using the van for our direct surveillance. Ethan's in charge here, and he tells me we can observe and record, access CCTV and drones from there, too.' Jay turns to me. 'Mary, I'd like you to visit the house, see if you can get any sense about where Patryk was taken, please.'

'Basically, do my usual?' I ask, a wry smile on my face.

'Absolutely.' Jay beams at me like a proud father, but then frowns down at my fingers. They're non-stop fiddling with my engagement ring. As soon as I see his gaze on my restless hands, I clench them into a fist then put them behind my back, like a child hiding something.

'Eileen said to tell you she's on her way down here,' Jay says. 'She should get here this afternoon. She had some things to tie up first, with her other work.'

'Oh, that's good,' I say. *Eileen always helps me to feel calm, and I need that right now. The sick feeling in my stomach is growing, second by second.*

Jay claps his hands together, sending the occupants of the room scurrying like so many worker bees. 'Right, then. Let's go see what we can see.'

'See what we can see,' I mumble. *Sounds good, Jay, but sometimes, that's not such a great idea.*

CHAPTER TWO

W e climb the stone staircase and Derek puts the key in the door, jiggling it around. Standing behind him, I linger on the doorstep of the small flat, enjoying the warmth of a tiny patch of sunlight. It's on the first floor. The basement apartment underneath has a pristine lawn, framed elegantly with a picket fence. I was sad to say goodbye to the 'B&B' near our future home, but I'd rented this flat in our fake names so we could keep up our cover story in the village.

'This looks like it'll be an adorable little flat, actually. The location's beautiful! Don't you think, *Henry*?' I say, gazing around as we approach it.

Derek blinks, but there's not much of a gap before he says, 'Yes. Gorgeous area. You did well finding it, *Teresa*.'

'Any luck with that door yet?'

Derek gives the key one more wiggle and the lock twists, finally granting us access. It opens to show a standard-looking hallway, and we enter, walking around the layout of the flat.

'Oh. Well, the outside is more impressive than the inside, I have to say,' Derek says.

'Yeah, I agree. The inside's mid.'

Derek furrows his brow. 'What's that mean? 'Mid?''

I grin. 'It's slang for mediocre. How do you not know that? You being a cutting-edge hacker and everything.'

'I don't know; slipping, I guess. Shall we have a proper look around and a quick drink? Then I'll nip out and get all our stuff from Rocky.'

'OK, yeah, c'mon then. I'll help. Why did Jay choose Teresa as my alias? I actually hate that name.' I say.

Derek chuckles, peeking behind the curtains in the bedroom, and I bounce on the double bed, wrinkling its pretty floral spread.

'Well, at least you're not Henry,' Derek says, peering in the wardrobe and pulling out drawers.

'Still better than Teresa. That name sucks.'

'Ah, come here, Terry. 'A rose by any other name would smell as sweet,' remember that.'

I purse my lips, accepting my kiss, then hold my arms out for a hug. 'What does that mean?'

'You don't know? I think it's a famous line from one of Shakespeare's plays. It just means it doesn't matter what you're *called*. It's what you *are* that matters.'

'Hmm, I really like that. I've never heard of it before. Probably because I skipped most of my school career. Hated it.'

Sometime later, Derek has set up his laptop as he wants, and is slouching around, scrolling on his mobile while I've unpacked all of our non-technical belongings neatly.

'What listening device is being planted, then? A lamp or something?' I ask.

He looks up from his phone briefly. 'Not quite. I told Jay the first thing I'd use is an earbud.'

'How d'ya mean? Hide a pretend one in there?'

Derek's lips twist into a smile, and he shakes his head. 'No, I mean just regular old earbud pros. They're already a potential listening device. You just need to access the control centre, tap on a particular icon, then place them in front of whomever you want to eavesdrop on. It's fine if we turn the volume up.'

'No shit? That's so cool, but also really scary. Would you ever earwig on me?'

'What? You mean would I tap into your riveting conversations with Marcie about your weirdo movie club? Er, no, beautiful. That's a hard pass from me. You can rest easy.'

'What? How dare you?' I smirk. 'We have many interesting conversations. You should be so lucky to spy on us – Monika, Christ! What're you doing here?' I say, one hand shooting to cover my heart as I flinch in shock.

Monika's stoic face observes us from the corner of the room. Despite the lack of warmth in her features, I notice she's holding hands with John. Somehow, that makes her expression seem tender. John stares out of his ruined face, and I can't remember how I ever found him threatening. *He actually breaks my heart now.* Saying nothing, I meet their gazes, and my own is stony with resolve. *I'm so sorry for what he did to you, John. Oliver is going down. No matter what. He won't get Patryk. We will get that little boy home you wait and see. I'll do whatever it takes, I promise.*

A knock at the door interrupts my contemplation. Derek and I stare at each other, and brows knitted, we both head towards the intrusion. So I'm not distracted by John and Monika, I close off my reception to the dearly departed, putting my powers on mute for now.

A tall brunette woman stands by the entrance. I crane my neck to look up at her sharply pointing chin and narrow nostrils. She's dressed in a tweed skirt and blazer, with a polo jumper. She has her arms folded across her small chest, and her foot is tapping. Clearly, her height isn't something she is conscious of, because she's wearing three inch black, patent heels. Not waiting for our greeting, she verbally interposes on us.

'Hello. I'm Victoria Bartholomew. You must be the holiday renters.' Her accent drips with privilege, and I get a better look at Victoria's long, horsey features. On closer inspection, I know my mum might have described Victoria as an 'unfortunate-looking woman.' I don my professional persona like a cloak of invisibility. 'Hello, Victoria, so nice to meet you. Yes, that's right. We're renting from Imogen and Saul. Are you the lady from the flat downstairs?'

Victoria's gaze drops to my shoes, then back up to my face, her thinly plucked eyebrows raised. 'The lady downstairs is correct. Imogen and Saul were considerate upstairs neighbours and I have their contact details. I trust I shan't have any issues with you during your stay.'

My, my Vicky... that's not very neigh-bourly, is it? Horse-face. Lips pinned together, I smile.

'Of course not, Victoria, and thanks for stopping by to introduce yourself. It's so kind of you. I'm Teresa, and this is Henry.'

'Pleased to meet you, Victoria,' Derek says. 'Sorry, but I'm afraid we have a viewing appointment and must leave now.'

Even though he's effectively dismissing her, Victoria responds more positively to Derek's statement than she does to mine. She grants him a tight smile, stretching her thin lips and giving her face a strained appearance. After we close the door on her, Derek and I turn to each other.

'Your mate Vicky looked like she needed to take a shit,' I quip, causing Derek to give a crack of laughter.

'She wasn't what you'd call 'warm,' was she?' Derek says.

'Hardly. She had a hair up her arse about something, I know that. Ah, well, forget her. Let's just get this show on the road. I have to find that psycho again.'

'Exactly, and I need to hear how Jay's team plans to stick the listening devices in Oliver's house... or on him.'

Derek holds out his palm to me as we cross the road. I give him an old-fashioned look, but accept it, and we swing it together as we pick our way across the cobbled path. Bird-song trills in the foreground like a dainty theme tune, and the serenity of our surroundings sweetens my mood, soothing me like a warm bath.

I point to a striking black-and-white plumage to the right of us, 'There's a magpie. I think that means good luck?' I smile at Derek, my other hand squeezing his gently in my pleasure at spotting the majestic bird. *Or something about luck?*

'I know, why don't we head back to the Bowles place again now, get it over and done with? That girl, Daisy, at reception seemed really nice. I bet she'd let us in again. Maybe she has some info or something about Oliver if we ask her.' *Then I won't have to pollute my psychic senses with Oliver's toxins if I link with him and might get some clues to help find Patryk.*

'Good idea, beautiful.'

'Thanks, D. See, I'm not just a pretty face, am I?'

Derek grins. 'You're smiling like you do when you've been on a night out with the girls. You look drunk.'

'Oi. I was feeling all loved until then. You ruined it. For yourself.' I pout.

'Oh my God, shoot me now - I take it back. What've I done?'

I laugh. 'Idiot. Anyway, maybe if Daisy lets something slip about Oliver, I won't have to get close to him again. By the way, I meant to ask you. Earlier, when you were talking about listening devices, you said it in plural form? Is there something else other than the earbuds you can use to listen in on people then?'

'Oh, yes. You can utilise quite a few things as listening devices, really; an air freshener, phone charger, smoke detector. I could attach something to his credit card if I could get hold of it, or his car key fob, a pen. I could even make use of a plug socket in his house.'

'No way? That's so mind blowing, but... Oliver will be well wary now because they asked him for his DNA sample. How can they get any of that stuff into his house without him suspecting?'

Derek and I step into the entrance of the private club, smiling at the young woman who greets us at the door. It's not the same *woman as before,* but they could have been sisters. Similar age, same clear, shiny eyes, and same bouncy ponytails. *Jane* is equally as friendly as her predecessor, and after hearing we were checking out the local area, she's just as eager to show us around. After dropping some hints that we're curious, however, it's obvious Jane doesn't know a word of gossip about any of the members. Or if she does, she's not letting on.

As we head towards the wood panelled common room, I return to our previous conversation, keeping my voice low as I suggest, 'Perhaps Jay could get someone in there using some kind of ruse?'

'Probably that's what they're planning. Ethan didn't say exactly. I'm thinking they could cause a flood outside, and Jay'll have one of his lot go in, pretending to be a plumber or something. Then they'd plant the devices.'

'Babe, you're *so* clever. Yes, something like that would be good. We can call Jay to check what he's gonna do when we get back. Meanwhile, I'll do what I came here to do. Get close to this guy and try to collect some psychic intelligence.'

We take a seat in one of the studded leather armchairs near the open fire. Holding my hands up and out towards the heat, I study the large room. After scanning the dozen club guests for Oliver's features, I can see he isn't here. The room is mostly filled with men, but there are also one or two women sitting with them. Just as there was a resemblance between the two greeters, Jane and Daisy, so too do the women present share similarities with Victoria Bartholomew. I note there are no spontaneous introductions, although we're the subject of covert scrutiny. The sneering looks and collective shut-out, tells me we are not being viewed as desirable club member candidates.

We chat with each other in the common room for another hour. No one makes conversation with us, except the girl who showed us to our seats, and the guy who offered us drinks. *Huh. What a bunch of stuck-up pricks.* 'This is dry-up, babe, and Oliver's a no-show. Let's just go back to the flat for now. We can stroll around town this evening and have a nosy. Also, we can check what time and how Jay's getting those gadgets in there and have a think about how I can link up with Oliver another way.'

'Yeah, alright. It's stuffy in here, and boring. Why don't we have a walk around now, then go back and shower together? Then we can get an early night,' Derek says.

'One track mind.' I roll my eyes, but I'm not complaining. An early night of cuddling and being close to Derek sounds like bliss, especially after being frozen out by the 'up-their-own-arse' brigade. I rise, gracefully holding out my hand towards Derek. 'Let's go, Henry.' I grin into his devilishly cheerful face. *Always so easily pleased is Derek. Despite his profession, his private life is an open book. His feelings are uncomplicated. I love that about him.*

CHAPTER THREE

The walk around the village is uneventful, and the tranquillity pours salve on the irritation I'd felt while we sat in the toff club. The people who stroll by, with their dogs, or just out for a walk, are friendly, greeting us as we pass. By the time we return to the flat, my mood's restored and my mind's made up. *I need to somehow psychically connect with Oliver again so I can help find clues about Patryk's whereabouts. If only I'd been prepared the first time we went to the Bowles Club. Now, the only way I can think of is to go to his home, but I can't think of a way to get in. Hopefully, Jay will come up with an idea.*

We call Jay, and Eileen takes over, asking, 'What are you thinking, Mary? Don't you think this is too much for you or Derek? You know, there are actual police officers who can and *should* take charge of this investigation,' she says, direct as usual.

Jay protests in the background, 'Eileen, come on, that's not fair.'

'Is it not, Jay?' Eileen asks. 'Oh, I think it is. You have these two out on a limb here, and you know it.'

A sharp silence rings in my ears and I push my hair behind my ear, nibbling my lower lip. *This is so awkward. I hadn't expected Eileen to respond like this to my question about how we could sneak into Oliver's home so I could forge a connection with him.* I tell her, 'It's OK, Eileen. We signed up for this. We want to help.'

'Yes, it's fine Eileen,' Derek adds. 'We know what we're doing.'

Eileen answers, her Scottish accent thicker and faster, and I know this signifies the strength of emotion she's feeling. 'With respect, Mary and Derek, no, you don't. You're not police officers, and this person might be a killer. God knows what he might have done to that bairn John, and he may still have poor wee Patryk. If you're not concerned about the strain on your mental health, then think about the physical danger here. In my eyes, you've both done enough, and it's time for you to go on home now.'

My heart floods with affection for Eileen, so plain speaking and full of fierce mother hen protectiveness for her chicks. *Scared as I am of Oliver, part of me yearns to agree with her, and I know that although Derek might not agree, he'd do what I want. He always does. The decision's up to me.* Behind my eyes, I see the desolate figures of John and Monika, standing earlier in the corner. I remember my promise and steel myself. 'No, Eileen. We won't leave until it's done. I can't go home. Patryk needs me, and so does John. Also, I know the police have superb officers, but they're not able to do what I can do, and Jay thinks that might give them the edge they need to find Patryk. If we don't stay, *maybe* the police will get Oliver eventually, stop him from taking another little kiddie. But poor Patryk will be gone. I know it, and I can't have it. I won't.' *I think about Errol, appearing, trying to tell me something but blinking away.* A cold cramp grips my heart, making my legs tremble, but I push my shoulders back, squaring them. *Whatever the cost, I need to stay.*

Derek holds my free hand, and it stops trembling.

Eileen's cracked whisper nearly melts my resolve. 'But what if something bad happens to *you*, lass? *I* can't have that.'

'Nothing will happen to me, Eileen. I'll have Derek with me, and Jay and a whole team of police officers available,' I tell her firmly. *If it's me or Patryk, it'll have to be me. I know love is waiting for me on the other side. I have nothing to fear about going home to The Blue. But Patryk's too young and he's suffered too much. He should get to go home to his parents, enjoy living some of his life.*

'We'll be fine, Eileen,' Derek chimes in. 'We'll be really careful. Plus, if you let Jay speak, he'll be able to tell us how we can go about things in the safest way.' Derek's voice is molasses on biscuits, and Jay's snort at the 'if you let Jay speak,' comment, reminds us all he's still there. He has not taken offence at Eileen's direct challenge to his leadership decisions. The detective inspector takes charge of the call again.

'Thanks for that, Eileen. For the record, guys, I would just like to say that your safety and wellbeing is important to *me,* too. It might not always seem that way, but I do care.'

'I know you do, Jay,' I tell him.

Jay clears his throat, and when he speaks again, it's back to business. 'Anyway, about planting these listening devices. Derek, that's not a bad idea of yours. We won't vandalise Redford-Bowles' property to get in, but what if we have a bogus gas technician? We could pretend there's a gas emergency and knock on a few local doors? Derek and Ethan can prep them for what to do. What do you think?'

I search Derek's face for his response, and he nods into my mobile in reply. 'Yes, that could work. It's not that difficult to place the items. If Ethan sets everything up, whoever goes in just needs to put them there and leave. Then you'd be able to listen in.'

'Great, I can choose an officer today, brief them with instructions and have them go in tomorrow.'

'That'd be perfect,' Derek says.

Jay's tone deepens as he says, 'OK. Mary, now about you going in... I have to agree with Eileen on this one. I don't think you should go into Redford-Bowles' house. There's no way I'd get the green light for that, and God forbid anything happened to you. My head would be on the chopper, and besides, I'd never forgive myself - whatever Eileen believes. Ethan is sorting the surveillance equipment, and we'll use that. We can covertly insert some devices that appear as though they belong in situ at Oliver's home. The operative I send can also leave an object they'll tell Oliver they'll need to collect at a later time. That way, he'll have had direct contact with it when he accepts it and hands it back. You'll be able to touch that object and we can utilise your gifts that way instead. Are you up for that? It's your call.'

'Sounds like a plan,' I say. *If I'm honest, I never felt happy about going into Oliver's home, so this way's much better.*

I hear Jay clap his hands together in satisfaction. 'Great! Come over to the house tonight and take a look at the objects we'll be placing in Oliver's. Maybe there's something that you'd prefer them to leave?'

'Yeah, good idea. We'll come in a little while when it's dark. We've got a right nosy cow downstairs from us.'

Jay says, 'No problem, text me when you're leaving, please, Mary. I have something I want you and the rest of my team to hear. It's an important reminder of why we're here.'

CHAPTER FOUR

T he village is hushed as we walk back to the flat adding a stillness to the atmosphere. Our footsteps echo against the cobbles as we walk, and I grimace as the puddles of rainwater flick up against my calves. *Eww*. My mouth feels dry, and I clear my throat before speaking, my voice coming out rusty. 'Well, that turned out to be a fun-packed evening.'

Derek nods, agreeing. 'Hmm. Very emotional. That poor woman.'

'I know. Patryk's mum is in pieces. It was so devastating to hear her, crying out, desperate for us to help find her son.' *It'd been so painful to hear the voicemail Patryk's mother, Iryna had left for Jay, but I understood why he'd shared it.*

As we near the stairs leading up to our rented flat, Derek squeezes my hand. I'd seen his own eyes had been brimming with tears as we listened to Iryna's message. Without knowing what we had planned for tomorrow, Iryna had contacted Jay. She'd been begging him to find Patryk, help him, pleading with Jay, 'Please don't forget my baby boy. He needs you. Please find him. Do what you can to save him.'

As we'd listened to the message, Eileen had gripped my hand, tears rolling down her face, and I'd stared back at her silently, speechless as I'd wiped my own tear-soaked face. *Unbearable*.

Derek said, 'We were only supposed to go over the listening devices and instructions. I almost wish Jay hadn't played the message to us all. I don't really know why he did that, to be honest.'

My smile is sad as I answer. 'I do.'

'You do?'

'Well, I think so? I reckon it was to fire us up,' I say, 'You know, so we understand the reality of the stakes.'

'Well, I think that's out of order. Jay knew it would devastate us all when we heard Patryk's mum sobbing her heart out. It's manipulative.'

'No, Derek, Jay was right to share it. We *do* need to remember Patryk and his parents. This isn't a game; a little boy's life is on the line. Eileen was right earlier when she said we're taking an enormous risk, but after hearing how broken Iryna is, we'll remember and know why we have to do this. We have to find Patryk, no matter what.'

Derek stops, still holding my hand and pulls me closer, dropping a kiss on the end of my nose. 'You're beautiful. Inside and out.'

Warmth zings between us, and Derek rests his forehead against mine. We pull apart, anxious to get back to the flat. Walking quickly, it seems like only seconds pass before we reach the house we rented, tiptoeing up the concrete stairs to the flat. Mindful of Victoria Bartholemew downstairs, we're careful not to make too much noise. Derek scrapes the key in the lock, and the sound seems overly loud.

'Shhh…you'll wake up the grinch down there,' I say.

The creaking front door makes me slap a hand over my nervous smile, and as we step inside and the door shuts, our gazes meet. Tension twangs between us. Derek gathers me to him, kissing me with reverence, and smoothing the hair back from my face. 'I love you so much, Mary.'

'And I love you, too, Derek.'

As we kiss, we move to the bedroom. There's no time for anything as our passion mounts, except for each other and the silent union between us. *We are one. Where Derek ends and I begin, I can't tell. We have no solid outline, and our lovemaking has morphed us into a single being. Transmuted. Love, bonded.* I notice a banging underneath us, and seated over Derek, I still my hips. He groans in protest, and I drop a kiss on his lips, silencing him. 'Can you hear that?' I ask.

'What?'

'That knocking noise underneath us?' I say.

We both listen intently. The clattering on the floor sounds out again, but this time, I hear the demand that accompanies it. 'Be quiet up there!'

'Urgh. It's that crusty bitch from the flat downstairs,' I say.

'No! What a cheek.'

Derek and I share a look, and then collapse in paroxysms of laughter.

'She's got a dog's chance of us stopping. Let's give her something to really complain about, shall we, D?'

'Most definitely. Come back here, beautiful.'

Heat builds steadily between us, until, thighs slick with sweat, I crumple. First, onto Derek's chest, where we share a hug and a kiss, and then onto my side, panting. The clanging from downstairs has subsided. Victoria apparently gave up her attempts to quench our ardour.

Derek goes to the bathroom, then returns and tucks the covers all around me.

'D'ya wanna take a shower together, D?' I ask in a drowsy murmur.

'No thanks, Mary. I'll have one in a little while. I need a drink first; I'm really thirsty. Want a cup of tea ready for you when you get out of the shower?'

'Yes, please, that'll be perfect.' I throw the covers off us both, and Derek chuckles as I do an awkward tiptoe dance to the bathroom. I shut the door to give me some privacy and start the water. Once the temperature is right, I step into the shower. After drying, I dress myself in my favourite cotton pyjamas, then brush my teeth. Shaking my head, I notice blue toothpaste in the sink, and bend down to sluice some water at it with my hand. As I straighten, I flinch as I catch sight of Errol standing right behind me. 'ForfupshakeEwwol.' My mouth is full of toothpaste, and I cannot annunciate the words I'm trying to say. I raise a hand to my heart, miming its pounding out of my chest. 'Wanwer.'

Errol's slight smile tells me he knows exactly what I'm saying, but I spit out the toothpaste anyway, rounding on him. 'What the actual hell're you doing, Errol? What did we say about you creeping up on me like this? You're out of order, man.'

'I know, Mary, but-' Errol's voice cuts out, and as I stare at him, my expression gurns, bewildered.

'Whatever's the matter, Errol?' I ask. 'Tell me.'

'I love you, Mary, and I need to-' Whatever my friend is trying to tell me is *expunged*, his words censored. Errol's features are grim, and as I try to work it out, his edgy anxiety transfers itself to me. As I watch him, his figure blinks. He blinks once, twice, before he disappears like a candle flame.

'What was all that about?' I wonder aloud. Meeting my own grey gaze in the mirror, I set about brushing my hair, pondering what Errol's appearance means. He wants to tell me something, and it's urgent. It will obviously affect the plan that the cosmos, or whatever, has for me. *The angsty bastard.* 'It's obviously something to do with this case, and my safety.'

Derek knocks on the bathroom door. 'Is everything OK in there?'

Unbidden, a picture of Patryk flits into my mind, and my fingers go to touch the hair that curls sweetly at the back of his neck. *An older boy now, he even has armpit hair. Next year, he'll go to big school.* My thoughts move to Iryna and her husband, the first time I saw them on TV. It was in the news interview, leaning on each other, their faces ravaged by grief. Finally, Iryna's strained voice from tonight, resonating through the room where Jay and the rest of the police were. Her desperate pleas filled the space, thick with sorrow. She'd been repeating herself, begging for help to find her son like a broken mantra that drew on my heart like a rusty knife. Looking down, I touch my hand to my own flat stomach. *I have to keep helping Patryk get back to his mum, no matter what.* I call out to Derek through the door, 'Everything's fine, babe. I'll be out in a second.'

'OK. Tea's out here when you're ready. I'm jumping back into bed.'

'OK,' I say, wiping my sweaty palms down my pyjama legs and slowing my breathing down. *It will be OK in the end. As long as Patryk gets to go back home to his parents, even if it means I have to return to The Blue.*

I get into bed with a childish hop that makes Derek smile, and I snuggle up to him, clutching him tightly. As I mentally unwind, I tap into our deep, shared bond of devotion, watching the vibrant hues our connection creates. My contented sigh captures Derek's attention, earning me a gentle kiss on my forehead and a caress on my head. 'My hair's still damp,' I warn him.

'I don't care. I'll take you anyway I can get you.' Derek scrunches his face. 'Are you OK, Mary? It was a lot to deal with tonight. You seem quiet.'

'I'm fine, don't worry.'

The arm that Derek's placed round my shoulder gives me an affectionate squeeze, then lifts to pick up his phone. He starts scrolling, quickly becoming engrossed in the internet.

I don't groan as I usually would at his addiction to the shiny black interface. Instead, I cuddle in closer to his side. Drowsily, I enjoy the interplay only I can see, strands that are flowing from us both, moving and drifting in the air like the fronds of a magical jellyfish. *Beautiful...*

CHAPTER FIVE

*T*ap, tap, tap, tap.

The nervous energy inside me hasn't dissipated since I woke up, making my stomach clench and cramp into a tight knot of tension. Hearing the tapping sound, I stop wiping down the kitchen's already clean worktops, turning my head to gaze at the window. Momentarily, my mood's lifted, and a smile of joy spreads across my face as I watch the pretty robin redbreast perched just outside. Its song chirps out amongst the other birds. I call out to Derek who's sitting at the table, staring down at the phone in his hand. 'D! Come look at this, there's a little robin at the window.'

'That's nice, beautiful.' The disinterest in Derek's voice is clear, and my face screws up in frustration. *He's not even looking.* 'It's really cute, Derek, come and see it before it goes.' Enthralled, I sneak towards the window, moving as slowly as I can, to avoid scaring it.

The tiny bird looks up, its gaze locking with mine. Then it flies away. 'Oh, it flew away,' I say. I linger by the window, craning my neck to see if I can spot it somewhere else. Even though I can't see it anymore, I'm able to hear birdsong outside the window. I fancy I can discern the voice of the tiny robin amongst it. I turn round to check if Derek's got up yet and frown at him as I feel the stress falling back upon my shoulders. 'You're still looking at your phone. You missed the robin, D, it's gone.'

'Oh. That's a shame, love.'

'Are you gonna look at that thing all day or what?' I ask, fed up with being ignored.

At my snappy question, Derek glances up, blinking.

I swear if he doesn't put that phone down for a change, I'm gonna lose my shit. 'What's the plan for this morning?' I ask. 'Do you need to be in here or in the surveillance van when they plant the devices?'

'I'd prefer to be here. I've hooked up with Ethan remotely, so I can also hear what they pick up. Jay said that someone called Peter will go in this morning, posing as a plumber.'

'They really did like that idea, didn't they? Are they pretending there was a gas leak in the area as you suggested as well?'

Derek's cocky grin says it all, and my annoyance at his dependence on his phone evaporates slightly as I'm flooded with pride at his professional competency. Thinking about last night, triggers a memory of Errol's apropos appearance and I feel my stomach tighten again. *We have to find Patryk. Get him home.* My fingers curl into my palms. I unfurl them purposely, then find my hand straying to the necklace my mum gave me, twisting it between my index finger and thumb.

'What's wrong?' Derek asks.

God, so much… 'I just hope it all goes OK and we find Patryk, that's all. I feel sick with worry. The devices aren't being planted til midday are they?'

'That's right.' Derek nods. 'I'm feeling edgy myself, Mary. Do you want to go for a quick walk around the village? Stretch our legs before it all kicks off?'

'Yeah, great idea. Also, what about if we go past Oliver's house, but keep out of sight, obviously.'

Derek holds out his hand to mine, saying, 'C'mon. Let's go.' He leads me towards the hallway, and as he does, my stomach cramps, and I hunch over. 'I'm feeling sick, Derek,' I say.

'What've you eaten today? Maybe it was our dinner from last night?'

'No… I don't think it's that. I think it's just nerves,' I say, then, 'Oh, yes…I need to text Marcie before we go.' I pull my phone from my back pocket and lean against the wall, 'Sorry, D, I'll just be two secs.'

'No worries, I'll just nip and sort out my hair while you do that then.'

I write a quick but heartfelt text to Marcie. Telling her how much she means to me, and how she was the first person to show me kindness and give me a good example of what a human being *could* be like.

I want you to know your friendship has meant the world to me, and I'll always be grateful to you. No matter where I am, I'll always love you as my soul sister, and part of me will always be with you. Please let Sophie and Rachel know they're also dear to my heart, that I love them both, and think the world of them. I know I don't have to ask, but please take care of Derek.

With a swallow, I push the green arrow, sending the message. *Hopefully, Marcie will be at work when she receives this text, and by the time she sees it…*

I rise, seeking Derek again. 'Come on, let's get this show on the road.' As I shrug into my coat, I turn to him, rolling my eyes as I notice his head's down and he's focusing on his phone again. 'Oh for God's sake, Derek. Lay off it for a while, aye?'

'What? Mary, you've literally just sent a text on your phone - how is that fair?' Derek says.

That's so frigging unfair, you're always on your poxy phone. I keep the words to myself, drawing in a deep breath and pushing away my rage. 'Look, what about if we both leave our phones here, so we're not tempted. We'll only be gone for half an hour, an hour at the most.'

Derek's jaw juts out and he doesn't answer right away.

As much as he's stuck to that phone, he'd better not say one word about leaving that thing here or I might throw the bloody thing out the window. Our gazes clash for a second, then Derek hands his mobile phone over to my extended hand. I move quickly back to place our two phones on the worktop surface I cleaned earlier.

Turning towards the door again, I start as simultaneously, the doorbell rings and Errol appears in the hallway, mouthing something. No sound is coming out, but his face is distraught. His usual smile's absent, his mouth turned down and his eyes wide. Errol's reaching a hand out to me, and speaking, but as has been happening so often lately, his voice is on mute. He must be blocked by the Universe again and unable to tell me what's wrong. *It's alright, Errol, I know the shit's probably gonna hit the fan in some way.*

Tiptoeing up to the front door, I stare through the spy hole, then mouth to Derek, 'Victoria.' *That's all we need right now.*

I contemplate if I should open the door or not. Our neighbour Victoria's standing on the doorstep. She has one foot rapping on the floor. She brings a slender but hairy arm upwards and glances at an elegant watch and exudes an air of suppressed disdain. Neither me nor Derek have seen any signs of aggressive behaviour, no kicking a cat when she walks by, or anything similar. But I hate her. I open the door, but immediately recoil as Victoria barks out her orders upon seeing me. 'Teresa. I've mentioned this to you and Henry before, but I insist you cut off the noise at nine p.m. This is beyond reasonable. It really is.'

I stare at Victoria, uncomprehending. My eye twitches and my hand flitters up to soothe it. I hate her voice. *Entitled cow.* My chin goes up, and I feel my small hands curl into fists as I work myself up mentally. 'It's Terry, not Teresa, and sorry, but what are you talking about? We don't even make any noise.' *I'm sure I've already told this woman to call me Terry.* My breathing quickens as I think about it. *Calm down, Mary, an argument with this woman might draw attention to us, and we definitely don't need that right now.*

Victoria's eyebrows are thin and razor-sharp like her eyes, and they raise up in disbelief, taking my temper with them. 'Well, I *am* sorry, but I beg to differ, Teresa. There have been several instances when I have heard an unbearable amount of clutter and banging from this apartment. It's simply unacceptable. I have tried to give you some neighbourly leeway, however, this has to stop. I won't have it anymore.'

My nostrils flare and I grit my teeth from shouting out my battle cry and ripping her neatly coiled hair off her head. *Bloody bitch-bag, I really can't stand her.*

Derek rests his hand on the small of my back, gently warming the area.

Relaxing my breathing, I adjust my inner eye. Usually in a rush to get in and out of our fake family home, I haven't given Victoria a psychic scan before. Detaching my attention from her dictation, I cast my focus out to her direction, just a little. I keep my focus loose, knowing I cannot completely zone out in front of her. Eyes wide, I reel back.

Victoria is emanating a cloud of inky aura I want to avoid. Hugging my waist, I shuffle backwards a few steps, glancing at Derek as I do so. The cloud snakes out towards me, as though it's seeking me out, its corrupt tendrils of oily umbilical slithering out towards me.

Eww, hell no, that will not touch me.

Victoria's eyes squint at my motion, and she smirks at me. *Has Derek clocked me moving back? It seems not, because instead of also backing up, he moves forward, now standing in between me and Victoria. No! I don't want that stuff touching him, either.*

Hands on her hips, Victoria is still talking, unaware of the change in whom she is delivering her dressing down to. 'You'll force me to contact the authorities. Do you understand what I am saying? I repeat; before nine a.m. and after nine p.m. are *sacrosanct*. I do not expect to hear *one sound* from this accommodation, or there will be repercussions.'

Frowning, I take a halting step towards Derek, to right his move and put him behind me. Instinctively, it feels wrong for me to allow someone so off in their emanations so close to my beloved. Derek can't see the smoky aura of crappy contaminants swirling all around him, but I can. I restrain myself from holding my nose, not wanting to breathe it in either.

Saying nothing to interrupt Victoria's monologue, Derek shakes his head almost imperceptibly, and puts out a hand behind his back, barring my way.

Victoria's tight lips pucker into a line, and she jerks her head around Derek's head to look at me. It's clear she dislikes me, and it's me she really wants to deliver the dressing down to.

With a frown, I look her up and down from behind Derek. Victoria and Derek are almost toe to toe, with Victoria slightly taller than my six-foot one fiancé. *Boy, she's a big one.* I peep down at her shoes, eyes widening at the size of her footwear. *They're mahoosive... no open toe sandals for you, milady.* A quick glance over my shoulder lets me know Errol has again vanished. *By choice, or by order of the Universe? If only I could work out what it is that Errol may not tell me.*

'So, I would suggest you make sure it does not happen again. Understand?' Head held high, Victoria smooths back her slicked back hair then turns, satisfied with the tongue-lashing she's delivered.

This is not a question; it's a statement.

Victoria pauses on the doorstep, and swivels back to face Derek and me. She's scowling at us and her gaze switches from one to another of us.

Stepping forward again, I squeeze around Derek and without a word of goodbye, slam the door without a second thought in Victoria's face. *Good.* 'Shall we go for that walk now, babe?' I ask Derek, eyes wide and tone innocent.

Derek grins, and expression rueful, shakes his head. 'What am I gonna do with you, Mary Jameson? Yeah, c'mon, let's go.'

CHAPTER SIX

T he village seems less quaint today, and the bite in the air makes our walk uncomfortable. The birds are not singing right now, and all I can hear are the sounds of my uneven breathing and my jeans scrish-scrashing together as I trudge along, Derek at my side. Even the brightness of the sun in the blue sky isn't cheering me up, making me squint against it.

'Have you ever noticed how nice it looks from inside on days like this? But you freeze your tits off as soon as you get outside. I hate that,' I say.

'I think it's pretty. It reminds me of a ski holiday advert. All sunshine and snow.'

'Exactly. Looks as though it's going to be eighty degrees outside, all sunny and shit. Then you get out there and it's minus ten. It's like the Universe lulls us into a false sense of security, then sucker punches you.' A flash back to another bright morning, filled with false promise comes to my mind. *When Marcie was discharged back at the Rainbow Unit… It was a morning just like this one.*

We march by dog walkers, and their smiling greetings contradict my morose theory. They don't seem bothered by the mendacity of the weather, either. When they've passed, I turn to Derek. 'It's like… it's all a big con.'

'The weather? You're talking about the sun shining on a chilly day? That's a con?'

'Well, yeah, sort of.' *Plus another little something else the Universe is conning me out of, like our life together. I feel like I might die today, Derek, and I love you so much. I know I have nothing to fear afterwards, but I don't really want to say goodbye so early. Plus, I'd really have loved to've been a mum - a good one, like mine was.* My lips purse, and it's such an effort to force back the words I want to say, I'm sure they're white with the pressure. I slip my hand in his. 'I feel like I should walk past Oliver Redford-Bowles place, just to see if I get any vibes from it. We weren't successful yesterday at the club.'

'Brr, babe, you're freezing,' Derek says. 'No wonder you're being weird and moany. Ok. Let's go walk past this psycho's house if we're going. But we'll have to be quick. Time's getting on, it'll soon be time for Jay's team to do their stuff with the devices, if they haven't already.'

'Yeah…' I murmur.

There'd been no other homes in the last fifteen minutes of our walk. Oliver Redford-Bowles house is isolated and luxurious, granting the kind of seclusion only wealth can bring. We stand, concealed by the gigantic hedges at the end of his impressive drive. Shifting my weight from side to side, I blow into my fingers, trying to warm them. *Should've worn gloves. And thicker socks.* 'My feet are like blocks of ice; they're freezing,' I say.

'Well, why don't we just go back to the flat then? You're not picking up anything, are you?'

My hand runs down my face as I consider Derek's suggestion for a few minutes. Then I cup the pendant on my necklace. It's been lying against my skin and feels warm to the touch. I take a deep breath, fortifying myself. *I don't like it one bit, but I know what I need to do. I feel it.* 'No, but I think that's because I need to be closer, that's why. I'm going to knock on the door.'

Derek narrows his eyes. 'Knock on the door? Why? We're supposed to get an object touched by Oliver, not go to his house.' He puts his hands up. 'Look, Eileen was right when she said to us Jay was wrong to get you and I involved. We aren't the police. We could get seriously hurt here, Mary.'

'Then you stay here, D. I love you, but I can't turn my back on that little boy, believing I could help. I'd never forgive myself. You wait here. Really, I'll be fine. I just want to get closer so I can feel Oliver's frequency and establish a connection.'

Derek nibbles his lower lip, which is something I rarely see him do anymore, then shakes his head. 'For crying out loud, Mary. This is putting me between a rock and a hard place. Can't we just give the police a call on our mobiles? Let them sort it?'

Our gazes meet and I know Derek's realised why we can't do that. *My insistence on leaving our mobiles indoors. I feel like such an arsehole right now, I could scream.* 'It's my fault, I know, I could kick myself. Anyway, I'm not supposed to be here and as far as the police know, their devices are in place, and everything's sound, but I sense something's off. It just feels like I need to get closer, or whatever it is will get worse. I have to form a psychic bond with Oliver, to be able to sense what he's up to. Let's come up with a reason for me to knock, maybe get inside.'

Derek's mouth opens, and he hisses, 'Jesus Christ, Mary, what? You want to go *inside* the house now?'

Silence rests between us, giving me the chance to absorb how scared Derek looks. I pin a confident smile on my face and try to look unconcerned. He can't hear my heart, banging against my chest like a jackhammer.

'I'll be fine, D. You can stay here and keep a lookout for me. If I don't come back outside within ten minutes, just run to the nearest house and ring Jay for backup.'

'Hell, no! I won't leave you alone to go in there. The nearest house is at least fifteen minutes away-What kind of man do you think I am?'

'A nice, sensible one, who doesn't go into serial killers' homes?'

Derek's expression freezes into place. Immediately, I know my choice of words had been poor. *Serial killer.*

'Well, I'm *not* completely sensible, because if you insist on going into that hell house, then I insist on coming with you.'

I sigh. 'Shit.'

'Exactly. Now let's just get this over and done with, so we can go home and have some spoons.'

Ah, bless him. Chin tilted up, I straighten my shoulders, then hold out my hand for Derek to take. 'I'm sorry to put you in the middle of this mess, D. C'mon, let's get this shit show on the road.'

Hand in hand, Derek and I walk down into the lion's den. As soon as we stop at the front door, I ring the bell. *What are the odds? It's one of those fancy bells, one that videos whoever stands on the doorstep.* Both our hands are trembling, and I remove mine and hop from one foot to the other.

A few moments later, the door opens to reveal Oliver Redford-Bowles himself, brows raised and a sneer on his face. He's attractive, with chiselled features and sandy blond hair arranged with a precise side parting. Brown eyes, almond-shaped and questioning as he looks down his nose at us. Face expressionless, he doesn't smile. I'm reminded of Victoria, and it puts steel in my spine. Brows wrinkled together, I widen my eyes and try to look pleading.

'Yes? Can I help you?'

'Hi, my name's Teresa and this is my fiancé, Henry. I'm so sorry to disturb you, but please can I borrow your toilet? Henry and I are on holiday and were out walking when we got lost. I'm so desperate now, so sorry to bother you, but I didn't know what else to do.'

His face is cold and unfriendly as he stares at me. 'You must have walked past the public latrines to get here.'

'Did I? Oh no, don't say that! My God, Henry, can you believe that? I'm so stupid! We haven't passed any other houses in ages and there's no way I can make it anywhere else, it's freezing out here.

Please, can I come in? I swear I'll be just a minute; otherwise, I might just disgrace myself on your doorstep?'

Oliver's thin nostrils flare, and the door edges closer towards being shut. For a second, I think he's going to slam the door in my face, but then his gaze flicks left and right. I haven't opened myself to receive yet, but I get the sense that he's considering his *public* persona. My intuition is proved correct when he speaks next. 'Of course. Forgive the mess.'

As we enter, I continue with my act, mimicking the unmistakable wiggle of a woman needing to use the toilet. As I shift my feet from one foot to the other, I purse my lips together as I note the look of disgust on our host's face.

'If you take the first staircase, it will be your fourth door to the right,' he says.

The *first* staircase. This place is massive, and cold as hell. *All that money and he can't splash out on some heating?* Without another word, I head towards the staircase, not wasting any time. *The sooner I get into the receptive mode and learn what has called me here, the quicker Derek and I can leave this place.* Leaving the men in the hallway, I take two stairs at a time, as quietly as I can. Their footsteps and voices tell me they are moving into another room, just off the hallway. *Not to worry, Derek, I'll be right back.*

'You find Patryk now,' a familiar female voice speaks out of nowhere.

'Jesus Christ!'

Monika's lucky she didn't make me scream out loud, jumping out on me like that. There's no clicking to warn me when she's coming through. I hiss at her. 'Shhh. What do you think I'm doing here? Now go away, you're distracting me.'

'Sorry.' Monika remains in place, staring at me, her face deadpan.

I peer round her, suddenly curious. 'Where's John?' I ask.

'He's not come here. It is…bad, for him.'

I want to cry at the thought of the little boy suffering, but I push the tears away, swallowing. *John's gone from here now, but he needs to be able to return to The Blue. To be healed and absorbed by love. Buck-up, Mary Jameson. Thinking about that won't help right now.* My breath whistles as I suck it in, then I whisper, 'Why are *you* here, Monika?'

Monika looks around, as though casting about for words to say. 'I want to say thank you and say what a good thing you do now. For John and Patryk... for their families. If you don't stop this man, then... more children... and families will suffer. Many. You understand?'

This is more confirmation that Oliver is the killer, and the bastard is downstairs with my lovely Derek. Breathing the same air, sharing the same space. I should just go down there, stab him in the eye, and watch him bleed out. Would I go to prison? Get a hold of yourself, Mary Obosa Jameson. I'd never find Patryk if I did that. I smooth my hair down, calming myself. *My primary goal here is the connection. To do that, I need to get in the zone, then search for Oliver's frequency.* With a sense of foreboding, I draw a deep breath. *Once I'm open to receive, I doubt I'll maintain a psychic neutrality for long. Monika's hints have only deepened my suspicions. If this man truly is the killer, I'm bracing myself for a shit storm of horrific emotions.*

One thready breath later, I pull the toilet lid down, and sit, quieting myself. Impassivity does not come quickly, but it does come. I cast my inner eye about, scanning for anything to do with Patryk or Oliver. With the abruptness of a sledgehammer, I receive downloads of scenes, a scatter gun of fear, rage, and warped hatred. Vomit unfurls itself in the back of my throat, making my tongue curl like a salted slug inside my mouth.

The listening devices. The police officer. Peter, posed as a plumber and placing the other devices all here in the house. Plugs and the plug sockets here and there are all fine. I see them, one-by-one, my mind searching. Then, I realise this is something new. *I'm seeing what could be. What might change. A potential future.*

There's a problem with something connected to the devices. Something that tips the balance in the wrong direction. There! I see it. It's a silver pen, heavy - exactly the type of expensive pen Oliver would own, planted on a table in the drawing room. In any normal household, it wouldn't be noticed, but not in here. Oliver Redford-Bowles is meticulous, and he'll know it's out of place as soon as he sees it. Flashes of him completing his ritual exercise sessions in his home gym, then going to the sauna.

'Twenty minutes of sauna a day, adds years to your life,' floods through to me. Images and blocks of thought are coming at me thick and fast now; I'm powerless to stop them.

Oliver, shutting the door to me, and to Derek. As he strides away, he wears a look of disgust on his face, like others wear a smile. He heads straight into the study to remove a key. Oliver stops suddenly, balancing on the balls of his feet. He is staring straight ahead at the wall, but he moves his head slowly, until he's looking at one thing. The pen. It flashes red in my mind's eye, the aura throbbing. Kaleidoscope thoughts flit from one screen to another in his mind, and I can see them. I can hear his suspicion and follow his lightning-fast association. Oliver's thoughts are broadcast to me as clearly as if he's speaking aloud to me, and I listen aghast, as I hear: '*That pen does not belong to me, and it wasn't there yesterday. Someone put it here. Who would do that, and why? The annoying girl and her chap? No, she went upstairs, and he never left my sight. Only other person it could be was the plumber who was in the area. This is an expensive make, not the kind most plumbers would have, or leave lying around if they did. The pen was in the drawing room. The plumber should not have been in here. He signed for the job at the front door with a biro. Come to think of it, the plumber was out of place, too. The way he stood, walked. Too upright and stiff. That plumber must've been an undercover officer. He put that here. I must be under suspicion. Knew*

296

I should've gotten rid of the child after they took that hair sample. They're sniffing around for evidence.'

Oliver resolves not to give it to them, walking out of the room at once to retrieve his car keys. The other key remains in his trouser pocket. Next, my visions show me Oliver in his car, and he's driving, but not for long. I try to focus my psychic attention to the scenery along the way and take a mental note of a big white lorry passing by, and two signposts I see. Oliver travels in silence. No podcasts or radio stations play. The only noise I can hear is a delicate scraping. It makes me cringe, the sound like a fork against a plate. I realise it is his teeth grinding together as he grits them.

After the car comes to a halt, Oliver changes out of his leather brogues, into some boots stored in the trunk of his car. He then strides through woods until he arrives at an old, stone cottage. The key fits, and he goes in.

My other-worldly sight watches Oliver as he heads down into the cellar. Here, the horror of what I see nearly repels me out of the moment, and for a second, I struggle to maintain the clairvoyant connection and the scene glitches in front of me like a mirage about to vanish. With a shudder, I force the link with this *potential future* to stay and remain present in the moment that's being shown to me. Despite the outward aged appearance of the cottage, Oliver has remodelled the cellar. Everything is shiny steel and glaring white. On the high island countertops, there are various instruments laid out, surgical ones. Nearby, a small boy sobs. It's Patryk, trapped like an animal in a large dog crate on the floor.

Oliver, expressionless and without a word, marches over to snatch a scalpel from the steel counter. Then, he drags the mewling boy out by his hair. Patryk, emaciated, struggles to hold his own weight, but he doesn't have to. One sharp arc ends his misery in a spurt of red, the copper stench of blood heavy in the air. Then Oliver's cold pleasure is the last thing the boy sees. When released from Oliver's hold, Patryk collapses, his limbs making a *whump* noise as he tumbles to the floor, boneless.

The vision of what might be is so abhorrent it throws me out, and as my stomach rolls, my hand claps over my mouth to stop myself from vomiting. I shake my head, trying to rid myself of the scent of copper. 'No,' I whisper, my attention back in the current moment, in the luxurious bathroom of Oliver's grand house. To the smell of bleach and potpourri.

I'll ring, Jay, he'll come, and - then I remember. *No! I left my phone indoors. Shit. What can I do?* My head tilts as I try to weigh up a myriad of options and decide my next move. *Will they know it's us if Jay and his team are listening in on the devices? I could shout out for help near a device, but how quickly could they get here realistically, and what would happen to Patryk if we don't guess where Oliver has him? Are there any planted devices where Oliver's taken Derek? I can't remember... Can I leave, beg a neighbour to use their phone to call Jay? No, this house is pretty secluded and by the time I'd done that, Oliver might have discovered the pen. In my vision of the possible future, if Oliver sees that pen, it's all over and Patryk will die.* A recollection of Errol flashes into my mind. His last appearance to me, he looked sad and desperate to talk, but was muted by the Universe. *That makes me think that if I take the pen away so Oliver never sees it, then somehow, things will work out so that I will be the one to die, but Patryk would be safe. It'll probably be an exchange - Patryk's life for mine. Him. Or me.*

Patryk's mum's voice message reverberates in my mind, followed quickly by Monika's. She'd said Oliver would take other little ones like Patryk and John, torture them, and kill them. *And Patryk would die.* A sudden insight suddenly strikes me. 'Gethymmore Wilcum.' A child's language – not 'Get Thymore Wilcum,' it was 'Get him, more will come.' *Oliver won't stop unless I do this. I cannot turn my back on these kids. Kids and animals. Maybe next time around I'd get the life I wished for.* I square my shoulders. *Next time, maybe.*

I flush the chain, and turn on the hot tap, running my hands under it. My reflection shows a white-faced witch with jet-black hair and storm grey eyes. My hair has grown without me noticing again. The sleek bob is past my shoulders and is winging its way to my chest. I tuck it behind my ears. *There's no time. I'll sneak downstairs, find this bloody Jonah-pen, and get the hell out of here. Who knows, maybe I don't have to die, maybe if I get the pen that will be enough, or maybe Jay will just turn up. I doubt he will though, unless he thinks we're in any danger, and he won't know that I need to get the pen... Shit.*

I take a couple of minutes to make sure I'm not in the receptive mode before I can leave. *Overwhelmed would not be good right now, this is not the place to be vulnerable.* I spot the other staircase, and creep down that one, using it to access the room I sense is close by. The doors are all closed, and I'm risking opening it to see Oliver and Derek. My heart hammers against my chest as I pull the handle down silently. As soon as I open the door, I spot the desk and the pen, just as it was in my vision. *Jackpot.*

Grabbing it, I creep back upstairs on swift tip toes, then shut the bathroom door loudly and walk down the first set of stairs normally.

The pendant on my necklace feels warm against my chest and comforts me, as I cup it, I give my engagement ring a swirl. *Patryk and the other kids would be safe now. Monika and John will be at peace. And I will be with my mum again, she'll be proud of me, I know.* She used to say I was special, 'beautifully and wonderfully made.' My heart lightens as I think of my dearly departed friends, Little Mary, Jo, Dolores, and Lou. It has been ages, and although I'm always glad for them, knowing they've moved on to exist in their highest joy, I often grieve at their loss with a dull ache.

Derek calls out as I walk down the stairs. 'We're down here in the kitchen now, Mary.'

The kitchen is no warmer than anywhere else I've been in the house, and I shiver as I enter it. Oliver and Derek both glance up. Derek's shoulders slump in relief when he sees me. A small smile curves across my lips until I glance at our host. His face is expressionless. My hand goes up to smooth my eye twitch, and as I do, I imagine the scars on my palms itch. *What's he looking at me like that for? Did he hear me go into the study? No way, Derek would've shouted out.*

'Well, thank you so much, phew. Relief! We won't take up any more of your time. Will we, dear?'

'No, no. We must get on now,' Derek says. 'Thank you so much for allowing my dear Teresa here to use the loo.'

Oliver's eyes widen, and his eyebrows raise. He tilts his head to one side as he regards us. Finally, a reptilian smile passes across his features, and it doesn't make him look any friendlier. I feel the chill of corruptness seeping out of him and take a faltering step back. *Something's wrong. He knows something.*

'Ah, come now, let me make you a cup of tea before you leave, won't you? It's unseasonably cold out there.'

'Oh no, we couldn't possibly take up any more of your time,' I say. My chest thrums, and I feel a tuning fork vibration again. I'm not in the receptive mode, but even so, the air around Oliver seems to shimmer as he moves towards the side with the kettle on it. I can't see him, but I have a sense that my friend Errol is fighting to get to me. I glance at Derek, frowning. His Adam's apple bobbles up and down in his throat.

'Please, take a seat and I'll make refreshments. I insist.'

Derek shrugs, maintaining eye contact with me, waiting to take my cue. *It's up to me again. I don't want to tip Oliver off before Jay has found Patryk. The police must be listening in; so maybe it will be OK.* 'Well, thank you then. That's very kind of you.' My lips almost twitch at the disbelief on Derek's face as I move toward the table to sit down.

'Wonderful. Henry, what would you both like, tea or coffee?'

'Tea's fine, thank you.' The misery in Derek's reply is so clear Oliver's brows fly up.

I try to reassure my fiancé with a smile, patting the table space beside me to encourage him. He seems to struggle to unstick his feet from the floor, remaining in the same place as before.

Oliver is the epitome of a gracious host, 'Lovely. And Henry, sugar, milk for you? How do you like your tea?'

'Milk with one sugar, please.'

'Magnificent.' Oliver has his back to us, moving from side to side as he bustles around with our refreshment.

'And for you, *Mary*?' Oliver swivels round as he says my *real* name, knife in hand as he pivots towards me.

Shock makes my thoughts move in slow motion. *That's what went wrong. Derek called me Mary when letting me know they were in the kitchen.*

'Mary, *run!*' Derek's shout snaps me awake.

Oliver's gripping a cleaver, swinging it so it will lodge itself into my skull. Instinctively, I raise my hands over my head, squeezing my eyes shut as I anticipate the death blow, but it doesn't come.

Disbelieving my luck, I open my eyes, jumping up from the table to take the hand Derek stretches out to me from his new position in front of me. It's then I notice the blood and time stops. A blob of red gurgles out of Derek's mouth, dribbling in thick globules down his chin. My blood turns to ice in my veins, freezing me on the spot. Then there is silence. Eyes wide, our gazes meet as horrified, we both gape at the knife buried in Derek's collarbone. *No.*

A flash of pain to the back of my head, and I fall forwards. My world turns black.

CHAPTER SEVEN

'Mary... Beautiful, you've got to wake up.' It's Derek, whispering close to my ear.

Dizzy, I open my eyes to the dark, straining to see him. Pain roars into my head from the blow it absorbed, and despair floods my heart as I realise my situation. Oliver's tied my hands roughly together with some rope, and my body feels contorted with an uncomfortable stiffness. I'm glad Derek is here with me, though. He confirms my woozy suspicions.

'We're in the boot of a car. You're alright,' Derek says.

'Head's spinning.' My stomach heaves and I mewl as vomit exits from me, an automatic protest at my unnatural travel position.

'It's OK, beautiful. Hang in there. You've got this.'

Remember who I am? Who said that... was it Derek, or did I think it? No matter, I just need to shut my eyes again now. Only for a minute. I blink back into the darkness, then smile. Derek's love for me is shining a light I can see behind my eyelids. It bathes me in its warmth, comforting me, and I draw fortification from it. *Derek.* I sigh.

He speaks again, his voice drawing me out of my sleepy state, 'I know it's painful, but you *have* to wake up. Please open your eyes.'

'No, D... tired.'

Derek's whisper is firmer this time, more insistent. 'You need to call out to Errol now. *Remember, Patryk.*'

I feel his words resonate inside me, pulling me towards consciousness. *Derek. Yes. Have to save Patryk.* My eyelids flutter open, and I see I'm in the shiny white room, made colder with stainless steel. Although the astringent scent of bleach stings my nasal hairs, the stench of piss, shit, and vomit overpowers it. *Rock, paper, scissors, shit. There's another smell I can detect underneath all of that, more insidious. The copper smell of old blood.* My stomach turns over. *Dear God no. I'm in the killing room I envisioned.*

I scan my surroundings, dizzily trying to take stock of my situation. Derek is out of my eyeline and isn't talking to me at the moment. My wrists are tied down to a stretcher, and my captor has his back to me, laying out tools methodically. The person's not speaking, and except for the sound of feeble crying, the room is as silent as the grave. Without seeing the face, I *know* the back facing me belongs to Oliver Redford-Bowles. My eye twitches and I scrunch up my nose to force it to stop as I absorb my position.

With a swallow, I turn my blinking grey gaze away from Oliver, trying to focus. Sweat runs into my eyes, stinging, and I screw them shut, wiping my face against my shoulder. More rope bites into my small biceps, and my hands have been bound at the wrist for so long they're numb. I need to get my circulation going again. As I flex my hands in their binds, they come alive, but feel alien to me. I wriggle my fingers, and it helps to loosen the ties slightly.

As I move my hands surreptitiously, I scrutinise the room with desperation. *Where the hell is Derek? I don't see him, but instead, I see someone else. Despite my circumstances, a surge of pure joy irradiates my heart. It's Patryk.* Pale and dirty, the small boy is crumpled in a cage on the floor, facing me. The image of his vibrant family portrait clash in my mind horribly with his present state: gaunt, eyes too large for his face, his hair once lively and curled, now lies dull and grimy. Patryk huddles in the metal cage, grubby and shaking, reminiscent of a traumatized dog. Blinking back tears I struggle to hold back emotion when I recognise the tattered rags he wears are remnants of his once pristine school uniform.

Rage burns, hot in my stomach, prodding me to try to get to him. Pins and needles shoot into my limbs as I renew my struggle against the binds. They bite into me, wrestling back their control. *I can do this, I'm double jointed... I have done this before; I can undo these ties. I know I can. Where's Derek now, and what did he say again? Errol! He said I need to call Errol.* 'Please, Errol, where are you? Please God, let Errol come now. Help me get this little boy out of here.' Remembering the last time I was in almost this exact position, I repeat the actions, swivelling my wrist as much as I can. I am nearly free when Oliver turns, catching me in my ministrations. 'What've you done with Derek, you freak?'

'Well, you're awake, I see, if suffering from concussion. That's fortuitous. It's a lot more gratifying when my work has a conscious recipient.'

'Fuck you, you psycho prick. Untie me, then we'll see how gratifying things can get.' I gather my breath screaming, 'Derek!'

'Unlikely.' Oliver's tone of voice remains as unchanged as his facial expression while we speak. Then he turns away nonchalantly, offering me his back again. The calm *kirching* of steel on steel punctuates the end of our conversation. *He's gone back to his work. Oliver is preparing his tools.*

Patryk's whimpering renews my desperation and pumps adrenaline through me. *I need to find Derek, have to get free, save Patryk, and get him the hell out of here.* 'Please, let Patryk go,' I beg, although my throat is dry and rusty. *Even if Oliver doesn't respond to my plea, I still need to try.*

'Don't be ridiculous.' Oliver doesn't turn his head to address me. 'Patryk is my guest of honour here. I never even locked the boy's cage. He's free to leave whenever he pleases. However, he's destined to become part of my experience. The jubilance of my magnificent expression. Basically, I'm enjoying myself.'

'You sadistic prick.'

The metal door on the crate is comprised of bars and is closed. It's impossible to tell if Oliver is lying from where I am. Still focused on laying out cutting apparatus, Oliver guesses what I am thinking and speaks again in light tones. 'Oh, I wasn't lying when I told you the door's unlocked. The subject has learned what happens when he attempts to escape, and he chooses to remain. But I'm getting ahead of myself. You'll see… in good time.'

Oh, for the love of God, can this man just stop laying out knives. How many does he have, for Christ's sake? Hang on… maybe I can grab hold of one if I get free?

Where the hell has he stashed Derek? He must be in the next room or something. I'll find him, and it will be alright. Mind buzzing with questions and possibilities, I've almost freed my hand. *Now, if I can just grab Patryk, then run and find Derek, we can locate a way out of this antiseptic hell hole.* Inside my chest, my heart bangs against my breastbone so hard it feels as though it'll burst through my ribcage. Blood roars in my ears, pulsating, and a fierce determination zings through me, lending me strength. I think about the heartbreak of Patryk's mum and father holding each other up, sobbing. Poor John's parents with their brittle grief and his dad, with the quiet devastation on his face. Monika, and what she said to me in my latest vision. Oliver has killed before, and he *will* continue to kill if I don't stop him today. I know he hunts the kids, stalking them, then snatching them. Driving them here in his cousin's van, where he takes his time to torture, then kill them.

The full connection between John and Patryk I don't know, but I do know the *why*. Oliver takes them for pleasure. He targets boys who share a loving bond with their families, with their mother in particular. Torturing the helpless is what he enjoys, is why he'll kill many more if I don't stop him. John and Patryk would be the first of many, and as the numbers of victims grow, so too will Oliver's sophistication. And his appetite for suffering.

I must stop that from happening, whatever the cost.

My necklace has slid around to the back of me, and I feel its warmth like a finger at the base of my neck. *My mum always said I was special. That I am loved - surrounded by love, in fact. It's always there, just waiting for me to tap into it. I know this to be true, and I also know I have nothing to fear after this life experience. I will miss my Derek though, and my friends... and I so wanted to be a mum.* The sigh I allow myself is silent, but deep, and cleansing. *This is the way it must be so I can save Patryk, let poor John rest in peace, and stop any more casualties from happening. Let it be what it's meant to be, then.*

I allow my eyelids to flutter down while I open myself up to the receptive mode, seeking guidance. When I open my eyes again, I see Errol. *About time! And who the hell is that woman with you, Errol?*

'We've hardly any time, Mary. This is Gaynor. She's a very gifted lady, spoken about on our side, and I finally found her. Amongst other things, Gaynor can move objects with her energy, and she wants to help.'

Like a poltergeist? Or like that guy that used to bend spoons?

'Mary, shut up and concentrate! Bend your wrist a bit more, that's it, keep going. Gaynor is going to help you with the rest, but she's still learning over here, and her power's limited, so you have to help, too.'

I feel the ties stop biting into me so much, and the blood rushes back into my extremities with painful force. *Bloody hell, that Gaynor is only doing it, she's freeing me, it's working.* My breath catches in my throat, not wanting to tip off Oliver by making any loud exhalations. Although he seems absorbed, he would notice, I'm sure. His focus is on the preparation for his 'magnificence of expression,' and mine is on Patryk.

Single-minded in my intent, when I feel the last string loosen on my arms and wrists, I spring up with stealth. My legs aren't bound, which makes it easy for me to slide off the surgical stretcher silently.

Standing, but not daring to move yet, I look for an obvious weapon. But Oliver has all of them by his side.

Patryk makes a pleading noise and the hope on his face nearly brings me to my knees. *OK. Sod this upper-class twanny. I must have had dozens of fights growing up. I can take him.*

As gently as I can, I step behind Oliver and clench both my fists, ready to hail him with blows.

Over his shoulder I catch sight of my face in the shiny instruments, realising my nemesis will also have seen my reflection. I leap back just as Oliver whips around to face me. He slices the air with the same scalpel I saw him kill Patryk with in my vision of a potential future, and I feel a line of fire spring up diagonally across one side of my face. *It burns.*

'Shit!' One hand automatically goes to my injured cheek, and the other reaches out to steady myself, landing on the cast-off rope on the stretcher.

Just as Oliver stabs at me again with the blade, I grip the rope with both hands, bringing it up to meet his wrists. A vein throbs at his temple as he exerts every ounce of his strength, but he still cannot bring the knife down and plunge it into me. Oliver's face remains emotionless, but his eyes burn with a hatred that singes me.

Errol and Gaynor are standing to one side, and I notice Gaynor focusing intently on something out of my eyeline. Errol's motioning to the left of me. Without a second thought, I react, using every bit of my strength to push one side of the rope further up and force Oliver in that direction. I spot the large bowl; Oliver probably intended it to collect entrails or something horrible. Well, no matter. *I can use it as a weapon.*

Oliver, outraged at being corralled, fights back with renewed vigour, stopping me from reaching it. I hear it circling the surface it rests on and know that Gaynor is trying with all her might to make it roll towards me. *Help me. It's not working...not yet.*

Patryk whimpers as my own hands get closer and closer to my face, and a smirk graces Oliver's features. Adrenaline courses through me, and I screech out my rage, leaning my head back, then bringing it forward as fast as I can. My forehead smashes into Oliver's narrow nose, breaking the thin bone there with a satisfying crunch. Blood instantly spurts out, and it's his turn to cradle his injured face.

His cry of rage is short-lived, and while he's distracted with stopping the bleeding, I reach out to grab the bowl, crashing it with force into his temple. Oliver falls to the ground, eyes closed.

'Weren't expecting that, were you, you mug?' I race over to Patryk, and he's trembling. *Please God, let the door to this thing be unlocked as Oliver said it was.* My hand shakes as I test it, then joy lights my heart when it creaks open.

Patryk seems stuck, unmoving in the doorway. I reach in, trying to pull him, but he resists, moving farther back with a mewling noise. *Shit. Oliver has conditioned him not to come out. I can't even begin to think how he has managed that.* 'Come on, Patryk. I won't hurt you. Come out now. Come with me.'

The little boy's eyes are all pupil, dilated, and, mouth gaping, he stares at me, then Oliver, who is lying unconscious on the floor. *But probably not for long.* 'The bad man won't hurt you if you come out now, Patryk. I won't let him. Come on, love, come with me, I'll take you to your mum and dad.'

'To mummy?' Patryk's voice is croaky and dry as he utters the babyish moniker. Hope reappears on his drawn features again, and he steps out of his tiny prison.

Anticipating the weakness in his unused limbs that would take precious minutes to recover, I snatch him up. He doesn't fight me. Instead, he wraps his legs around my waist, and winds his arms around my neck, trustingly. Although he's emaciated, he's still a ten-year-old boy, and my slight biceps protest as I perch him on my hip like a small child heading to the exit of the pristine killing chamber. *I won't be able to carry him this way for long.*

The open door creates a slice of light. Outside the stinging white of the room is a corridor with walls that resemble a cave. *It's pitch black. For God's sake, can nothing ever just be easy?*

'Mary, down this way, quickly!'

'Derek? Thank God!' I head towards Derek's voice. I look at Patryk, telling him, 'Sweetie, I need to put you down now, OK?'

With a slow exhalation, I help Patryk find his footing, gently testing if his weakened limbs will hold his weight. They do. We remain anchored for a few precious seconds, allowing Patryk's legs to accustom themselves to standing again. Then, gripping his small palm in mine, I draw him firmly toward the faint echo of Derek's voice. My free hand stretches out in front of me in the inky blackness, tracing the dark, chilling walls, guiding our steps through the unseen labyrinth. Beneath us, water pools and splatters with each footfall. Patryk's hand quivers in mine with such force it makes my arm jitter. 'We'll be out of here soon, love,' I reassure him.

'OK,' he whispers.

'Mary, this way-hurry,' Derek urges me on, closer to him.

I pick up speed, and in the dark, miss an object that trips me up. With a cry, I land flat on the floor, putting my hands out to feel whatever broke my fall. I recoil as I touch skin and fabric.

Stomach heaving, I scrabble to rise again. Floundering, I slip on the lifeless body, dumped here in the corridor, slick with blood. I retch, covering my mouth without thinking, then realise my hand's sticky and scrabble to get up on all fours, heaving. My eyes have adjusted to the lack of light, enough so that now I can make out a face.

It's Derek's body, dumped out here in this dark tunnel, like trash.

My piercing scream echoes against the walls, and I do not, cannot stop. *Not my Derek, please, not my Derek.* My mind and body reject this unbearable reality, too awful to grasp. Derek's spirit waits beside me, and I gape at his upright form, then the one beneath me. Disoriented, I put a bloodied hand to my forehead as he speaks. 'I'm

309

so sorry it went this way, beautiful. I love you so much, and I always will.'

'No, no!' I scream repeatedly until my voice abandons me and I can only mouth the word, refusing to accept the truth that's confronting me. *Derek's voice in the car boot with me, waking me up. My Derek, here now, soothing me, loving me. Derek on the ground. Dead. I knew. I knew. I didn't want to admit it had happened, because it was supposed to be me, not him. Never him, he is so good, so much better than me. I can't bear it -* darkness reaches out to claim me, drawing me into its smooth embrace.

As I lose consciousness, from a long way away I hear Errol saying, 'Wake the hell up, Mary!'

Derek pleads, 'Mary! Get up now and save this boy!'

Then finally, Monika, 'Save my grandson. I beg.'

Ignoring them all, I fade into the dark recesses of my mind, where its cocoon keeps me safe. I'm not coming back. I'm staying here. Then, Derek calls to me in the dark.

'Mary... I know, love, we had all those wonderful plans for our future. I'm so sorry to cause you this pain, my beautiful.'

'D, I can't cope with losing you. Anything but that. It was supposed to be me. I thought the choice was me or Patryk, and the rest of the kids Oliver would go on to murder. Never you... I can't be without you, D. I love you so much.'

'I love you too, Mary, but you have to do this. You need to shut down any psychic links to me right now.'

The idea of severing the connection between us is unthinkable.

'No, Derek, I won't - I can't!'

'You can, and you have to. Do it for me, and for all the kids that Oliver will kill if you don't. For the future good.'

My immediate rejection of the idea wavers under Derek's urgent pleading. 'I wouldn't even know how to do that. We're soulmates, connected forever. Could I even do that?'

'You can, baby. Do it like you close yourself off to the receptive mode. Just focus solely on all things on the Derek and Mary wavelength and let me go. Please, I'm begging you. If you don't get out of here right now, this will all be for nothing. My death will be for nothing.'

Even in my unconscious mind, my grief is overwhelming, it reaches the core of my being, and I sob, heartbroken. *Close myself off to Derek. Lose him forever, or Patryk and those other kids die. The Universe is so cruel.*

'Mary, please, do what I say and set me free. I'm going home now, back to The Blue, so you can close yourself off to me. Just shut your feelings down and get up, *please.* I love you, adore you, forever, but we had our time together. *This* is the way it's supposed to be, the best way it can be, and I'll always be a part of you. I'll always love you.'

'Derek, no, please don't leave me, I'm begging you … how can I live after this? What will I do if we can never be together again?'

'Mary. You need to shut down to me. *Let me go.* Then you go and you kick some fucking arse!'

'Derek! You never swear!' Despite Derek's heart-breaking message of goodbye, his use of profanity shocks me, perversely provoking an urge to grin. *He always makes me smile. Made me smile…*

'I know, baby, but the situation seems to call for it. Close yourself to me, please, Mary, you need to leave this place. Errol will help you when you ask. Save Patryk. Live for me… Goodbye, beautiful, I'll love you forever.' Derek's presence fades, and in my mind, I hear a faint echo of the song he used to sing to me... *I was made for you...*

I have to do this. I have to let Derek go. With the grim determination of a surgeon amputating a limb, I close myself off to Derek.

Once it's done, my eyes open slowly, immediately becoming aware of the voices ringing out. They shatter the perfect darkness that had lent my mind its protection and the comfort of Derek's presence. I no longer feel the overwhelming devastation I'd experienced before passing out, but my wholeness feels diminished somehow. It's as though my emotions are a decayed tooth, and every inward breath makes it whistle with sensitivity. Derek's absence continues to grate on my soul until I do as he directed and shut down every thought and emotion concerning him. *Numbness.*

Patryk's diminutive presence looms close to mine. 'Have armpit hairs, getting a big boy.' His thoughts from the day of his abduction re-enter my mind, triggering a sharp pang of affection and melancholy. His voice is small and raspy, but I can still hear it. 'Please... lady... please, he's coming.'

Disjointed splish-splash footfalls sound out in the dark, and Patryk's little fingers grip and shake me, his distress mounting.

Errol appears and leans in close, his voice intense. 'Stand up, Mary. Stand up right now.'

A pulling sensation at my shoulders accompanies Errol's command, and my hair lifts upwards. Swallowing my grief and focusing on what needs to be done, I accept Patryk's help as he stands back, tugging at me.

'Everything will be OK,' I say, knowing it will not. *Nothing will ever be OK again.* I take a half step in the direction I hear Oliver approaching, my lip curling. *That vile creature should pay for what he's done. He doesn't deserve to live.*

'I want my mummy.' Patryk's plea pierces my heart, stopping the bloodlust that threatens to overtake me. The words remind me of myself at his age, wanting nothing more than to be with my mum again. *Patryk will survive this and be with his parents again. This all has to be worth it. I won't allow Derek's death to be in vain.*

Without another word, I change course again, pushing Patryk in front of me and heading to the small dot of light I can see ahead of us. *Just like the saying tells us, there's light at the end of the tunnel.* We run towards it. As we approach the opening, Errol and Gaynor appear, standing at the end, pointing behind us. Comprehension smashes into me, and I stop dead, pivoting 160 degrees and coming face to face with Oliver. I raise my arms, shoving him away with such force it propels him backwards, hitting the ground with a thud in the dark. Leaving him to stumble on the floor, I swing back around to Patryk, driving him closer to the exit. The beckoning daylight makes me squint as we get nearer to it. Patryk stops trotting along and stands still, covering his eyes with both hands. With a deft but gentle touch, I remove them, then hold his wrist, moving quickly along again with him in tow. 'We're nearly there now, Patryk. Soon be out of this tunnel,' I say.

A backwards yank on my hair forces me to jack-knife and automatically let go of Patryk's hand. I'm dragged back into the tunnel, and the light recedes.

'Run, Patryk!' I scream.

Thank God, the little boy continues to run on without me.

Oliver is back at me again, chopping at the air beside my head, and I see light bouncing off a knife that is significantly larger than a scalpel. His injuries have robbed him of his previous precision, and for that, I am grateful.

Not wasting time grappling with the hand that clutches my hair, I shift, twisting inwards, then deal his leg with a vicious back-kick to the knee as hard as I can. With a shout, he lets go of his hold on me, dropping to the floor as he holds it, in foetal position. Without hesitation, I boot Oliver's stomach, and as soon as his arms move to protect his midriff. I toe-punt his head. *Once, twice, three times a charm.*

'Argh,' Oliver cries out against the blows, and moves his hands back to his head. It's too late; I already have access. With no remorse, I stamp on his cranium, stilling his movements. I don't wait to find out if he's still breathing. Instead, I use his incapacitation to sprint fully out of the tunnel. It doesn't take me long to spot Patryk's stumbling

313

form, running in the wooden area, as fast as his weakened legs will allow.

'Patryk, Patryk, wait!'

He turns, swaying on the spot, and as I reach him, he puts his arms up to me, reverting to his babyhood. I try to pick him up, but this time, I don't have the strength, so instead, I kneel and hug him tight. 'It's OK, it'll be OK. We'll find a road. Someone will come.'

CHAPTER EIGHT

O ur feet crunch through the dead leaves that adorn the floor of the woods, and I notice the birds. Unaware of any suffering or peril, they sing happily in the surrounding trees. It's cold and I shiver, wishing I had a coat or something warm for Patryk with me. 'It's still daytime,' I comment to Patryk, as we trudge along.

Because of my vision, I know the cottage Oliver took us to is only a short drive from his house. The wooded area is secluded, and I wonder how long it will take us to spot a road and a passing driver.

Patryk continues to walk, but I can see he's fragile. Emaciated, he looks as though a stiff breeze could fell him, and his skin is a pasty grey colour. Splodges of caked blood mark his face and body. He has dried faeces all over him, and part of his right ear is missing. Tears flood my eyes and I grit my teeth. My fingers run over the tips of his and I wince as I realise that some of his fingernails are missing. I keep my grip loose, desperate not to cause his sensitive nail beds anymore pain, but Patryk seems unaware. He holds my hand tighter.

Not knowing if Oliver is dead or alive, I don't want to chance stopping to check Patryk over. We can't risk being caught. 'The birds are singing nicely, aren't they, Patryk?'

'When will I get home?' Patryk's voice is a croaky monotone.

'Not too long now, love. Hang in there.'

We carry on limping along together for a few minutes before we spot a road, and I decide to stay silent, conserving my strength until

I have something concrete to impart. It doesn't take long. 'There! Look, Patryk, it's a road. Oh, thank God, that means it won't be long 'til someone drives past. Then we can flag them down.'

'Then I can see mummy?'

'Yes. Then you can see your mummy.' My heart constricts, and as I put my free palm to my chest, tears well up. *No, I can't allow myself to release my feelings yet, because then I might unleash all of it. And that would not be good.* I blink my eyes clear again, before Patryk can notice, leading us to the road in a few brief minutes.

'Is that a car coming, lady?'

I squint and push my hair back out of my face. *'Lady?' Ah did I even introduce myself to Patryk?* My memory is foggy of our meeting. *It seems so long ago now.* 'My name's Mary,' I say absentmindedly as I peer at the tarmac, then I say in a suddenly light tone, 'I think you're right, Patryk. It *is* a car. Come on, let's get their attention.' Holding Patryk's hand, we move towards the approaching vehicle, and I wave an arm in the air, flagging them down.

As the car comes to a halt just down from our position on the road, my heart, previously constricted, swells with jubilance. Then, as I peer at the person behind the wheel, I give a funny half-laugh, wondering at the strangeness of fate. *'Victoria?* No way.'

Well, it appears the good old Universe has a twisted sense of humour. My stuck-up neighbour is apparently whom the cosmos has chosen in the role of saviour. How will I explain our grubbiness and Patryk's prison camp appearance? I shrug. *Who gives a shit? That's not important right now; this is an emergency.*

'I'm so glad to see you, Victoria. I can't believe you came along just when we needed help. This is perfect.'

True to character, Victoria's staring at us both through the open window, down the barrel of her nose. She doesn't look impressed.

'Can you take us to the police right now, please, Victoria? It's an emergency.'

One eyebrow raised, Victoria says, 'Yes. You'd better get in.'

'Thank you,' I say.

Victoria looks around us, and the car's locking system disengages as she grants us access to the sanctuary of her Range Rover. 'Get in the back, please.'

Taking Patryk's trembling hand, I walk nearer to the car, eager to get us to safety. He doesn't move, rooted to the spot.

Surprised, I glance down at him, then crouch to his eye level, drawing him closer. His entire body is shaking. Victoria looks impatient, and I don't trust her not to just drive off and leave us here. 'It's OK, Patryk, this lady will take us to the police.'

Patryk's head shakes, 'Nnnno,' he says.

'Yes, darling. I know you've been through so much, but please love, hang in there with me. We're nearly there. The police can take us to your mummy.' I gather him into my arms, instinctively wanting to comfort him. His breath tickles my neck as he leans towards my ear as I scoop him up, carrying him into the car. After settling us both in the back seat, I speedily put both our seatbelts on then slam the door shut.

Without a word, Victoria speeds off with such force that my head jerks. I turn to look out the rear window, checking that Oliver's not following us like some kind of demonic nightmare.

He's not there, we're safe. Heart hammering with relief to be free, I laugh out loud, ruffling Patryk's hair. *Patryk's shaking like a leaf.* 'We're going to get you home, Patryk. Back to your mummy. We're nearly-' I break off, looking out the window at the woods to the side of us. *What the hell? Is that Oliver's cabin I can see in the distance? Victoria's driving us back to the frigging tunnel.* Horrified and confused, I look back down at Patryk.

He's still trembling, eyes wide and shell-shocked as he stares unblinking at the back of Victoria. As I study him, a dark stain appears in the front of his trousers. At the sight of his terror, comprehension strikes me and my entire body flinches with the strength of it. Immediately, a savage rage descends upon me, curling my lip. *Victoria's in on it.* Without second guessing myself, I lean forwards, wrapping both arms around the headrest and her neck in a chokehold. Victoria's hands come up, gouging my face and catching my sliced and bloody cheek. Adrenaline is flooding through me and although her fingers are red with my blood, I can't feel anything. She claws at me to drag my grip from her neck, and as she does, the car swerves, revving loudly as her legs straighten and her foot pushes down on the accelerator. The car revs loudly and surges forward, shooting past the turn off to the cottage and tunnel, continuing along the road.

Patryk begins to scream.

Still restrained by my seat belt, I'm half standing, straining forward as much as I can for more leverage. Removing one arm from Victoria's neck, I leave the other crooked around her neck, so I can seize control of the steering wheel. Victoria takes the opportunity of my weakened hold, twisting in her seat and jerking my hand away. As she manoeuvres herself, her foot slips from the accelerator, and I glance through the windscreen, realising we're now off road and spotting the tree. A millisecond later, I snatch my arm back, just before Victoria's driver and passenger seat air bags are deployed, shielding her face and knees. Protected by our seatbelts, Patryk and I are boomeranged by the collision.

The car's occupants are silent as its engine cuts out.

The air bags begin to deflate immediately, and I see Victoria squirming in her seat. As fast as I can, I vacate the car, wrenching open her door and wrapping one hand around her ponytail and the other on the shoulder of her blouse, then, I drag her sideways. She shifts in her seat, pulling and scratching at my face, resisting my efforts to rip her from the vehicle. As she moves, the rapidly deflated air bags allow me to catch sight of the hammer and rope laying against the passenger seat in the foot well. I try to wrestle her hooked and bony fingers from my hair and stop her from gauging my eyes, but then I stop.

Placing one of my hands on the steering wheel and the other at the back of Victoria's head I smash her forehead down against the dashboard with force. Her head hits the radio, turning it on, and a thrash metal music fills the car, its furious tempo keeping pace with our altercation.

Quickly recovering her equilibrium, Victoria lashes out at me, still fighting to remain in the driver's seat. Patryk's screams have run dry, and he now sobs quietly in the background. Incensed by his sorrow and fear, I put my right foot on the door's trim at the bottom of the frame. Then, I pull with all my strength.

Crying out, Victoria drops out onto the hard soil beneath us, and as she does, the momentum makes me also fall backwards. I land on my back, the air whumping out of me and black spots dancing in front of my eyes as the back of my head vibrates in pain. My hand explores for a second, then ignoring the throbbing tenderness, I roll over to my side, pushing myself to my knees. Exhausted and dizzy, I call out to Errol desperately. *I have to save Patryk. God help me. Errol! Where the hell are you? Help me.*

Taking advantage of my momentary incapacitation, Victoria is up again, and stands above me. Her foot arcs backwards as she prepares to kick me, but anticipating her strike, I grab hold of her ankle and tug it out from under her. She screams as she drops, but I don't wait to watch her fall on her back, instead jumping into the car in the driver's seat and slamming the door.

Once inside, the music from the radio still screams all around me, almost drowning out Patryk's wails.

Victoria's not far behind, quickly returning to her feet and opening the car door to try to haul me back out.

Oh no sister, no way. Swinging 'round to face her, I grab both sides of her face and fingers clenched, I pull her towards me, headbutting the bridge of her nose. The crunch is simultaneous with the blood that pours from Victoria's nose, and she staggers back with a gulping scream of agony. Following up on my advantage, I turn and

319

kick her as hard as I can. I'm roughly aiming for her midriff, but hear a hard 'clock' noise, when my foot hits the bone of her hip and she falls again to the floor.

The keys are still in the ignition, and I twist them, turning the engine over. As I do, a draft of frigid air alerts me to the back door opening, and I turn around horrified to watch Oliver reaching in for Patryk. Cowering in the corner, Patryk's still belted in and can't get away. He's clearly too panicked to think of unclipping himself. Instinct takes over, and I leap through the gap in the seats. Grabbing Oliver's outstretched arm, I bend it around the seat, attempting to break it, and as I do, I shout out, 'Undo your seatbelt, Patryk. Run!'

Still hanging onto Oliver's writhing arm, I register the click of a seat belt buckle being undone, then Patryk's door opening and see him run into the woods, through the rear-view mirror.

There's no time to feel relief as the driver's door opens again and I'm set upon by Victoria, a two-hundred-pound scratching cat. An image flashes in my mind, and I release Oliver's arm, fending off both assailants as best I can, and bending quickly, I snatch up the hammer from the floor, then swing it awkwardly towards Victoria and Oliver, hindered by the cramped confines of the car. Both of them veer back, but then I see Victoria stumble round to the passenger seat. *Errol, for Christ's sake where are you? I can't manage both of them by myself.* With no other option, I sprint into the trees after Patryk.

I'm coming, Patryk.

The woods feel like a maze filled with hidden threats and I'm in a poor condition to meet them. The back of my head is screaming out in pain, the skin on my hands and face are torn and bloody, but my resolve is unbreakable. *I will get Patryk to safety, uncover the truth.* As I run, I trip over often, stumbling and sometimes dropping to my knees. Adrenaline lends me the strength to get back to my feet, but I feel it waning. *I need Errol, where is he? This situation's so bad.* Victoria's surprise connection to Oliver, her attempted attack of me and Patryk swirl in my mind. *I need to find Patryk, and get help, real help, and fast. How had Victoria known to come here so quickly? Found us here on this dirt path? Only one answer made sense. After recovering from my head stamp, Oliver must've returned to the torture room and called for reinforcements. Victoria. Cheval maléfique.*

Spotting Patryk's stumbling form is just in front of me, I cry out in gladness, 'Patryk, I'm here. Wait.'

At my call, the little boy turns around and his look of relief morphs into an expression of panic. Pivoting, I shield myself as my assailant rains down hits to my forearms with a thick stick. The pain drives me down to my knees as I feel a snap in my wrist, and it radiates up my arm, searing me. Victoria has the upper hand now, and I can't lower my defence. Too late, I realise I must've dropped the hammer and not noticed when I fell in the woods. Now, I dare not drop my arms for a second, and I can't find the energy to fight Victoria off and run. A single tear runs down my face. *I need to save Patryk, he can't suffer anymore.*

The woodland is hushed, and I hear a set of footsteps approaching me, the uneven weight shift sounding unnaturally loud as it crunches the leaves on the floor. I watch as Oliver moves unsteadily, walking closer to me with his big knife in his hand. He stops about two metres away from me, a smile playing around his lips as he observes Victoria bludgeoning me.

Errol's voice is welcome as he says, 'I'm here, Mary. Quickly, do as I say. Drop to the ground, roll out the way, then push up onto your hands and knees.'

Knowing that as soon as I lower my arms, Victoria will pulverise me with the massive stick she's holding, I hesitate to obey my friend.

'Do exactly what I say, Mary. Trust me,' Errol demands.

Sucking in a deep breath, I do what he says, dropping, rolling, and pushing in fluid motion. Shockwaves of agony flow up my wrist and forearm.

Errol wastes no time giving me more instructions. 'Face them both now, and unlock the receptive mode. Do it now, Mary! Visualise

321

the pain the boys suffered, channel it. Just like you did when John came to you at the séance.'

I had not rolled far from my attacker, and Victoria's brief confusion at my movement is now over. She raises the stick again, but Oliver has now reached her side, and he stills her hand.

'I want to use the knife on her, take my time,' Oliver tells her.

Nose broken, face a mask of blood and cuts, Victoria smiles.

Errol says, 'Mary, open yourself to the receptive mode. You won't be alone. Trust me.'

My bottom lip trembles but I obey Errol, latching onto the feeling of protectiveness I hold for the two boys. *My life for theirs.* My shoulders and breathing relax. Click, click, click... Instantly, I'm in the receptive mode and marvel as I observe and allow. *Time is moving slower this side than it is in the land of the living.*

Gaynor stands once more with Errol, and her eyes are closed, hands are palm up. Monika is also there, holding hands with little John.

Gaynor bids me, 'Focus on your feelings for John and for Patryk. We'll do the rest.'

My body jolts as though electricity is slicing down the crown of my head, jittering as though lightning is striking me. Oliver and Victoria stare down at me, menace in their expression and death in their hearts. The corruption, discord in their psychic signatures is so jarring my ears ring with it, and my fillings vibrate in my mouth.

Empathic link achieved. The first thing I experience is the loss of John's parents, then come wrenching hunger pangs and crippling fear.

I double over at once.

'Mummy is so lovely; she will worry about me. Daddy, please take care of Mummy. Ow, it hurts... please stop.'

Luckily, the time misalignment between Oliver and Victoria and the reality I'm experiencing, means they're moving in slow motion, out of sync with what's happening to me. I can't stop sobbing and don't notice the snot and tears that run unchecked down my face. *No, please no.* Pain-filled eyes search out Errol, my hand stretched out in appeal to him. *Make it stop. It's too much.* If he could cry, he would cry right now. I know this.

My friend touches his companion's arm, and somehow, she grips his hand. The arbitrary thought, *I didn't know spirits could touch*, occurs to me.

Oliver's feet move in slow motion as he steps towards me, lips as curved as the blade in his hand.

Errol clutches Monika's hand, and with the other one, she still holds John's. Gaynor glides over to me, then moves to stand behind me and I know that because of her presence, Oliver's knife will take longer to cut into me. Without preamble, Gaynor clasps my temples, and I jolt, flinching. I picture jump leads charging a car engine. I'm brimming with energy, and although I'm the bridge of an emotional transfer, I experience a complete disconnect from what is going on. Gaynor is bidding me: 'Good, that's it. Allow all that feeling to swell and build inside you. I know it's painful, agonising, but you need to accept it. That's right Mary, now *throw* it at them. Throw it all out, *right now.*'

'What? How?' I ask.

'Embrace the connection between you and the boys, and the pain of their families. Pour all their hurt, all their pain back out. Visualise it like an arc of electricity, funnelling back to its original source. Send it right back to Oliver and Victoria, where it started. Do it with love.'

I already have lightning in my mind's eye, so the comment hits the right button. Raised onto my knees, I obediently follow Gaynor's instructions, angling my palms towards the oncoming executioners. One facing Oliver, one towards Victoria. The victims' terror, agony and fear are transmuted back to the duo. It's a conveyed stream of consciousness that I send out on a frequency. A bizarre communion

323

between myself, the dearly departed, and their murderers. The transfer stops them in their tracks at once.

Victoria screams out immediately, like a banshee, tearing at her hair and ripping at her own eyes, as though she aims to expunge herself from the sights she's seeing. Running in a wild frenzy, she rams into the solid trunk of an old oak tree, knocking herself unconscious instantly.

Oliver is different. He doesn't scream out loud like Victoria, but his mouth gapes and he sways, gulping like a fish. Oliver takes two faltering steps backwards as the thought waves I'm projecting hit him like a tsunami. He still has momentum, but he's no longer coming forwards. Instead, he's staggering sideways, as though trying to get away from me, then about a metre in front of me, he drops to his knees, making swiping gestures around his face, as though he's stuck in front of a bees nest and is trying to swat them away. Like a sleepwalker emerging from a dream, Oliver blinks and looks around him. Something in his eyes looks dazed and unfocused, making me believe he's experiencing everything his victims had endured. His arms go up, as if to protect his face. I know he's trying to shield himself from the worst of it.

'That won't help. The cuts will still come. Then the fire, and the burns. The fear and grief. They will also come.' I speak my thoughts, feeling as though I'm far away and my voice is coming through me, not from me. The psychic link is still holding, and Gaynor's work isn't yet done.

She says, 'Oliver has not seen the full horror yet.'

John's screams of pain and rage become audible over the tearing and shearing noises that are building only in my mind. As John's cries become less prevalent, Oliver's distress mounts.

Satisfaction swells in my breast, as I realise the suave sadist is being stripped of his malicious intent. The experience is also doing something else; it's providing him and his helper a silent gift that keeps on giving. A psychic transfer of emotion and experience between the living and the dead. The pain is being passed, taken from John and sent back to its originators.

Oliver's gaping mouth opens and his eyes widen in horror. He shakes his head, begging for this to end. It does not, and as Gaynor steps around me, I realise that for Oliver and Victoria, it will never end. The echo of what their victims felt has trapped him and Victoria in limbo until they can truly feel remorse for what they did. Which will probably be never.

It's horrific. Brutal. But totally what they deserve.

Gaynor ends her connection by removing her contact with my temples, and steps around to the front of me and I collapse on all fours. As my gaze shifts from the two now slack-faced murderers to Gaynor, a shiver makes its way up my spine.

Gaynor says to the other spirits, 'It's done.'

'We did it, Mary,' Errol says.

Although Patryk has been saved, and I'm alive, Errol's voice is sombre and joyless. Derek is gone forever, and I'm empty. There are no tears, and with dry eyes, I regard Gaynor and Errol. Getting up slowly, with blood dripping from my face onto my broken wrist as I cradle it, I call to Patryk. I can hear him rustling in the trees as he hides. *Such a good little boy.* 'Come on, Patryk, let's get you back home to your family.'

Patryk speaks from behind a thick tree trunk, but he doesn't emerge. Voice quivering he asks, 'What about the baddies? What if they come after us again?'

'Don't worry about them, love. They can't run anymore, and they'll never be able to hurt you, or anyone else, again.' I stare at Oliver and Victoria for a second. Do I detect a shine of horror in their eyes? A glimmer of awareness? The trapped souls of the Rainbow Unit's former patients spring to my mind, making me shudder about what I've done. Then, I think about Patryk's missing fingernails and ear, little John's burnt face dumped like trash in the canal. And my

Derek. Heroically taking the death blow that was meant for me. I shrug. *Fuck these arseholes.*

Turning away, I hold out my hand to Patryk. He rushes over, wrapping his arms around my waist tightly. I bend down and kiss the top of his head lightly, then smooth his hair as I straighten, tapping him on his shoulder. 'We still have Victoria's car, hopefully it will still go, then it won't take us long to get to the nearest police station. Let's get going.'

The sound of sirens assaults the quiet of the woods cocooning us, and as we near the car, the flashing lights make us both squint.

CHAPTER NINE

J ay sprints to meet us, his voice sounding frantic as he calls out from the roadside. 'Mary, where's the suspect - where's Oliver?'

My voice is flat as I tell him, 'It's OK, Jay. He can't hurt anybody else. He's down there - Victoria too.'

'Your neighbour, Victoria?'

At my nod, Jay takes a quick look around my shoulder and sees the gaping duo of child abductors wandering around aimlessly.

Still clutching Patryk's hand, I remain rooted to the spot, while paramedics arrive with stretchers, then, as we refuse to lie down or let go of each other's hands, they take our vital signs and attend to our wounds, gently cleaning Patryk's many injuries, stopping the bleeding on my face and inspecting my wrist before stabilising it with a splint. My blank gaze flickers as I register Jay and his officers stomp off through the woods to read Oliver and Victoria their rights and take them into custody.

Patryk and I are still having our wounds assessed and treated when the police return, looking baffled. 'What's wrong with them?' an officer asks, nodding at our assailants.

Jay shrugs, scratching his head as he regards Oliver and Victoria, meekly shuffling into the police vehicle under escort without speaking. They looked haunted, wearing matching expressions of terror etched into their faces. He stares at me. 'How did you neutralise them like that?'

'I had help,' I say, not bothering to deny that it was something I did. There's no remorse in my expressionless face. *They deserve exactly what they've got ... every bit.*

The paramedics give Patryk and I sippy cups filled with a lemon solution, as they shepherd us towards the ambulance, eager for us to get hospital attention. Jay wipes his palms down his trousers, then stretches out a hand to me. 'We didn't have the hallway properly rigged, so only heard some of what went on at the house. In the kitchen. We came as soon as I realised you were in there. I intended to make you leave, but by the time we arrived there, the house was empty, and we saw the blood. There's no poxy CCTV or anything down this neck of the woods, and we hadn't put a tracker on Oliver's vehicle, so we couldn't find it straight away. I'm so sorry, Mary. I didn't know where he'd taken you.'

'It's OK, I understand.'

'He registered the cottage in Victoria's name, so we couldn't find it. In the end, we barged into that stupid gentleman's club and just asked around about him. Apparently, this cottage is the couple's summer retreat. Victoria is the real owner of that flat above her you rented and she must've been the one who picked out the victims for Oliver. Both John and Patryk had stayed in the flat on holiday. You found the killer, straight away, we just didn't realise. I'm so sorry, Mary. I can't believe...' His voice breaks, and there are tears shining in my friend's eyes I don't acknowledge.

Instead, I stare him square in the face, my own features as still as the rest of me. 'It's not your fault, Jay.' My reply is dull and lacklustre. *I sound like a robot.* 'Oliver is the kitchen kid I saw in my dream. His adopted mum was vicious, and so was he. He despised boys with strong motherly bonds because he couldn't have it. Victoria knew what pleased him, and actively sought victims that would suit. Don't blame yourself, Jay.'

It's my fault Derek got killed. It was my idea to leave the phones indoors, and I should've told him my guess about Errol's fading in and out being connected to danger. If I'd warned Derek, and he thought my life was at risk, he would've argued against me taking the case. He would've said nothing was worth losing me. Like I've lost him. Forever. Derek...

I still have hold of Patryk's hand, and within minutes, we're settled and making headway towards home.

Paramedics bustle inside the vehicle, assessing and treating where they can, asking questions. For the time being, Jay's the only one capable of communicating with them. Neither Patryk nor I engage.

On autopilot, I have my arm around the small boy's shoulder, and the two of us huddle close. We have a blanket each covering our shoulders, but my teeth still clatter like castanets.

Now and then Patryk whimpers, 'Mummy,' and of its own volition my hand soothes him, stroking his hair. 'Shhh. We'll see Mummy soon. It's OK.' I force the words out through the chattering of my teeth, making them sound out over the name that resounds in my head.

Derek, Derek, Derek, Derek... his name is not just a word, it's a low vibration of loss that pounds through me, like the crashing waves of the sea. I say nothing and leave my arm around Patryk. My teeth continue to chatter, and I fight the dizziness that assaults me.

Jay stares at me, his face wet with tears.

'Eileen will be at the hospital, as she's your nearest relative, and now your next of kin, we called her. I can contact Marcie, too, if you'd like.'

Marcie? Eileen? At first, I am hard pushed to remember who Marcie and Eileen are. When I do, there is none of the usual rush of affection that usually accompanies their names. I have no emotion left inside me to assign to anyone. *Empty.*

Time passes and we reach the hospital, pulling up at the emergency entrance slope designated for ambulances. I'm not aware if the time has gone quickly or slowly. A bubble of shock is cushioning me, blocking the pain that would be too much for me to manage right now. The same bubble also interferes with my thoughts, making them hazy and muddled. I yawn as we pull up.

'Sleepy?' Jay asks.

I shrug, and Jay squints, wiping a hand over his face to dry his cheeks. He gives a decisive nod, then gets up and crouches down in front of me. His voice is low and intense.

'I'll never forget what you've done for this boy, for this family, Mary. The sacrifice… God, I'm so sorry. I couldn't have guessed. I'll always be right here for you, whatever you need, Mary. Anytime.'

Derek, Derek, Derek, Derek…

Jay turns to Patryk, who's small face is nearly hidden by my blanket. Jay tells him, 'Patryk, the station called your mum and dad. They're at the hospital waiting for you already. They're so happy you're safe and excited to see you. You ready to go see them, Patryk?'

Patryk blinks, wide eyed. 'Mummy and Daddy?' he says, sounding much younger than his ten years.

The paramedic tending to Patryk says, 'Yes, you'll be with them any minute, Patryk. How's that?' She wipes Patryk's face, then gently encourages him to drink more fluids then lie down on the stretcher. He's not as dirty as he was before, but still a far cry from the well-kept little boy in my vision. I stare down at his trousers, tearing up. The ambulance staff couldn't remove them because he'd become so distressed. Now, he's lying on the ambulance stretcher, in his torn-up trousers caked in filth. My eyes brim with tears. Such a stark contrast from the proud schoolboy in his pristine uniform, so lovingly cared for.

We're both shivering as we leave the ambulance and move towards the entrance. Patryk remains on the stretcher, but I want to walk, and stumble down from the van. Instantly, staff shepherd us to the entrance. They find a wheelchair for me, but I resist all efforts to guide me into it. Mine and Patryk's hands stay clasped together, and

I hobble along beside the stretcher making slow progress along the concrete path.

Inside the hospital, I'm suddenly aware of heat, and perspiration breaks out all over me, face and body. My breathing comes in quick bursts, and my vision becomes blurred.

'Mummy! Daddy!' Patryk calls out.

'Patryk!' his mummy says. 'My God! Thank you, Jesus.'

His dad opens his arms, rushing towards the stretcher. 'Son!'

Patryk releases my hand as his parents run to engulf him in their fierce embrace. All three sob, and as I glance around them, I see everyone around the family watching the reunion looking choked with emotion. The upsurge of love whooshes at me, primitive in its power. The ripples of it catch me with the edge of its groundswell, making my lips curl up as I close my eyes. It's majestic. Pure gold, then blue.

The Blue is here, filling the space of every in-between, until it transforms into just everything.

John's here. His damaged features, once so frightening to me, are now healed and beautiful once more. I feel he is at peace, smiling as he waves at me. Monika is with him still and touches a hand to her heart, then to her lips. *Thank you. He has loved ones come to meet him, family.*

Once more, I have an awareness of the feeling of connection with The Blue, with all things. I know my higher self yearns to accept the connection. To be transformed by love.

To be with Derek, but not yet. I can't go yet. I promised him to live.

I disconnect, closing down all things extra sensory, and immediately collapse, landing on the hard floor with a loud thud like a marionette with its strings cut. Unconscious.

CHAPTER 10

'Mary, let us in. Please, it's Derek's funeral in a couple of hours. We can take you.' Marcie calls through the letterbox and her voice, usually so chirpy, is hoarse with crying. 'Mary, please. Why won't you let us help you? It's been two weeks since...'

As I've done every day since I got back from the hospital, I ignore Marcie. And all my friends. *I'm no good to them anyway; they're better off without me. Everyone is.* I drag the brush through my hair, then let it fall. It clatters sharply against the dressing table, a jarring sound on this day of muted whispers and sombre shadows. My black dress, chosen with a care that now seems macabre, clings to me, elegant yet constricting. *I want to look smart for the funeral, for Derek. He always called me 'beautiful.'* I smooth the material down awkwardly, with only one trembling hand. The other one's broken and rendered useless by a cast and sling that holds it immobile, another painful reminder of that horrific night. My gaze drifts back to the dusty glass in front of me, and I stare at the bandage marring my cheek. Its once pristine white is now tarnished, the edges frayed and clinging to my skin with a desperation that mirrors my own. *There'll be a scar underneath, probably a deep one. Derek probably would've had something admiring to say about that too. God, every thought seems to whisper something about the life we should've had together.*

A familiar face appears behind my reflection. Errol. He's the only one I can't shut out, and he's been with me since the night Derek was murdered. Errol's good-looking features look strained, and he's shaking his head. 'It's no use, you know, Mary. Building walls around yourself. Cutting off love. That's not what Derek would have wanted,' he tells my reflection.

Outraged, I hiss into the mirror, nostrils flaring, 'Don't talk to me about what he would've wanted, Errol. He would've wanted to *live*, that's what he would've wanted. But he's dead now. Dead and gone… and I don't even get to speak to him in the afterlife, because he had to go. I had to close myself off to him so he could go on to The Blue and I could get on with saving Patryk.'

'I'm so sorry, Mary… so very sorry. I tried to warn you, but I couldn't…'

I hold his gaze in the mirror, my own face expressionless. 'I know you tried, Errol, but I misunderstood. The stupid Universe wouldn't allow you to spell it out, and I messed up. Because of that, Derek is gone and now, I don't give a toss about my own life anymore. That's the truth of it. And now I couldn't care if I live or die, except Derek told me to live for him. So, I will.'

'Mary, please, don't say that. Things will get better, I promise. Just please, hang in there.'

'How am I supposed to do that, Errol? What exactly am I supposed to hang onto? What do I do now? Anyone who gets close to me dies. I'm a frigging Jonah.'

Errol covers his mouth with a hand, but I hear his soft groan of distress. He doesn't speak again as I get ready for Derek's funeral, allowing me my silence.

Before long, the funeral car comes for me and I leave quietly, sitting in the long car by myself and staring out the window. Derek's body is already at the crematorium, awaiting me. *This is the last time I'll ever see him.*

I stand greeting people outside the front entrance of the crematorium. There's a sizeable crowd, most from work, but some from his personal life. I'm pleased they came, proud of my late fiancé, and honoured so many people are paying their respects to Derek. *Derek.* My bloodshot eyes meet those of Marcie and Eileen and for a second as they move forward towards me, my composure nearly breaks. Blinking, I swallow my grief, pushing it down, and giving them a wan smile to show I'm coping. I'm glad when they move on, allowing me to steel myself again. When I feel the gentle touch of Sophie I flinch away.

'Hi, Mary, where do you want us to sit?' Rachel asks me.

'The front row, with me,' I tell her. Sophie's at her side and I know they'll let Marcie and Eileen know.

After they pass by me, I try to mentally reel my emotions inwards, enough so I can greet the oncoming guests. I say the same to everyone, tone monotonous. 'Thank you so much for coming,' 'Thank you so much for coming,' 'Thank you so much for coming.'

When the attendants advise me it's time, I go inside. Derek's casket is already inside, at the back of the room, framed by some heavy gold curtains on electronic runners. As I walk down the aisle, I pass Jay. He's seated himself at the back of the room, no doubt castigating himself and taking the blame for Derek's death onto his already burdened shoulders. I slow down, staring at him, but he doesn't meet my gaze, keeping his own eyes downcast. *Ah, Jay, it's not your fault. This is all on me. Derek died because I'm not safe to be around, I'm like a poison.*

Sophie, Rachel, Marcie and Eileen are seated in the front row, and I head towards my friends. Looking around, I'm satisfied with what I've managed to orchestrate for Derek's final goodbye. The place heaves with flowers, and Derek's favourite playlist is on loop through the building's speaker system. The minister says a few words. *It's time for the eulogy.*

The lilies are beautiful, but they're letting off a strong odour that's triggering a migraine. Gritting my teeth against the pain, I glide past an enlarged photograph of Derek, sitting in his favourite chair at home, phone beside him, laptop balancing on his knees. There was nothing special about the day the photo was taken. I just remember it was a happy day and I like that picture of Derek, his big puppy dog eyes shining. In his casket, I've placed a photo of us in his hands, together on the day of our engagement, arms wrapped around each other, grinning. *We were so happy.* My bottom lip wobbles as I climb the pulpit to deliver the eulogy, and I taste blood on my tongue where I've bitten my lip. The blood reminds me of the smell in Oliver's torture room, and I stumble on the carpet, quickly righting myself despite having the imbalance of my arm in a sling. The hand that holds the microphone trembles, and I straighten my shoulders, lifting my chin to face the mourners. I wrote everything down on cards so I wouldn't forget and fudge it up. *I don't want to get it wrong. This is my last chance to tell people how wonderful my dearly departed fiancé was. Derek deserved the best, not to die so young – something I'll always be responsible for.*

'I'd like to start by thanking so many of you for coming today. For those few who don't know who I am, my name's Mary. Derek was my fiancé, and the love of my life.' *And the man I got brutally slaughtered.* 'Derek and I met in hospital. It was a difficult time for both of us, and I wasn't a gracious person. I'm not an amiable person. Right from the start, though, Derek called me 'beautiful,' because that was all he ever saw in me and in others. Beauty. When I was in a bad mood, he cheered me up, made me smile. He was just that kind of person.'

My stinging gaze moves around the parishioners, and automatically, I make eye contact with Marcie. As she meets the devastation in my haunted eyes, her whole face crumples and she sobs, overcome with emotion. I don't react, except to move my gaze somewhere else. I'm lost in a world of my own. It's a struggle to continue, but I know I must. I clear my throat, feeling strangled. 'I was so proud of Derek. He was the perfect man. Handsome, gentle, and clever, with a hilarious sense of humour. He was also a man who always put others first. If there was something that was important to you and Derek loved you, he'd move heaven and earth to see things worked out your way. He was always on your side.' *And that's why I ended up getting him killed.*

Marcie's heartbroken wailing drifts out to me over the sea of faces, but thankfully, it doesn't have the power to break the spell of composure I'm under.

'Derek never got angry or mean, and if you were in a bad mood, he had a way of cheering you up with just a few words. Derek was the kindest, most gentle-natured person I've ever known. And he'd do absolutely anything for those he loved. He gave me unconditional love and was one of the few people to do that since my mum died.' *Because I don't deserve to be loved. Because anyone who gets close to me gets hurt or dies.* I close my eyes momentarily, placing the hand that holds the microphone against my stomach briefly to stop myself from gagging. *Those stupid flowers are making me want to vomit. The smell is so strong.* I swallow the lump of grief that's welling up in my chest. *No, I won't freak out now. I must do this for Derek. I want to do him proud. Keep going, Mary Obosa Jameson.*

I bring the microphone back up to my lips, saying, 'Derek was shy, and although he only saw the good in everyone, I never understood how he never saw it in himself. He was calm, clever, and talented, and the type of person who was always giving. Right until his last moments.' I hesitate, pushing away the macabre thoughts and images that rush into my head. The very last moments I was present for. 'I, and everyone who knew him, will always love him. Derek was too good for this world, and that's why I'm sure he'll have passed on to a better place. Surrounded with love, forever. Au revoir, mon coer. I'll see you again one day, D.' My voice breaks then, and my chin wobbles, as I stare over the rows of chairs and people. I allow random thoughts to distract me from my pain. *Ah, there's Dave, Sean, and Bertie from Derek's Seattle job he did a few years ago, and there's Poppy and Micah, we went to their barbecue last summer. Ethan from Jay's team came too. That was nice.* My gaze circles back to Marcie; she hasn't stopped crying. *I'm a bad person.* My grief starts to rise, its force wobbling my belly as it seeks to find its way out. *No. I can't cope with anyone else's grief right now. I'm not strong enough. Marcie and our friends' suffering is too raw and painful to witness. Especially because it's all my fault.* Finished with my public goodbye to Derek, I step down from the dais, legs like cotton wool, and sink back in my allocated seat next to my friends.

Sophie's voice is low, but still audible even over Marcie's bawling. I keep my head straight, my eyes on the coffin displayed in front of us. Despite purposely distancing myself since that terrible day, I'd called and offered my friends the chance to say a few words during the service. They'd all declined. Sophie'd said she preferred to say goodbye to Derek in her heart, and in her own way. 'Mary, please… talk to us. We love you. We're your family,' Sophie whispers to me, voice catching.

Lip trembling, I shake my head, no. Drawing myself up in my seat, I brace myself against the tender affection I hear in her words. *I need to keep it together for Derek. Just a little longer.* 'No, Sophie. You need to stop contacting me. All of you.'

'What? No way.' Sophie touches my hand and I snatch it away as though scalded. 'Yes way. I can't be around you. *Any of you.' It's not safe for you. I'm not safe for anyone to be close to.*

The uncomfortable looks and whispers from a few of the mourners tell me that without realising it, my volume's increased. *Christ, my composure's cracking. My friends aren't going to give up. Well, that's OK. Derek had insisted on being joint tenants with right of survivorship of the flat, so ownership of it had passed to me as soon as he'd died. I didn't even have to wait for probate. The mortgage had life insurance attached, again with me as sole beneficiary, so it was paid off in full. Derek had the rest of his assets in a living trust, so I have enough to just purchase the house in Hampshire outright. Once the funeral's over and the legal tape's sorted, I'll disappear, move into the house. They can't be around me anymore. I won't risk their safety. I love them too much.*

I hear Eileen, seated behind me, shifting in her seat, then feel the warmth of her hand as she places it on the back of my arm. Without a word, I move forward in my chair, so it drops away, and I focus on the rest of the service. Seizing back control of my emotions, I lower my voice to a hushed decibel again, speaking to Sophie without turning my head to look at her. *I need to give Derek the funeral he deserves. Classy. It's the least I can do after getting him murdered.* 'I need space. From everyone… for a while, please.'

Silence greets my words as Sophie digests my plea. From the corner of my eye, I can see Rachel beside her, taking her hand and nodding. Closing my eyes, I breathe a sigh of relief.

'OK, but just know that when you're ready for us, we'll be here. Derek was my best friend, but we love you too, Mary,' Sophie says.

My chin wobbles again as Sophie's equanimity breaks, and she, too, dissolves into heartbroken sobs. Rachel comforts her, and I can feel her ire in my peripheral vision. Then that too evaporates. *It probably crossed Rachel's mind how she would be if it were Sophie in the coffin.*

Derek's closest colleagues take turns to extol his virtues, and it's time for us to say our last goodbyes before the cremation. As I requested, the minister lets everyone know that all of the mourners are invited to the wake that I've arranged after this service at a local hall.

As the golden curtains close on Derek's casket, our special song plays. It's the song Derek used to sing to me, and a single tear rolls down my face as the words ring out eerily. 'I was made for you…' I stare at the curtains behind which my Derek is being laid to rest. *That should be me in there. Not poor, faultless Derek. Love of my life.*

I clench my hands, then grip the sides of my seat, restraining myself from leaping up and running to the dais where Derek lays, trying to stop this from happening. *And I can't even talk to him. What's even the point of being a medium?*

After a few minutes, when I'm sure I won't make a scene, I stand up on shaky legs. Despite my attempts to distance myself from my friends, they gather round me. Eileen comes in first, taking both my hands in hers. When she speaks, her Scottish accent is the strongest I've ever heard it. 'I'm so sorry, lassie, so sorry. If you need anything, if you want to come and stay with me for a while, you just let me know.'

I nod, keeping my face downcast as we're joined by Rachel, Sophie, and Marcie. Sophie hugs me, then is occupied as she comforts Marcie, the two hugging and crying. Rachel stands near me and Eileen, studying my pale, gaunt face, and red-rimmed eyes. After a second, she says, 'Don't freeze us out, Mary. Sophie's right. We all loved Derek, but we love you equally. We don't want to lose you too. If you need anything, anything, we're here for you.' Rachel puts her arms round me, standing stiffly.

'Thanks, Rachel, I appreciate it.' *And it's true. I do appreciate their friendship. So much. I just know that I don't deserve it.*

Outside the crematorium, the weather is cold, the wind biting into my face with angry breath. I'm glad about the punishment. *I deserve it.*

The minister speaks to me, but I'm numb to her words, glancing around blindly until my gaze settles. I inhale sharply, recognising a woman. It's Patryk's mum, Iryna Challance.

She bows her head but is staring at me with a guilty expression on her face. Without speaking to her, I know she's another person who's feeling as though they're to blame for my loss and I don't like the idea. *She doesn't need to feel like that.*

As the crowd disperses to attend the wake, I move towards her, dreamlike. As we meet, Iryna's words spill out in a rush. 'I'm so sorry for your loss, Miss Jameson. I wanted to come, show my respects, but didn't feel I had the right to come to the service for your fiancé. I read about your loss in the newspapers, and I'm so sorry. I never got the chance to tell you how grateful we are and to thank you for what you did for my baby boy. I'm so sorry. I didn't know... The voicemail I left, it was my fault for begging you all to help. I had no right.'

I shake my head, then say, 'You had every right to do that, Iryna, and please don't blame yourself. It wasn't your fault. Don't think that. I chose to get involved because it was the right thing to do. And it's Mary.'

'You're very gracious. You can't believe... the depths of our despair... I... but of course, you can, you know...'

There's an awkward silence in which Iryna's pale face floods with pink, and I press a hand on her arm, telling her, 'I understand, Iryna. Honestly.'

'Mary, I don't know what else to say, but if there's ever anything you need. A favour, money, absolutely anything. We want you to please call on us. It's yours.'

The emptiness in my eyes tells Iryna there won't be anything I need again, but I smile and thank her all the same. 'Thank you,' I say. 'How's Patryk doing now?'

Iryna's gaze drops from mine, and she fiddles with her handbag, getting a handkerchief out and dabbing her eyes. 'Patryk's... adjusting. He won't sleep alone anymore or go out much. And one of us needs to be with him at all times. That's why his father didn't come today. He wets the bed, and sucks his thumb, but the doctors say this behaviour's normal after such trauma, and we all hope that with love and time, he'll recover.'

'Bless him, I'm sorry to hear that, Iryna. Patryk showed me how very special and brave he is when we were together. I'm sure he'll recover in time. After everything he went through and survived, I know he's one tough little cookie. A fighter. I'm glad he has such loving parents to support him; he deserves the best.'

Tears brim in her eyes again, and she nods, moving towards me as though she wants to envelop me in a hug. I step back, my heel wobbling on the dirt. The action makes me look round to see if anyone saw, and I realise that most of the people have gone from the courtyard now, having gone on to the wake or to their homes. Only Jay, Eileen, Sophie, Rachel, and Marcie remain. 'I should go now, Iryna,' I tell her politely. 'Thank you very much for coming. I appreciate it. Please give my very best regards to Patryk, and your husband, of course.'

'I will, and please remember, Mary. If you ever need anything. Anything at all, please don't hesitate. If we have it, or can do it, it's yours.'

The hall I rented for the wake is within walking distance, and I relish the idea of having that time to myself. After going to my friends to request they go on ahead, I use the toilet attached to the crematorium, then ready myself to leave, heavy thoughts buzzing round my foggy brain. Iryna's visit was unexpected, but I was glad she came because despite my grief, I'd been wondering how Patryk was, hoping he was ok. It threw up a question, if I had known the *real* choice, would I have chosen Patryk again? Or Derek? I like to think that I'd have found some middle choice.

Errol and Gaynor stand waiting in the courtyard for me, the two of them holding an identical sombre look on their faces.

In my mind, I hear Errol's words from earlier, telling me to 'hang in there, because things will get so much better.' *I doubt that, Errol. I doubt that very much.*

AUTHOR'S NOTE

Dear Reader,

I'd like to dedicate this book to my beloved Auntie 'Bad-Ass' Gill, who was one of the nicest people I'm sure I'll ever know. Happy Birthday Auntie, love you lots xxx.

Thank you all so much for joining me on this continuation of Mary Jameson's story. I hope you've enjoyed reading *Psychic Echoes*. What were your thoughts on the ending? If you appreciated it, then you might be pleased to hear I'm already working on Book 3 in the series. You might also have guessed that this book wasn't just about the thrills; it also aimed to celebrate diverse main characters. Because, I believe that stories like this one can help champion diversity across all genres of literature.

If you were entertained by *Psychic Echoes* and by the company of its characters, I'd be grateful if you could consider sharing your thoughts with a review. As an independent author, my resources for marketing are quite limited, so I deeply rely on word-of-mouth from my loyal readers. A review from you means so much to me. It helps other readers to find this series and supports me in writing more stories that bring us together.

Thank you again for giving me your reading time, and for being a part of this story's life. Remember, my inbox is always open and I love to hear from my readers!

Warmest wishes,

JP x

ACKNOWLEDGEMENTS

First, I'd like to say a massive thank you to all my readers (in particular, my mum, Rosemary) for your willingness to dedicate your reading time to *Psychic Echoes*. It means everything to me.

A heartfelt thank you to Zach Bohannon, my editor, for his invaluable insight and guidance, to Christian Bentulan, for capturing the story's essence and creating such a wonderful cover, with special thanks to Susan Keillor and finally, my friends and family, whose unwavering encouragement has been a source of relentless motivation.

Thank you all so much.

Warmest wishes,

J.P. x

Coming soon...

Psychic Feelings: Book 3: A Supernatural Thriller

After a devastating loss, Mary Jameson retreats into solitude in Hampshire, haunted by her sorrow and a belief that she brings danger to those she loves. In an effort to protect her dearest friends from her perceived curse, Mary secludes herself, accompanied only by the echoes of her nightmares and the watchful eyes of her spirit guides, Errol and Gaynor. But when a close friend suffers a brutal attack, Mary is drawn out of isolation into a harrowing mystery that tests her powers and resolve.

In this gripping third entry in the series, Mary forms an unwilling alliance with Adam Saxon, a police officer connected to the unfolding mystery. As they untangle a web of secrets, Mary's quest to protect those she loves leads her into the heart of darkness, challenging her perceptions of fate and friendship.

In *Psychic Feelings*, suspense and the supernatural intertwine to weave a tale of courage, loss, and redemption. Join Mary Jameson on her most perilous journey yet, where the past haunts the present and the line between friend and foe is as thin as a whisper.

In a world where Mary's curse is her strongest ally, can she embrace it to expose the truth before it consumes her and those she bravely allows close once more?

Also by J.P. Alters

Psychic Voices: Mary Jameson Book 1: A Supernatural Thriller

Psychic Training: Mary Jameson Book
1.5: A Supernatural Short Story

Psychic Echoes: Mary Jameson Book 2: A Supernatural Thriller

The Twisted Fates: Unearthly Lessons in Darkness

*Coming soon: Psychic Feelings: Mary Jameson
Book 3: A Supernatural Thriller*

www.jpaltersauthor.com

Printed in Great Britain
by Amazon

42538764R00198